For Kenneth –

All the best.

FIRE BELL

IN THE

NIGHT

GEOFFREY S. EDWARDS

A Touchstone Book
Published by Simon & Schuster
New York   London   Toronto   Sydney

 Touchstone
A Division of Simon & Schuster, Inc.
1230 Avenue of the Americas
New York, NY 10020

First Touchstone trade paperback edition September 2007

TOUCHSTONE and colophon are registered trademarks of
Simon & Schuster, Inc.

For information about special discounts for bulk purchases, please
contact Simon & Schuster Special Sales at
1-800-456-6798 or business@simonandschuster.com.

Designed by Elliott Beard

Manufactured in the United States of America

10   9   8   7   6   5   4   3   2   1

Library of Congress Cataloging-in-Publication Data
Edwards, Geoffrey S.
    Fire bell in the night / Geoffrey S. Edwards.
        p. cm.
    "A Touchstone Book."
    1. South Carolina—History—1775-1865—Fiction.
2. Fugitive slaves—Fiction.   3. Charleston (S.C.)—Fiction.
4. Race relations—Fiction.   I. Title.
PS3605.D884F57 2007
813'.6-dc22   2007025415

ISBN-13: 978-1-4165-6424-9
ISBN-10:   1-4165-6424-1

For Mom

But this momentous question, like a fire bell in the night, awakened and filled me with terror. I considered it at once as the knell of the Union.

—*Thomas Jefferson, 1820,*
speaking of the Missouri Compromise and its effect on the
nation, dividing the country into North and South

PREFACE

ᕫ

The Mexican War ended in 1848, but the American victory was hollow. The land ceded in defeat—the New Mexico Territory and California—became the source of a political powder keg. Slavery once again divided the country. The new lands did not fall under the tenets of the Missouri Compromise, which, thirty years before, had imposed an artificial border between North and South, free states and slave. The tenuous balance offered by that compromise was now upset. There were fourteen free states and fourteen slave. The new lands threatened to tip the balance to one side's favor. Neither could afford to lose.

An all-southern convention was scheduled for the summer of 1850. There, the South would be poised to secede from the Union were California and New Mexico admitted as free states. Many in the North promised such an action would force an armed response.

Meanwhile, in Texas, a border dispute arose. An armed standoff between federal soldiers and Texas militia was taking place on the banks of the Pecos River. The Texans wanted their promised land.

The federal troops refused to budge. The slave-owning states were prepared to come to the aid of their southern brother should conflict erupt, an act that also would have precipitated Civil War.

This was the precarious state of the Union. This was the Crisis of 1850.

FIRE BELL
IN THE
NIGHT

PROLOGUE

〰

END OF APRIL, 1850

Someone tossed a pine log onto the campfire. It hissed and popped, and sparks swirled in the updraft like fireflies.

My Lord.

Ten men arose and moved wordlessly away, single file down the dirt path. Their black forms blended with the night.

My Lord.

The eyes in the circle watched stiff backs and clenched fists as the men disappeared one by one into the trees. In sadness, those in the circle picked up a chant set to the rhythm of a heartbeat. Had they seen the men's faces, they would have been afraid.

> *My Lord. My Lord. My Lord.*
> *For better days ahead,*
> *My Lord.*
> *For better days a plea,*
> *My Lord.*
> *For better days ahead,*
> *My Lord.*

Come sound the Jubilee,
My Lord. My Lord. My Lord.

Jebediah Jones had a key to the toolshed. His ingenuity and resourcefulness never failed to impress his fellow slaves. That he could produce the needed key now, at this time, seemed an omen. They waited silently, barely breathing, listening to the rattle of metal against metal with night sounds all around them.

My Lord. My Lord. My Lord.

There was a click as the hasp opened, then the long slow creak of the hinges, frighteningly loud. Then Jebediah was inside the shed, passing out tools. He chose for himself the only ax. It glinted silver in the moonlight and reflected like a pale lantern on his features. He face looked so different now that his friends barely recognized him. His normally lazy eyes looked strange, red almost, but not from tears. His voice had a tight quality, devoid of inflection. The men circled around him as he went over the plan one final time.

"Everyone remember, it's Gantry we go afta' first. Solomon and me will slip up to his cabin and do what need be done. The rest of y'all wait behind the trees over yonder." His monotone whisper broke off as he pointed to the west. "Afta' we's done, we'll meet up by his cabin and make our march on the house. Since none of us is sure where the massa sleeps, we'll split up once we's upstairs and look for the bedroom. Then we kill him and his missus." He looked around at the group, his steel gaze meeting each man's eyes—they glowed like moonstones. "Understand?"

The youngest of the group, Christmas, leaned forward; his words were soft. His finger shot up toward the sky. "Th-the moon be right fo' this, Jeb?"

Big Jim, the man beside Christmas, jerked down the arm. "Don't never point toward the moon," he growled. "Makes for bad luck."

Jebediah took a step forward, reinforcing each man with his rigid, emotionless bearing. "Ain't none of that matter. No moon, no stars, nothing. Only matters when a man think it does. Y'all understand?"

With that, he turned and walked toward the overseer's shack. Nine men fell in behind him, in step to an internal cadence.

My Lord. My Lord. My Lord.

Mrs. Smythe had brandished the silver soup ladle at face level as if it were a key piece of evidence. It gleamed in the sun, and the boy still could not keep his eyes off it.

"He was holding it behind him, looking guilty as sin, Mr. Gantry. And I said, 'How dare you! How dare you!' " Her voice rose with pious outrage.

"There now, Mrs. Smythe. You just sit yourself down." The overseer bobbed his head as he spoke, then drew a porch chair into position for the lady of the plantation. He noted with alarm the color in her cheeks and the droplets of perspiration on her upper lip. "Don't distress yourself, missus. I'll get to the bottom of this."

The lady collapsed into the chair in a fit of dizziness, grimacing and wrinkling her nose slightly as Gantry spoke too close to her face. He had not taken but two drinks this morning, hair o' the dog, but Mrs. Smythe always looked like she had caught a whiff of something disagreeable. She fanned herself rapidly with her hand. "All this aggravation will be the death of me."

Gantry narrowed his eyes and turned to the gangly field slave. He changed the volume and timbre of his voice. The coating of syrup was gone. "What were you doing up here at the house in the first place, boy? You know you don't belong here."

The thirteen-year-old stammered, having trouble getting started. Then the words poured out in a rush. "Sir, Bessie called to me when I was bringing up the firewood. Told me to hunt for some mint leaves, right quick, and bring 'em to Cook in the kitchen. I ain't never been in the kitchen before, sir. Went through the wrong door—"

Gantry held up a hand to cut him off. "You *knock* on the door, boy. You don't just open it."

"I did knock, sir, but—"

"This is a nightmare," Mrs. Smythe declared. "A complete breakdown of authority."

"I'll get to the bottom of this, ma'am," Gantry soothed. He then resumed his interrogation. "What were you doing with that spoon in your hand?"

"I saw it on the table, sir. It was so shiny. I was looking at my face in it. Then the missus come, and I . . ."

Johnny Walker was unraveling fast, and his servile decorum was crumbling. His eyes now flashed from Gantry, to the spoon, to his mistress, like a bee trapped indoors, bouncing off the windows. Gantry knew he had to get the boy out of there, or the lady would have one of her "spells."

"I've heard all I need to hear from you," Gantry barked. He turned to the lady. "I'll take care of this matter from here on, Mrs. Smythe. Don't trouble yourself no more. I'll see that this boy won't be bothering you."

She sighed and shook her head. "No one understands what I have to deal with. It is just one thing after another."

Gantry grabbed the boy by the collar and marched him down the steps, away from the house.

The ringing of the bell had brought the slaves in from the near fields. They convened the back of the big house at a round dirt patch the bondsmen called Hell's Circle. The mansion formed the backdrop, two stories of pristine white showered in midday light. Its gracefully curving walks and hedges seemed an extension of the gently rolling landscape. The old folks said that even after fifty years, the manor looked as fine as the day they helped build it. It seemed a waste that such a dwelling now housed only four permanent residents: the master, his wife, and the two young children. The house slaves, of course, did not count.

Gantry now sat on the steps of the covered back porch, where the slatted railing seemed to form the maw on the face of the great white creature. Above, sun glinted off the thick panes of the two second-story windows of the porch wing, which looked down like angry eyes. Under the sun's full glare, it was almost impossible to look at them. "Just as well," the elders often whispered. "Our eyes ain't meant to see such things." And Johnny Walker had not been meant to get too close.

The boy now stood fidgeting in the center of the dirt circle. He did not speak, and neither did the forty or so slaves who ringed the periphery. They avoided looking at him and at each other, preoccupied instead with the distant trees in blurred focus, the endless blue of the sky, and the red dust at their feet.

Gantry's boots stirred up the dust as he approached, and the boy seemed to shrink a little, as if he hoped to disappear into his baggy clothes.

"Ain't no reason to be scared there, boy," Elijah Gantry said calmly. "If you just admit what you did and apologize to Mrs. Smythe, there's no reason this has to be bad."

"Sir, I's very sorry that I upset the missus, but like I said, I just picked up a couple pieces to take a closer look, that's all."

The boots paced back and forth in front of the boy. The older slaves knew that what Gantry wanted here was a confession of guilt and quick justice—just like in the Bible.

"Be not deceived. God is not mocked," he intoned forcefully while pointing at the heavens to indicate a direct quote. "For what a man soweth, so shall he also reap!"

The boy's confused look showed that he wasn't getting it, so Gantry stepped closer to make his point.

"Boy, Mrs. Smythe told me she caught you stealing that silver. You put it behind you and slipped it into your pocket. Now you wouldn't be calling Mrs. Smythe a liar, would you?"

Johnny Walker rooted in his pockets with his hands, mute, his chin quivering slightly in indecision.

Gantry resumed. "Well, if you ain't calling her a liar, then you must be admitting that you was gonna take it."

"But, sir, I wasn't gonna take it. I just wanted to get me a closer look, that's all. I promise."

Never certain of the temperament of a drunken Gantry, known to sway from jovial altruism to overt cruelty, the slaves stood frozen in anticipation of his response. When he heard the boy's continued claim of innocence, the crocodile smile melted from his unshaven face.

Gantry's fury erupted. He ran at the boy and delivered a blow flush to the side of his head, dropping him to a knee. As a collective gasp resonated among the spectators, the overseer tugged Johnny Walker back up to his feet by the collar of his shirt and began a succession of punches to the stomach, each creating a hollow noise like a thumped melon. Gantry released his hold on the slave, allowing him to drop awkwardly to the ground, but the onslaught did not end. Gantry delivered a succession of well-placed kicks, circling the young slave as each new position offered a ready target. The overseer finally stopped when the boy drew himself into a whimpering ball, then stood erect over his victim with a smirk.

"That ought to teach you a lesson," he said, panting. He began to stuff his shirt tail back into the confines of his belt.

Those forced to witness the beating had averted their eyes and held their tongues. Now they began to buzz as Johnny Walker rose gingerly to his feet. The boy's action was more a breach of etiquette than a testament to his manhood. He simply did not know that he was supposed to stay down. As the boy's face rose level with Gantry's, the overseer's eyes changed.

"Back to the ground," a slave yelled out.

"Please, sir," a woman pleaded to Gantry. "The boy be all messed up. He don't know what he's doing."

Johnny Walker swayed back and forth; he was fighting a battle with each leg to simply remain upright. Gantry reached over and grabbed him by the back of the neck, and he went limp like a cat. The overseer pushed the boy's chin up with the other hand. One eye was swelling shut, and the trail of blood and saliva that dribbled from his mouth moved in and out with his uneven breaths.

Elijah Gantry smiled with only the mouth. "You just don't get it, do you, boy?"

Johnny's response came out slurred and barely intelligible. "Sir, honest. I didn't mean to do nothing."

Gantry seemed to cringe a bit, and he gritted his teeth. He pushed the boy back to the ground and fingered the coiled whip on his belt. He appeared to vacillate, as if the Puritan in him wanted to purge the usual admission of guilt, but the overweight drinker was unequal to the task. He then straightened with an idea.

Gantry removed his hat and cast his gaze skyward. "Oh Lord, help me. I do all I can for these people, and this, this insubordination, is how they respond to my kindness. But, as you say in the Good Book, 'those who do not obey their masters shall reap My wrath.' " He turned his attention back toward his worldly audience. "Well, then, if that's how its got ta be. Walt! Robinson! Come over here."

The two summoned field hands strode through the mass and met a foot from the downed boy.

"I want y'all two to take this boy and put him in the box."

Walt and Robinson looked quickly at one another but did not move. Walt, the taller man, dropped his head and removed his large-brimmed hat. He used the back of his hand to wipe away the accumulation of sweat on his brow before shuttling a quick glance between Gantry's face and his boots.

"Begging yo' pardon, sir, but there ain't a cloud in the sky, and it's mighty hot today. Not like normal fo' this time of year. Don't you think—"

"I know what the damn weather is. I don't need no nigger to tell me what I already know. Now pick up that boy and take him to the box. Now!"

The two men backed away from the overseer and attended to the boy, Walt and Robinson each taking a knee and putting an arm underneath Johnny Walker's shoulders.

"I swear, Walt, I wasn't fixing to steal nothing. Honest," Johnny whispered.

"I know, I know. That ain't important now."

The onlookers watched silently as the boy was carried off, both feet dragging behind him, stirring up the ash-dry dirt and leaving a ghostly trail.

A hundred yards away sat the box. It was Elijah Gantry's newest correctional device, and he would proudly tout it as the only one in all of Habersham County. A rectangular structure, six feet long by four feet wide, the box was anchored in a ditch between two dirt walls. A thin layer of metal covered its braced wood frame. Gantry had overseen its construction during the previous winter after his return from a buying trip to Savannah. He called it "the cooker." Slaves had asked how it worked, but Gantry was uncharacteristically inscrutable. Instead, he had offered a demonstration three weeks ago, just before the weather turned.

Bartholomew had been caught stealing food, and he was sentenced to spend two hours in the box. He thought he had gotten off easy. Upon his exodus, however, the slave declared on wobbly legs that it was "too hot in there fo' the Devil hisself." Bartholomew was not one to pass up a chance at a good yarn, and he said that while in the box, he had heard pounding from down below. "The Devil was openin' hisself a chimney straight from Hell, right into that box." Some believed him; most did not. But subsequently, no slave would walk within fifty feet of the box if they could avoid it.

It was now late April, and the heat of summer had come early. And today there were no clouds to lessen the sun's wrath.

As Gantry stood on the compact earth before the box, the men could see the shimmering waves of heat rising from the metal. Gantry shook his head a little and scratched his beard. "Let's go ahead then."

Walt bent his head to the boy's ear. "Don't you worry now, son," he said. "We be back in no time to spring you."

Robinson continued. "Remember now, the Good Lord be in there with ya. You remember that."

For the first time since the beating, Johnny's face showed awareness and fear as Walt slowly pulled the door open with his free hand and the blast of hot, stale air fell against their faces. Robinson fanned his free arm in front of them in a futile attempt at ventilation. Then the two men hunched down, careful not to touch the sheet metal as they slid the boy halfway into the box.

"Remember now, son, we be back directly," Walt reiterated, grasping the boy's arm firmly for reassurance.

Johnny Walker dragged the remainder of his body inside and immediately curled into a ball. Gantry walked over and slammed the door, lodging a stick between two pieces of metal as a makeshift lock.

"Let's not dally about then. There's work to be done."

Gantry dusted off his hands, walking past the two men and toward the somber gathering near the plantation house.

He turned once, briefly, to call out a warning. "Sufficient unto the day is the evil thereof!"

No one was sure exactly what he meant.

It was late afternoon by the time news of Johnny Walker's predicament filtered to the far end of the plantation. Jebediah Jones had been tilling his patch of the "northwest forty" when Nat had come over from the adjoining field with the news.

Jebediah had been born on the Smythe plantation close to thirty-five years ago and had worked the land since he was ten. From childhood, two droopy eyelids had given him a perpetually sleepy expression, and exceptionally long arms and legs had made for a gangly look, ensuring that his clothes never quite met wrist or ankle. His parents had resigned themselves early to the fact that he would never be a handsome man.

Sensing the need to enhance his desirability, his parents invested in the boy's education, which was no mean feat, as it was illegal to teach a slave to read. They both hired themselves out in their free time to raise money, and eventually found a free black woman willing to tutor the boy. Blessed with a quick mind, Jeb soon mastered the simple reading primer and graduated to the Bible.

But Jeb did not confine himself to book knowledge. He listened when the old folks talked. He showed them respect, and they told him secrets—about planting and hunting, about the old proverbs and traditions, and of the poems women liked to hear at courting time. As Jebediah drew respect from the community at large, girls his age became intrigued.

He chose to marry Prudence, a fine-looking and well-built slave girl whom he admired equally for her free spirit. For Prudence, good-natured laughter came easily. She was also clever; she patched and trimmed Jebediah's old clothes with scraps of fabric in bright and pleasing colors. Over the years she had borne him four children, three boys and a girl, and been a good wife. They shared their cabin with Johnny Walker, an orphan whom Prudence had seen fit to raise as her own.

Upon hearing the news of Johnny's punishment, Jebediah, for the first time that day, took stock of the weather. After dealing with the Georgia heat for so long, day in and day out, he had developed a certain tolerance for the oppressive conditions, knowing how to work himself optimally without falling ill from too little water or too much sun. But the box? That changed everything. Jebediah turned his head toward the unclouded sky, squinting his eyes even further shut. Suddenly it was hot.

"Don't ya worry, Jeb," Nat soothed, placing a hand on Jeb's shoulder. "I'm sure the boy be just fine."

Jebediah remained silent, staring statuelike toward the house.

Nat continued, sensing the man's line of thought. "Ain't no good gonna come by you running back there and stirring up a hornet's nest. I'm sure the boy be back in your hut resting anyways. All that's gonna happen if you go charging back there is that you and Mr. Gantry is gonna have a date at the whipping post."

Jebediah's eyes regained focus, and he swiveled his head toward Nat. Jeb looked into the man's kind eyes. Nat was talking sense, and Jeb knew it. He also knew that each foot of ground he tilled and each breath he drew would come hard until the driver called them in.

"Day be almost done," Nat said, noticing the lengthening shadows.

"Ain't done soon enough."

He counted to force the time to pass. He moved his lips and said the numbers under his breath. What did the Good Book say? That a day in God's life was like a thousand years? Well, he would just have to wage his own private battle with time; he would not let it play its cruel tricks on him.

". . . Nine sixty-two. Nine sixty-three."

"Bring it on in!" the slave driver trumpeted in his throaty baritone.

A long procession of field hands fell in line for the walk home. They soon broke into a sad melody to which the slap of feet on the dusty road served as percussion.

> *This ain't Christmas morning, just a long summer day,*
> *Hurry up, yellow boy and don't run away.*

Grass in the cotton and weeds in the corn,
Get out the field, 'cause it'll soon be morn.

Jebediah did not join in. Nor did he fall into line as he would on a typical day. He walked briskly down the road—running was forbidden—and over the large hill that was the high point of the Smythe land.

The hill was called Harold's Hill after the late master, father of the present owner. The Georgia clay glowed red below Jebediah, and just to the west, the great pine forest marked the border of the plantation. The road ran along the forest for a considerable distance, and close enough to provide a view of the long dark rows between the tall loblollies. The wall of trees seemed like an ocean to a man who had never seen the sea. It started near the house and ran deep into the far reaches of Georgia herself.

Many a discontented slave had spent time hiding in that forest of pine, only to return when the food ran out or the weather turned. Most received a beating for their disobedience, but many said their time out there was punishment enough. One could walk for miles in any direction and have no sense of change or progress. Jebediah wondered if the interminable pines drove men mad.

He continued his brisk walk down the hill, gaining speed as the incline became steeper. He stopped briefly at the work shed and returned his hoe to the driver in charge.

"Clear your patch today?" the mulatto named James asked curtly.

"Aye," Jeb responded. "Most."

"Well, make sure you finish that up on 'morrow. Ain't but a week till we gotta plant."

Jeb turned his head away and nodded. After the driver waved him on, he returned to a quick pace and headed for his cabin. The path forked by an ancient oak at the base of the hill. The lane led on to the big house, while the right path led to a collection of slave cabins on the east side of the plantation.

Jeb considered himself a fit man. But his chest had gone tight when he got the news about Johnny Walker, and his breaths came shallow. He felt a bit weak in the knees, and his strides came up short, like he was running in water. He forced his mind away from that line of thought and back to the thud of his feet on firm ground. He started to count again—this time the number of strides per breath. He was coming to the slave cabins now, twenty-seven of them, all cut from the great bordering pines.

The Jones cabin was located in the middle row, down toward the far end. Hanging on the door to his home was a carved sign that read "Jones Family"—a present Jebediah had made for his wife following the birth of their first son.

Jebediah reached the door and charged in, out of breath. Hoping to see Johnny Walker, he instead saw his wife seated in the good chair with his oldest boy, Ezekiel, standing beside her. Prudence bounced to her feet upon his entrance, rushing to the side of her husband. She still wore her field dress, a long white cotton garment tied at the waist with a hemp belt. Her collar was cut low in a V, stretching down her chest. The dress was sleeveless, and dirt smudges ran down both long, muscular arms. Her hair was tied back and hidden underneath a white bandana, with a few locks slipping out over both ears. Her dark, beautiful face was swollen under the eyes, and tears stained her cheeks.

"Oh, Jeb," she cried. "What is we gonna do?"

"Where is the boy at?"

"That's just it," she said, struggling to talk between sobs. "Mr. Gantry beat him good and put him in that box. No one was meant to—"

Jebediah grabbed her around the upper arms and clenched. "I know all about that. Where is the boy at *now*?"

"Oh, Jeb. He's still in there. Mr. Gantry ain't never taken him out."

Jebediah let go of Prudence and dropped his head.

"What we gonna do, Papa?" Ezekiel asked anxiously.

The father drew a long deep breath, then spoke gently to the boy. "Now ya listen. You go eat, and take your momma with ya. In the meantime, I'll be figuring a way to get Johnny out."

"I'll help you," Ezekiel said.

"No," Prudence interrupted, her voice calm now. "You listen to your papa. You come with me and get some food."

Prudence leaned forward and kissed her husband gently on the cheek before starting for the door. Once they had left, Jebediah sat in his chair, clutching his head as he tried to work out a course of action.

Accustomed to having few options, he soon decided that his best plan was to find Gantry and somehow convince him to release the boy. Jebediah knew that Gantry was suspicious of his intelligence, but he also knew what Gantry wanted most—to feel important. Now he believed that if he showed the proper deference, the respect that Gantry yearned for, the overseer would bow to decency and let the boy out. He grabbed his hat and left the cabin.

Jebediah had no idea where to find Gantry at this time of day, but he figured his cabin was as good a guess as any. Rounding the hedge of azaleas that formed the border between the manor grounds and the slave paths, he caught sight of four slaves moving quickly toward him: Solomon, Walt, Big Jim, and Thomas West, the last being his cousin.

"Assume y'all heard about Johnny Walker," Jebediah opened.

"Aye," Big Jim answered in his deep voice. "That's why we was out looking for ya."

"Have you seen Gantry?" Jebediah asked. "I'm trying ta find him ta see if I can plead my case."

"That's what we came to talk with you about," Walt replied. "Saw Gantry not an hour ago leave with that house-nigger Gemmins to ride up into town. Lord only knows when they're coming back."

Jeb ran his hand across his face and forced himself to take a deep breath. He had just lost his most viable chance to free Johnny Walker.

"C-c-cousin."

Thomas West had opened his mouth, and Jebediah could see him working himself up to talk. Stuttering was common among slaves, but for Thomas West it was almost incapacitating.

Jebediah put his hand on his shoulder. "Sure there, Thomas."

"I d-don't think he sh-should be in there m-much longer." The slight man's brow was wrinkled with the effort. "So, w-what you th-th-thinking we should d-do?"

Jebediah looked his cousin in the eye. "I s'pose there's only one thing *to* do. We've gotta go get him out now. Ourselves."

"I was hoping you was gonna say that," Solomon said. "It's why I brung this here hammer. Figuring we can break off that lock with it."

The other men nodded in agreement, and the group now doubled back toward the plantation house. The decision to act had calmed Jebediah, but the proximity of the box now began to increase his dread. The rising fear again clutched at his throat and weakened his legs. It was the same feeling brought on by his nightmare, one based in experience. It was the time he almost drowned.

It had happened the year that Ferson Creek, swollen by heavy rain, had almost wiped out the bridge by the South Road. Jebediah had been part of the work detail, and had been ferrying supplies through knee-deep water upstream from the bridge. Fatigue had set in, Jeb had lost his footing, and the dark green current had carried him under the bridge to the deeper water downstream.

The rushing sound in his ears had been deafening, and the shouts of the men onshore, the distorted babbling of demons. His eyes had been wide open, and he could half see his arms thrashing before him. When he thought he would burst, he had taken a breath of the water. Something in the ancient part of his brain screamed that if he did it again, he would die. Panic had propelled him high enough to cough up the water and seize a breath of air.

Jeb surely hadn't known how to swim, but he had seen men do it. Fighting terror, he had lain flat and flailed with his arms and legs, trying to grab breath when his head was free of the surface. Somehow, amid the fear and the choking, he had made slow progress toward the outstretched hands on the shore. He knew he had to press on like that now; make his legs work, make his mind work, and get to the boy.

The five men cut across the grass, the dirt path, and Hell's Circle without uttering a word. The big house was a drowsy creature now, the outside mottled with gray and purple shadows. There was a light in the glassy eyes, but little movement; Mrs. Smythe prided herself on running an orderly home, and all slave activity after dinner cleanup was frowned upon.

All five slaves approached the box in a straight line, with Jebediah at the front. He walked over to the door of the box and began to fiddle with the handle as Walt strode to the side and flapped his fingers quickly against the roof of the device.

"Still hot," he whispered. "But ain't like before."

"Give me the hammer, Solomon," Jebediah said. He tapped it lightly on the roof twice. "Don't ya worry, Johnny. We'll have you out in no time."

Jebediah pounded upward at the stick lodged between the metal of the door. Within seconds the tool did its work. He tossed the hammer to the side and pulled the door open, releasing a wave of hot, foul air on the group.

"Johnny," Jeb said forcefully. "You alright?"

Without waiting for an answer, he slid both arms in, reaching for the boy. He stopped. His hands had encountered a form too hot to be human.

"Ah, no," Jebediah gasped quietly. "Big Jim, help me."

Big Jim jumped down into the ditch and joined in the effort to remove the young slave from the box. The two men reached in and were able to pull him out by the legs. Then Jeb knelt beside him.

"Oh, God, no," he breathed.

The boy laid motionless, his shirt soaked with sweat and vomit. His face had a kind of gray, washed out look to it. His skin remained hot to the touch. Jebediah quickly put his ear to the boy's chest and his hand over the mouth.

"Sweet Jesus," Big Jim lamented. He was looking at the dried blood on Johnny Walker's fingers. The boy had tried to pry away the metal.

"H-he alive?" Thomas West asked, frightened.

"Aye," Jeb whispered. "Heart and breathing's quick, though. Too quick." He stood up and looked about him as if he hoped to spot tangible help for the boy. He settled on the men around him. "We got to get him back to the cabin right quick. Thomas, run back and get Mary Watley and her daughter and tell 'em to get to my cabin."

Thomas West nodded and sprinted off, defying the rule.

"Big Jim, help me get him up."

Big Jim helped to place the boy in the cradled arms of Jebediah. As the group hurried back toward the slave cabins, Walt walked next to

Jeb and held the boy's head level. Jeb refused at any point to hand the boy over, as hard as it was to bear him.

As Jeb pressed on, the heat of the boy's body was a constant admonition that he should have come straight in from the field when he heard the news—Gantry or no Gantry. It might have freed him from the heat sooner, it might have made a difference. Now he could only keep his legs working, carry the boy home, get him some help, make him safe.

He was passing the cabins now. They had a hazy look, like they were under water. He wondered if he was crying. Sound was distorted too. There was clapping and banjo playing somewhere up ahead. People were talking, and children were squealing as they ran about in their play—but only up ahead. When he came even with his neighbors, when they saw him carrying the boy, the pitch of their voices dropped, like the passing whistle of a night train. The sounds of cabin life were lower and slower behind him.

Jebediah stumbled through his open door and gently set the boy on the floor in the center of the cabin. Prudence stood off to the side, her hands on her cheeks, quivering. The children all froze in place, their young eyes fixed on Johnny Walker.

"Zeke," Jeb said from his knees with a calm force. "Get your brothers and sister and take 'em outside. Go to your uncle's cabin. Stay there."

Ezekiel obeyed without an argument, gathering the entranced children and escorting them outside; not an eye left the boy before Zeke closed the door behind him.

Jebediah was scared. Never before had he been struck with such a feeling of helplessness, of pure uncertainty, that leveled him as he knelt beside the boy he had raised for the last eight years.

His eyes remained on Johnny Walker's face, for he could not muster the courage to look at his Prudence. He had no answers. The most influential slave on the Smythe plantation was ashamed; ashamed he had not better protected the boy and, moreover, ashamed he did not now know how to save him. Prudence seemed to understand. She did not utter a word, thereby sparing him the effort of speech. She simply knelt down beside the boy, placing herself by his head, and began to gently rub her hand forward and back across his hair. Jebediah did not feel her glance upon him, and he was grateful, for he feared he would break if their eyes met.

Despite the aid of Mary Watley and her daughter, who repeatedly administered an herbal brew and sponged the boy with cool water throughout the night, Johnny Walker died in the early morning, before sunup. He passed with his surrogate mother and father clutching his hands and quoting passages from the Bible, neither having left his side from the moment he entered the cabin.

Prudence, with a voice as cool and calm as a spring Sunday morning, sang a hymn as Jebediah wrapped the boy in the good family blanket.

> *No more rain fall for wet you, Hallelujah,*
> *No more sun shine for burn you,*
> *There's no hard trials,*
> *There's no whips a-cracking,*
> *No evil-doers in the kingdom,*
> *All is gladness in the kingdom.*

No one spoke much at the communal breakfast, for the grief was too fresh. Soft words and gentle touches were replaced by a growing unease when the call to work was late in coming. When the house bell rang instead, it came as no surprise.

Jebediah could see Gantry sitting on the porch steps. The overseer waited until all were assembled before hauling himself up and shuffling across the grass. He looked like he'd had a bad night. His eyes were puffy, and lank strands of hair fell from behind his ears. If he had a comb, he had lost it. The buttons and buttonholes of his shirt were not lining up, and his belt had also gone missing. His left hand was now permanently stationed at his waistband. He cleared his throat and spat.

"I assume y'all know why we're here," he opened.

Before continuing, he pried his eyes open to their widest and scanned those present. What he saw must have surprised him, for his eyes narrowed and he shifted position as if uncomfortable. Jebediah glanced at the slaves around him. They were not looking at their feet or the sky, as was typical. Every slave's gaze was focused on the overseer.

Gantry increased his volume. "You are here because one of you, or more than one of you, defied me." He began to walk back and forth. "Yesterday, I sentenced the boy Johnny Walker to time in the box 'cause of his thievery. Yet, when I returned last night to release him, what did I find?" He paused. "Nothing. No one. The boy was gone. This just ain't acceptable. Now, I expect those of y'all that participated to step forward so that you may receive your punishment."

Jebediah felt Prudence squeeze his hand.

Gantry coughed, and then raised his voice. "If one of you does not step forward, then I'll be forced—"

Jebediah parted the two slaves standing before him and strode to the edge of the dirt circle, cutting short Gantry's threat. Big Jim, Solomon, Walt, and Thomas West followed immediately. The five men formed a line, all with their chests extended and their chins high, proud in their defiance.

Gantry moved toward the men, one hand on his pants and the other on the whip, stopping five feet away.

"Well, Solomon, I certainly ain't surprised to see you had a part in this. But I'm disappointed in the rest of y'all." If Gantry expected some sort of response, he received none. He looked right at Jebediah, who now looked past him. "So tell me, Jebediah, where's that boy of yours at now?"

Jeb did not answer or move, though his will was fighting a war of great proportion. He wanted to speak but he knew he dared not, for his level of control was by no means certain. Instead, his throat was clenched so tightly that it hurt, and his pulse began to beat in his temples.

Gantry's voice deteriorated into a growl. "I said, where's the boy at now?"

"He be dead sir," Walt muttered.

Elijah Gantry's mouth half opened, and he furrowed his brow. "Dead? God have mercy," he muttered, then stood silent for a time. He looked at the ground, the slaves, then back to the house. "But if he hadn't tried to steal Mrs. Smythe's silverware, none of this would have happened."

His own words seemed to embolden him, forcing back any guilt. "All of you remember, in the end it is not me, but the Lord God who passes the final judgment on your actions. However, do not let anyone say I have no compassion. There will be no whipping today." He swung around and started toward the house.

Jebediah felt oddly disappointed. He had never been beaten—ever. Yet, strange as it seemed, he had wanted the punishment now. The sting of the lash was a tangible pain that he felt he could face squarely and overcome. Perhaps it could displace the unfocused pain tearing at him from inside. He began to relax the tensed muscles that had held his body rigid and treelike before the overseer. Fatigue overcame the disappointment, and his entire body began to ache.

Gantry stopped after about ten paces and turned to face the group. He looked like he was having second thoughts about the whippings.

"I'll discuss what happened with Mr. Smythe and come up with an appropriate punishment," he warned. "But, for now, there's work to be done. We got to get the fields ready. Jebediah, you may take one other man and dig the boy's grave. Y'all can have the funeral next week after the field is planted. The rest of y'all get back to work."

He clapped his hands twice to dismiss the group, then shuffled off in the direction of his shack.

Jebediah and Thomas West made off for the storage shed to get a shovel so they could get on with burying Johnny Walker.

William Smythe made no bones about his lack of interest in the day-to-day operations of the plantation. After all, that is why he paid good money for an overseer, so that these things could be handled without his ever dealing with them. Farming was not his raison d'être—a mantra he repeated almost daily—and outside of griping about his slaves with other gentlemen at social gatherings, he was content to go through life without discussing them at all.

William Smythe had not put down cash for a new slave in years, so it never failed to amaze him that at each Sunday meeting he saw faces he could swear he had never seen before. He guessed it was because he never really looked at his slaves, but of course, they rarely looked at him either. If they did, it was certainly not with the filial love stressed by the preachers; the looks more closely resembled indifference. That suited Smythe just fine. He let Gantry preside over the roast pigs and barrels of bourbon. He let his dear wife keep track of the little darlings' names at baptisms. Outside of his personal attendants, he would be hard pressed to name five bondsmen under his control, and those would be the playmates of his youth.

Unfortunately, the continuing drought now threatened his self-prescribed lifestyle. For the last year and a half, his financial base had deteriorated as the Georgia ground dried up; meager cotton harvests and dropping international prices combined to strip the region of much of its wealth. After last year's poor harvest, and in the midst of a dry spring, William Smythe was forced to look at the books.

The situation had him in a permanently foul mood. Not only were his hunting trips fewer, country rides shorter, and parties less frequent, but that jackal of a wife was constantly nipping at his heels about money for the latest fashions or new English furniture for the house. He rued the day of his marriage, and when pushed would openly declare it, forcing the woman into a fit of hysterics that he rather enjoyed.

He glanced up briefly at the knock on the open study door. It was Gantry, unkempt as ever. If the man was not going to bother to wash his clothes, the least he could do was hang them up. The man obviously lacked the perspicacity to note his employer's example—every day a fastidious three-piece suit and a meticulously tied cravat.

"May I come in, sir?"

"Stomp your feet first," Smythe replied. "I don't want that infernal red dirt scattered throughout my study."

Gantry pounded his feet on the floor mat and tromped in gracelessly. He stopped three feet short of the desk and loomed over Smythe silently as the planter kept his eyes on the ledger.

"How's your family, sir? Your lovely children?" Gantry opened.

Smythe raised his hand, palm extended, and held it there for many seconds, offended by the overseer's interruption. Then, finally, he raised his eyes in concert with the lowering of the hand, stopping his gaze on the unshaven face of Elijah Gantry.

Smythe hated insipid small talk, especially from those who did not at least equal his social rank. He rolled his eyes and went straight to business. "Gantry, I called you here to discuss your wanton disregard for my property." Smythe gently rubbed his manicured mustache and paused for effect.

"Sir, I must protest. I ain't messed with any property of yours."

"But you have, *Mr.* Gantry," he said, twisting the *Mr.* in such a way as to make it offensive. "You see, I put you personally in charge of the welfare of all my slaves. *My* property. And yesterday, you saw fit to, how should I say this . . . disregard a slave boy's welfare. Now that boy is dead, worth nothing, and you sit here with the audacity to say you haven't *messed* with my property?" Smythe glowered but kept his tone even.

"Sir, the boy was fixing to steal Mrs. Smythe's silver."

"A punishable offense, for certain. But death? I find that a little extreme, don't you agree, Mr. Gantry?"

"Yes, sir. I will be more careful in the future."

"Indeed you will, and you will also be fined. While in ten years you could not possibly be able to afford to pay me what that boy was worth, you will still take some responsibility. A dollar-fifty a month from your salary."

Gantry fiddled with his hands. "Yes, sir."

"Good. Now, there is another pressing matter. Unfortunately, as you know, financially we are not what we were just a couple years ago. This—"

"I know, but that's all gonna change. I can feel it, sir. Rains are coming."

The planter slammed his hand down onto the desk, forcing Gantry to jump back. "This is important," he declared forcefully. "In order to stay economically viable, we are going to have to make drastic changes. I just returned from town, where I made a deal to sell off five of our women slaves of childbearing age to a man interested in taking them west. Mississippi, I believe. I know this will be an unpopular decision.

However, without an infusion of cash now, this plantation will not survive until the next harvest. In order for food to remain on our tables, the sacrifice must be made."

"I understand, sir. Do you know which five you want to sell?"

"I have a list of names here, based on my records. I picked out five over the age of twenty-seven—no sense giving away young ones if I don't have to. Also, none with children under three." He handed the list to Gantry, who looked down at the names. "Have them ready this afternoon. You will take them to town yourself."

"Yes, sir." Gantry pursed his lips, then spoke. "You know, sir, one of these is a widow, but the rest is married women. I could—"

Smythe held up his palm. He allowed a hint of venom into his voice. "If you had done your job better, this action would not be necessary. My decision is based upon sound business reasoning. The buyer won't exactly accept eight-year-olds or eighty-year-olds, will he?" He paused while Gantry shuffled his feet. "According to my records, these are the best ones to go."

"Yes, sir."

"One other thing," Smythe said, his eyes returning to the ledger. "I don't want there to be a horrid scene with them and their families. Crying and the like. You know as well as I do, darkies get far too emotional. Make sure you remove them subtly, as to not arouse suspicion. The last thing I need with this headache is to hear little children whimpering all day long. Do you understand, Gantry?"

"I do, sir," Gantry answered. The overseer started for the door, then stopped for a moment, eyeing the list.

"What now?" Smythe snapped.

"Nothing, sir." Gantry walked out the door and down the hall, dragging his boots on the carpet.

Prudence wasn't home when Jebediah returned after the long day. She had been one of the five women hired out to the Berger plantation for the afternoon to clean out the chicken coops. Jeb walked the children down to supper, and at dusk, when Prudence still hadn't returned, the children began to grow alarmed.

"No need ta worry," Jeb told them. "None of the women is back from Berger's yet. They got 'em a late start. Nat said Gantry didn't come pick up your momma and the others till after midday."

"The road over to Berger's goes by Ferson Creek," Zeke said to his father out of earshot of the other children. "Ain't that where they seen the panther tracks?"

"Aye, folks say they seen 'em. So my guess is, if the women finished up late, they'll probably bring 'em back early on the 'morrow."

Jeb was saddened at the thought. He would have welcomed the comfort of Prudence's low, gentle voice, the peace he felt when he held her.

He read to the children from the Scriptures before bedtime—one of their favorite stories, Daniel in the lion's den. When all but Zeke were quiet and sleepy, he left them in his charge and walked down to join the folks by the campfire at the commons.

There was not much talking going on. Old Mosley was strumming his banjo, and most were just listening. After a few nights, Jeb knew that folks would start telling their stories about Johnny Walker. How he wouldn't eat anything green, about the time he hooked a big ol' fish and put it on Granny Bev's line when she was sleeping, and how he tried to act like a man when he was scared. But it was still too soon.

There were three or four folks gathered around Hannibal, who was conjuring with some chicken bones. He was shaking them in his jar and tossing them out in the dust. After a few minutes, those around him got to buzzing. Christmas left the group and came over to sit beside Solomon, one down from Jeb. He spoke in a low tone.

"Hannibal says something ain't right."

"Do tell." Solomon nodded as if the young slave was stating the obvious.

"He don't know what it is yet," Christmas went on, "but he thinks it be bad."

Jeb turned away from the conversation. He didn't place much credence in Hannibal's predictions, but he avoided contradicting him. The conjurer made dozens of predictions every week, but folks only seemed to remember the ones he got right. Tonight the prediction gave Jeb a hollow feeling nonetheless.

A commotion began over by the first row of cabins. Hetty's beau,

Damon, a free black man who bought and sold rags among the plantations, had just come by to see her. After the first deep rumble of his voice, hers came in high-pitched and agitated. "No! That ain't right. You're lying!"

He grabbed Hetty by the shoulders, and she started wailing. He started shaking her, and Jebediah called out, "What ya doing down there?"

Damon let go of Hetty and walked slowly toward the group. The men at the fire stood up. Damon had always been an outgoing type, but now he did not seem to know who to look at. He kept glancing among the men, then his eyes settled on the fire.

He spoke in a low, even voice. "This afternoon, early on, I was over by Wilmont. A white man had a wagon of women he said he'd just bought. They was setting out for Mississippi. I recognized some of 'em and went on over to see Sheriff Maston. Told him I knew some of 'em was from the plantation around here, and I asked him if it was legal. I give him stuff free, so he don't mind talking with me. He said Mr. Smythe had signed the papers good and proper, and Gantry had brung 'em over himself this morning.

"I recognized two of the women." He looked at Big Jim. "Your Sally was there, and so was Prudence." He glanced at Jebediah, then looked away.

"It can't be!" Big Jim's sister jumped up. "They's working at Berger's. Just for the day."

"You ain't met Sally but once," Big Jim said. He sounded mad at Damon. "You gotta be mistaken."

Damon's voice was low and sad. "The sheriff got no reason to lie."

"How many?" Walt asked. His voice did not sound like it came from him; it cracked when he spoke. He grabbed Damon by the arms. "How many women was in the wagon?"

"There was five."

There were shouts and cries of grief all around him, but Jebediah just stood very still.

"No." He shook his head. "No." His voice wasn't loud or even agitated, but the inflection was wrong. It rose up at the end like a question.

The others were yelling and looking at him, and he was just standing there. Then he heard the water rising. It was rising fast, coming up around his head. Folks were still talking loudly to him, but he was very calm, just listening to the water coming.

He thought he saw Prudence for a moment in the faces pressed around him. But he knew she was gone and not coming back. "Not my Prudence. Oh, my Lord." He heard his own voice saying it. But then it was drowned out by the sound of the water and the sound of his heart hammering in his ears. He started to kick hard, fighting for the surface, but the water was pulling him down . . . down . . .

He should have realized it before. It wasn't so bad if you stopped struggling and just let it wash over you—if you breathed it in, very deeply.

Jebediah himself was a little surprised at how steady his voice sounded as he discussed the course of action with the men. As the nine who had decided to leave the campfire moved ahead down the path, Jebediah stood facing Thomas West. Thomas was working up his courage to speak.

"J-Jeb. You s-sound real c-calm like. B-but are you alright?"

Jeb looked at his cousin for a long moment. "Thomas, I love you like a brother, always have and will fo'ever. But now there's something I have to ask of you."

"Sh-sh-sure, Jeb."

"Don't come with us tonight. Now hear me out. The children be too young to fend fo' themselves, all except Zeke. I need you to look after 'em." He stopped and looked into his cousin's eyes. "Please, Thomas, will you do this for me?"

Thomas West nodded slowly. Jeb stepped forward and grasped the man in his long arms, squeezing him tightly before kissing his cheek.

"God bless ya, Thomas. Now go back to the campfire. Stay there till the others return to their cabins. Then you go ta yours and stay inside till it be morn."

Jeb walked to his door, leaving Thomas West alone on the warm Georgia night.

"I l-l-loves you t-t-too, Jeb."

My Lord. My Lord. My Lord.

• • •

Eight of the slaves hid in the woods as they were told, while Solomon and Jeb walked toward the overseer's hut. There was no stealth in their actions. Jeb thought that if you were about to kill a man, there should be nothing sneaky about it. As they reached the doorway, both men stopped and looked at one another. Solomon was working his mouth. Jeb could see that he was trying hard to swallow. Jeb put a hand on his arm and raised his eyebrows in question. Solomon took a couple of quick breaths, then nodded. Jeb turned back to the wooden door and delivered a fierce kick just below the handle. The latch splintered, and the door fell open with a crack.

"What in God's name," the voice from the back of the room rasped, muddled by sleep.

The light of the full moon was at their backs. The two men could see Elijah Gantry quite clearly, but he was squinting at them, moving his head from side to side as if trying to figure things out. Their long shadows fell upon him as they approached. Gantry fumbled for the oil lamp on his nightstand and managed to light it as the men stopped just feet away. Jebediah Jones, ax in hand, met his startled eyes with cold indifference. Then Solomon leaped forward with the knife.

Solomon thrust twice, to the stomach and the chest, bloodying the overseer before the man was able to throw the attacker off onto the floor. The blood was spurting out of the chest wound, and Gantry looked at it as if surprised. He tried to stop it with his hand. The eyes looked up at Jebediah.

"Please," the man gasped.

Solomon was now back on his feet. He stood motionless, looking at Gantry. The blood was welling up, and Gantry started to twitch, then flop around like a fish. Solomon kept trying to swallow. Two pairs of terrified eyes looked to Jebediah.

He slowly raised his thumb to his neck and ran it quickly across his throat. In a moment it was over.

The two slaves found the others where they waited by the edge of the woods. Both men carried torches they had lit from the lamp in Gantry's shack. Jebediah saw his companions' faces in the sharp angles of light and shadow cast by the torches. They first studied Solomon, covered in blood but uninjured, then Jebediah. The faces changed as they looked; he watched them harden into masks of resolve. Then the men moved on to the house.

They approached from behind the azalea hedge, moved along the side of the house, and came at it from the rear. The light of the torches reflected on the darkened windows as they passed.

Jebediah climbed the porch steps and the men followed him. They walked right in through the unlocked kitchen door.

The kitchen boy, asleep on his pallet by the pantry, heard them enter. He made no sound, but followed their progress through the dining room, where the torch light glinted off glass panes of the china cabinet and the silver service on the sideboard. Their shadows followed them like giants; the china rattled as they passed.

He watched them move into the open front hall, where two staircases began on opposite ends of the room and arched inward to meet at the second-floor landing. Each torch led half the men up an opposite staircase; the two black symmetrical snakes with heads of fire wound up the steps at the same moment. Then they disappeared into the upstairs hallway, leaving only light and shadow.

The boy heard Missy Margaret's sleepy, high-pitched voice call out, "Mammy, is that you?"

Then she started screaming, at first like she did when her brother threatened her with a frog. But after that, like nothing he had ever heard. And then little Massa Robert started screaming too.

Grown-ups were yelling, but he couldn't tell who they were or what they were saying. And above it all, the missus's little dog kept barking and barking. He put his fingers in his ears to block out the noise, until one by one, the voices stopped.

And then he heard it, and the hair prickled on his neck, and he shivered clear down to his bones.

"Ah-ooo, ah-ooo, ah-ooo," the little dog howled on and on in the darkness.

The men split up after they left the house. Some took the road that led away from town, while others took the path into the north woods.

Jebediah shuffled back across the plantation, entering the cabin where the "Jones Family" sign hung slanted on the door.

Inside he sat in his chair, watching the children sleep for a final time; their heavy breathing, like God's whisper. He stood, then walked up to the children, placing a gentle kiss on each forehead, hoping to God that one day they could forgive him for what he had done. Thomas West would look after them. He was a good man. And in spite of his stutter he was a whole man.

Jeb knew that the waters had claimed him. They had swept away all that he had and all that he had been, including that part deep inside that masters and overseers had not been able to touch. There was nothing left of Jebediah Jones.

Only from the top of Harold's Hill could one have seen the shadow slip across the far fields, disappearing into the great dark forest of pine.

ONE

❦

Horace Simpson looked at his pocket watch for the third time in the space of half an hour, then snapped it shut and absentmindedly let the braided fob slide through his fingers. He regarded it for a moment as it began its slow, pendulous arc, then abruptly snatched it back and stuffed it into his pocket.

The body of the hanged negro he found that morning had swung in the same manner, as the wind had toyed with the corpse, its hands tied behind its back and its legs tied together. The gusts had blown the body in a circular fashion—the motion occasionally interrupted as the feet had bumped the trunk of the oak. With each gust, the rope had creaked like a porch swing.

Simpson ultimately helped to cut him down, for the young man from the mayor's office obviously had no stomach for it.

"This isn't normal," the man stammered.

Simpson did not doubt that the young man was unaccustomed to dealing with hanged bodies; he kept swallowing every few seconds, wiping his mouth with the back of his coat sleeve as if the nausea might overtake him.

"Do you know who he is?" Simpson asked.

The clerk nodded. "His name is Lawrence Mills . . . a local cabi-netmaker."

"And what did he do?"

"Probably nothing." The young man made several attempts to cover Mills's face with a discarded feed sack, but the wind kept blowing it aside. "There have been rumors of unrest among the negroes here in the city. Mills's name came up, but we knew at City Hall that there was nothing to it. We were pretty sure that a competitor implicated him just to cause him trouble."

"Looks like he succeeded," Simpson remarked with more than a trace of sarcasm.

The clerk's face was earnest as he met Simpson's eyes. "Charleston is not usually like this. Things just aren't normal right now—not since the killings over in Habersham County. Civility is part of our upbringing here. We treat each other with common courtesy. . . ."

Simpson found himself smiling as he recalled the young man's remarks. How typical of Charleston that a civil servant would describe a lynching in terms of a social faux pas. Simpson guessed that the young man had not worked at the mayor's office very long. In his own experience, visiting Charleston as he had over the years, he knew that lynchings were rarely isolated incidents. They seemed to be the result of too much steam building in the pressure cooker. A black would step out of line, commit a crime against a white man, and the whole city was thrown into an uproar. Black "troublemakers" were rounded up; a few might get some sense beaten into them, and a few might be lynched. After all, to the men who perpetrated these acts, it was not a life—it was just a nigger.

This particular civil servant, clearly a more sensitive type, had obviously been rattled by the incident—so much so that he had subsequently spilled a great deal of information to a wily out-of-town reporter. Characteristically, Simpson took satisfaction in manipulating the situation entirely to his own advantage. How else could he have landed *this* interview; he alone of all the reporters in town?

Simpson avoided the impulse to recheck his watch and glanced at the sun instead. He again took stock of his surroundings.

He was on one of several wharf-lined spots of land jutting into Charleston's natural harbor. The bay was calm today, more reminiscent of a lake than a sea as it gently lapped at the skirts of the barrier islands to the east.

The eight spires of Charleston's grand churches presided over the city. The irony was not lost on the reporter. New York City had many imposing churches, certainly more than Charleston, yet New York's other tall buildings limited the view to one or two spires from any perspective. Here in Charleston, however, one was hard pressed to find a spot where one could not see all eight—a constant reminder of the omnipresence of the Almighty. This, in a town one northern theologian had dubbed "the unholiest city west of Constantinople."

The steeple bells were always ringing for one reason or another. They announced the hour of the day and the beginning and end of church services. They rang for births, deaths, fires, and ships in peril. The locals always seemed to know what they signified, but the constant ringing was anathema to a visiting reporter. Simpson never knew if he should be resetting his watch or dashing off to cover some catastrophe. He ultimately resolved to ignore them altogether.

But the bells were blessedly silent now, for Charleston was napping. Curled up in a blanket of summer haze and surrounded by green pines and blue waters, her peace was only disturbed by the busy cicadas whirring to each other in the heat, and irate seagulls calling out taunts as they vied for position near the wharf where the fishing boats docked.

The wharves on the finger of land where Simpson stood were deserted. The hoists and dollies were locked away in a nearby warehouse until the shipping season. "Sandman's Storage," the wind-routed sign read. Simpson chuckled at the irony. He had checked out the interior of the building upon his arrival and found that it presently housed two militiamen sleeping off a drunk. Both were armed to the teeth. Each napped with his shotgun laid out beside him like a favorite doll, and one had a daunting array of knives lined up in decreasing order of size like instruments in a surgery.

Some of their blue-coated cohorts were making busy on a wharf on the next finger of land about a quarter-mile north, calling to each other in lazy backwoods drawls as they set their hoists in place. "Like water sloshing around in a gutter," Simpson liked to say when describing southern speech to his fellow reporters. "Most of what they say seems unintelligible unless you know the secret." Here Simpson would pause and wink. "I have discovered that after about three of their bourbons, it all becomes crystal clear."

Simpson bought the mayor's assistant a drink after their grisly encounter. He probed for inside information on the trial and on the political machinations of the locals. He queried the young man about the presence of the militia in such large numbers for the trial. The clerk seemed loath to speak of them at first, as if their coarseness was yet another blot on the city's character.

"You're right," the young man finally conceded quietly. "There are more of them here than we need for the trial. But you must remember, the Smythe plantation is less than a hundred miles away. We were not sure at first if the uprising there was the beginning of a general insurrection or, at the very least, a spark that might set off a similar incident."

"From what I have heard," Simpson countered, "the incident in Georgia hardly seemed an uprising. Ten dead, weren't there? Four of the Smythe household, the overseer, three of the house slaves, and two bounty hunters. All within twenty-four hours. A murderous rampage, yes. But I do not see evidence of a vast conspiracy . . . and they caught all but one of the murderers."

"That's just the point. They didn't catch the ringleader, Jebediah Jones. Rumor has it that he is roaming the countryside, recruiting an army."

"Don't you find it hard to believe that runaways could be present anywhere in such numbers? If even one escapes, a posse of bounty hunters is on the trail immediately." Simpson shook his head. "I can't believe that runaways are massing in numbers anywhere."

"It isn't really runaways that people are worried about. You must remember something, sir. We have about twelve thousand negroes here in Charleston, a number almost equal to that of the whites. Most are law-abiding, I give you. But there are a few bad apples . . ." He glanced around to see if anyone appeared to be eavesdropping, then lowered his voice. "I'm sure you have heard of Denmark Vesey."

"I have."

The young man sighed and shook his head. "For some reason, the fear never goes away."

Simpson understood. He guessed that it had come ashore with the first slave ships, like a plague transported with the cargo. For the slaveholder, the fear was incubated with the hatred of the heathen souls they could not, *would not*, assimilate—a hatred that would one day rise up and exact a terrible revenge.

Thirty years ago, their worst fears were almost realized. Denmark Vesey, a slave who bought his freedom after winning the lottery, apparently formulated a horrific plan—an uprising involving hundreds of slaves and free blacks. Simpson had stumbled across old newspaper accounts while sharing a bottle with a couple of cronies deep in the tombs of the *Tribune* one cold winter night. Piece by piece, investigators exposed the threads of a plot to murder all white slave owners and seize control of Charleston. The blacks would then commandeer the ships in the harbor and sail to Haiti, but only after their vengeance was complete and Charleston lay in smoldering ruins. Slaughter was avoided only because two slaves had misgivings and revealed the plot to their masters. Subsequently, hundreds of conspirators were arrested, and over sixty were hanged, including Denmark Vesey. The severity of the threat and its chance revelation raised goose bumps on the reporters. Simpson could only imagine the effect on Charleston's whites— the folks with the keys to the shackles.

"So the militia were called up right after the Georgia uprising," Simpson continued.

"Shortly after, yes. The governor activated them for our protection."

Simpson leaned forward. "What did your mayor have to do to get the governor to cooperate? Your governor never grants anything without a quid pro quo. I also understand that there has been a history of conflict between those two offices."

"I really wouldn't know anything about that, sir."

• • •

At that point the interview ended. Then, this morning, a messenger arrived, offering the most unlikely of interviews—one so important Simpson had trouble concentrating throughout the day. The rendezvous was to be here, at this isolated location, at 3:00 p.m.

But Simpson's contact was nearly one hour late—unacceptable even by southern standards. An idea now began to gnaw at the back of his mind. What if he had been drawn here for some other purpose? What if no one was coming? He looked back at the city and stared for a long moment. Had someone dangled the bait of a secret meeting to keep him from a real scoop back there?

When the fire bells began to ring, they did not surprise the reporter. He had already begun to retrace his steps toward town. A plume of smoke was rising at the south end of the city. Simpson guessed that it was just blocks from his lodgings.

A sound behind him caused him to turn his head, and for a moment he froze.

"My God! What is going on here?"

The militiamen were standing stock-still also, staring right at him. Even at a distance, their expressions and body language were unmistakable. Within a few quickened heartbeats, Simpson leaped to the realization that the sole intent of the appointment was to deliver him to this place, and that his promised contact would never arrive.

He turned and began to run, aware that he had probably uncovered the best story of his career, but might never escape to tell it. He did not look back behind him, just at the rising plume of smoke to the south. He ran until the shuffle of his shrinking strides was swallowed by the thud of footfall around him. He was approaching the first block of buildings, the first paved street. Now he only needed to round the corner and melt into the crowd.

Then came the explosion—or maybe it was only in his head— sparks and darkness. When the light came back, he found he didn't hurt—not really. But he knew beyond doubt that his body was irreparably broken.

As the light began to fade, he willed himself to focus on the face bent over his. Then maybe he smiled a little at the final irony that the Prince of Darkness should prove to be a young man with blond hair.

TWO

JUNE 30, 1850

Y ou be walking in dead man's shoes," Toby intoned. Characteristically, he did not explain himself. He just kept sweeping dust and scraps of paper from under John Sharp's desk while John pushed back his chair and lifted his feet clear.

"I'm pretty sure these are mine, Toby," John responded with a smile.

The wrinkled black man had a habit of dropping ominous lines like that when he and John were alone in the building at night—remnants of folklore from the dark days of Toby's youth, mingled with gossip about the day's headlines.

"You know what I mean. Going down there. Taking his place when they done gone and killed him." Toby stopped sweeping and looked hard at John, squinting with just one eye. "On the plantation where I grew up, when a slave died, if he had him a pair of shoes, them shoes was passed on. Not to kin like his other belongings. The shoes went to him that they fit."

"That seems like a practical arrangement," John commented.

"But they wasn't always a blessing, them dead man's shoes. You had ta watch 'em, else they could take you down the same path as him that had 'em before—straight to the grave."

"You can be sure that I'll watch where I'm walking, Toby," John replied. "That was Simpson's problem. From what I hear, no one killed him. He just wasn't looking where he was going. There was commotion in the street, and he ran out in front of a fire wagon."

Toby nodded slowly. "Seems to me there's as much commotion as that in New York, and Mr. Simpson done alright here." Toby locked eyes with John and his voice fell lower. "You see, you gotta be careful in Charleston—even more than the other southern towns. She's different. She's a Jezebel." His voice fell to a whisper. "And if you ask me, that whole town is headed straight for hell."

Now, as John Sharp stepped from the train onto the platform of Charleston station, the blast of heat convinced him that the city was already halfway there.

John set down his suitcase and checked his breast pocket for the address of his local contact. He looked about for a carriage for hire. The train's passengers and the locals who had met them were dispersing in all directions, like a handful of marbles dropped on a sidewalk—all but two men who were bucking the flow. John had spotted them leaning against the wall on the shady side of Charleston station, but now they roused themselves like lazy alley cats and wound a slow approach through the crowd. John glanced around at the porters and the few remaining passengers. They were all looking at him. The trajectory of the two men was clear.

"You there, sir. Don't be a-walking off." It was the nearest of the approaching duo.

John glanced briefly over his shoulder, then back at the man who had spoken. "Are you addressing me?" His tone was crisp yet polite, suggesting an obvious case of mistaken identity.

"Yessir, you."

The leader stopped a few feet from John, one hand on his hip, the other in his pants pocket. He wore a half-buttoned blue wool jacket over a dingy undershirt and shapeless gray pants. The younger, dim-looking man hanging just behind him was similarly attired, but had opted to forgo the formality of a jacket. His right hand was also shoved deeply into his pocket.

"I'll be needing ta know your name and your business here, sir," the man with the jacket said, puffing out his chest a bit.

John decided that the man's posture was a bluff. While he himself might be on unfamiliar ground in a strange town, these men seemed distinctly out of their element addressing a man beyond their class. As their eyes examined John thoroughly from derby hat to three-piece-suit to polished shoes, their expressions wavered between pretense of authority and outright discomfort. Any semblance of confidence came solely from the one blue jacket they possessed between them.

John opted for a businesslike response. "My name is John Sharp. I am a reporter for the *New York Tribune*."

The men's reaction was akin to that of fishermen who had watched bobbers all day and finally had a nibble. The man with the jacket quickly withdrew a pencil and scrap of paper from his pocket. He marked the paper with deliberation.

"Shaaap," he repeated, drawing out the name like a yawn. He moved his tongue to facilitate transcription, then nodded toward John's brown leather suitcase as he replaced the paper and pencil. "You're gonna have to open that." There was more confidence in his tone now, as if the play was beginning to follow the script.

"Perhaps you could explain why," John prompted.

"I'm the law. Gotta check for contraband."

John handed over the key. While the inspection of a gentleman's baggage was unseemly, to say the least, John was more interested in discovering the nature of the men's odd assignment than challenging their authority. He watched their expressions closely as they opened his bag. They were obviously disappointed to find an orderly array of folded shirts and pants.

"What were you looking for?" he asked.

The men glanced at each other but said nothing. John decided that the remaining desultory pokes through his underwear were strictly a formality. Whatever they were looking for was large enough to have been apparent from the moment the bag was opened; large, but probably not heavy.

Just as the man in the blue jacket began to close the suitcase, the encounter took an odd turn. The younger man stepped forward and deliberately kicked dirt into John's folded clothes. The leader's head snapped around to take in John's reaction, while the youngster backed away with a snide, self-satisfied look—like a small sneaky mongrel that had managed to get in a nip while its target's back was turned.

"Terribly clumsy of you," John remarked coldly, reclaiming his key. As he shook the dust from his clothes and closed the bag, the two men walked wordlessly back to their spot by the depot, sauntering slowly as if nothing untoward had transpired.

John glanced about with the aim of securing a carriage or assistance with his bag. But no one was looking at him now. The passengers and carriages had departed. The trainmen were making ready for their next run.

"Porter!" John called to a group of ragged black men lounging on the far side of the platform. They had assisted passengers with their bags, but now the men fidgeted. They looked anywhere but in the direction of the New Yorker. John was a marked man.

He withdrew a handkerchief and wiped his forehead. He was contemplating toting the bag across town himself when the rapid slap of bare feet on hardpan road drew his attention to the approach of a gangly black boy of eleven or twelve. The boy stopped about a dozen feet away, then stiffened to attention like a soldier on parade. He initially focused on John's shoes, but he was apparently a curious sort, for he hazarded a peek at the traveler's face.

John put the handkerchief away. "It is hot here," he commented.

"Yessir," the boy said, nodding. "Folks say the devil takes vacation here in the summer . . . especially this one." The eyes flickered a moment, then made a quick scan of the horizon as if searching for something—a reflexive response to superstition, perhaps. His next words were softer. "You be needing a porter fo' your bag, sir?"

"Actually, I was hoping to find a carriage for hire."

The boy shook his head. "No chance fo' chasing one down. They's long gone."

John gave the boy an appraising look. A thin frame hid beneath an oversize outfit like a turtle within its shell; only the boy's hands protruded from two rolled-up sleeves, and his head peeked out from a tall collar that rode just under his chin. His pants sat well above the waist in the grip of suspenders, integral supports that clung to his chest and fanned his shirt wide to both sides. But what the boy lacked in size, he apparently made up in diligence. The face was all business.

"Very well." John glanced at the folded notepaper he retrieved from his breast pocket. It bore the address of his lone contact here in Charleston. "Do you know how to get to Tradd Street? Number 107?"

The boy nodded enthusiastically. "Yessir. Only 'bout a mile from here."

"Then it looks like I have hired myself a porter."

The boy eagerly hefted John's bag. If he was at all fazed by its weight, he did not show it.

"What is your name?"

"Samuel. Samuel Grass."

"Nice to meet you, Samuel. I am John Sharp. So shall we get under way?"

"Yessir, just this way, sir," Samuel said, removing one hand from the bag and using it to point left onto Washington Street.

They ventured onto a street lined with nearly identical wooden houses standing elbow to elbow. None rose more than three stories, and each hid a long body behind a narrow facade. The blocks ahead promised more of the same. Apparently, Charleston's reputation for flamboyance did not extend to architecture in this part of town.

The city's odor was another story—a deep breath of the hot, heavy air nearly triggered John's gag reflex. The smell was like none he had ever experienced, a mix of several distinct odors. He took an analytical breath through his nose, attempting to identify the ingredients of the atmospheric stew. He spotted the wharves as they crossed a side street and heard the faint yells of the stevedores. The smell was definitely reminiscent of the New York waterfront—of waste from fishing boats, garbage, and bilge water. His imagination added decaying semitropical vegetation and rich alluvial mud to the mix, and possibly a dead alligator. He had never seen or smelled one, but he just knew that one of the dead creatures would stink like this.

But the smell was not all that was "off" in Charleston. John glanced back toward the station, which was now obscured from view.

He turned to the boy. "Those men who spoke to me back there, do you know who they were?"

Samuel also looked over his shoulder. "Don't know their names, but they is militia."

"I see," John replied. "Are militia usually at the station?"

The boy hesitated. "No, sir. Just the last few days. When the train be a-coming."

"Do you know what they are looking for?"

The boy glanced at John's face, then furrowed his brow. "No one be telling me."

John could not help but smile. Toby back in New York used that line, too. It was a good dodge, but it also meant he had acquired knowledge by other means. He just wasn't talking—yet. John knew he could always get people to talk. The boy would open up before they parted company, just like everyone else did.

"Time will be a problem for you," Robert Haggerty, editor in chief of the *New York Tribune*, had remarked two days earlier as John took the chair opposite his desk. "You will not have much of it to get to the bottom of this assignment. Simpson would have had over a week to get the background I wanted on this trial, but he managed to get himself killed his third day in Charleston."

Haggerty picked up a cable on his desk and scowled, then tossed it back. He glanced at John. "Did you know him?"

"I had met him only briefly."

"Well, Simpson was a good reporter, but he had a tendency to drink more than was good for him. That may have been his undoing."

"What happened?" John asked. "I've only heard rumors at this point."

"He was apparently chasing down a fire. Fire bells were ringing, horses were spooked, and Simpson managed to get run over by a fire wagon. Died right there on the spot." Haggerty shook his head. "It was broad daylight, for God's sake."

The editor gave John a hard look. "If I send you down there, I assume from your background that you will not fall prey to the same pitfalls as Simpson?"

John treated it as a rhetorical question and nodded in response.

Haggerty rose and walked to the window. "Well, I picked you for the job for more than your character. The piece you turned in on Astor Place makes me think that you can deliver what I'm looking for.

"The people down there are making a statement with this trial; I'm just not sure what they are saying or what they are trying to accomplish. They could have dispensed with the matter quickly, and no one north of Mason-Dixon would have noticed much one way or the other. But that is not how they chose to handle it."

John opened his notebook. "Do you already have an angle? Did Mr. Simpson give you anything?"

"No, but I'll tell you generally what I'm looking for." Haggerty walked back to his desk and sat down. "I am not looking for a mere transcript of the trial. If that was all, I'd just send down one of the usual court reporters. Rather, I want to understand the social and political ramifications of this situation—what rich and poor, white and negro, think of the crime and the accused. Northern and southern perspectives on this are so different—they are indicative of a widening gulf between us. I want to know how far this impasse over slavery will take us. How diligently will these people fight?" He paused and stared at John. "And can they win?"

Haggerty smiled. "And I will need you to uncover all of this in a few days. Are you up to it?"

John chuckled. "Sure." He paused, then raised an eyebrow. "And Mr. Simpson?"

"You were briefly with the penny press before you started with us."

John nodded.

"Well, it would be natural that you would be thinking along those lines, given your past experience. But I already have it on good authority that Simpson's death was truly accidental." The editor pursed his lips. "And there is another reason I don't want you dogging Simpson's footsteps." He picked up the cable and handed it to John. "I debated showing you that. Simpson sent it the day before he died."

Strange unrest here. STOP Hornet's nest. STOP Key interview tomorrow. END

John just looked at Haggerty.

"Don't ask me what in the hell that means. I sent Simpson down there to cover a trial, and I get this cryptic nonsense. I wish to God the man had spent the money I gave him on his cables.

"But here is the crux of the matter. Charleston has its social problems. Hell, so does New York. You have worked in the Five Points—I don't need to tell you. Incidents trigger flare-ups; feuds can turn volatile. But sometimes poking a stick into a hornet's nest is not worth the danger—not when there is already a significant story."

Haggerty tapped his finger on his desk for emphasis. "Do not become sidetracked in Charleston. I am interested in one story down there, and that is the trial. Peripheral issues interest me only as they relate to those proceedings."

John paused. "So who is the defendant?"

"Some poor bastard named Darcy Nance Calhoun."

John continued his walk toward downtown Charleston, mulling over the unusual nature of his assignment. It was the polar opposite of most stories. The specifics—the who, what, and where—of the crime in question were generally known. It was the *why* that pitted two societies, indeed two of the Commandments, against each other. It was the *why* that would ultimately decide the fate of the defendant.

As John had considered the assignment on his train ride south, he was cognizant of the level of respect his editor had shown in him by not assigning an angle. Many major stories started simply with an editorial premise, and the reporter was sent to gather the facts that fit. This task was infinitely more challenging. Now, he would begin to search for the reasons that made two cities view a trial so differently. What was it in the nature of this place, its people, and its recent history that made an action that New Yorkers did not consider a crime at all a capital offense in Charleston?

John was jolted from his thoughts by the tolling of a bell. A grand white steeple behind the near row of houses began to reverberate. Just below its peak and to the right, another, virtually identical, began to peal as well. Soon all the bells of Charleston joined in, a cacophonous symphony that stopped John in his tracks. No wonder horses were spooked in this town.

Samuel turned once he noticed that John had stopped. He looked at him quizzically. " 'Tis three o'clock. That's all."

Before they could proceed, a disembodied metal wheel rim rolled out from the narrow corridor between the homes, followed by a jostling group of urchins, black and white, armed with sticks. They stopped when they got a look at John and conferred in a huddle. A small blond boy broke off from the group and approached.

"Please, sir. Can you spare some change fo' an orphan, sir?" he asked.

John looked at the boy, who regarded him with deep-set, saucer eyes. His cheeks were mud-streaked, his shirt misbuttoned, and he had a small cut above his chapped lips. The boy's expression was so pathetic that John dug his hand into his suit pocket, pulled out a penny, and then handed it to the child.

"Thank ya, sir," the boy replied before running off.

Immediately he was replaced by four others, the echoing cry of "Please, sir" now bombarding him incessantly.

Samuel walked up behind the group of boys and clapped his hands. "Go on now. Git. All y'all. Git!"

The tallest of the group, a white boy with lank brown bangs that nearly covered his eyes, withdrew an object from his pocket—a clothespin with a bit of string attached. The boy dangled it in front of Samuel and set it to swinging. Samuel snatched it away and stuffed it into his own pocket.

"Y'all git! *Now!*"

The boys scattered at the sound of Samuel's order, squealing and giggling, then re-formed on the heels of the blond boy, their metal hoop rolling before them.

"Thank you, Samuel," John said as the two walked back to where the boy had set down the suitcase.

"It's no trouble. You gotta be careful 'round here. Folks ain't always what they appear to be. Like that boy you just gave the penny. He ain't no orphan. In fact, if there was a real orphan in that crowd, I'd be mighty surprised. They is just a scamming. They can tell who's a foreigner."

"I figured as much."

"They'll steal, too," the boy continued. "Just as sure as looking at ya."

John smiled. "Yes, I know. Where I come from, we have people like that as well."

Samuel picked up the baggage, lifting from the legs and stumbling a couple steps forward, waiting for momentum to take control. John realized with amusement that his contribution to street theater had been misinterpreted by the boy. Samuel obviously now considered his employer naive and in need of protection. The response was indicative of an honest and conscientious nature. Samuel might be a reliable source of information.

He had another thought. "Samuel, do you think they knew *I* was a foreigner?"

"Oh, for certain. Yessir."

"And why is that?"

Samuel turned his head upward and squinted at John. Apparently, the foreigner's demeanor told him that he could forgo the typical etiquette. "Can't really explain it, except to say that you just look out of place, sir. Sort of like a hound in a coonskin."

John could not help but laugh, and Samuel flashed him a smile.

John glanced at the people about him in the street and immediately noticed a difference in demeanor. The gentlemen and ladies strolled as if they were part of the matinee show of some pageant. With no hint of deference to carriage or wagon, they walked as if the tide turned on their schedule. Even the laborers, black and white, moved with a lazy kind of ease.

He did notice a difference among the blacks, however. In dress, they varied as much from each other as did their white counterparts, yet all observed certain conventions. At John's approach, the well-dressed black woman with the parasol stepped into the street as readily as the washerwoman with the laundry basket balanced on her head. While whites regarded him openly, blacks never lifted their gaze above his shoes. The reporter wondered how he could successfully gauge black attitudes when that segment of the population would not even look at him.

John and the boy paused at an intersection to allow a carriage to pass—an exceptionally fine one, new and gleaming black, a rival of the most opulent John had seen in New York. Its four white horses were perfectly matched, and the liveried black driver and footman as stiff as statues. Leather trunks were piled high at the rear. The nearest oc-cupant was a young woman attired in cream silk and fine lace. Her .glance fell momentarily on John as she passed, then, with a blink, moved on.

Samuel saw John looking at the carriage. "It's one of the planters' families. Probably returning to the city fo' the sickly season. Most of the low-country plantation owners has them a place in Charleston. They come here in the winter for the social season, and in the summer for the sickly season."

"This is the sickly season?" he asked.

Samuel nodded. "Ain't nothing for you ta worry 'bout, though. The sickly season, I mean. They say ya can't catch the country fever or yellow fever 'less you go to the swamps or the backcountry."

John did not feel particularly reassured. He knew his face was flushed from the heat, and he could not imagine that a backcountry swamp could smell any worse than downtown Charleston. He re-moved his hat and ran his fingers atop his head; his short blond hair was dampened from sweat.

"Cabbage leaves," Samuel announced from a couple steps behind.

John swiveled and looked awkwardly at the boy. "No, thank you, I am not hungry."

"No, no. Not to eat. To wear."

John's expression forced Samuel to elaborate.

"See, ya soak the leaves in cool water fo' a time. Then, when you is ready to go somewhere, you take the leaf and you put it in the top of your hat. It ain't work with all hats, but it'd work with yours."

"And people really do this?"

"Yessir, not all the time, but on the hot days, sure. Helps keep you cool."

"Interesting," John muttered, cautious not to dismiss any remedy that might somehow alleviate the sweltering heat.

At the next intersection, Samuel looked back at John. "Sir, if I might ask you a question. What sort of business you have here in Charleston?"

"I am a reporter for a newspaper in New York City. I was sent here to cover a story."

"What story is that?"

"The trial. Darcy Nance Calhoun's."

Samuel glanced up at John but didn't respond.

"What are folks saying about that?"

"Don't rightly know." The boy set down the bag and switched it to the other hand. "Nobody's been saying nothing to me about it. That's for sure."

They walked in silence for a distance, advancing slowly down Meeting Street. John noted that the buildings were growing larger and more opulent. Just ahead was a truly grand structure, even by New York standards—a hotel in the Greek Revival style with a facade of more than twenty powerful columns, supporting first a balcony, then three more stories rising to the pediment, from which a flagpole extended well over the street. The building dwarfed the fine carriages parked on the street. The doorman was an exceedingly tall man with an ebony face and a dazzling white uniform resplendent with brass buttons and gold epaulets. He intoned greetings in a deep bass drawl just audible over the sounds of the street.

A flower fluttered to the pavement from above, followed by a gentle exclamation of regret. A white glove appeared against the black wrought iron of the balcony railing, and a young woman peeked over at the sidewalk below. She wore a white dress with an impossibly tiny waist and a full hooped skirt. A parasol framed her auburn hair. A gentleman looked down also. No one would have mistaken the man for a New Yorker unless he had a career on the stage, yet he appeared representative of his class in Charleston. Every element of his appearance spoke of flamboyance—a looser cut in his coat and pant legs, wide lapels, a flowing silk cravat, and a tall stovepipe hat perched atop his long, wavy hair. His comment made the girl laugh—a soft giggle quickly covered by the glove. They stood there for a moment looking down at the street, she casually turning the parasol with her fingers as he puffed on a thick cigar. The smoke hovered just above their heads, swirling and stagnating with no breeze to disturb it. Then the man offered his arm, and they turned to walk across the landing, moving so effortlessly that they could have been gliding on a sheet of ice, with no extraneous movement save the twirling of the parasol.

"That's the Charleston Hotel," the boy announced, interrupting John's preoccupation.

"Magnificent," John replied, still looking at the girl.

"They have silk sheets on every bed and a gas lamp in all the rooms."

John smiled. "I believe it," he said, noting the five new gaslights in front of the hotel.

"I know a boy that works there. He makes him some good money. Thinks he can get me in as a bellboy in a year or two." Samuel nodded to himself and smiled at the thought.

After a moment, John glanced at his watch, then up and down the side streets. He wondered where everyone was. It was half past three o'clock, and John knew the population of Charleston to be over twenty thousand, yet the foot and vehicle traffic was amazingly low. No major northern city's streets would be so deserted at this hour.

"Why is it so quiet around here?" he asked Samuel.

The boy looked puzzled, as if unsure of the question. "Well, it's the heat of the day . . . afternoon heat." He looked up at the sky, squinting toward the sun. "Most folks try ta stay out of it if they can. They do their running 'round in the mornings or toward the eve. Things'll start to get busy in about an hour. You'll see."

"Is there much activity at night?"

"Used ta be. Not now. All the black folks gotta be off the streets before sundown. As for other folks, well, I can't really say for sure. Just think they stay in at night."

"Do you know why?"

"Pa says folks is afraid. Some faces they be used ta seeing in the daytime suddenly makes 'em scared at night."

"And what would happen if a black was caught on the streets after dark?"

"Nothing good, that's for sure. Since I ain't know no one that had it happen to 'em, I ain't fo' certain. But I heard rumors." Samuel walked up closely to the reporter's side and began to whisper. "Heard folks either got sent to the workhouse, or they got hung."

John stopped walking. "Blacks are hanged for breaking a curfew?"

"Seen 'em hanging there myself," Samuel whispered again. The boy pulled the clothespin and string from his pocket as if to substantiate the point.

John regarded the object silently, now realizing the macabre nature of the street urchin's taunt.

"Tell me about the workhouse," he continued.

"That's where they send all the black folks that start trouble or raise a fuss. Used to be just for slaves, but of late they be sending free folk there too. On account of rumors of folks stirring up trouble."

"So it is a jail."

"Not really. 'Cause they work 'em there." Samuel separated himself from John and stepped off the sidewalk, into the street, as a white man approached. Once the man had passed, he rejoined John and continued. "They beat 'em good, too."

John considered the boy's statements, saying nothing. It was chilling to hear a boy talk so dispassionately about hangings and beatings, rumor or not.

John was no innocent. For several months before starting with the *Tribune*, he had been a correspondent for the *Intruder*, one of the first of the penny press tabloids. He had witnessed and described for the masses murdered corpses, notorious prostitutes, and the violence of the New York slums. It had bothered him, but this bothered him more.

Before leaving for Charleston, John had visited the *Tribune*'s archives of other periodicals in an attempt to glean current information on the city. The *Charleston Gazette* was conservative, to say the least. John found a wealth of information on crop and livestock futures, local horseracing, weather prognostications, and the social comings and goings of ladies who did not appear to have first names. There was little mention of the upcoming trial and certainly no stories of hangings for curfew violations. Charleston had its dark side, but one wouldn't know it from the *Gazette*. John was curious about a society for whom the sensational was no longer news.

John and Samuel stopped for a wagon to pass on the cross street before them. A row of men, all black, lined the periphery of the wagon bed, their legs dangling over the side, their arms entwined in the fencing that surrounded them. A second tier stood in the middle—five or six men teetering precariously back and forth as the wagon bumped along the uneven road. They rode in silence, their faces emotionless. It was their eyes that sent a chill through John. No flicker of movement betrayed acknowledgment of his presence; their focus did not seem to extend beyond the cart. No aspect of the scene around the men seemed to make any difference to them whatsoever.

"Who are they?" John asked softly, standing still even though the wagon had passed. John had seen a fair number of blacks going about their business thus far on the walk from the station. He knew that Charleston had a large population of free Negroes. These were the first men he had seen confined.

Samuel seemed glad to have the chance to rest his arms. He set down the suitcase. "Think they is slaves. I sure ain't know none of 'em. Lots of times folks who own slaves will hire 'em out to do work for other folks. These could be from the rice mills. Or, maybe they been down fixing the bricks by the East Bay, who knows?"

"Are they fenced in to make sure they do not escape?"

"Escape? No. Heck, where would they go? Besides, a man could jump over that fence if he really wanted to. No, it's so they can pack as many as possible on the wagon without none of 'em falling off."

John had seen slaves before. He had seen them while on a trip to Washington—chained, transported through the capital like frightened cattle. He had been shocked and angry, as were the citizens around him. Here the reality of it came home—empty sightless men, invisible men, unnoticed by the strolling gentlemen and fine ladies, by the seamstresses and shopkeepers, and even by a free black boy eager to earn his two bits for carrying a bag. The sight was not noteworthy to the locals, it was normal.

Life in Charleston moved languidly about him, like lilies floating on the surface of a tranquil pond. But evil lurked beneath the surface. John felt a rising dread in the pit of his stomach and a chill in spite of the afternoon heat. What had Simpson thought of this place? Had he been lulled by the lazy lifestyle? Intrigued by the strange racial dynamics, and distracted by the pretty ladies . . . until it killed him?

Maybe it was the faint smoky smell that John had noticed for the last few blocks that made him think of Simpson. After all, the reporter was on his way to a fire when he died. The source of the smell was just ahead—a two-story white structure, formerly identical to its neighbors, which now bore irregular black borders around its windows and door—evidence of a gutted interior. Reporters were always chasing down fires, but Simpson never made it to this one. John glanced back at the quiet street. He tried to envision a chaotic scene, a charging wagon.

"Did this building burn three days ago?"

"No," Samuel replied. "It burned last week."

So this was not Simpson's fire. John peered into the building, then at the walls of the neighboring businesses, noting the singed trim and blistered paint.

"As close as these buildings are to one another, it is amazing that the whole block didn't go up in flames."

"Yessir. The fire company, they is quick. They gotta be." The boy seemed uncomfortable. He picked up the heavy suitcase and walked several steps, offering John the cue that they should move on.

Instead, John pulled a notebook and pen from his pocket. "Do you know where the other fire took place?"

The boy shifted from one leg to another. "Which fire?"

"The other one," John repeated. "The last one."

"Don't know which one you be talking 'bout." The boy wrinkled his brow. "There's been lots of fires."

"How many?" John asked with intrigue.

Samuel leaned in to whisper. "Sir, I overheard a couple of men talking this morn. They was talking 'bout the fires. This one here makes thirteen, they said. Thirteen in the last month."

"That's incredible." He scratched the number down on paper. "It doesn't seem that dry here. Certainly not dry enough for that many fires."

Samuel shook his head. "Sir, these ain't natural fires. Folks been a-setting 'em."

"Arson?" John said, excited. "Thirteen cases of arson in the last month? Who is doing it?"

"That's just it. Ain't no one know for sure. But the white folks say it's the black folks doing it. People on edge about it, sir. More than you know. Sir, I don't think it'd be a good idea to be standing here no longer on account of—" Suddenly the boy froze, his eyes fixed over John's shoulder.

John turned slowly and met the gaze of a man who stood but five paces away. Something was wrong about the eyes—the pupils were too large, the irises too pale. Two black dots stared out at him from a white sea. The look was pure malice.

"What do ya think you're doing here?" The words came out as a hiss, for the man barely moved his lips when he spoke, as if the thick tobacco-stained beard surrounding them held them immobile.

John expanded his view to take in the uniform—the blue wool jacket buttoned from beard to waist with a mismatch of colored buttons. It was soaked through at the armpits. John had no desire to get any closer.

"Do I have to ask again?"

It was the second question that struck a nerve in John, for it labeled the man more clearly than if he had carried a placard. John could recognize a bully. God knew he had seen enough of them during his stint in the Five Points. But John wasn't part of this world—the man had no real power over him. John had his credentials.

The reporter gave the slightest of half-smiles and took a step toward him. He looked directly at the eyes.

"I am John Sharp. I represent the *New York Tribune*."

The man flinched a little. The eyes were processing. They went hard again. "What the hell is a Tribune?"

"It is a newspaper. I am a reporter. I understand you have had a rash of fires here."

"I can't see that that is any of yo' business."

"What does this make? Thirteen?"

"I ain't been counting. I won't have you nosing 'round—"

"It's my job. Now perhaps you will tell me who is in charge of the local fire department." John put his pen to his notebook.

"Damned if I know." The man's teeth were set. John thought he would have put his ears back if he could.

"Where's the firehouse?"

"King Street." The man nodded off to John's right. "Now get along."

John took one last look at the eyes. "Much obliged." He turned to Samuel. "I've seen all I need to see here."

As they started back down Meeting Street, Samuel was obviously having trouble with the bag.

"I'll give you a break for a block or two," John said, taking the suitcase from the unresisting boy.

They walked in silence until they blended into the increased street traffic at the intersection of Cumberland. Samuel periodically glanced back over his shoulder, then seemed to settle down amid the clamor of the street vendors and peddlers hocking their wares.

John thought it best to offer some reassurance. "Samuel, you don't have to worry about what happened back there. I am a reporter, and reporters ask questions. Sometimes it annoys people, but it's part of the job. You were obviously only carrying my bag. Don't let it bother you."

The boy nodded. "Yessir. It's just that Charleston ain't normal right now, sir. Ain't nothing like normal. People be suspicious of all folks that ain't like 'em. And, sir, you ain't like no one."

They came upon Tradd Street just a few blocks down from the site of the fire.

Samuel motioned to a two-story building. "That's 107, right there. Should you like me to wait for ya, sir? I can look after your bag."

"That sounds fine, Samuel. I should not be more than twenty or thirty minutes, I believe."

"Oh, time is no problem. Curfew's not for another four hours, 'bout." Samuel found a small covered spot on the sidewalk where he seemed happy to set the bag and rest.

John straightened his coat and tie in his reflection in an adjacent store window, and thought for a moment that he saw a blue uniform behind him across the street. When he turned, it was gone.

THREE

ᕽ

John paused in the foyer of 107 Tradd Street. The entrance of the building bore a street number only, no clue to the nature of the business within. Inside, a sign mounted over a connecting door announced, "Whorter Shipping Company," and as if to substantiate the claim, a small ink drawing of a clipper ship occupied the adjacent wall. The only furniture was a dusty hall tree.

John hung his hat on a hook and used his hand to coax his damp hair into a more presentable state. He withdrew his notebook from his pocket and glanced at it. Other than some possible questions for his contact, John had little to go on beyond the address and the name Arthur Mahan.

When following leads for a story, it was not uncommon to connect with relatively anonymous sources. It was extremely strange, however, when the nebulous source was the contact provided by his editor.

"The man jumps at shadows," Haggerty said. "After Simpson's death, he agreed to provide local background on the story only under conditions of utmost secrecy. You are not to mention his name to anyone, and under no conditions are you to quote him or reveal him as a source."

"How will I recognize him?" John had asked.

"He will be the only man at that address who is expecting you. He is middle-aged, a former New Yorker—and," Haggerty confided as if providing the key to identification, "he is a bastard. Abrasive as hell."

Now, as the man was his only source in Charleston, John was determined to make him his new best friend. He assumed a businesslike smile, tugged on the bottom of his jacket, and rapped twice on the door.

"Come in."

John entered a large room where shafts of light from two rear windows illuminated dust motes from floor to ceiling. The room was cluttered, but it also revealed unmistakable signs of prosperity—an assortment of chronometers, an oak desk, several leather chairs, and a well-crafted model of a brigantine on the mantel over the fireplace. A bizarre gargoyle perched on a pedestal to one side of the desk.

Standing behind the desk was an older man with thick crescent eyeglasses just below the bridge of his nose. Unlike the other gentlemen John had encountered so far in Charleston, this man was clean-shaven, though his dark brown hair did conform to the billowing southern style. His lean build was offset by a chubby face that was showing signs of age—sagging beneath the eyes and creases around the mouth. He did not smile.

"Good day, sir," John opened. "My name is John Sharp. I'm with the *New York Tribune*."

The man dropped his chin and eyed John over the top of his glasses. "Do you have any idea of the difficulty that your newspaper has caused me?" The man paused just long enough for John to open his mouth. "Imagine! Having the police pound on your door at eleven p.m. and then drag you out of bed to identify a body."

John's expression must have shown his confusion, for the man stopped to elaborate. "Your fellow reporter, Simpson, died in late afternoon. It took the constable a good seven hours to turn up this address among his effects. Then he just couldn't wait until morning to drag me into this." The man spoke with truculence and the hint of a southern accent. The unrefined nature of the drawl made it ugly, like a rudimentary attempt at a foreign language.

John attempted to commiserate. "That must have been very disturbing for you, sir."

"Disturbing? You don't know the half of it." He gave an exaggerated sigh, then pointed to one of the high-backed leather chairs across from his desk. "Take a seat. You and I have important matters to discuss, and limited time to do so."

As John seated himself, the man shuffled through a desk drawer, pulled out a long cigar, and lit it. "Cigar?" he asked as his own sat stuffed in his mouth.

"No, thank you." As the man appeared absorbed with puffing on the tobacco, John continued. "Sir, I'm sorry but I have yet to learn your name." He hesitated a moment, recalling his editor's admonition. "Could you be Mr. Whorter?"

"Wrong, Mr. Sharp. That scoundrel passed away five years ago." He appeared to smile at the thought of the scoundrel's demise. "I was forced ta keep the name for business reasons. Southerners ain't much for change. More a curse than a blessing, I believe. No, Mr. Sharp, my name is Mahan. Arthur Mahan."

"A pleasure to meet you, Mr. Mahan."

The man continued to puff at his cigar while scrutinizing John. "How old are ya, Mr. Sharp?"

"I am twenty-two, sir."

"Twenty-two," he repeated. Then, under his breath, "Closer to the womb than the world at that age. And tell me, how long have you worked at the *New York Tribune*?"

"A year now," John replied patiently. He was beginning to like the gargoyle.

"Hmm. Let me guess. Your uncle sits on the board of directors. Or wait. Is it that your father's company advertises religiously in the *Tribune*?"

John smiled, waiting until Mahan was finished to reply. "Neither, sir. I previously worked for the *Intruder*, and some articles I wrote caught the eye of Mr. Haggerty. He subsequently hired me."

"You came from the penny press, eh. The sole goal of those papers is to peddle smut to the dregs of society." Mahan gave John an appraising stare. "What made you decide to become a reporter? You look more like the type who would be studying law, or some other worthy profession."

John paused to take a long look at the gargoyle . . .

The decision to pursue a career in journalism had been made after a bleak train ride home at the end of winter term at Yale. For the first time in his life, John had let himself in the front door of his own home. He carried his suitcase himself, and set it down on the silk carpet. The carpet and chandelier were the only remaining furnishings in the entry hall; inverse shadows, like ghosts, marked the spots where the gilt mirror, the Stewart portraits, and the pair of Ming vases had been.

Footsteps approached from the sitting room, making a strange echo through the empty house.

"Mother."

She smiled. "You look taller."

She did not. John was amazed at how she had diminished in his few months away at school. Her colors had faded too, like a painting hung in sunlight too long.

John hugged her. "Where is Father?"

"He's at his office. He still stays there most of the time."

"You've had to deal with all of this yourself?" He made a vague gesture at their surroundings.

"I have had Fuller. He just left with a load of boxes. He'll be with us until next week. The Sinclairs offered him a position."

"Come. I'll make us some tea."

She led him through the empty dining room, where depressions in the carpet marked the footprints of the grand table and sideboard. She saw him looking.

"They're really all just props, John. Like at the theater. They aren't of real value. They change with the scene."

John was silent for a moment. "And our roles?"

"Each of us will find a new one." Then she smiled. "You're young, and you have your wits about you. You will get to write your own."

• • •

John slowly returned his gaze to Mahan. "I was always a pretty fair writer," he said. "It seemed worthwhile."

Mahan stood and walked over to a cabinet to the right of the desk. "So Robert Haggerty hired you himself. His history of decision making certainly does not curry in your favor. But, over the course of time even a fool will make a fortuitous decision, given enough chances."

John sat silent. It was difficult to formulate a response to a statement that could be either an insult or a compliment. John realized that he was actually beginning to enjoy Mahan. He could hardly wait for the next salvo.

Meanwhile, Mahan picked up a silver tray, bearing a decanter of amber liquid and two glasses. He carried the tray back to the desk and set it at the center.

"Tell me, Mr. Sharp," Mahan said as he sat down, "why were you picked to replace Simpson down here? Logic would dictate that a reporter with more seniority would've been picked for something so important."

John chose not to mention his own relative abstinence from alcohol. "Perhaps it is because I like to dig beneath the surface." He looked Mahan in the eyes. "I value solid background in a story."

"Is that right? Well, young Mr. Sharp, I must give you credit. 'Cause so long as you can stay out of harm's way, you may find yourself with quite a story here. Quite a story indeed." Mahan leaned forward and began to pour from the decanter. "Bourbon, Mr. Sharp?"

"Thank you, but I drink very little, and rarely during the day."

The man continued pouring into a second glass. "Then you must learn, just as I was forced ta learn upon moving here. You see, Mr. Sharp, there is not a situation that southern gentlemen don't use as an excuse for a drink. Business or pleasure, celebrations or grievings, rarely will you find a man without a drink in his hands. An abstainer is noticed—and suspected." He handed a glass to John.

There was no way to turn down the refreshment after such a speech, and John Sharp, who usually confined his drinking to an occasional beer, took his first sip. The bourbon burned his throat like coffee off a stove and brought a flush to his cheeks.

"Interesting," John muttered, returning the glass to a spot on the desk.

"An acquired taste," Mahan replied, swallowing half the glass in one gulp. "Well then, Mr. Sharp, enough chitchat. We'd better get down to business. What do you plan to do with Simpson's body?"

John almost choked on his drink. "He hasn't been buried yet?"

"No. Haggerty never bothered to wire instructions or the funds for the necessary arrangements." Mahan continued, "Simpson didn't much care for the South, ya see. Told me he could never bring himself to live here, as I do."

"You knew him well then?"

Mahan shook his head. "I was his contact for local background when he came here on assignment. I preferred to keep interaction to a minimum." Mahan took a puff from the cigar. "It is not wise to be associated with a Northern newspaper. Down here everyone equates the northern press with Garrison and that damned abolitionist paper, the *Liberator*."

The thought seemed to rekindle his ire. "Now Simpson walks in front of a fire wagon, and everyone, right up through the police department, thinks I'm some kind of northern spy. Then you show up— I just hope no one spotted you."

John thought it best to return to pressing matters at hand. "I think Simpson should be buried down here right away. The heat—"

"There isn't a problem with that." Mahan waved away John's look of skepticism. "The local morticians here have been experimenting with a process. They kind of pickle 'em, and the body keeps for weeks. It allows time for bodies to be shipped home for burial, or for loved ones to come for a funeral."

"So Simpson has been . . . pickled?" At Mahan's nod, John continued. "Well, then, I guess I'll cable Mr. Haggerty and ask for instructions."

Mahan glanced at one of his many clocks. "Now we best be moving things along here, Mr. Sharp. Tell me what you know of the trial you were sent here to cover."

John pulled the notebook and pen from his breast pocket. "Very little, Mr. Mahan. I know that a white man is to be put on trial for assisting a runaway slave. I know that if found guilty of the crime, the man is likely to be hanged. I know that the trial is to start tomorrow. That's all."

Arthur Mahan took another gulp, emptying his glass. "If," he spoke softly. "*If* he is found guilty. My dear Mr. Sharp, make no doubt about it. The man *will* be found guilty. You are not about to be witness to a fair trial. You have come ta Charleston for a lynching."

"If it is a foregone conclusion, why the pretense of a public trial?"

"I suppose it is to appease the southern concept of fairness. Or sport. Though there is little entertainment in shooting a caged animal. I also guess it has something to do with the way things will appear in the North. Few things are as important to a southerner as appearance, regardless of what anyone may tell you. Many know that this story has created a firestorm among the Yanks, so southerners will do all they can to at least appear just."

"Yes, but they must know that if the man is found guilty and hanged, northern outrage will only increase."

Mahan nodded. "Certainly. But then they may cower behind that bulwark that always protects 'em. Legality, Mr. Sharp. A southerner would stone Jesus himself, then show up bald-faced at the gates of heaven with the argument that under Roman law he was justified in his actions." He picked up the cigar from its ashtray and puffed thoughtfully.

"Adherence to the law is important to them, then," John remarked, making a note. "Will you tell me what you know of the alleged crime and the arrest?"

"The accused's name is Darcy Nance Calhoun. A fine cracker name if I've ever heard one. The locals are having fits over his last name being the same as their esteemed late senator, John C. Calhoun. Though, were I the prisoner, I'd be taking steps to see that no one thought me a relation of that blowhard separatist, regardless his old rank in society." He poured himself another glass of bourbon and with a simple gesture urged John to pick up his. "Darcy Nance ain't from Charleston. He's from a little farther down the coast. A search party trailing the runaway came across his cabin in the woods. Someone noticed something suspicious, and when they looked inside they found the slave they were after. That's about it. They brought Calhoun up here to Charleston for the trial, and if everything goes according to plan, all of it should be wrapped up by the beginning of next week."

"Quick justice."

"Oh, make no mistake, young Mr. Sharp. None of this would be happening were it not for that slave uprising some weeks ago in Habersham County. That's gone and thrown everyone into a panic the likes of which I haven't seen since a slave took a hoe to his overseer and killed him about five years back. Darcy Nance is just playing the part of fortune's fool. Were it not for the elevated temperament of the citizens, he'd be looking at a little jail time and nothing more."

"I read about the slave revolt," John remarked. "A reporter from the *Tribune* was in Savannah on another matter and did a piece on it. We have gangs in New York who inflict more damage than that in any given week. These people must be very fearful."

"You have no idea," Mahan responded. "It was necessary to call up the militia just to maintain order."

"Yes, I encountered two of them at the train station and had a run-in with another just a few minutes ago."

Arthur Mahan slapped his glass down on the desk. "You've had a run-in with the militia?"

"Well, perhaps that was overstating it."

"Did they follow you here?" he asked, springing out of his chair and walking toward the window.

"No," John answered, mildly taken aback. "Two of them went through my suitcase at the station, and another accosted me as I was taking some notes."

"You're certain they didn't follow you here?"

"I can't imagine why they would."

Mr. Mahan poked his head out the window, scanning the street below. After a time, he retreated and turned toward John with a look of distaste. "Mr. Sharp, you do not grasp the gravity of the situation. You are here as a reporter, and you will leave this city and her troubles behind you in a short matter of time. I, on the other hand, live here. And while my presence is tolerated, it is far from accepted. If I continue to be linked to the northern press, my business will surely fail.

And perhaps far worse. Tell me, what did you do to attract their interest at the station?"

"Nothing. They watched me as I got off the train. I apparently don't dress like the locals. As I said, they wanted to look in my bag. Do you have any idea what they were looking for?"

Mahan exhaled loudly. "I can guess. We have been swamped with abolitionist propaganda lately. They may have thought that you were smuggling in pamphlets. They confiscated reams of them at the post office." The shipper shook his head. "I really can't afford to be involved in this."

"I understand," John answered. "I will certainly exercise every caution—"

"You should. For your own sake. But this is to be the last meeting here between the two of us. Hopefully the last meeting at all." Mahan returned to the chair, his face lightly flushed. "If you have any questions, ask them now. Your opportunity for honest answers in the future will greatly diminish."

"Very well. Simpson's death. Are you certain it was an accident?"

"Absolutely. There were about fifty witnesses. Next question."

"Then what can you tell me of the recent string of fires? I heard there have been thirteen cases of arson in the last few weeks."

Mahan's eyes turned from the window to the reporter. "Good, Mr. Sharp. I see you are doing your job. Unfortunately, you now know as much as I. Of course, the rumors circulating are that it's the work of the Negroes, but I find it hard to believe that the blacks are that stupid. There is an early curfew, and any Negro caught on the street after dark is imprisoned. Any caught setting a fire would be hanged immediately. The Negroes have their faults to be sure, but I find it hard to believe that so many have such a wanton disregard for their own lives."

"Then who is doing it?"

Mr. Mahan shrugged his shoulders. "I don't know. It could be a group with a political agenda, or just a maniac with an affinity for bright lights—maybe even someone in the militia. They certainly have their share of undesirables, and there are so damned many of 'em." Mahan's voice grew reflective. "Mr. Sharp, did you walk here from the train station?"

"Yes, I did."

"And what did you notice of the buildings?"

"I noticed beautiful churches and hotels. Most of the houses I saw, however, were plain, uniform, and old."

"Did you by chance notice how close together the buildings sit from one another? Especially the closer you got to downtown?"

"Yes, I did."

"A fire's best friend—buildings that close. One properly placed spark could wipe out an entire street, from one end of town to the other. That's why fire is so feared. Almost as much as the Negroes. Perhaps that's why white Charlestonians try to group them together. To turn two enemies into one." Mahan stopped and flicked a large ash from his cigar. "What is your next question, Mr. Sharp?"

John glanced down at his notebook. "This might strike you as odd, but I was wondering about something I saw at the Charleston Hotel as I passed by. There was no flag on the flagpole. Was it an oversight, or is there larger political significance?"

"Good, Mr. Sharp. A reporter worth his salt would use this opportunity to judge the true temperament of these southerners. So, was the flag absent for a reason, you ask." The man stood up, arching his back as he stretched. He then removed his glasses and began to rub the lenses with a handkerchief pulled from his pocket. "I am going to let you in on a theory of mine, Mr. Sharp. I happened to meet with another shipper several months ago. We had both noticed something strange. A number of southern men of influence had recently booked passage through us for the capitals of Europe—ostensibly for tourism. Yet they didn't take their families, and they apparently didn't do any buying or selling either. They brought no cargo back with them and did not arrange for later shipment, either import or export.

"My associate speculated that the business was political. He thinks they were drumming up support in the courts of Europe for the southern cause." He raised an eyebrow. "I think that we're onto something. Just take a look at the situation in the Southwest. Right now, we have federal troops and Texans lined up toe-to-toe on the New Mexico border with plenty on both sides just itching to fire the first shot. Now I give you that a gentleman from Charleston would rather eat outside standing up than share his table with a filthy Texan. Yet in some asinine brotherhood of slaveholders, these same gentlemen would be willing to take up arms and die for one another if the cause so required. So you ask me if the missing flag was just an error. I tell you that southerners do not make errors of etiquette."

John paused to let that sink in. Mahan's clocks chimed the half hour.

" 'Tis four-thirty," Mahan said. "We should hurry this along."

"Very well. I just have some logistical questions. Will it be difficult to get into the courthouse tomorrow?"

"I've made the arrangements for you. The trial starts at one o'clock, although southerners rarely run on time. Regardless, arrive at least fifteen minutes early. Outside of the court there should be two men ushering folks in. One is extremely short with an enormous nose. His name is Roberts. He'll be expecting you."

"Thank you. Will there be a lot of reporters there from the southern papers?"

"Ha! Southern reporters? Why no, sir. The only other reporters you will see will be from the North, like yourself."

"Why is that?"

"The papers here avoid reporting on topics that might be interpreted as incendiary. They don't miss an opportunity to print libelous stories of the North, but they somehow remain averse to discussing the local problems. In the days following the Habersham County uprising, do you know what the lead story was? Weather predictions for the upcoming season. Can you imagine? Not a single word appeared locally in print about the uprising. Not a word. When the trial is over, they'll print the outcome. That's all."

Seeing from Mahan's body language that he was ready to end the interview, John rose. "Could you tell me where the wire office is? And also, I would appreciate it if you could recommend decent lodgings."

"The wire office is a block down from the courthouse on Meeting Street. You can't miss it. As for lodgings, might I assume that the cheapskate you call your boss did not give you enough money for a room at the Charleston Hotel?"

"You assume correctly," John answered with a grin.

"Well, then there are a couple of adequate boardinghouses along State Street near the Cooper River. McClellan's is all right. Simpson stayed there. You have an attendant waiting with your bags?" John nodded. "Then he will know how to get there."

"That sounds fine, thank you." John downed the last sip of his bourbon. While the taste had not improved, he now enjoyed the numbness it offered his throat. It also loosened his tongue. "Mr. Mahan, you have been of great assistance. If I may ask, why do you choose to live in Charleston? Like Mr. Simpson, you don't seem particularly fond of the city."

"I'm here for one reason, and that is business. You might be surprised by the number of northerners who are here in Charleston for the same reason. You see, Mr. Sharp, southerners prize their gentility above all. And business is typically the last option for any gentleman of proper stock. There are not enough native sons willing to do what's necessary for the economic health of the city. That's why they tolerate my presence, and the presence of those like me. But be assured, I'll always be an outsider here. A necessary evil, so to speak."

"I see."

"But enough of me, Mr. Sharp. Since you feel relaxed enough to ask me a personal question, allow me the opportunity to offer you some advice." He blew out a final puff from the cigar and then squashed it deliberately into the ashtray.

"I'd be grateful for any help that you could offer."

"Try to maintain a low profile. Your appearance aside, don't draw any undue attention to yourself by announcing exactly what you're doing here. Certainly everyone will know you are a northerner. But northern travelers come through Charleston all the time for business. Disguise yourself in that regard, and you may avoid unwanted problems. Additionally, you may wish to avoid certain areas of town after nightfall. While it would be presumptuous of me to advise a young reporter to stay home at night, I do recommend that you avoid the wharves and the waterfront bars." He paused, reading John's expression. "I know what you're thinking. You're from New York. And there is nowhere more dangerous than the slums of New York. However, never before have you been to a place where more people inherently dislike you, without ever having met you. The upper classes here have their breeding, which will protect you, but the lower classes do not. Therefore, heed my warning."

"I understand." John stood up and set his empty glass back on the tray. "And thank you for the bourbon, Mr. Mahan. It was an interesting experience."

The older man nodded politely, then followed John to the door. "If you need to meet with me in the future, I advise that you send some sort of messenger. I will then make the arrangements."

"Very well, and thank you again."

John stopped abruptly in the doorway. He turned back to Mahan. "This ideological impasse between North and South, do you think it could actually come to separation?"

"If events continue in the direction they're headed, yes. For one thing, we have the wrong captain at the helm. I'm referring to President Zachary Taylor. I can't begin to state the depth of hatred these people have for him. He was a southerner, you know. Born in Virginia, owned a plantation in Louisiana. These people see him as a turncoat, a former slave owner who is intransigent on the issue of admitting new territories as slave states. He wants his plan or nothing—no compromise. That does not bode well for any of us." Mahan turned back toward his desk. "Good day, Mr. Sharp. I wish you well."

FOUR

Samuel?"

The street scene had changed during John's short interview with Mahan. Tradd Street now buzzed with the sights and sounds of commerce. The sun had dipped behind a canopy of oaks lining the parkway, and Charleston's dormant population roused itself to complete its daily business. A key player was missing, however. Samuel and John's suitcase were nowhere to be seen.

John glanced nervously about and subconsciously patted the suit pocket that contained the little cash he carried on his person. His brow furrowed in consternation as he glanced back at Mahan's office window.

"Samuel!?"

John strode to the spot under the canopy where he left the boy. A worn white stone and scratched doodlings on the sidewalk indicated that the boy had sat there for a while. There was a child's drawing of a dog with a stubby tail and enormous teeth, and a partial figure of a stick man. The man was missing one leg below the knee—Samuel had stopped abruptly.

John felt a rising concern that had nothing to do with his luggage. He began to move quickly, looking behind wagons and carts and down the corridors between buildings. Mahan had certainly managed to pass along some secondhand apprehension. Had the militia actually tracked him here? Were they responsible for the boy's disappearance?

John spotted a pair of militia now; they were perched on the stoop of a storefront just a few doors down. John forced himself to stop, check his pocket watch, and feign a yawn.

One of the men, a sallow youngster with patchy blond whiskers, began walking toward him. He stopped directly in front of John and began to overtly sniff the air.

He grimaced. "I smell me a Yankee," he announced loudly.

John managed to swallow the bile rising in his throat. "I'm not a bit surprised," he said through a plastered smile and clenched teeth. "I don't suppose you could tell me where to find a cool drink?"

"About two hundred miles north!" The militiaman laughed as if surprised by his own wit. He turned to his cohort, who nodded in approval.

Victory obviously achieved, the youth brushed John with his elbow as he walked past him to a fruit cart and helped himself to an apple.

"Hey, Smitts, grab one for me!" his companion called, still laughing. The Yankee was apparently forgotten in favor of purloined fruit.

The sound of uneven footfall, the slap of bare feet on pavement, now drew John's attention from the opposite direction. Samuel, loping with a two-fisted grip on John's suitcase, appeared from behind a wagon parked halfway up the block.

"Samuel, where were you? Didn't you hear me calling?"

"I'm so sorry, sir. Got ta playing ball with some other boys up the block after ya didn't come out for a while. I didn't see you come out 'cause of the wagon. Ain't never happen again, sir. So sorry, sir."

The relief John felt somewhat diffused his irritation, and he managed a smile for the boy. "It is all right, Samuel. Just stay close from now on. I still don't know many people here."

"Yessir. Where now, sir?"

"I want to go to a boardinghouse over on State Street, and I understand that the courthouse is on the way. I am interested in seeing it."

Samuel pursed his lips. "There be a commotion there. Everyday, 'bout this time."

"Why is that?"

"It's 'cause the militia be drilling out there. Changing of the guard, I think."

John nodded. "That's all the more reason that I would like to take a look."

After the last insulting altercation with the militia, John had glanced briefly at the few townsfolk around him who witnessed the incident. For the most part, their expressions mirrored his own embarrassment. John guessed that the citizens of Charleston were no less class-conscious than the people of New York. And in New York, civil servants with a measure of authority generally knew their place. Based upon his experience, militia here did not—and that could mean that they were as confused about their role here as he was. It also made them dangerous. John wanted a chance to observe them from the crowd's perspective.

As the traffic backed up at the intersection of Broad and Meeting Streets, John sent Samuel ahead to wait for him half a block beyond St. Michael's Church.

John threaded his way through traffic to join the edge of the crowd. He peered over the heads of the assembly to take in the courthouse, a large square structure with four second-level pilasters providing the only ornamentation on the facade. John recalled reading a description of the building by Charleston writer William Gilmore Simms. He said that it made no fuss and challenged no man's admiration. As far as John was concerned, that about summed it up. The graceless edifice seemed far too stolid for the citizens it served.

He turned his attention to the crowd. Based on Samuel's statement, he expected to find a group of spectators looking for a little entertainment at the end of their workday. But John was instantly aware that these folks were not here to catch a parade. Their body language was all wrong. They stood squared off against the building—perhaps a hundred and fifty of them—shoulders tense, feet planted, arms half bent at their sides. John had a feeling that the crowd intended to put on a show for the militia—not vice versa.

"So when are y'all gonna do something about the fires?!" A mild-looking little man crested the ruckus to shout the question, his voice high-pitched and strained. He was about twenty feet away to John's left. John moved in closer.

"Damn right, Clyde," his neighbor commented. "It's about time we had some answers!"

Murmurs of agreement spread out from the man like ripples on water. The townsfolk alternately voiced outrage and reassurance, shifting and swaying, then gradually subsiding.

"Who do you think is responsible?" John quietly asked a couple standing next to him, who had nodded to him upon his arrival.

"The blacks have got to be doing it," the man answered softly, but with surety.

The wife nodded in agreement. "You just can't trust any of 'em anymore." She looked to her husband. "I walked into the kitchen this morning, and Cook was slicing bread. She looked up at me with that knife in her hand, and it chilled me to the bone."

A woman just beyond her leaned in. "And have you seen the way they look at you in the street these days? None of us is safe."

"The question is," the first man rejoined, gesturing toward the building, "when are they gonna get off their duffs and do something about it? Are they gonna wait till the Negroes burn this whole town to the ground?" He turned back to look at John. "You're from up north, aren't you?"

The man implied no malice, and John responded truthfully. "Yes, sir. I am from New York."

"Well, the Negroes almost did it up there, didn't they? They set fire to New York and almost burned the whole place down."

"That was a long time ago, back when slavery was legal. . . ." John let his voice trail off as he realized the implication of his statement. The last thing he wanted to do was incite further fear of blacks. "Poor whites were involved, too," he added.

"Didn't it start like this? With different fires all over town?" The man leaned in close. "How did they figure out what was going on?"

"Well, as I said, this was a long time ago, before Independence," John replied. "I think it was just chance that the plot was uncovered. Some loose talk was overheard."

"How many was involved?"

"Well over a hundred."

"What did they do with 'em?"

John had read of public atrocities and medieval torture exacted on the blacks involved. He kept his reply simple. "They hanged most of those who confessed."

"Sounds like a tried-and-true solution." The man shook his head. "When you think about it, folks up there ain't much different from folks down here. They don't hesitate to take action when it happens in their own backyard."

John moved forward toward the courthouse, hoping to obtain a clear view of the militia. He used his reporter's skill to elbow his way through cramped bodies and squeeze between united shoulders until he was just a row shy of the front.

The militia were lined up just off the courthouse steps; four rows of men with about fifteen men per row. They were a ragtag group. Their blue coats varied from sky to navy, and the mismatch of firearms buttressing their shoulders could have belonged to any backwoods hunting party. Their only common attribute was poor grooming; to a man, they looked badly in need of a haircut, shave, and bath. As individuals, not one of them would have garnered respect.

But right now, they were not individuals; they were a unit. "Hut, two, hut, two, hut . . . ," barked the corporal. The boots stamped in unison to an even cadence. The men had enough training to execute their maneuvers with a degree of precision. When ordered to halt, they stared at the crowd as one, eyes fixed. These raw conscripts were on their way to becoming soldiers.

Individuals in the mass continued to air their grievances—from lack of refuse collection to curfew violations. Children of all ages moved in and out of the throng, watching the event as if it were some form of theater. Some of the boys mimicked the movement of the militia with playful joy as others seemed to revel in the rowdiness displayed by the adults . . . and the rowdiness was growing.

"Let's face it, folks. They ain't gonna do nothing! They're too busy protecting the niggers and that nigger lover in there, Darcy Nance!"

John couldn't see the man behind the voice. It came from somewhere deep in the crowd. But he felt a change in the group as the name resonated. He heard it repeated all around him. He saw fists ball and arms flex. John observed that the crowd was in motion again—seething and bubbling like the contents of a stew pot. Swirls of aggression built up and then vented in angry outbursts. The men grew unabashed with their language, and the women unembarrassed by it. As if in response to some subconscious cue, the crowd began to press forward.

"Present arms!"

John's head snapped back around. With a slap, the militia presented their rifles in concert, chest high.

John felt a lurch in his stomach and a sudden catch of breath, as if he had been pushed backward off a stoop without knowing the distance to the ground. His arms braced at his sides—to break a fall or stop the crowd's advance.

"Hey, fella! Are you all right?"

John managed a nod, but remained fixed on the militia. He searched for signs of breakdown, a flickering of the eyes as they looked out at the crowd or a rifle stock shifting toward a shoulder. Just one barrel leveled toward the men . . .

"Folks up there aren't much different from folks down here."

"What seems to be the problem here?"

An officer with salt-and-pepper hair and a gray beard moved forward on a chestnut stallion, forming a barrier between the militia and the vanguard of the citizenry. His back was ramrod straight, and his hands motionless as they gripped the reins in his lap. He wore a full uniform, gray in color, which fit him well. His collar bore the insignia of a colonel, and the rows of ribbons on his chest proclaimed meritorious service and valor in combat. The heel of one polished boot moved slightly, and the horse arched its neck and moved smartly along the line of militia, to the end, then back to the middle. The colonel turned his head to face the crowd.

He stared out impassively at first, allowing the crowd to get a good look at him. Then he returned the favor, first sweeping the crowd with his gaze, then singling them out as individuals. The crowd quieted. John was aware of the sound of his own quick breaths.

"We was wondering why y'all is protecting that bastard Darcy Nance, instead of dealing with him." It was the same voice that had earlier incited the crowd, but the force had gone out of it.

The colonel frowned. With no apparent signal from the rider, the horse reared impressively, as if affronted by the question. The colonel calmed his mount, then directed a stern look at the man. "You know better than that, sir. That is an issue for the courts. As far as I know, he's not even in Charleston."

A murmur swept through the crowd, and there were a few isolated boos.

The officer raised one hand. "Now y'all need to break it up," he ordered like a lecturing parent. "It's time to be heading home for your supper." As if to emphasize the point, he took a leisurely look down at his own timepiece.

Incredibly, the crowd began to segment into clusters and then to dissipate. The corporal marched off with two rows of militia. The colonel and his mount sauntered away in the direction of Cumberland. John remained with an expression of incredulity and slowly withdrew a handkerchief to wipe the sweat from his face and neck.

John caught up with Samuel a couple of blocks down, on the corner of Cumberland.

"Not far from here, sir," the boy said as the two resumed their walk. "To the boardinghouses. Just a couple of streets over."

"Fine." John looked about him. The people around this area were behaving normally, with no hint of tension nor sign of conflict. He relaxed a bit. "Quite a scene back there, Samuel."

"That right, sir. You all right though, right, sir?" the boy asked, looking at John's face.

"Oh, yes. I am fine." He paused. "Samuel, as I was at the courthouse, people there seemed especially agitated. Mad, I mean. I thought it best to warn you that you may wish to head straight home tonight and not go out if at all possible."

"Yessir. Thank you, sir. But, I'm wanting to tell ya that . . . Well, today. Ain't nothing different happening than any other day. It's always like that 'round the courts at this time in the afternoon. When the militia change, that is. Folks get all riled up. Starts to yelling and cussing, mostly 'bout the blacks. We know to stay away 'round that time." Samuel turned his head down and looked to his feet. "Can't much blame 'em, what with all the goings-on. I's worried too."

"What are you worried about? That you will be arrested?"

"Naw. On account of I ain't done nothing wrong. My momma says, 'Ya keep your nose clean, and the rest of your face shines to like it.' I figure it works the other way, too. If you are doing something you shouldn't, your face shows that too. I keep my nose clean, sir. So I's guessing the white folk can tell I ain't up ta nothing."

"So what is it that you are worried about?"

"I's worried 'cause lots is happening that don't make no sense."

"I can understand that. I guess that's why I like my job. I try to gather information so that things start to make sense."

"How do you do that?"

"By asking people questions. By listening and keeping my eyes open."

"Folks pay you for that?"

"They do."

The boy walked along silently, apparently mulling over John's strange occupation.

John and Samuel stood opposite a building that bore no resemblance to the Charleston Hotel. The unadorned wood-frame structure had all the charm of a warehouse.

As they crossed the street, John dug into his pocket and found a coin, a quarter dollar, and pulled it out. "Samuel, your help has been of great assistance. I would like it if you'd continue to work for me over the next day or two." He reached out his hand and gave the boy the quarter.

Samuel's eyes popped. "Two bits. Of course I will. Thank you, sir."

"There will be another two at the end of my stay. I would like you to meet me here tomorrow, just before ten." They stopped just off the sidewalk in front of the boardinghouse. "If I have any errands or places I must go, you can help."

"Of course, sir. Would you like me ta wait for you now? Make sure you get settled?"

"No. I will be fine from here." He reached over and took the suitcase from the boy's clenched hand. "It is best you get home now."

"Yessir. Thank you, Mr. Sharp."

Samuel turned and began to walk briskly, his left hand tucked tightly into the pocket in which he held the quarter.

"Samuel," John called after the boy. Samuel turned. "If you could possibly find me a couple of cabbage leaves for tomorrow, I would greatly appreciate it."

The boy smiled wide, showing his teeth. "Yessir. I'll bring 'em with me in the morn. Bright and early, ten o'clock."

"Yes," John said with a grin. "Bright and early, ten o'clock."

FIVE

⌒

McClellan's Boardinghouse provided John with a clean room, a decent bed, and a writing desk facing a window. Getting the window had been no small feat, for in Charleston, windows were apparently only available in rooms with an eastern exposure.

"It is a matter of good manners," the innkeeper had explained. "The breeze comes from the east, so all of the porches face in that direction. Folks wouldn't want to look down on a neighbor's private porch from a room facing west. That would just be rude."

So John had paid extra for the breeze and an appropriate view. He dropped his suitcase on the bed. He was tired and hungry, but despite that, he could not lessen the pang of excitement the city had instilled in him. He laid out his writing materials and hung up his clothes. Then he walked over to the window, where he looked out at the church and neighboring houses for quite a time.

A knock at the door drew him away from the window. "Is that you, Mr. McClellan? Is dinner ready?"

No one answered. Instead there was another knock. Three short taps, a pause, then two harder taps—like a signal.

John hesitated just behind the door, slightly surprised by the interruption. Who would not announce himself?

He swung open the door. Leaning against the frame was a short young man, his hands stuffed casually in his pockets, forcing his suit jacket to retreat. The tight fabric of his vest fought against the buttons, rippling the garment at the waist. John looked up at the face. The blond man was grinning from ear to ear, proudly displaying a broken smile most would be reticent to share. Even more startling was his blackened left eye, a fresh purple and yellow wound that made John wince.

"What took you so long, sport?" the visitor asked in a lowbrow New York accent. "I was beginning to think you had a lady in here."

John remained openmouthed as the stranger stood upright and walked past him into the room, trailing the overwhelming smell of cheap cologne.

"You lucky devil," the visitor exclaimed. "How did you manage to rate a room with a window?"

"I do not know. Sir, might I ask—"

"Hotter than the hinges of hell, my room is. No window. How any of these people can live in this infernal weather I don't understand. No wonder they are so agitated."

"Yes. Sir, forgive my forwardness, but might I ask who you are?"

"Oh, pardon me. Have I not introduced myself?" He dusted his hand against his trousers, then extended it. "Owen Conway's the name. In town from New York. I was just downstairs, and our proprietor informed me that another New York reporter had checked in. Well, as soon as I heard, I had to make a point to stop by. Good thing I did, too. Else, how would I have known you had a window? Much more comfortable to dally about in here."

Mr. Conway swung his feet up and stretched out on the bed. John stared slack-jawed at the two filthy shoes on his bedspread.

"And you?" he asked.

John remained transfixed on the shoes.

Owen Conway picked up on John's discomfort. "Oh, that," he said offhandedly, sitting up and swinging his feet back to the floor. "Don't worry about the blanket. You won't sleep with it. Too damn hot. Heck,

I've had to resort to sleeping in the nude. Don't tell the ladies, though." He grinned, then continued. "But now it is you who goes on without an introduction."

"Yes," John answered slowly. "My name is John Sharp."

"A pleasure, Mr. Sharp. So tell me, which paper do you write for?"

"The *Tribune*, Mr. Conway. I write for the *Tribune*."

The other reporter whistled in appreciation, then turned serious. "I am sorry about the death of your colleague. He had the room right next to mine. Simpson, wasn't it?"

"Yes," John replied. "Did you talk with him at all?"

"I'm afraid not. In fact, I never actually had the pleasure of meeting him. He was out when I checked in. Then, the following day we learned that he had died." Conway shook his head. "Terrible accident—so pointless."

"You say he had the room right next to yours. Has anyone stayed there since?" John asked. "I need to ask Mr. McClellan to have a look around. I'm hoping to find his notes."

"Afraid you're out of luck there, sport. A man already came by for his effects. That's how McClellan got the news. I had a look around myself after he left." The Irishman paused to chuckle at John's expression. "All that I found was an empty bottle—not even a libation to mourn the man's passing."

"And which paper did you say you wrote for?" John asked.

"I write for the *National Police Gazette*."

Both men laughed.

"So you work for the *Police Gazette*. A first-rate scandal sheet."

Conway flinched in mock pain. "I abhor the term. We simply provide the working classes with the news that interests them most. A public service."

"Please, take no offense," John replied. "I'm an alumnus. I was with the *Intruder* for a few months, as a matter of fact."

Owen Conway flashed his crooked smile. "Quite a leap, Mr. Sharp. From the *Intruder* to the *Tribune*. You should be commended. Might I ask who you had the goods on?"

"No. No blackmail, Mr. Conway. I simply wrote an article that caught the eye of the *Tribune*'s editor."

"An in-depth review of ladies' fashion, perhaps," he offered. "Or an expose on bogus remedies for the ague?"

"No. I was at Astor Place."

Conway's face melted into a sober expression. "A terrible day. Some other time you must tell me of it. Perhaps over a pint."

The Irishman repositioned himself on the bed as John walked to the open window, planting himself in the path of a light breeze.

"So tell me, Mr. Conway, are you also here to cover the trial?"

"It's Owen," he answered. His feet were now back on the bedspread. "And ostensibly, yes. But I'll be frank with you, John. I truly have little interest in the trial or its outcome. It merely presents a backdrop for what I'm really after."

"And what is that?"

"Well, this is the way I see it. What do my readers most want to hear about? Scandal, plain and simple. Prostitution, murder, corruption, fighting . . . And what is better than scandal? Someone else's scandal—your neighbor's dirty laundry. Especially if you don't like your neighbor. So as soon as I heard what a ruckus was going on down here, I couldn't resist. I figure there's a whole series of articles that could come out of this."

"And has Charleston lived up to your expectations?"

Owen smiled wide. "It's better than I imagined. There are fires. More fires than you could ever believe. There are mobs on the street everyday, always just about ready to riot. There are hangings. Add the bordellos and bars, and there's enough dirt down here to fill a book. It's a writer's dream."

"Yes. But does the situation here bother you? Are you afraid of what's going to happen?"

"Bother me? Naw. Can't say I've got a lot of empathy with the Negroes. Just can't relate to 'em. And I've certainly no sympathy for the rich whites. Pushing folks to the breaking point just so they can squeeze out an extra buck here and there." He paused and smiled. "They all must learn to strike a pose at an early age, but not one of them seems capable of pronouncing a consonant. If you ask me, all these southerners deserve each other." He paused to take out a cigarette, which he held in his mouth, unlit. "And afraid, you ask. I can handle myself just fine. Grew up just west of Centre Street, right outside the Five Points. Work in the Points on most days. That's the reason the *Gazette* hired me. I'm not scared to mingle there. But I must tell you, John, once you've seen the Points, there's nothing down here that can scare you or shock you. Heck, I don't have to tell you. You probably worked there from time to time yourself."

"Indeed," John answered, tossing a box of matches to Owen. "However, my contact down here offered me a warning. He said that here, 'never have so many people disliked you without ever having met you.'"

Owen removed the cigarette and laughed. "You forget yourself, John. Perhaps that is the case for you, but you overlook the fact that I'm Irish."

"Yes," John said with a smile. "Quite right."

Owen sparked a match and lit his cigarette, then pocketed the matches.

John continued. "I must say, Owen, that I'm rather surprised the *Police Gazette* would subsidize your trip here. My experience with the *Intruder* taught me that those editors are about the tightest bunch you'll ever meet."

"They aren't paying for it. This excursion is entirely at my expense."

"How are you able to afford it?"

Owen sprang forward and rhythmically slapped his knees. "Let's just say that I'm quite resourceful."

"You don't mean to imply that you steal?"

"Heavens no," he answered with mock outrage. He then pounced to his feet. "I just do whatever I need to get by. My eye, for example. You may have been asking yourself what predicament yielded so unsightly a souvenir."

John nodded. "I must admit, I am rather curious."

"Contrary to what you're thinking, it was no drunken brawl or confrontation with the local authorities. I merely entered myself in a couple of prizefights last night. Made a dollar and fifty cents doing it too." He shook his head slowly back and forth. "Amazed the heck out of these crackers. They kept insisting that I fight, certain that I'd get my skull bashed in. But no matter who they kept putting in there, I kept winning. They don't fight well drunk, these southerners. Quite wild and prone to mistakes."

John studied Owen Conway. In spite of his average size and lean frame, the man's confidence and scarred knuckles attested that he could hold his own.

"I see," John responded. "But one fact contradicts your story. And that, Owen, is the blackness of your eye."

Owen prodded the wound with his index finger, wincing slightly. "This is true. A fault of my own, unfortunately, and not due to my opponent's dexterity. I had the cracker pretty well whipped when I let my guard down. A beautiful redheaded lass caught my attention, and I began to woo her. The next thing I knew, the bruiser threw a rabbit punch that got me. Smack!" He slapped his fist into his open hand. "Quite embarrassing, as a matter of fact. Not to mention unattractive."

"And the redhead?" John followed up with a smile.

"I'm sorry to say, she slipped through my fingers." He sighed, then placed his hand over his heart. "That, my friend, was far more painful than the punch."

Conway's face perked up quickly. "Hey, you know what, sport? I've got a great idea. Got me a little inside tip from a nice young lady named Mildred that works in a bordello down on Elliott Street. She told me that every night, one or two of them society types sneaks down there. What do ya say you and I go down there later and scope it out? Trail anyone who looks too well dressed for their own good. Quite a scandal it would make. Plus, if no one does show up, there are certainly worse places we could wait."

John paused a moment. "An inviting offer. But I'm afraid . . ."

"Or what about visiting the saloons? I've heard of one in particular. The Fighting Cock. Only the worst elements frequent there, from what I'm told. I bet we could scrounge up some interesting stories. Quench our thirst at the same time. What do you say, sport?"

John looked at Owen, whose blue eyes were rounded with excitement. His childlike enthusiasm for visiting the town's least desirable haunts was amusing, if not inviting. But the endless hours on a rock-hard train bench had taken their toll. John ached, and yearned for a hot meal and quiet, comfortable surroundings.

"Your offer is enticing, Owen, but I'm afraid I will have to decline. The train ride wore me out, and my remaining energy is reserved for a visit to Mr. McClellan's dining room table."

"Completely understandable, sport. No explanation required. I felt quite the same on the day I arrived. Of course, somehow I did wind up at Mrs. Asbury's house on King Street until the early-morning hours. Amazing. The house looked completely normal from the street, but once inside, I found myself in an opium den. Tell me, John, what is it about opium that invites young women toward toplessness?"

John's shock was sincere. "Certainly I do not know."

"Yes," Owen said distantly, his eyes glassed over. "Well, no matter. However, I must insist that you at least join me for dinner. There is a small hall just down the block. What d'ya say, sport? You up for it?"

"But what about the food here? Isn't it included in our rates?"

"It is nothing short of ghastly. Mr. McClellan, God bless him, cooks the food himself. The man is a horrendous chef; nothing he makes is edible. He insists upon providing a boiled potato for me with every meal. Only for me, everyone else gets rice. It's as if I were starving and living in Galway. I simply can't stomach another potato."

"I see."

"Also, I'm set to meet with two other northern reporters I've met since arriving. One's from Boston, the other Philadelphia, I believe. Nice chaps. A bit older than you and me, but entirely pleasant."

"Very well. That sounds worthwhile. When shall we go?"

"Why, immediately, John." Owen paused to glance briefly around the room. "A word of warning though, sport. I'd be careful about leaving anything of value here in the room. McClellan seems an honest sort, but my first night here, I heard someone bumping around in Simpson's room. I just assumed it was him returning late. Of course, I learned the next day that he was already dead by then." Owen shrugged dismissively and smiled. "Just a bit of advice, for what it's worth."

• • •

It was beginning to grow dark as the two men walked down State Street. Owen directed John toward a seedy one-story shack sandwiched between two taller structures. The shingle was missing from the brackets on the facade, but the smell of roasting meat provided a more compelling invitation to the travelers than any advertisement. A pair of peeling blue doors offered a riddle. Between them was a hand-lettered sign reading, 'Wrong Door,' with an arrow pointing to the one on the right. John hesitated a moment to sort through the logic, but Owen immediately jerked on the 'wrong' door and urged John forward with a sweeping bow. The interior was dim, and the patrons hunched over their tables like rows of insects feeding in the dark. At the sound of the door, all heads turned toward the two men. Their eyes flashed yellow in the reflected light of the lanterns. Owen treated them to his dazzling smile.

"Garçon, table for two," he quipped loudly.

"Sit your damned selves," a barmaid bellowed in return.

Owen laughed and turned to John. "Delightful folk, aren't they? Make you feel like family."

John ignored etiquette and took in the contents of the trestle tables. Greasy fingers ripped apart whole wood-roasted chickens and generous slabs of ribs slathered in a sauce that smelled of vinegar, mustard, and hot peppers. John was ready to elbow a stevedore aside and go for it, but Owen plucked at his sleeve.

"I think our associates are seated at the back. Shall we?"

John nodded and followed as Owen cut a path toward the rear. Halfway there, Owen stopped and let loose a great laugh.

"Well, I'll be. John, follow me. There's someone I want you to meet."

Owen approached a table occupied by two menacing-looking fellows. The nearest had protruding brow ridges, a receding forehead, and significant bruises. Owen slapped him on the back.

"Hello there, Hedge. You're looking a mite bit worse for wear tonight."

The man scowled and huffed.

"You see, John, Hedge here is one of the fellows from last night.

We boxed at the Sand Pit. Quite a whipping you took, Hedge. I hope you're not feeling as poorly as you look."

Hedge slid his chair back from the table, poised to rise. "A lucky encounter, I assure you," he growled. He cracked his knuckles for effect.

Owen smiled. "Oh, Hedge." His voice took on a winsome brogue. "Please do not blame it on something as whimsical as luck. At least blame it on the alcohol. Or your mood, perhaps. Luck is something for ladies at the racetrack."

Hedge turned to his companion, locking eyes with the man. John thought it was a bad sign.

"Forgive me, Hedge, for my lack of manners. I have yet to introduce my friend. Hedge, this is John Sharp, a colleague of mine from New York."

John extended his hand, which went ignored. It was probably for the best, considering the quantity of sauce on Hedge's paw; still, the signal was unmistakable. John nudged Owen.

"Perhaps we should go to our table," he suggested.

"In a moment, John." He turned back to the two men. "Hedge, now it's you who are forgetting your etiquette. You have yet to introduce your friend."

"This here is Bull." Bull leaned forward a little closer to the candle. He had enormous shoulders and no neck. His chin appeared to rest directly on the front of his undershirt, which was in full view as the man's jacket was slung over the chair behind him. He squinted briefly at John and Owen, then apparently lost interest, returning to the more important matter of divesting a corncob of anything edible.

Hedge's good eye took on an evil gleam. "Maybe you'd like to have a go at Bull in the ring tonight. That is, if you're willing ta put your money where your mouth is."

"As enticing as that is, Hedge, I'm afraid I'll have to decline. I am quite worn out from last night, you see. A bit fatigued after throwing so many punches. But I have a much better idea. My friend Mr. Sharp here might be up for it. Ten times the man I am. Why, he's whipped me all over New York State on numerous occasions."

"Horse manure!" It was Bull.

"Bull says your friend don't look much like a fighter," Hedge observed.

"Looks can be deceiving," Owen replied. "Up north, they call John here the Cannon. John, tell em how you got the name."

"Cannon? No one—"

"Stop being modest there, Cannon. Tell 'em."

John froze, like an actor with no line. "Because of my time in the artillery," he offered feebly.

"All right. Well, if you're not going to tell them, then I will." He grabbed John's right arm and held it up. "He got the name because this right hand here hits like a cannon. Sent many a man to the hospital, it has. And it ain't like one of them children's cannons you all have down here in Charleston. This is a full-fledged, New York twenty-pounder."

"Horse manure!"

"Bull here says our cannons are every bit as big as yours."

"Naw." It was Bull. Apparently the translation had missed a nuance. He eyed John. "You don't look like you could whip cream, kid. But I'll give ya your chance. Fight's gonna have to wait for a week and Tuesday, though. I got eleven more days of wearing the uniform."

John looked back at the chair. The coat was blue—militia. "Suits me fine," John ad-libbed. "A week and Tuesday." He gave Owen a murderous look.

Owen slapped John on the shoulder. "You know what, fellows?" he said. "My friend Cannon here would like to buy you two gents a round. We'll have the barmaid bring it over."

Hedge and Bull each gave John a look that revealed a new perspective.

"Awful kind a ya, Cannon," Hedge replied. Bull grunted in agreement.

"Think nothing of it."

Owen rapped on Hedge's back once more. "Good to see you again, Hedge. You too, Bull. Hopefully we'll run into you two gents later."

"Going to the Fox Trot. Maybe we'll see ya there."

"Perhaps we will." Owen winked. "Depends on our luck with the ladies."

• • •

"What, pray tell, was that all about?" John asked as they drew out of earshot.

"The nickname? Well, I certainly had to trump 'Bull.' It can't compete with Cannon. I'm certain there's no bull in the country that can stand up to a cannon."

"Yes, but why were you picking a fight with those men?"

"John, I was doing nothing of the sort. These men down here fancy themselves a tough breed. I'm merely trying to fit in. They prey on weakness, these tough sorts. So the solution is to show none. Right there, Cannon?"

John just laughed.

They located their fellow journalist at a small table in the far corner of the hall. Prescott Woodridge appeared to be in his early thirties, deeply tanned, with a nose one size too large for handsome. His clothes were well made, but a year or two behind the style. When John and Owen arrived, he was either engrossed or distracted—drawing lines on a napkin with the tines of his fork.

"Hello there, old chap," Owen greeted him. "Why are you sitting back here all alone? Where is Mabry?"

"He couldn't make it," Woodridge replied. "He apparently had a bad run-in with some boiled peanuts. That will teach him to try unfamiliar foods in this heat."

Owen made introductions. Woodridge was a freelance writer out of Boston. A curt barmaid stopped briefly to take their order. John sent two glasses of ale to his new thug friends.

John gave Owen a look. "You don't think they'll stop by to thank us?"

"Not a chance," he laughed. "The Fox Trot has the easiest ladies in Charleston."

If any of this was of passing interest to Woodridge, he did not let on. He polished off the last third of the pint in front of him in one pull, then reached for the one he had standing by.

"How long have you been in Charleston now, Mr. Woodridge?"

"Four days," he answered, wiping his mouth with the back of his hand. "And yourself?"

"I arrived just today."

"Your paper certainly didn't give you much lead time on the trial." Woodridge stopped abruptly, then shook his head. "Sorry. I just made the connection. You're replacing Simpson, aren't you?"

John nodded.

"I'm terribly sorry. I ran into him a few times in the bars. He seemed a decent sort."

"Did he talk with you at all about what he was working on?" John leaned forward. "Arriving so late, I had hoped to follow up on his leads."

Woodridge shook his head. "I'm afraid I can't help you there." He returned his attention to his drink, then spoke almost as an afterthought. "I will tell you this, though. I did some checking on his death—just in case there was something . . . suspicious. He was a fellow reporter, after all. I felt I owed him at least that."

"What did you learn?"

Woodridge looked back at John. "He ran into traffic without looking. Pure and simple. He was coming out of a section of houses, as the fire wagon came down Fisher Street. The roads are narrow there. Plenty of folks saw it happen. Some people on their way to the fire stopped and sent for a doctor, but he was dead on the spot. Just thought you'd want to know . . ."

The barmaid appeared with their food; roast chicken, blackened and crisp on the outside, and something called pulled pork, a shredded roast meat liberally doused with sauce and dumped on a slice of bread. It was incredible, with a mouth-burning kick that merited another order of ale.

"So have you been to Charleston before, Mr. Woodridge?"

Woodridge rested his elbows on the table and leaned forward a little. His eyes were bright now from the ale. "I have been here a number of times. Charleston has had a checkered history, and it is a reporter's job to follow trouble." He paused to fish a smoke out of his pocket. "The city gets like this sometimes. Little things will set it off."

John kept his voice low. "I understand that a slave revolt just south of here in Georgia may be at the root of the increased tension—the reason the trial is taking place. Can you tell me anything about the ringleader, Jebediah Jones? There are quite a few rumors circulating about him."

"I dare say," Woodridge agreed. "Before I came down here, I tried to track down the one that he was educated in Boston and then sent south to foment insurrection among the slaves. I found no record of him whatsoever among the abolitionist societies. In fact, the only black in the city by that name was a seventy-year-old cobbler."

Owen snorted. "A typical outcome of serious legwork."

"Did you learn anything down here?" John asked.

"Most of the free blacks won't talk much. Two who seemed credible said he was born on that plantation and worked there all his life. They didn't know what made him do it."

"What became of him? Really. I overheard a variety of speculation on the train."

"It depends on who you talk to. I have heard that he was able to flee north with the help of sympathetic blacks. I have heard that he hides in the backwoods, hunted, barely able to survive. I have heard that he is dead, killed by whites—that the truth has been covered up for political purposes."

"What about the rumor that he is raising an army?" John asked. "One numbering in the thousands that is waiting to attack one of the major cities—Savannah or Charleston?"

"The man would have to be another Napoleon—with a magician's skill. How could one hide and provision a black army in the thousands without detection?" Woodridge shook his head. "There is no such army. But if there were, it would be nice if they rescued this poor sap who goes on trial tomorrow."

"Do you think the trial's outcome has been predetermined; that the man will be found guilty?"

"Absolutely. They'll hang him." Woodridge's voice had an odd, flat quality. He leaned back in his chair. He compressed his lips and let his eyes travel over the room, as if cataloging the faces of those who would do the deed. He made as if to speak, then took another long drink of ale.

"I have heard that a show of legality is very important to the locals," John said. "Southerners think the law is on their side in this."

"Whose law?" It was more a statement than a question.

"Well, even the northern states recognize the Fugitive Slave Act." Woodridge leaned forward again. He looked at John with a kind of ale-induced earnestness. "Do you think God ranks his Commandments?"

John and Owen glanced at each other, unsure of where he was going with this one.

"I mean, do you think that forgetting the Sabbath is as bad as adultery? How about stealing versus killing?" Woodridge looked at John and Owen, apparently judging from their quizzical expressions that he had made a logical leap the others weren't quite following. He shook his head. "I'm just trying to say that there are two kinds of laws—moral laws and those enacted by men in power to fit their needs at the time. I just think that the Fugitive Slave Act does not measure up to 'Thou shalt not kill.'" He made a self-deprecating shrug and signaled to the barmaid for another round.

"I think I get your point," John said. "To the southerners, slaves are property. Aiding a runaway slave is a property crime—like passing along stolen goods. Yet the punishment is commensurate with crimes against a person—like assault or murder."

Woodridge didn't respond, evidently feeling he had said enough on the subject. He withdrew a cigarette case from his pocket and offered a hand-rolled smoke to John and Owen. Both declined.

Owen's attention now seemed drawn to the buxom young barmaid who had delivered their last set of drinks. He stood.

"If you gentlemen will excuse me for a few minutes, I have some business I must attend to."

Owen departed, and John attempted to engage Woodridge on another subject. "Owen mentioned on our way here tonight that you were in Texas. That you covered the Mexican War."

Woodridge nodded. "I was there for several months. There were few surprises—I saw what I expected to see." In response to John's raised eyebrow, he continued. "My father was a military man. He served with Jackson at the Battle of New Orleans. I grew up with countless stories of military campaigns."

The older reporter seemed distracted. He shifted in his chair and traced patterns with his finger in the spilled salt on the table. After a minute or two, he looked up at John as if surprised he was still there. "You asked me about the Mexican War. My old man and I had very different opinions about it. He was all for it, a major proponent of Manifest Destiny. I was dead set against it. Of course, everyone knew we would win. That was not the issue. The real question was what would happen after we *had* won."

He took another sip of his ale, and John waited for him to continue.

"For thirty years now, an invisible line across our nation has, at the same time, divided us and tenuously held us together. The forty-second parallel."

"The Missouri Compromise," John said.

"Yes, Mr. Sharp, the Missouri Compromise. In my mind, a treacherous and foolhardy pact that simply tabled the issues, leaving the problems to the next generation—our generation. Every state above the line was to be free. Every state below it, slave. If a free state was admitted then, quid pro quo, a slave state must also enter the Union in order to maintain the balance. Well, everyone not blinded by lust for land had to recognize the peril that would result from our victory in the Mexican War. Here we are, two years after the war, and Pandora's box has been opened. A great expanse of land is now ours, the fruits of our victory, *and all of it falls below the forty-second parallel.* So, whom does it belong to, Mr. Sharp?"

"Well, if one adheres to the spirit of the Missouri Compromise, the new territories would go with the South. They would be slave states."

He nodded. "The South believes this unequivocally." Woodridge slapped the table for emphasis. "And the North cries foul. They cannot allow the slave states to outnumber the free, or they risk being outvoted on every congressional issue. And only so many northern states can be created to counteract them. So, what is to happen?"

"I've heard a different compromise suggested," John said. "One in which the citizens of the proposed states would vote on whether they wished to be free or slave. I believe it is called 'squatter sovereignty.' "

"It will never happen. The South can't allow it. The plantation system just isn't practical in the new territories, New Mexico and California. There is no need for slaves because the plantation system cannot exist on a large scale under the arid conditions. Therefore, that possibility is out of the question."

"Do you think some southern states might threaten secession to get their way?" John asked. "It has worked for them before."

Woodridge snickered. "Like New England did with Madison back during the War of 1812? He sure managed to get that peace treaty signed right quick, didn't he?"

John turned his hand palm up. "South Carolina seems to raise the issue every time they reach an impasse in Congress. It used to make Jackson so mad that he threatened to hang John C. Calhoun."

Woodridge's mouth twitched at the thought. Then he leaned forward and dropped his voice to a whisper. "I think it's for real this time."

"You think so?"

Woodridge nodded. "I think they really mean it." He took another sip and continued earnestly. "Look, for instance, at the lack of revelry here surrounding the Fourth of July. It's almost as if they have already broken away in their hearts."

"But the president wouldn't let that happen, would he? It would mean war."

Woodridge gave John an odd little smile. His face looked flushed in the candlelight. "You may recall that I told you I opposed the Mexican War."

John nodded.

"Have you ever seen a man killed?"

"I'm not sure what you mean," John responded. "I have seen a number of dead bodies, but certainly nothing like what you would have witnessed as a war correspondent."

Woodridge shook his head. He sat back a little and rubbed his forehead. A lock of hair fell down over one eyebrow. He leaned forward again and looked at John with an odd expression. "I saw a man die today."

John said nothing. He just stared at Woodridge.

"I was in the north end of town. I came across a crowd of about twenty people running and pushing. I followed, and watched them merge with another group in a circle in a vacant lot. I heard a kind of yelping sound. At first, I thought it was a dog. I thought maybe someone had cornered a mad dog. I climbed up on a porch to get a better look.

"They had this Negro in the middle of them. They were screaming. He was yelping—that same damned yelping. They took turns hitting and kicking him. He fell, and I saw a lot of flailing going on. They picked him up and dragged him toward me. They were holding him up. There were a lot of people watching.

"A minute or two later I saw a man come running up. He had a militia uniform on, and he was carrying a long rope. That's when I was certain of what was happening.

"They tied the Negro's hands, and someone took off his belt and used it to tie his legs together while they threw the noose over a tree branch. He was looking around at everybody like the whole thing was crazy. His eyes were real wide.

"That's when he looked at me. I swear to God, he looked straight at me. I don't know if he thought I had some authority, dressed up as I was, standing up on the porch. He seemed to think I could do something.

"They lowered the noose and put it over his head. Then the sound changed—he started to wail, nothing coherent. He just wailed and wailed. Some were laughing, some were screaming. My God, it was loud." Woodridge licked his lips and looked down at the table. "For whatever supposed atrocity this man had committed, there was no gallows to offer mercy. No quick death. He was pulled up, tug by tug, until he dangled about four feet off the ground. To see a man tortured like this . . . To see the muscles in his arms go rigid, and his feet bounce up and down in search of a floor. His neck strained beyond conception, the veins so thick they looked like pulsing fingers. His mouth, always open, fighting for a breath, gasping at imagined air. And the eyes. His eyes bulging out as if they were ready to explode. And then . . . Snap." He pulled his hands apart sharply. "God's abrupt and delayed compassion."

He reached for his glass, finding it empty. John slid his fresh ale to within Woodridge's reach. He took another voracious gulp.

"I'll never forget the way he looked at me—and I didn't do a damned thing."

When Woodridge finally looked back up at him, John found that he had no words. He could only look at the other man silently.

Woodridge gave that odd smile again. "So you wonder if people are ready to start killing each other. I personally am ready for blood-letting on a massive scale. In this case, on this issue, it may be the only solution. War is coming, Mr. Sharp."

As Woodridge finished, John became aware of Owen's silent presence just outside the light from their table. Judging from his expression, he had caught the end of their conversation.

Woodridge arose and took his leave, suggesting they meet again after court the following day. As they watched him make his way toward the door with the excess deliberation of the inebriated, John was suddenly aware of his own overwhelming fatigue.

"Owen, I am more than ready to call it a night. I'm going to head back to McClellan's."

"But, sport, the night is still young, and I'll be damned if I'm going to let it end on this note . . . all dark and depressing. There's fun to be had."

"I'm just not sure that I could find fun right now, particularly in this town. Not after listening to Woodridge. I feel like I'm looking down into a pit."

Owen shook his head. "The guy was sending signals all night that something was eating him. He wasn't like that when I met him yesterday."

"I'm sure anyone would have been shaken by what he witnessed."

"Still, you know as well as I do that Woodridge couldn't have done anything to stop that lynching. That mob would have turned on him, too."

John nodded. "Sometimes it's a tough call."

"And some people just don't handle it well. They can't prepare themselves for the foul things they'll see in life. I believe it's the curse of intelligence."

"How so?"

"They think too much. Can't just accept what they see. They have to dissect it. Why did it happen? How could they have stopped it? With dumb folks, they just see it and take it. That's what happened, period. It's why all the best soldiers aren't that bright. And it's why fellows like you and me live such happy, contented lives." He chuckled and slapped John's arm. "Look, sport, you just got here today. You really need to see the other side of it." He tapped John on the chest. "You know—balanced reporting.

"I know what you could do to clear your head. Take a walk down State Street, then follow Broad Street all the way to the East Bay. Don't stop until you get to the water. It's worth seeing. Trust me."

"I'll think about it," John answered. "I'll see you at the courthouse tomorrow, right?"

"Right," Owen responded, but his attention had already wandered to the barmaid who had earlier caught his eye. He winked at John. "Now, I'm going to see if *I* can't turn this night around."

John found himself making the turn onto Broad Street rather than taking the short route back to the boardinghouse. He wasn't sure if it was curiosity or Owen's barb about balanced reporting that provided the incentive, but as the breeze from the sea began to clear his head, he was glad of his choice.

Broad Street dead-ended into East Bay at the far eastern side of the peninsula. Only a string of dock stands to his left separated John from the water. He could see the silhouettes of ships at their moorings: cutters, steamers, and all the small boats, their wood groaning and creaking with quiet voices undetectable during the day. Now, sounds on water were amplified by the night's stillness.

As he walked, John was joined by increasing numbers of pedestrians. Indeed, the street traffic of nighttime Charleston was the inverse of the day's activity; commercial areas were relatively deserted while the better residential areas buzzed with activity. Ladies and debonair gentlemen emerged from their homes, dressed up, but with no apparent destination. They ambled about with a graceful nonchalance, exchanging greetings with friends and neighbors on their verandas as they passed.

"Evening, Mr. Carter. Evening, Miss Jane."

Mr. Carter touched the brim of his hat, and Miss Jane inclined her head and dipped her fan. "Why, Mrs. Matheson, how delightful ta meet your mother last Sunday. I hope she is well."

They congregated in small knots and then dispersed, only to regroup again a few houses down.

The reporter subconsciously squared his shoulders and adjusted his pace to avoid overtaking everyone on the street. He had passed an invisible social line some blocks back. These were all people of means, and John was a guest in their world.

He was attracted to a glow up ahead, just off the street, where the docks ended. It looked like the eastern horizon just before sunrise. As he rounded a curve, the source of the glow became evident.

These were the mansions of Charleston—two and three stories tall, some narrow, others wide—nestled next to one another for the entirety of the street. Some showcased porches and balconies on all three floors. Exquisite windows of beveled glass reflected light like crystal. Here was Charleston's architectural genius; tucked in this corner of the peninsula and reserved for the privileged.

John found himself at the edge of an expansive public park, well ordered and immaculately maintained. A discreet plaque on a stone pillar proclaimed "White Point Gardens." Oaks, cedars, willows, and even an occasional palm presided over a rich variety of cultivated flora. He walked along the perimeter, at the seaward side of the city mere feet from the Atlantic, where waves clapped softly on the battery wall. Enough of the aura from the homes filtered through the trees to create an abstract painting of reflected light on the water's surface. Off in the distance, John could make out the sound of the harbor buoy, tolling faintly on the salty breeze. It brought a feeling of pure peace.

Through a curtain of weeping willows ahead, John glimpsed a fantasy beginning to unfold. He ducked inside the shelter of the soft wands for a better look. There, a parade of stately carriages were lined up, one after the next, before the homes of the south Battery. The mansions were bathed in light, the collective light of gaslights and a thousand candles; enough to make white walls luminous and gardens vibrant with color at the edge of night.

Amid the light, the Charleston aristocracy glowed a light yellow. Well-built blacks in fine livery assisted their masters and mistresses from the carriages with professional decorum. The partygoers dressed with a formality that more than matched their counterparts in New York. The gentlemen's formal wear hung with flawless drape, regardless of size or build. Ebony canes, manipulated with each step, expressed individual style and character. The women were breathtaking, with their tiny waists and full hooped skirts. The dresses answered to the ladies' choreographed movements in time; a delayed response no more noticeable and no less exquisite than a graceful echo.

John followed the procession as it approached its destination, a three-story white mansion with extended balconies on the first and second floors. The attendees moved deliberately, but with a dreamlike fluidity. The only quick actions were performed by the footmen, and even they managed a certain grace.

John closed his eyes to absorb the sounds of the party. He smiled to himself with the knowledge that he had done this before. Subdued chamber music floated from the house. A waltz. The bass clef of the men's speech harmonized with the cello, while the pitch of the ladies' laughter joined the violins. Above it all was the falsetto of tinkling crystal glassware, as precise and clear as the tones of a triangle.

He began to imagine the conversations. The phrases that drifted toward him were barely intelligible, just below the threshold of understanding. Of what did they speak? Certainly of nothing so dire as war or civil unrest. Not in mixed company.

There seemed to be a general bonhomie and graciousness that transcended that of New York parties. This was an elegant gathering of a group of friends. There was an inordinate amount of laughter; the men's deep and hearty, the women's playful and coquettish. And while it was possible that it could be attributable to the guests' running start on alcohol hours before, John preferred to think that it sprang from an unabashed friendliness and goodwill.

His thought was interrupted as a steward walked outside and discreetly rang a small bell. The guests began to filter back indoors for dinner. He had heard these southerners operated on a much later schedule. John could picture imported china and silver on linen, fine wines and exotic foods.

Soon, all were inside, save a young gentleman who idled at the rail of the second-story balcony. He stared out toward White Point Gardens; perhaps beyond it, to the sea. John momentarily felt uneasy. While the young man did not look at him, he still felt as if he was being intrusive. But he could not make himself turn away.

The man smoked a small cigar, exhaling wisps of smoke that dissipated on the breeze. He appeared preoccupied. Troubled, perhaps. Then, the sound of door closing presaged the arrival of another guest, a young woman whom John had not noticed until now. She was beautiful, all grace and sophistication. The jewels on her ears and around her neck flashed intermittently as they captured the light, highlighting her faultless skin. Her hair was done up with style, but left two long curls that tapered down in front of her ears and glanced off her powdered cheeks. Amid a lull in the breeze, John thought he detected the scent of gardenia mixing with the jasmine of the flowers. He was certain the fragrance was hers.

She took the young man's hand impulsively and awarded him a full and unreserved smile. Seconds later his mouth began to move, and she slowly dropped her head. When she looked up again, she wasn't smiling. She spoke. He answered, and she lowered her head again. He placed a finger just beneath her chin and raised it slowly. Their eyes met.

Suddenly they both turned toward the house. A sound from inside interrupted. She lifted her skirt a little, scurrying away from the gentleman and out of John's sight. After watching her disappear, the young man again faced out toward the ocean, standing frozen, impossible to read. Then, following an exaggerated breath, he turned and vanished as well.

John shook his head and smiled. "You're a fool," he whispered.

•   •   •

As John walked home, he thought not of the problems that had brought him to Charleston, nor of the strange and intense scenes that he had witnessed earlier in the day. He simply replayed images from the gala, reliving them over and over again. It was like coming home . . . after a very long time. This night, a mere glimpse of such people erased a thousand of their faults.

SIX

John woke up from a sound sleep, sweating.

Bong!

The nearest steeple tolled an alarm, an ominous warning that reverberated through his small bedroom, making his heart race.

Bong!

He fanned at the imaginary blanket, an item that he had discarded hours ago, and stood up. He rubbed his eyes, momentarily disoriented, then staggered toward his open window. In the distance, he heard scattered shouts.

"Fire! Hurry up!"

Bong!

"Down on Beaufain! Hurry! It might spread!"

John rested a hand on the ledge and studied the skyline. He saw the nearest steeple off to the left, the spire seeming to quiver from the successive tolling. He panned right.

"Water!" someone distantly cried.

Then he saw it. To the north. An insidious yellow-orange light. Small, at this point, but emitting a smoke blacker than the darkness.

John heard a rumble in the distance. He could see flashes of lightning on the horizon far to the south. Rain would be a blessed relief. But based upon the lapse between the flash and the thunder, the storm was too far away to help douse this fire.

Bong!

The sound of men running, the slap of shoes on brick, increased on the street below. He saw lamps lit in dozens of surrounding windows. He grabbed his trousers and dressed hastily as he stood by the window. He might not know his way around Charleston in the dark, but he had no doubt that he could find his way to a fire.

Bong!

John watched for a few minutes longer, attempting to identify landmarks to work out a route to the blaze. Then he saw men walking back slowly, and lamplights began to flicker out. The fire must have been contained.

The smoke continued, however. John could smell it. Distance filtered its pungency, leaving the same acrid aroma he had noticed earlier on the street.

Then the tolling ceased.

The rain never came.

SEVEN

〰

In the morning, a pall hung over Charleston. It was manifest in the form of an overcast sky—ash gray clouds that connected to form a blanket over the city. The air was heavy with a humidity that fell like a fog across the quiet streets. Off to the east, in the Cooper River, a lone steamboat cut through the choppy water, the hum of its engine supplying a gloomy dirge.

John had expected to hear a commotion over last night's fire. He found nothing of the sort—no cries of outrage or promises of retribution. Instead, citizens moved through their daily routines as if by rote, their faces reflecting a resignation born of fatigue.

After a breakfast of dry cornbread, fatty bacon, hard-boiled eggs, and weak coffee, John walked downtown to the wire office, only to find it closed. No one was stirring at City Hall, either. He returned to the wire office and rapped on the window at eleven o'clock. The annoyed telegrapher begrudgingly let him inside. John's message to his editor had been succinctly worded but comprehensive; he reported satisfactory contact with Mahan, advance word on the trial, a brief description of Charleston's political climate, and a request for instructions concerning Simpson's remains. After the trial, he would wire ahead the outcome, then catch the first train back to New York to deliver his full report.

John glanced at his pocket watch. It was only late morning, and he was already stewing beneath the weight of his black wool suit. It could turn out to be a long day.

When John returned to his boardinghouse, he found Samuel waiting for him by the front steps.

The boy wore the same oversize outfit he had worn the preceding day, but added a satchel slung over a shoulder.

He spotted John and walked quickly toward him.

"Good morning, Mr. Sharp. All's well I hope."

"Yes, Samuel. It is good to see you."

"You too, sir. Sure everything's all right, though? You had ta run somewhere or sump'n?"

"No," John answered. He would have laughed had he not been so uncomfortable.

" 'Fore I forget. I brung you these here cabbage leaves like ya asked. My mama, she done set 'em ta soaking last night, so they should be cool fo' a bit." He took off the satchel and began to pull one out.

"Thank you, Samuel. And please thank your mother."

"Ain't no botha'. Hopefully, it'll help. You look a might bit hot."

Samuel extended the large leaf as John removed his derby hat. The boy took the hat and spread out the leaf inside, insulating it as well as possible.

"That should work fo' ya now, sir. Work fo' a few hours at the least. Got me another one when that one ain't working no more. You just let me know."

"Yes," John replied. He placed the hat back on his head and immediately felt the coolness on his sweaty hair. Even if the sensation proved only temporary, it was still worth it for the immediate relief. "Samuel, I believe that these cabbage leaves might actually work."

"Of course they work, Mr. Sharp. I wouldn't have given 'em to ya if they didn't." He looked at John expectantly. "So, where to, sir?"

"Actually, I won't need you anymore this morning. I just stopped by the wire office, and now I'm heading back to my room."

"I can do stuff like that fo' ya." Samuel's voice was eager. "Stuff like going to the wire office. I been thinking, I could do the running and fetching for ya while you's in town. That way, you can relax in the shade where it's cool."

John chuckled. Right now the idea was appealing.

"You said you was paid fo' keeping yo' eyes open. Well, maybe I could be an extra pair of eyes moving 'round town. Folks is used ta seeing boys like me running errands. They don't pay us no mind."

John considered for a moment. It could be useful to have the boy do some of the legwork, as his time in town was so limited. But with the city's climate of fear, he couldn't take a chance on getting the boy in trouble.

"I'll tell you what," John said. "I can use you for some errands, and you can keep your eyes open for me. But, except for the errands, you can't tell anyone what it is you are doing."

"Yessir. 'Course, sir."

"All right. You told me before that you heard folks say that there were thirteen different fires here in the last month. I want you to sit down and think about how many you have seen for yourself when you were running around. Picture them in your mind and try to remember what street they were on. If you heard of a place where there was a fire but you haven't seen it, you can run by and take a look, but otherwise don't count it. I only want to know about recent fires, ones I could still go by and see; ones that haven't been rebuilt yet.

"But this is important, Samuel. Don't let anyone see you looking at the buildings. Just walk on by like you were doing something else. And don't ask any questions. Do you understand?"

The boy nodded eagerly. "Yessir, I understand. I'll tell ya 'bout the buildings I's seen and I'll be real careful."

"Good," John replied. "You can meet me back at the boarding-house by twelve thirty, before I have to leave for the trial."

And, with that, Samuel Grass was off like a whip.

As John entered his boardinghouse, he was met by the proprietor.

"A letter for you, sir," McClellan said, waving a white envelope. "A gentleman brought it by earlier this morn. Said it was important."

John's stomach churned just a bit. The only people he knew here were certainly not the type to deliver letters. "Thank you, Mr. McClellan. I think I'll take this into the parlor."

"You go right ahead."

John seated himself at the table in the next room and pulled the letter hurriedly from the blank envelope. It read:

Mr. John Sharp,

I apologize for the impersonal nature of this letter. Unfortunately, extenuating circumstances have left this my sole option. I am leaving Charleston, Mr. Sharp. Immediately, as a matter of fact. As you receive this correspondence I shall have already set sail on the Osprey, *a small cutter bound for New York City. I realize that my departure leaves you now with no contact in Charleston. For that I apologize. However, I feel the immediacy of my leaving is of grave and utmost importance.*

I assume that you most likely saw the fire of last night. The fire that ravaged a building on Beaufain Street. That building was owned by Whorter Shipping Company!

Do you still wonder who is behind the fires, Mr. Sharp? I hope this incident opens your eyes to the danger you face. I do not believe that this fire was in any way an accident. I have no enemies. That leaves a clear deduction; it was my contact with the New York Tribune *that now endangers me and my holdings. First, Simpson. Now you. It is obvious, Mr. Sharp, that words slipped from your tongue when they shouldn't have, and you were then followed to my office.*

Hopefully, my refuge will be temporary. I shall return when the situation changes back to one of normalcy. I have left a few dollars in the envelope in case you come across an unexpected difficulty. Be wise with it.

Heed my warning, Mr. Sharp. These are dangerous times in Charleston, and you are now alone here. Be frugal with your trust,

for these men hide a devious agenda behind their social pleasantries.
May God watch over you, sir.
    Sincerely,
        Arthur Mahan

John pulled the money from the envelope, three dollar bills, then tucked the letter back inside. He sat still in the chair, digesting the disconcerting news. Could Mahan's allegation be true? That the Whorter Shipping Company was targeted because of him? He felt unnerved and confused. Was he truly in jeopardy? If so, he had just sent Samuel on a potentially dangerous errand. He drew a deep breath, attempting to sort it all out.

McClellan approached him, stopping a few feet away. "Everything all right, Mr. Sharp?" he asked, watching the envelope crumple in John's fist.

"Yes, yes, fine," he stammered.

"Oh, good. You looked a mite bit bothered for a moment. Had me worried it was some unfortunate news."

"An acquaintance had to leave town unexpectedly. That is all." John stood up. "I think I shall go up to my room now."

"Very well, sir. Oh, also, Mr. Conway came down here earlier and asked me for the key to your room. He said you wouldn't mind. So I gave it to him. Hope that's all right with you."

John answered, preoccupied. "Yes, that is fine, Mr. McClellan." He stopped at the stairs and turned. "A black boy named Samuel is running errands for me. I would like to speak with him when he returns."

John pecked at his door, opening it in increments to avoid a possible obscenity. Two boots dangled off the bed, a safe sign that clothing had not been discarded. He then swung open the door, revealing Owen and only Owen. It was a measured relief.

Owen stirred in the bed. "Hey, sport," he garbled softly, then coughed.

"Hello, Owen. I see that you are comfortable."

"Quite. I hope you don't mind my presence. I simply couldn't get a moment's rest in my room. The heat. I woke up repeatedly stuck to the sheets." He leaned up and propped his head against his left arm, revealing tight creases across the body of yesterday's clothes.

"No, it is no problem," John responded flatly. He sauntered to the window, tossing his suit jacket and hat on the dresser.

"What time is it?"

John stared out on the city. "Just before twelve."

"Whew. I got in kind of late. Wound up at a few taverns till the wee hours of the morning." He yawned. "How 'bout you? Did you come right home after the Battery?"

John nodded without turning.

"Quite a sight. I knew you'd like it." He stood and adjusted his suspenders with a snap. "So, you feeling better today? Fully rested after a good night's sleep?"

After a moment, John shrugged his shoulders. "I did not rest that well, actually. The fire bell, it woke me. I had a hard time getting back to sleep after that."

"The fire. I had forgotten. 'Twas quite a crazed scene. People running helly-nelly all over the place."

"You saw it?"

"Just the tail end, unfortunately. They seemed to have it under control by the time I arrived." John kept his back to Owen, who took the opportunity to begin a series of stretching exercises. "Good gracious!" he exclaimed, staring at his pant leg.

"What is it?"

"These filthy southerners. They insist upon chewing tobacco. Quite a disgusting habit, as a matter of fact. They then attempt to spit the remains into these brass pots all over the place. And distance is no deterrent. They'll try a shot from a good twenty feet away. Problem is, when they drink, they always miss." Owen lifted his leg. "Look at this. There are brown stains all over the bottom of my pants."

John turned and faced Owen, whose right leg was now in his two hands, mere feet from his hunched face. John could not help but laugh. "Really, Owen. Of all these people's odd traits, I find it strange that the one that most shocks you is their use of tobacco. Their society is crumbling around them, for goodness' sake."

Owen dropped his leg. "Yeah, well their crumbling society isn't ruining my pants now, is it?"

While Owen continued to obsess over his clothing, John returned to the window. His momentary amusement dissipated as he again considered Mahan's letter. He convinced himself that he bore no guilt. How could he have known that he would be followed?

"Hey, I'm talking to you," Owen said loudly.

John swiveled and looked at the Irishman.

"I asked, what have you planned for today?"

"After I eat, I'm going to the courthouse." Owen looked to him as if he expected an explanation as to why. "The trial starts this afternoon," John continued. "At one. Are you going?"

"Of course. Do you think I'd miss the chance to see these hayseeds get all worked up? Today looks like an excellent day to dig up some dirt."

John nodded. "Well, I am going downstairs to eat. Are you coming along?" He moved toward the door.

Owen picked up yesterday's jacket. "Yeah. You don't think I'd miss the chance for another potato."

At lunch, John sat quietly at a table in McClellan's dining room, still preoccupied with Mahan's letter. When the food arrived—a heaping plate of pork, rice, and corn-dodgers—and John made no motion to begin eating, Owen dropped his silverware and fixed John with a look.

"All right. So tell me. What made *you* turn into a crotchety old bastard like Woodridge? Did you see someone hanged as well?"

"No," John responded. He considered for a moment, then dug through his pocket to retrieve Mahan's letter. He handed it across the table to Owen. "This is from my contact here in Charleston. I'd like to have your take on it."

Owen reached for the letter, soiling it with smudges of grease from his fingers. He flipped the paper open with his free arm, shoveling spoonfuls of rice into his mouth with the other. As he read, an occasional grain would slip off his chin and drop over a word, an encumbrance that he sacked with a quick flick of the wrist. After he finished reading he chuckled, then tossed the paper dismissively back to the center of the table.

"So?" John asked.

"My take is that your contact, Mahan, jumps at shadows. You aren't taking this seriously?"

"Why wouldn't I? Didn't you read what it said? The fire may have been a direct result of my presence."

Owen dropped his spoon, which bounced loudly off his plate. "The fire. Because of you? That's preposterous. The Negroes are the ones starting all the fires. Every cracker down here says so. I hardly think the Negroes are going to follow you and burn down the houses you visit, regardless of how poorly you tip."

John flinched from Owen's unrestrained volume. He pressed his hands down just above the table, an indication for Owen to quiet down.

"Wow, you really believe this. Well, don't worry," he said in an exaggerated whisper. "I don't see any of the blacks in here. I think you're safe."

"It's not necessarily the blacks doing it," John whispered in return. "According to Mahan it's the whites. The militia perhaps. I must admit, there is a chance that he's right."

Owen made a muffled hum as he swallowed another bite. "So let me get this straight. The *whites* are the ones slowly burning down this city. That's absolutely ridiculous." He shook his spoon at John and laughed. "The first thing you look for in a case like this is motive. The whites have absolutely nothing to gain from burning their city to the ground. The Negroes, on the other hand . . . Well, let's just say quite a few of them would dance around the bonfire."

"I'm not so sure. Samuel, the boy I hired, says there's anxiety and confusion over the fires in the black community. As a result of the fires, blacks are arrested and made scapegoats for curfew violations. Does that sound like a cause for celebration?"

Owen shook his head dismissively. "I don't buy it. To hear them talk, no Negro down here has ever lifted a finger against a white. But Woodridge's lynching victim, and the scapegoats you refer to, do you think all of them are completely innocent? No black has ever committed a crime? For every Negro boy who says he's guiltless, thirty men of power would disagree. Who do you think knows more?" Owen swallowed a bite and smiled. "The next thing you know, you're going to tell me the whites are the ones who caused the fracas down in Habersham County. Really, John, the weather got to Mahan, and now it's getting to you."

John was not in the mood for Owen's humor. He rubbed his eyebrows inward, stopping to pinch the bridge of his nose. A headache was oncoming, a dull, hollow pain just behind his eyes.

Owen became less flippant. "All right, for argument's sake, say it is the whites. Say they are the arsonists. Even if that's the case, there's still no reason to believe that this had anything to do with you. John, there were over a dozen other fires before last night. As far as I know, none of them occurred in any building you had ever set foot in. If the fires are connected, your logic is flawed."

John removed his hand from his face and nodded slowly. Owen made sense. This place was obviously unsettling him. He needed an outside source to ground him, and Owen was perfect.

John picked up his fork. "So you think Mahan's fire had nothing to do with me?"

"I'd bet your life on it." Owen grinned.

John shook his head. "Guess I got carried away."

"It may have had something to do with that absurd letter from your contact. I do believe that whoever wrote it most certainly yearns to be a writer himself." He dropped his voice to a baritone. " 'Do not trust these people. They are the devil in disguise.' How dramatic. It is akin to the sleazy literature so popular with the ladies in the North."

"Yes," John said, suddenly ravenous. He picked up his silverware and began eating quickly.

"One thing is glaring, though," Owen observed. "And that is the abnormally grand opinion you must hold of yourself. To think all of this trouble suddenly sprouted over you. As if Charleston was Utopia until you stepped off the train. Why, I don't think even Garrison himself could cause such a stir if he came down here waving a gun and whistling 'Jimmy Crack Corn.' Not the same sort of trouble Mr. John Sharp can muster."

John laughed out loud. Mahan was definitely wrong. John was not alone in Charleston.

After lunch, Owen went upstairs to retrieve his notebook, and John walked out onto McClellan's front porch. He found Samuel sitting beside the stoop. The boy leaped to attention as he approached.

While Owen had helped John place Mahan's letter in perspective, the sight of Samuel renewed his worry over the fires. He could be endangering the boy by sending him to collect information on so sensitive a matter. Especially if Samuel asked questions: of his neighbors, his family, his friends. He walked the boy over to a bench in the shade by the side of the building. John sat down, and the boy sat cross-legged on the ground.

"You can still run errands for me," John began, "but I don't want you reporting on the fires anymore."

"Did I do something wrong?" the boy asked, his brow twisted.

"No. I just don't want to take a chance on anyone noticing what we are doing." He could see that the boy was crestfallen. "I am very interested in what you learned, however." He flipped the boy a dime and took out his notebook and pen.

Samuel grinned as he stuffed the coin in his pocket. "Well, I remembered all the places where I seen the fires—the ones that just happened. The ones that ain't been fixed yet. Then I ran over and took a look at four I be hearing about but didn't see for myself."

"Good," John said, his pen poised over the notebook. "How many are there?"

"Eighteen."

"Eighteen?" John muttered to himself.

The boy nodded. "Some of 'em be from last month."

"Do you know if anyone died in any of the fires?"

"I didn't hear that nobody did. Folks would've been talking 'bout that had it happened."

John looked back toward the porch. Owen had not yet emerged. "You probably don't know any addresses, but do you think you could tell me the streets they were on? In case I want to take a look at them myself."

"I can tell ya real good how to get to 'em." Samuel moved in close and watched intently as John made notes of most of the locations. John was very pleased. Samuel obviously had an astute pair of eyes and an excellent memory.

John's next question was casual. "Do you know how many of these were black people's homes?"

Samuel shook his head. "None of 'em."

John straightened and sat silently for several seconds. No black homes. Not one. That fact suggested that either blacks were setting the fires or someone wanted it to look like they were. He thought of the fires of New York. He thought of Denmark Vesey.

John heard the front door bang shut and Owen's footfall on the front steps. When he spoke again, his voice was very low. "Samuel, you didn't tell anyone, did you? No one knows you were checking the fires for me—not your family? None of the boys you play with?"

"I did like you told me. I didn't tell no one." The boy was obviously worried over what he saw in John's face.

"It's all right," John said. "But whatever you do, don't talk to anyone about the fires."

EIGHT

☙

Printers Row, the epicenter of New York's publishing industry, was nestled neatly along a strip in the heart of the city's commercial district. On his way to work, John would walk beneath the towers of mercantilism, six- and seven-story structures that had begun to sprout with the commonality and rapidity of garden weeds. The sprawling Astor House Hotel was one of them, its registry commonly filled with the names of eight hundred guests at one time. So was Mathew Brady's Daguerrian Gallery, the halls decorated with the callow beginnings of the new-sprung "still photography." There were less progressive establishments as well, hatters and haberdashers, embroideries and exporters, that helped the New Yorker to feel less alien among the new-age ingenuity. No building, however, captured the public imagination as did P. T. Barnum's American Museum, located just off the corner of Printers Row, on Broadway.

The museum's design was nothing uncommon. Yet all others, even Astor's grand hotel, stood in deference. Barnum had soaked the building in a rusty red paint, then festooned it with brightly colored posters—"transparencies," he called them. There were Indians in their war paint, midgets in the hands of giants, and a dancing monkey clad in full military dress. A portrait of a hot air balloon seemed as if it might fly right off the building. Some of the posters were in excess of thirty feet, causing gawkers as far as three blocks away to stop, amazed at the oddities P. T. Barnum had brought to them.

The facade was an advertising spectacle, and an outbreak of anticipation swept through the streets with each whisper of a new attraction. No talk of politics or discussion of business would outdo the arrival of a two-legged dog or the twenty-five-inch midget, General Tom Thumb. The same questions would bounce from corner to corner in response to the rumors. "Do you believe it?" "Can it really be?" The inquiries left Barnum to prove his prowess over and over again, a burden he was happy to accept, along with the price of admission.

It was during these times of heightened expectancy that John had come to truly enjoy his morning commute. Weekends brought numbers to the museum, with Sunday turning out a prodigious crowd of workingmen on their day off. John would often come a bit early and watch the throng congregate on the sidewalks as the excess spilled into the street. The hum of excitement escalated with each passing minute, as tempered voices soared into outspoken chirps of high spirit. All men spoke and none listened.

Barnum added a bevy of superfluous barkers who wandered about the crowd in red-and-white barber-pole striped shirts, stirring up the fully cooked.

"Astounding and amazing!" a professional voice boomed. "See the world's thinnest man, and his wife, the world's heaviest woman!"

". . . that's right," another trumpeted. "A new species of cow with four horns . . ."

"Let your eyes be the judge! Human or animal? Negroid or Mongloid? Come see the What-Is-It!"

As it grew close to eight o'clock, the crowd would begin to implode, the peripheral stragglers burrowing their way into the jumbled mass. Pushing and pulling became common, forcing the entire beast to lurch left before it was able to overcompensate with a massive tilt to the right. Fists were seen everywhere, not to be thrown—although that would not be out of the question if it meant improved position—

but balled up and gripping the money that the spectators could not wait to hand over. It was a charged dynamic, a designed chaos. Then the doors opened. The crowd pressed forward like an entire armada squeezing into a canal at once, slowly disappearing into New York's chamber of wonders. Just watching it was wild entertainment.

From the distance of one block, the gathering around Charleston's courthouse seemed curiously similar to a Barnum production. A horde of noisy, animated southerners enveloped the broad building, hollering and yelling in their low, slow tone as many waved their hats in the air. The courthouse caught and reflected the voices, projecting the turbulent echo back into the street.

A fence of blue-suited militia marked the perimeter. They imposed an arbitrary and invariable border, more concerned with holding their initial position than providing adequate space for the crowd. One young private flashed a crooked smile as he swung the butt of his rifle out in front, taking pleasure in boxing the knees of any attendee who strayed too close.

"This is great," Owen said with a nudge.

"Though potentially volatile."

"Yes. Let's hope."

As they moved closer, a man hailed them from the other side of the street. The scrawny individual was covered by a threadbare cotton smock, his face partly concealed by the curtained brim of his hat.

"Moonshine!" he whooped, his pitch addressed directly to John and Owen. "Homemade! Best in all the low country. Ha-penny and it'll warm y'up."

John scoffed. "I can't believe warming up is an appealing proposition to these people. It is so hot here that I am surprised the rivers haven't begun to boil."

"Nonetheless," Owen replied, raising one eyebrow, "it does sound tempting. Moonshine. What do you think? My treat." Without waiting for an answer, his feet led him away from John, toward the peddler.

John followed reluctantly. The ragged huckster rubbed the rope over his shoulder between his thumb and index finger, flicking back the dangling brim with his other hand.

"You Yankee boys want ya some moonshine?" he asked.

"You bet," Owen answered. "Two cups."

John recalled hearing that homemade liquor in the South was not an altogether safe proposition. Severe stomach illness and even blindness had been attributed to the crude distilling process. This man's appearance offered no testimonial for the product. "It is safe, right?" he blurted. "The moonshine?"

The peddler stared at him quizzically as he swung the rope off his shoulder, revealing a large ceramic jug. "Safe? The moonshine? 'Course it's safe." He shook his head dismissively as he lifted the tethered tin cup that dangled from the jug. "Now what you do after it, that's another story."

"Perfect." Owen lifted the drink and downed the contents. He cringed after swallowing, then rattled his head. "My good man, I see nothing to disprove your claim that this is indeed, the best moonshine in the low country."

"Told ya," the man replied, taking back the cup and dipping his fingers to the bottom. He ran them around, escorting the wasted drops from the tips of his hand to his mouth, where they were sucked clean.

John was mildly disgusted, wishing he had chosen to go first. Too late to back out now, however. Owen had already sacrificed his penny. He took the replenished cup from the peddler's hand, tipped it, and felt the liquid collect against his closed lips. They began to burn. Better to swallow it whole, he decided, and suffer the pain all at once. He emptied the cup in two large gulps, then exhaled the burning byproduct. The perimeter of his view went briefly black, and for a moment the loss of vision seemed a genuine possibility. It quickly cleared. "Whoo," he spat.

Owen laughed and slapped John across the back. "You see, John, there is a wild character hidden inside you after all. You are much more appealing when you let him loose. What say you? To the courthouse?"

The reporters waded forward, throwing their bodies into the mix. As the crowd funneled into the courthouse vestibule, it produced a heat of its own; collective bodies and collective breath. Fortunately, with the mention of Mahan's name and an impromptu bribe to the man named Roberts, the two reporters were able to break free of the crowd and gain entrance to the second-floor corridor.

They walked into a large courtroom, easily accounting for half of the building's width. Framed portraits of somber dignitaries lined the walls—distinguished men, but if portrait size meant anything, not the bureaucratic giants who presided over the downstairs lobby. A balcony packed with spectators ran the length of the opposite side of the room. Its counterpart ran directly overhead; equally full, judging by the commotion above. Massive arched windows admitted the outside gloom at the far end of the room. Before it, a stately desk, perhaps four feet off the ground, presided over the room like a throne.

Owen led John toward the third row of benches.

"Why so close?" John asked.

"In case people throw things. I want to see them splatter."

John shook his head. "A refined thought. Perhaps you should be sitting upstairs."

The boisterous clamor of the balconies was contrasted by the churchlike quiet down below. Here, well-dressed men sat with restrained dignity, never speaking above a whisper and limiting their movements to a simple hand gesture or the crossing of a leg. Owen, completely out of his element, fidgeted restlessly as he studied his surroundings.

"Oddest-looking courtroom I've ever seen," he announced, a little too loudly.

"It is modeled after Parliament. In Britain," John whispered. "This building has been here for quite some time, and once served as the colonial assembly house."

Owen looked askance. "And what? You conduct tours here or something? Honestly, John, the things you choose to remember perplex me."

With the upstairs packed to capacity, the lower level remained comfortably sparse. Only one or two people entered at a time, filling the benches slowly. One man's entrance captivated all, however, as he glided in at fifteen minutes after one o'clock. He wore a light cream suit of a flamboyant cut, accented with a slightly darker vest and a gold tie. The outfit perfectly complemented his bronzed face and amber mustache. He wore the unmistakable aura of wealth. Watching him, the balcony murmured as a whole, pointed fingers shooting up like salutes. He did not seem to notice the attention. Perhaps he had grown immune. He simply removed his Panama hat and nodded slightly, acknowledging all present.

As he slowly moved up the rows, John grew uncomfortable. He offered a quick prayer that the man would not sit near him, the collation of their clothes enough to conjure the image of a chessboard. The gentleman passed each bench, offering a pleasantry; a subdued "Good day" for an acquaintance, the use of a name for a friend. He looked down John's row with a discreet smile and bowed.

"Father," he said, eyeing John.

"That's rich," Owen cackled, gripping John's shoulder. "*Father.*"

John slid his back down the bench, sinking into an embarrassed hunch. "Who do you think he is?" The question hinted of rancor—an enmity from the sting of the faux pas.

"Heard the people upstairs saying the name Aubry. I've heard it before. When I was out drinking, one of the fellas was telling me about the ABCs of Charleston. It stands for Aubry, Breckenridge, and Campbell. Supposedly they are the three most powerful families in town. What do you call them? Oligarchs?"

"I see no reason to worship the man." John sulked. "He is dressed like a potion salesman."

Owen smiled. "Now, now. That's not a very brotherly thought for a man of the cloth."

"Besides," John said looking in vain for an open window, "his courtroom positively stinks."

The downstairs was now near capacity, and an impending excitement trumped even the smell. The lawyers soon entered, strolling down the aisle, past the small wooden gate cordoning participant from spectator. They sat behind desks: two representatives for the defense, three for the prosecution.

"All rise," a bailiff shouted from beside the tall judge's desk.

The shuffle of bodies coincided with the arrival of a gray-haired, thin-lipped judge who ascended the steps to his bench. He sat perfectly centered between the American and South Carolina flags. The state flag was noticeably bigger.

The judge briefly surveyed the courtroom, then looked back at the bailiff and nodded. The court officer walked to a partially concealed door along the far side of the room, opened it, then backed away. The court drew a collective breath.

A sheriff appeared first, then directly behind him a wiry but solid man, his hands manacled before him in large cuffs. His head was slightly dipped, displaying his mouse brown hair. While an effort had been made at grooming, stubborn cowlicks poked out erratically, clumps not used to the coax of a comb. A thin line also ringed his head, a pronounced indentation produced by the tight grip of a hat.

For a moment the courtroom was silent as everyone studied the accused. Then, a solitary "boo" rang out, followed by countless other cries of disdain. As wordless condemnation rained down from the balcony in powerful unity, Darcy Nance Calhoun raised his head to look at the crowd.

With each surge in the catcalls, he hunched forward his shoulders just a fraction, bracing as if a physical object had been hurled. Still, he was far from cowering. He looked less like a beaten man than one filled with interest, peeking up at the rafters like a squirrel from its hole. His gaze darted about the courtroom, and though he seemed frightened, he was not afraid to lock eyes. His stare descended to the lower level, stopping momentarily on those who stuck out: the lawyers, Mr. Aubry, the odd man in the black suit.

John studied the eyes that met his, bright sky blue irises filled with a furtive curiosity. He was clean-shaven, revealing a seasoned tan on top of his light complexion. Two large ears poked through his hair and stuck out almost sideways, features that were just short of comical. The lines at the corners of his eyes and mouth were evidence of good humor. The face did not seem at home carrying a grave expression.

The judge banged his gavel, his indulgence having met its limit. The crowd hushed.

Owen leaned in to John and whispered beside his ear. "I expected a bit more from the devil."

As the murmur tapered to silence, the sheriff led Darcy Nance to the far table of lawyers. He unlocked the prisoner's cuffs, then picked up a sheet of paper from the desk. Standing next to Darcy, he began to read loudly.

"Hear ye! Court is now in session in Charleston County, South Carolina, on this first day of July, in the year of our Lord 1850—Judge Thomas Castille presiding. Here stands the accused, Darcy Nance Calhoun, who is of no relation to the late senator John C. Calhoun. May God rest his soul."

"Amen," mumbled the assembly.

"The accused stands charged with violation of the Fugitive Slave Act of this nation, ratified by Congress in the year of our Lord, 1793. That on the date June 2 of this year, the accused assisted in the attempted runaway of a slave belonging to Mr. Giles Irwin of Chatham County, Georgia. That he attempted to harbor and assist this property in its deception. And that, when specifically confronted by a group of citizens pursuing the property, he lied on its behalf. So are the charges brought before this court."

"Very well," the judge followed. "Thank you, Sheriff."

The sheriff nodded and walked away from the prisoner.

The judge leaned forward in his chair and looked directly at Darcy Nance, speaking slowly. "Mr. Calhoun, I understand that you have been assigned counsel. Mr. Smith, the man just behind you, will represent you in this case. Do you understand that?"

From where John sat, he had a good view of Darcy Nance in profile. As he listened to the judge, deep lines wrinkled his brow in an apparent effort to process the information. The common furrowing over time had made the lines permanent.

"Yes," the man responded slowly, in a deep voice and backwater tongue. "I mean yes, Your Honor."

"Very good. And am I to assume that you find said counsel satisfactory, Mr. Calhoun?"

Darcy Nance nodded along with the cadence of the sentence. After the judge finished, he paused and turned, rotating his entire body to face his lawyer. They shared a glance, and Mr. Smith nodded. Darcy again faced the judge.

"No, Your Honor."

The courtroom stirred, causing an animated strike of the gavel. "Excuse me, Mr. Calhoun. Are you telling me that you are *not* satisfied with your counsel?"

"Yes, Your Honor." He became flustered at the judge's tone and began to trip over his words. "I mean, Mr. Smith, the lawyer, he seems . . . I mean, he seems nice and good and all. Talked with me and everything. But I's saying that. Well, I want me a different rep-re-sentation."

The courtroom hummed, and the reporters present went scurrying into their pockets for pen and paper. All except Owen, who sat wide-eyed with a huge smile.

The judge, obviously taken aback, allowed the spectators their brief outburst as he removed his glasses and rubbed his hand across his face. The mounting distemper was short-lived and protocol restored as he swung down the gavel twice.

"Order," he yelled. "Order." He tightened his eyes and stared wickedly toward Smith. "When did your client make you aware of his discontent, sir?"

The lawyer took a step forward and cleared his throat. "Just today, Your Honor. I received a letter late yesterday on behalf of my client." He picked up a paper from his desk and extended it before him. "It is from another lawyer, offering Mr. Calhoun counsel."

With a flick of the hand, the judge gestured for the bailiff to bring him the document. He took it and read. As he finished, he exhaled, then lifted his glasses just off his nose and stared toward a man seated in a far row of spectators. John followed the judge's gaze. He had singled out an older man, dressed in a plain dark suit, his face resigned to perpetual wrinkles. John could not read his expression. The youngest of the men at the prosecutors' table apparently could, however, for he arose quietly and retreated to join the older man.

"Do you know who that is?" John whispered to Owen.

"His name is Mayfair, and he just happens to be the mayor of this fair city. Word has it that he appointed Castille. These folks are all in bed together down here."

Judge Castille resumed his examination of the letter, and after a moment the young man returned to the prosecutors' desk and conferred with his associates.

"Will counsel for the defense please approach the bench?" The judge nodded to the chief prosecutor. "You too, Mr. Alford."

The portly man seated with his back to the reporters rose and walked forward, as did Smith. Darcy Nance began to follow. Smith stopped, turned, and made a shooing motion with his hand. He spoke loudly enough for the crowd to hear.

"You just stay over there. You weren't invited."

Darcy inched backward toward his spot amid a ripple of laughter. John could not help but feel sympathy as he looked at him. He seemed utterly alone.

John was now grateful for Owen's choice of seats. As the courtroom began to buzz with the sound of muffled conversation behind them, the reporters could still make out the discussion at the bench.

"What does this country rube know of law?" It was Alford, the prosecutor. "How can he differentiate between one lawyer and another?"

"It does not take a man of great intellect to figure out that his lawyer is not altogether on his side." Judge Castille took off his glasses and flipped them onto the desktop, then turned to look hard at Smith. "I did not care for your expression as you dangled that letter before my face."

"Can you blame me, Your Honor?" the lawyer protested. "I don't relish being associated with the least popular man in Charleston."

"It's your job, damn it! No one asked you to have the man over for brandy and cigars. Your responsibility was merely to represent him in a competent manner." The judge exhaled. "Can you grasp the problems that you just created? Had you done your job, the man would not be looking to an outsider."

"If I may ask, Your Honor," Alford interjected, "who is it that wishes to provide counsel? Who sent the letter?"

With his index finger, the judge pushed the letter toward him. "A northerner. From Philadelphia."

Alford snapped up the letter and read quickly. "You should not allow it, Your Honor. If Darcy Nance is not happy with Mr. Smith, you can appoint someone else. *From Charleston.* If you accede to this, this courtroom will become nothing but a forum for Yankee grievances."

"I am aware of that," Judge Castille replied softly. "But I think that I have to allow it. The law says that he is entitled to any representation he wants."

"But this lawyer, this Coulter, he is not interested in the welfare of Darcy Nance. He is more intent on promoting his political agenda than defending a client. Look, it says so right in the letter." He reached across the desk and skimmed the page. " He says, 'This is an excellent chance to strike a blow on behalf of all men, regardless of color.' Can we afford to have such a man come to Charleston amid the present tension? Can you imagine his influence on . . . well, the more susceptible of our community?"

The judge hesitated before responding. When he did, it was barely audible. "Yes. The *timing* really concerns me."

Alford was slow to respond as well. "You could deny the request on the basis that it is simply a stalling tactic. The lawyer is in Philadelphia, and the trial date for this man has been set for weeks. He cannot just show up and demand more time because his lawyer is still days' travel away."

The judge shook his head. "I can't make the problem go away that easily. We don't want ground for appeal; something that could draw this procedure out over several months."

"Of course you're correct," Alford responded. "We don't want that. It kind of defeats the purpose." He shrugged. "What I don't understand is why Darcy Nance would want anything to do with the man Coulter and his cause. Darcy's as slow as molasses after a hard freeze.

So why would he throw in his hat with Coulter and issues far beyond his capacity? It is not his cause."

"You read the letter." The judge looked at Smith, who had been silent throughout the exchange. "When was the last time anyone treated him so civilly?"

Castille looked past the attorneys, and his eyes swept the courtroom. "You gentlemen may return to your seats." He arose with a single bang of the gavel. "I am going to take a brief recess."

John glanced back toward the mayor, but he was no longer in the courtroom.

In the judge's absence, conversation held at a steady rumble with only an occasional volley from above. Darcy Nance remained the only man standing throughout the hiatus. He shifted his weight from one leg to the other, his discomfort apparent in the rootless maneuvering of unsure hands.

"Seems as if these people were right," Owen said. "This guy is a loose wheel. Look at him. He's busy carrying on a conversation with himself."

John stared at the face; the furrowed brow, the moving lips. The way in which Darcy stressed certain syllables with a flex of his neck did not seem compatible with Owen's assumption that he was babbling like an idiot. John was certain that it was recitation.

"He's not crazy. He's praying."

"How do you know?"

"I can just tell. He looks just like my grandmother when she was in church."

The judge reappeared from his chamber after only a few minutes. He wore a grave expression. The crowd hushed, leaving only the thunder of hundreds standing and sitting at once. As all settled, the judge stared long at the defendant, then tipped his gaze down to his desk.

"Before we continue, Mr. Calhoun, let me make sure that the court understands your request. Once again, for the record, you are saying that you are unsatisfied with your present counsel, Mr. Smith."

"Yes. Yes, Your Honor."

"And instead of having me assign you different local representation, you wish to have this man, Mr. Coulter, from Philadelphia, come all the way down here to be your lawyer?"

Numerous voices throughout the court spat out the word *Philadelphia* with the inflection of an obscenity.

Darcy Nance waited until it was again quiet. "Well, Mr. Smith here said that man don't mind. Coming all that way and all. If he don't mind, I'd sho' like to have him."

Judge Castille exhaled. "Very well, Mr. Calhoun. I surely hope you understand what you are doing here and the gravity of this situation."

Darcy furrowed his brow. "I know my life be on the line, if that's what ya mean, Your Honor."

The judge looked to Darcy's lawyer. "Mr. Smith, I am putting you in charge of contacting this man, Mr. Coulter, immediately, and letting him know of Mr. Calhoun's wishes. He has one week. *One week* to arrive here in Charleston and become intimate with the details of Mr. Calhoun's defense. I will not allow any sort of continuance after that point. If he is not prepared, then I will appoint new counsel. Maybe reappoint you, Mr. Smith. Do I make myself clear?"

"Yes, Your Honor."

"Then this court is in recess until one week from today, Friday, July 8. Sheriff, you may take Mr. Calhoun back into custody. We are adjourned."

"All rise!"

John slapped his pen against his notebook. "Looks as if our trip here may last a bit longer than expected."

"Traitor!" a voice shouted from the balcony. "Yankee-loving traitor!"

"I'd say we just got a bit less popular," Owen remarked.

John stood up and looked to Owen. "If I might make a suggestion. I think it would be in our best interest if we were to exit with these men seated around us. One can never guess exactly who the mob will choose as a target. But I believe they will act reasonably around their upper class."

"Yes. That seems prudent."

The two men moved to the aisle, then fell in just behind Mr. Aubry and an entourage of the wealthy. The backup by the door caused them to start and stop repeatedly.

"Do you think you will be able to stay for the trial's duration?" John asked.

"I don't see why not. I can uncover as many scandals here as back home. And this seems a bit more interesting." They inched forward. "What about you? There's no chance the *Tribune* will call you home, is there?"

"I doubt it. Though I'll likely hear my editor rant and rave about the additional expense. I'm sure he will not let me forget how much money he is investing in me, and that I had better produce something great in return."

"Cheap bastard."

As hoped, adequate room was provided throughout the stairwell and vestibule for their exit. The commoners were held back on the balcony until the lower level was cleared, then kept at bay a bit longer while the privileged dawdled leisurely downstairs. Owen and John were among the first to emerge from the courthouse, strolling outside into the humid afternoon stew.

They studied the surroundings. The militia was still present; still arranged in a semicircle around the courthouse. Many were slumped over, squatting, or even seated, displaying little or no military discipline. There were very few civilians who had as yet gathered outside for news of the trial. After all, none would have expected so quick an outcome as this. It was only 2:15.

Owen rubbed his hands together and spoke excitedly. "I've got a feeling something is going to happen here soon. Not exactly sure what. Or how bad. But something."

"I doubt it. There is quite a concentration of militia here. Yesterday, the crowd backed down when confronted by their officer. I'm sure there will be some whooping and hollering. I doubt anything more."

Owen shrugged. "Maybe."

They walked across the street, just beyond the edge of the militia's perimeter, and turned. The well-dressed began their unhurried departure, again pausing just in front of the building before sauntering toward a row of carriages that lined the side of the courthouse.

"So why do you think he did it?" John asked. "Why would Darcy Calhoun want to be represented by a northern lawyer?"

"I was just thinking about that myself. It doesn't seem to make a whole lot of sense. All I can figure is that it is a push for more time. He probably knows what's coming. Hanging at the end of the rope isn't a real pleasant thought. Maybe this way he can at least breathe for another week."

"Hardly an idyllic week, though. In prison, guarded by those who despise you. I wonder if there is not something more to it than that."

"Regardless, any chance he may have had at a lesser sentence just evaporated. I'm sure they're already stringing up the noose."

As the last of the carriages clopped away on the cobblestone, an ominous rumble came from the building's entrance. The noise awoke the militia, who hopped to their feet and assumed a military stance. Then, from beneath the arched doorway, the men began to appear. One of the first outside sprinted into the middle of the street. He yelled to the knots of people outside the building, to the militia, to anyone who would listen.

"That judge done put it off!"

"They're bringing an abolitionist lawyer for Darcy Nance!"

Men continued to pour out of the entrance, but instead of moving away from the building, they stopped dead in their tracks, as if the prime vantage point was right outside the doorway. The rest of the vacating spectators spilled out around them, also stopping, creating a logjam of angry bodies. Many who had not attended the trial now began to flock from all directions. They converged on the line of militia, which was now sandwiched between the two faces of the crowd.

A piece of debris sailed by. "This is rapidly getting out of hand," John muttered to Owen.

"I don't know, John," Owen answered mildly. "Maybe they're just fixing to do some whooping and hollering. I'm sure the militia—" Owen stopped, tugged at John's arm, and pointed toward the center of the crowd. "Does that guy have a gun?"

"Good Lord, he is waving a pistol around in there," John said aghast. "What does he intend to shoot at?"

"Probably the Yankee bastard in the black suit."

The gun went off—apparently fired into the air. A crown of white smoke lingered above the center of the ruck.

"Hey, look," Owen directed. "Do you see that?"

At the far side of the commotion, a group of about fifty men broke off. They drifted away from the courthouse, west down Broad Street, accompanied by the sound of splintering wood and breaking glass. Owen and John hustled along their side of the street, hoping to get a better view of the melee.

The ruffians took out their frustration on the surrounding buildings. Trash that had been discarded during the earlier revelry became ammunition. Glass bottles, cups, tin cans, and leftover food flew at homes and businesses. Eyes that had stolen glances at the rioters from behind curtains or through cracks of doors now vanished under the assault. The officer from the preceding day was nowhere in evidence. The militia did nothing.

"Don't you love it?" Owen called to John. "This town is turning into one giant bar fight."

"It stands to reason when they sell moonshine in front of the courthouse," John called back. "What's up with the three of them?"

John gestured toward an unkempt trio in the center of the street. They were conspicuous in their stillness, standing entrenched like a bulwark against a tide. The immobility was eye-catching. The man in the middle pointed a thick branch skyward. His face was covered in sweat and euphoria.

"It's a-calling to me," he sang out to his companions. "It's a-calling to me!"

"What's calling to him?" Owen asked, looking skyward.

"Nothing up there," John laughed. "It's probably the genie in that little brown jug."

The man again pointed skyward, then, with cheering encouragement from those beside him, he wildly heaved a brick toward a grand round window on the second floor of the house across the street. Amid the silence of bated breath it struck, shattering a third of the window and leaving a jagged wound. The small band erupted, shrieking approval as they jumped about, vaulting into one another rapturously. The exuberance over the ruination ebbed as shouts continued to ring, and the fickle crowd dissolved to the insatiable cry of "More!"

The sounds of damage were muted by the turn onto King Street as the legion of men disappeared around the corner. John turned back toward the courthouse. There the crowd was still increasing, with hundreds now filling the wide intersection of Broad and Meeting Streets. An indiscernible chant, arrhythmic and coarse, screamed out like the voices at a racetrack urging their wagers toward the wire.

Owen ran back to John's side. "Hurry up! We're losing 'em! You don't want to miss the story."

As John looked in both directions, a man ran past, carrying two large crates toward the assemblage at the courthouse. The crowd parted for him as if he was expected.

Owen, his mouth half open with incredulity and excitement, could not keep still. "Well," he prodded, his arms and legs twitching.

"I believe that someone is preparing to give a speech. It could be important."

"You're going to stay here and watch some guy on a soapbox rather than follow the riot?" He shook his head and laughed. "Let me know how it turns out." He began to give chase. "I'll meet ya back here."

"Be careful!" John shouted.

Owen waved his right arm without stopping.

John moved swiftly toward the intersection, where the crowd was arranged in a circle. The swell now spilled into the cross streets. He rose up on his toes. He could see nothing but the backs of men's heads and the tops of buildings. His vantage was useless, and elbowing his way into the crowd seemed impossible. He worked his way around the outside, searching for an opening. There was none. He was missing the action.

"Damn," he yelled out in a rare moment of frustration. No one near even flinched.

As he continued around, he spotted the top of a gaslight stanchion well above even the tallest man. There was his solution. Get higher. He jogged toward the pole just as a unified cheer rang out. John tapped into skills that had lain dormant since childhood. He managed to shinny up until his feet found a grip on a narrow ledge. John now found himself well above the crowd, able to see everything all the way down to King Street.

A man stood perched at the center of the assembly, atop the crates that had been hustled in. His dress set him apart from his audience, a fine blue three-piece suit that hugged his heavy build. He waved his arms high above his head in the manner of a politician. The group applauded and roared in anticipation of the speech, settling only when the speaker trumpeted his powerful tenor.

"I came here today to speak of justice. A justice of the people that stands against the immorality of felons. Justice that preserves the peace and offers a warning to those who might think to break our laws. Darcy Nance broke the law! But Darcy Nance has escaped justice!"

An aggressive roar that echoed the discontent arose and seemed to reverberate off the surrounding buildings. John clung tighter to his pole.

"Today we have received no vindication! Today we have received no satisfaction! Our leaders have forsaken us, and for what? So that the Yankees can come down here and teach us about their law? They do not respect our institutions, yet are more than willing to engage our legal system. And yet legality is not their goal—quite the opposite. Their motive is not justice, but its subversion. They would sit at *our* table and force us to drink from *their* cup of righteousness. If it is not to our taste, then they would raise a knife to our throats and say, 'Drink more.' For you see my friends, they hide behind a false bastion of morality. They announce their opposition to slavery, but wish to make us slaves to their will. And their goal is none less than to make us all dogs to their policies. And I, like our late Senator, John Calhoun, will not stand for it!"

"Nor I," a man shouted in response, and the cry echoed throughout the crowd.

The speaker waited until the crowd settled. "I wish to address a serious matter today. The question of whether or not we should cut all ties with the northern states and proceed to exist independently. I ask you, how long must we live under their oppression? How long must we suffer the repeated insults of their heavy-handedness? I say no more! I say we cut the straps that bind us to their yoke!"

John felt himself slipping a little, whether from his sweating palms or from the buffeting cries of sedition. He wished he could transcribe portions of the speech, the direct quotes that would add texture to his story, but that was impossible in his present position. So he squeezed tightly, pulling himself back up, resolutely trying to hold on to both the pole and the words.

"Northerners call such statements as mine treasonous!" the speaker shouted defiantly.

"No. No," the crowd answered.

"I respond by saying that other men lived here who were also branded with the label of traitors. Like us, they spoke out against the injustice foisted upon them. They too demanded rights ensured them by God and law. And when those rights were withheld, they rose up in revolt against the oppressors." He stopped and wiped the sweat from his face. "Today we call those men patriots. And, in time, history will vindicate our cause as well. I call for American separation!"

The gathering teemed with a frenzy much different than the rowdy elation of the vandals. This was angrier, a building pressure like steam in an engine. This was more dangerous.

The speaker crested the yells. "I do not call for this break groundlessly. As the great Thomas Jefferson wrote in the Declaration of Independence, 'a decent respect for the opinions of mankind requires that we should declare the causes which impel us to the separation.' Thus, I will do so here. First, the northern politicians in congress push forward proposals seeking to undermine southern principles. The most recent attempt, the Wilmot Proviso, is a blatant undoing of compromises hard won in the past. It seeks to limit slavery in those new states wishing to accept it. It calls to abolish slavery in Washington, D.C. And it seeks to cement northern domination in the legislature for all time to come.

"But their effort to undermine our society does not stop in the halls of Congress. No, these Yanks also infiltrate our society with dissident agents. Agents that comb the countryside with poisonous messages of rebellion, inciting the slaves with hollow promises of freedom and the impossible rhetoric of equality. There is the true reason behind Habersham County! Certainly it was not an event, so hideous in its planning, that would sprout independently from the simple mind of an African.

"And the bloody abolitionists attack our citizens as well. They continuously inundate us with inciting mailings, denigrating our order and stirring up the weak-minded. Indeed, even the postmaster general has had to step in and disallow the continuation of this devilish literature in hopes of maintaining peace and order. When we got wind of these pamphlets, all of us, you and I, did what any good citizen would do. We confiscated them and consigned them to the bottom of the Cooper River. Would that all northern imperialism could be drowned so easily!

"And I ask again, would the actions of the wicked Darcy Nance have ever happened if not for the seeds of upheaval sown by the North? I say no. In our tragedies lie our vindication. In that evil, we see their complicity. And in our separation, we shall be justified!"

The speaker watched with a small smile as the audience vociferously yelled its support. As they calmed, he continued, his voice still loud, but now almost conversational. "So different a people are we, North and South. Our customs and habits remain foreign. So why do we remain forged in a sickened alliance? There is no justifiable reason. Yet will they let us separate peacefully? No matter how elegant our argument or good our reasoning, I fear the answer is no. Therefore we must face the unwelcome idea of war. A war to be fought on our soil and in our cities—for we shall not invade them. And while their soldiers shall fight for their lives, we fight for something much more. We fight for our way of life. Our livelihood. And as they face the bitter repulsion that comes from such a noble cause, their aggression shall cease. The war shall not be long, and we will be victorious!

"I end by saying this. The rights of the individual states are dead, buried alongside the graves of the proud men who worked so hard to ensure them. The North now wishes to colonize those they can't persuade, and do so under the cry of 'Americanism.' They say we are all Americans. I scoff at such a proclamation! I belong to South Carolina!"

Handkerchiefs were waved and hats tossed in approval. The speaker stood stone still above the storm, basking in the scene before him. The cheering continued, louder. He waved once more triumphantly, then jumped down from his podium and disappeared into the crowd.

John climbed down from the light pole. What now? Once the cheering ended, then what? No invading army approached the city. There were no aggressors to repel. The spring was coiled. John awaited its release.

Not far away, near the perimeter, behavior had begun to deteriorate. A pack of men drew upon two young militia now completely separated from the rest of their unit. They pressed on them, the soldiers retreating in slow, cautious steps, trying to hold the converging pack at bay with their rifles. An agitated member of the crowd disregarded the threat and strode into the muzzle of a weapon, spit and sweat flying from his face as he blasted the two with incomprehensible words of contempt. Unwilling to escalate, the militia surrendered, lowering their arms, dropping their weapons. They were soon encircled.

The crowd closed in. One man reached out and tore the insignia from the shoulder of a blue tunic. Another tore the bandanna from the neck of the second soldier. This seemed to initiate a new diversion for the crowd. They pushed the two soldiers back and forth among them, ripping at their clothing as the two men cowered submissively.

One of the soldiers found his voice. He was but fifteen feet away, and John could just make out his words.

"Why are you doing this? We're here to protect you!"

He received no intelligible answer, and John could only puzzle at the reason himself. Perhaps the militia were now perceived as protecting something else.

Someone had the second soldier by the neckerchief. His tunic had now been completely torn away, but the kerchief refused to come loose. The soldier had skinny, pale arms, and he clawed at the kerchief himself—grasping, panicked. Shouts rang out from the far side of the crowd. The pushing increased, and rocks and bricks were launched haphazardly into the air. And the bell from St. Michael's, just above them, began to ring. It was three o'clock.

A running man approached the crowd. He yelled into the melee.

"The wharves! They're taking him to a boat! Darcy Nance! Hurry!"

There was an instant of quiet, then the clamor arose again and the far side of the crowd started to move. The march toward the wharves began. John backed away as the crowd set off down Broad Street. He placed himself just off the corner and just out of range of the wash.

Men attacked the street side by side, at least fifteen across, and so deep John could not see their end. It seemed his stay in Charleston might be short, after all. For if this group reached the wharf before Darcy's boat left, he was sure that no trial would be forthcoming.

As the men pounded past him, John saw a tall pole raised at the center bearing the crowd's standard, a dangling effigy of an indeterminable figure. John assumed it represented the unfortunate Darcy Nance. Only as the hay-stuffed body turned toward him could he see the sign around the neck. The block letters read GARRISON.

But the crowd bore with it another inert figure. Close to John, just feet away, the helpless militiaman was still being dragged along by his neckerchief—still held upright by the press of the crowd. His mouth was open but unmoving, his eyes bulging in terror, his undershirt covered in vomit. A chance shift in the crowd left no one between him and John.

John seized his chance. He grabbed at the shoulder of the man's shirt and twisted the fabric around his hand, then he chopped hard with the side of his other hand at the wrist of the man gripping the bandanna. He managed to break the hold, but John felt himself being pulled into the throng. He refused to let go, tugging against the current, alternately losing and gaining ground. He felt a sharp blow to his shoulder and turned in time to catch a glimpse of a brick an instant before it crashed into his forehead. Sparks flashed through total blackness, and John felt himself jerked backward by strong arms. The last thing he remembered was tightening his grip on the soldier's shirt.

He woke up in a recessed doorway with a plump woman leaning over him.

"Good grief," she whispered as she dabbed his head with a dish towel. "Harold," she hollered, turning her head back inside. "Bring me some water."

John stared out at the street, still dizzy. It was mostly clear of people, but strewn with garbage, much as if a parade had swept through. He sat up.

"You take it easy now," the woman soothed. "You took a real nasty bump on your head." She handed him a cup of water.

"Thank you," John muttered, dazed and unsure.

A small crowd began to gather around the building, glancing curiously at the injured foreigner. John reached up with his fingers and slowly poked at his wound. It hurt like crazy and his head throbbed, but it seemed that the bleeding had stopped, his fingers now coated in a sticky red.

"What happened to the soldier?" he asked.

"Some other militia carried him off," an old man said. "They's taking him to a doctor."

A man pushed through the edge of the crowd. It took a few seconds for John to realize that it was Owen.

Owen rushed up to him. "Sweet Jesus," he said, kneeling next to John. "Are you all right?"

John nodded.

"What in the hell happened?"

"I'm . . . I'm not exactly sure. I was caught in the crowd. I got hit with something. A brick, I think."

Owen cringed. "Phew. Judging by the looks of your head, I'd say the brick got the better of you." His smile went unreturned. "And if that wasn't enough, then someone had to go and throw rotten vegetables on you." Owen reached up and picked a cabbage leaf off John's head.

John patted the top of his hair. His hat was gone. Evidently the leaf had stuck. "Actually, I put that there. It is supposed to help keep you cool."

Owen stared at John worriedly, as if he was speaking gibberish. "Sure, sure. Here, let me help you up. We'll get you back to McClellan's and fix you."

John took Owen's arm and stumbled to his feet. As he stood he saw his pants, one leg ripped completely from the knee down. "Aw heck. My suit is ruined."

Owen slapped at his back, cleaning off the dust. "Don't worry about that, sport. We'll get you a new one."

John continued to stare at his leg. "It was a great suit. I loved this suit. Really helped me fit in down here."

Owen smiled, then began to laugh. The release of tension was welcome, and soon both men dissolved into helpless laughter, to the utter confusion of the surrounding southerners.

A tall man, impeccably dressed, stood wiping his hands on a white handkerchief just feet from the Regan Bakery on Broad Street. He watched the two Yankees laughing as they limped off. His face was expressionless. He nonchalantly turned toward the man next to him, a stocky red-haired man with a pockmarked complexion, who handed him his beautifully carved cane.

"Rogers," he said in a monotone. "I want you to follow him."

Rogers nodded.

"You know what to do."

Rogers nodded again.

The tall man watched as the servant walked slowly up the street, hands in pockets, whistling tonelessly.

NINE

"You're sure a lucky son of a gun," Owen had told John a few hours before, just prior to leaving him alone in his room.

"And why is that?" John answered wryly, his pulsing headache and aching leg leaving him less than cheerful.

"Because now you're in God's good graces. You just had a pretty close call, I'd say. And God always smiles on you after a run-in like that. You know, the guy who gets his hair parted in the thick of battle always lives to tell about it. It's the poor soul who doesn't see a minute of fighting that gets drilled right before the flag of truce goes up. So consider yourself lucky. Heck, you could probably walk right down Main Street, arm in arm with Frederick Douglass, and you wouldn't even draw a scowl." He smiled wide.

John sat still for a moment. "As much as I would like to test that hypothesis, I have an incredible amount of work to do. Unfortunately, almost being trampled to death by a pack of angry southerners is not an excuse my editor will accept in place of an article. So, if you'll excuse me."

"Of course, of course," Owen answered, backing toward the door. "I'll come back later tonight and fetch you when it is time to go out."

He closed the door before John had a chance to object.

John stared after him for a moment in disbelief, resting the good side of his head on one hand. Go out? *Tonight?* After the day's events, how could Owen even consider that a possibility?

While he certainly could use a drink, he knew Owen did not intend a rendezvous at the Hunt Club. There would be no cognac sipped from crystal glassware. No smell of cedar and premium cigars. No polite interest from the well-bred as they questioned him on his harrowing afternoon. Rather, he was certain that Owen's destination would include spilled beer, cuspidors, and tasteless advances from women of ill repute. The offer was preposterous.

He dismissed the thought and set to writing. Over the next hours he composed, rewrote, and edited, driven to make his first piece from Charleston an insightful account. With the exception of five brief interruptions—one by Samuel, bringing news from town, and four by McClellan, who could not grasp either the situation that had left John beaten or his repeated assurance that he was fine—he worked steadfastly on the piece until well after dark.

At the end, when he read over his first article, John felt a strong feeling of accomplishment. In his first hours in the city, he had actively searched for an angle for his reports. Now, a little over a day later, he realized that the best angle was no angle at all. Participants in this conflict carried preconceived notions like cumbersome baggage. John resolved to seek out the truth—to observe, to listen, and above all, to keep his mind open.

Oddly, his raised spirits began to overcome his physical exhaustion. He still hurt, but as he crossed his bruised leg and felt the throbbing across his shin, he smiled. The pain was almost welcome, a testament to what he had endured. A dash of invincibility swept over him, perhaps due to Owen's power of suggestion, and he began to revel in it. Now, what his friend had earlier suggested, the chance to rub elbows with the worst Charleston had to offer, was undeniably enticing.

By the time Owen charged in, John was dressed and ready to go. He walked up to the visitor and slapped him on the arm.

"Hey, sport," John said, grinning. "What took you so long? I was beginning to think you had called it a night."

Owen stood with arms akimbo and squinted. "You all right?"

"Of course I'm all right. Just eager to see the town's sights. Where are we headed first?"

Owen checked John's eyes to see if they focused. As they locked back, he laughed. "How about Ryan's Reef? It's down near the wharves. Heard not a night goes by where a major fight doesn't break out there."

"Seems like our kind of place," John replied. "I could use a bourbon."

They walked along the wharves by the East Bay under the pale illumination of scattered streetlamps and intermittent moonlight.

"I must give you credit, John. Your decision to stay by the courthouse was a good one. You've got a hell of a lot better instincts than I do."

John poked at the swollen wound on his forehead, his reward for good intuition. "I don't know if I'd call it a good decision," he mused. "But tell me, what happened with the group you were following? Did they cause a great deal more havoc?"

"Naw. As soon as they ran across a few bars, they broke up. It was all but over by the time you left."

"Is that when you came back?"

"No," Owen answered with a sheepish grin. "I had a couple of pints with 'em first."

John laughed. "Somehow, I am not surprised."

"But I meant to tell you, the mob that set out after Darcy Nance came up empty."

"Yes, I heard. Samuel told me that they did not find him."

"Scared the Lord out of a few of the fisherman down there, though. Heard they stormed a boat and dragged 'em all off. Tore the thing apart looking for the rascal."

Owen led John right onto Elliott, a narrow side street cut between two rows of tall, rotting buildings. The block was almost pitch-black; even the moon seemed to avoid it. A solitary lamp halfway up the road lit the tattered face of the building behind it, but little else. Nearer, a lone man inhaled from a cigarette as he leaned against a door. As the fire crept up the rolled paper, the man's face glowed in the reflection, his catlike yellow eyes fastened on the travelers.

The faint but appalling smell of urine lurked in the alleys. John rummaged through his coat pocket for his handkerchief, then cupped it over his mouth and nose. They began to pass assorted bars and taverns, nondescript establishments advertised only by the murmur of voices behind a wall and a ray of smoky light seeping from beneath their doorways. Just ahead, a door crashed open and an old man exited, singing a rousing, garbled tune as he wobbled about drunk. He backed into the side of the building, and his legs gave way, his song replaced by raspy giggling as he landed on his rear. It did not take long for the singing to resume.

> *He was a saucy sailor boy*
> *Who'd come from afar,*
> *To ask a maid to be the bride*
> *Of a poor Jack tar.*

"What sort of tune is that?" John whispered from behind the kerchief.

"You got me. Wouldn't bet that it's a hymn, though."

Two men stood farther up the street looking up at a window. Their faces were partially illuminated by its light.

"I wonder what they are looking at," John said.

"Me too. Ryan's Reef is in the basement of that same building. Above it is a whorehouse." Owen walked up behind them. "What's going on?"

Neither man broke off their gaze. The man nearer laughed an answer. "Miss Mabel has her a customer."

"Good heavens." John sighed, rolling his eyes.

He walked toward the sidewalk, leaving Owen and the two others craning upward in anticipation. In front of the building, a stairway led down from the street to a door. Black painted letters on the wall read RYAN. John stood on the lip of the top step and waited impatiently, listening as the rhythmic creak of Miss Mabel's bed captivated the gapers.

Owen soon had his fill and joined John at the top of the steps. "Do you notice anything unusual around here?"

John looked up and down the street with a smile. The putrid smell, the drunkard still searching for the correct key as he tripped over a song, these two voyeurs leering toward a dim bedroom, hopeful of a glimpse. "Where would you like me to begin?"

"No, no. The steeples. Can't see any of 'em, can you?"

John checked the skyline. Indeed, none were visible. "No. Not a one."

"They say that's why Elliott Street is so corrupt. It's the only place in all of Charleston where God isn't watching over you."

"A comforting thought."

They descended the narrow, bowed steps of uneven proportion, the last one no more than six inches deep, then stopped in the well just beside the entrance. Above the door an old oar hung slanted, nailed to the wall, its paddle etched with writing. John squinted and mumbled its words.

"Landlubbers in search of beer, you will find no quarter here." He paused. "Perhaps we should not—"

"Nah," Owen interrupted, leaning his shoulder into the door. "It'll be fine. Anyway, I'm sure it's just a joke." He walked in before John had a chance to rebut.

Inside, candles enclosed in nautical lanterns staved off the darkness with all the effect of spit in the ocean, reducing the bar to only shadows. John felt his way along a wall and found himself eye to eye with a bizarre carving that hung from a nailed string. The carving was of a disproportionate black face about the size of a fist. John shuddered as the realization took hold. The hair gave it away. Real hair. *It was an actual shrunken head.*

This relic was not behind glass. This was not an oddity. It hung from the wall like a trophy, an object to brag about. John felt sinful even in the presence of those who had obtained something so ungodly. He knew with certainty that he did not belong here.

Across the room a row of men stood lined up at the bar, their heads all swiveled in concert toward the outsiders. Their faces were sharp, the mixture of light and shadow accentuating their hawkish features: noses seemed longer, scars more impressive, and the sneers more pronounced. They shared not a collar among them, and all wore the loose, untailored pants common to the decks of ships and prisons.

Owen grabbed John by the arm and led him toward the end of the bar. He slapped his hand on the wood and shouted a greeting. "Ahoy."

There was no response. Unfriendly eyes watched them as a fat barman limped their way.

"Y'all want something?"

"Indeed," Owen answered. "A bourbon and a moonshine."

The bartender reached beneath the counter for a bottle and two glasses without breaking his curious gaze. He filled both from the same bottle, then slid the glasses across the wood.

"The house special would be fine also," Owen said, laying coins on the bar. He handed John a drink. "Let's find a seat."

John faced the cramped room. A few occupied tables lined the walls. He leaned in behind Owen's ear. "What exactly are we doing here?"

"Out for a good time. And these are all sailors. After a few drinks they become a real talkative sort. They can probably give us some good dirt."

John panned left to right. Not a word interrupted the silence. John felt he stood a better chance of interviewing the mayor. He took a sip of the liquor, a powerful drink that tasted of metal, then followed Owen, joining him at the side of a long table occupied by two sailors.

"Mind if we join you?" Owen asked.

They looked up, saying nothing. The nearer man dipped his head slightly in acknowledgment, showing a glimpse of a small gold hoop on his ear, still mostly obscured by his long, unwashed hair. John and Owen sat down opposite them, resting their drinks on a table lacquered with a patina of grease.

"I'm Owen, and this here is Cannon."

"James," muttered the man with the gold earring.

"Pint," replied the other, showing a gold reflection inside his cavernous mouth.

Following a stretch of uncomfortable silence, the sailor James leaned forward in his seat and overtly peered at their faces. "Y'all fighters?"

John looked at Owen, whose face still exhibited colorful bruises from his boxing foray. He knew he looked much worse.

"We dabble," Owen answered.

The sailor nodded slowly, responding in a mixed accent that was half southern and half indiscernible. He talked around a cigarette balanced in his lips. "Ain't looking like y'all is any good at it."

Owen cackled. "Yes. I suppose it would seem that way."

Owen's exuberance forced smiles from the sailors. Their expressions immediately filled John with relief, and he took a large sip of his liquor in celebration.

"Y'all sure do dress strange," said the long-haired sailor. "Y'all from England or something?"

"No," John answered. "New York."

Pint sat forward. "I was in New York City 'fore. Went up there in the summer of '48. Remember 'cause one of the crew I was with got gutted right there in the harbor. A loading hook up'n got stuck on his shirt. Clear lifted him off the ground five feet, slicing him open all the way from stomach ta chest. Then his insides just start falling out all over the deck. And all the while he's just screaming like a stuck pig. Turns up dead in just seconds. Real nasty scene."

Owen broke the long silence that followed. "Yes. It is a beautiful city."

John took a long pull, then headed back to the bar. "I'm getting another."

"Good idea, Cannon. While you're at it, why don't you freshen us all up." He turned to the sailors. "Cannon's a real generous sort. Always insisting on getting people drinks."

As he returned from the bar, balancing the four glasses in his hands, a lively discussion had broken at their table. Owen was lost in a story, his arms flailing as he animated the details.

". . . so he's surrounded by these thugs. Easily ten or twelve of 'em.

And they are all waving about bats and sticks like they're ready to kill him. Then this one poor sot hits him in the back. *Whack!* But he turns around without even looking and decks him. Out cold. It kind of stunned the others for a minute. But then, they got even madder. Somehow, somebody trips him, and I lose sight. Keep in mind, I'm still fighting through hundreds of folks to get to him so I can help. But yeah, he falls and I can't see him. Figured they were giving it to him pretty good. Kicking him and punching him. But you know what happened next?"

The sailors, enthralled, shook their heads no.

"He's up and back on his feet. Fighting like a tiger. And now it's *him* that's throwing *them* down to the ground. One after the next. Swinging so fast he looks like he's got octopus arms."

The sailors laughed. John set the drinks on the table. Owen paused to catch his breath and wet his tongue.

"What are you talking about?" John asked, taking his seat.

Owen slapped him vigorously on the shoulder. "Well, I was just telling these men about what happened to you today by the court-house."

John just shook his head, which the sailors apparently interpreted as modesty.

"Sure wish I'd a been there ta see it," said Pint.

"As do I," echoed James. "See why they calls you Cannon, I guess. But tell me, how come if ya did so good, your face is looking so bad. Looks like you got kicked by a mule."

John ticked his head back and forth, still awed by the audacity of the claim.

"You want me to tell them?" Owen asked, gleaming a smile as he looked at his friend.

"Please."

"Well, it was just about over. Most of the thugs had already tucked tail and run. I'm about twenty feet from Cannon, and I see something flying through the air, well over the crowd. I look at it, and it's a block of concrete. It's heading right for Cannon. He never saw it coming. Did you, Cannon?"

John paused. "No. In fact, the power of the blow did more than just batter my face. It also damaged my memory. It's a good thing I have Owen here to jog it." John pulled in tight beside Owen's ear. "I can't wait to read one of your articles."

"It is quite a story," Pint said. "Hopefully we'll get a chance to see ya fight one of these days."

"Yes. That seems to be a growing sentiment around town. You should be able to catch my match with a fellow named Bull a week from Tuesday." John took another hefty pull from his drink. The metallic aftertaste had dissipated. The liquor now had him jovial and a bit high. He looked at the sailors. "Is it always like this in Charleston? I mean, is it always this . . . violent?"

James shrugged. "It ain't no ballet," he said, pronouncing the *T.* "But it ain't normally as messy as this. Not at this time a year."

"Why this time of year?" John followed.

"This be the slow time. Ain't much shipping during the summer. Most of it comes in the spring and fall. That's when a lot a extra folks be in town. Sailors and such. It gets more raggedy then. Violent, I guess you could say."

Pint slammed his drink. "Right now there ain't much sailors 'cause there ain't much shipping. Except for local stuff. To and from the plantations. Out to Morris Island."

"I didn't think that there was much out there, at Morris," Owen commented.

"There ain't," James said. "Somebody's fixing ta build, I guess. Naw, it's the militia being in town that's causing the uproar."

Pint agreed. "They think they is high and mighty. The ones here in town. But they's just local crackers with new blue jackets. They think they can order folks around. I kicked one's arse myself day before yesterday."

"I thought they were supposed to be keeping order," John observed. "Because of the fires."

"That's a good one. More likely they is setting 'em themselves."

"The unit by the courthouse yesterday looked pretty professional," John said.

"Some is," James answered. "I got me a cousin that got called up. Says they be drilling pretty good. Not in town, though, there ain't room for it. But them in town—they is always drunk and disorderly."

"Here's to drunk and disorderly!" Owen raised his glass. James and Pint laughed, and they all downed the dregs.

Owen broke character and bought the next round. As they drank, Owen and John listened to the sailor's stories of better days; of a long haul to Marseilles, of rough ports in the Caribbean. The time passed quickly and, to John's surprise, quite enjoyably.

The bar itself came to life when three women walked in some time later. The sailors throughout whistled and yelled, shouting catcalls so profane John blushed in embarrassment.

"Ladies come to this bar?" he asked in amazement.

"They ain't ladies," Pint responded. "They is whores."

The prostitutes made friendly with those by the bar, socializing so long as the potential for profit existed. When the prospect waned, they moved along, showering the next in line with flirtatious attention.

"Hey, Cannon," Pint said. "What does New York women look like?"

The curious nature of the question confused John. "They look just like any—"

Owen slapped his leg beneath the table and spoke. "A finer-looking group I've never found. Most are tall. With legs so long and thick you could tie a boat off on 'em. And the redheads. Whoo. They are literally one in every three. And all have round, ruby lips that match their hair perfectly. Friendly, too. Talk to just about anyone."

"OO-eey," Pint gasped, swallowing the fantasy. "That true, Cannon?"

"Yes," he said, facing the rapt sailor. "They are quite comely."

"I have to go back up there. New York City women sound perfect."

John caught Owen's eye. He showed a smug smile of civic pride.

After another drink, John settled into complacency. The nature of this place was so aberrant, it was entertainment in itself. It did not hurt that he was also comfortably drunk. Owen, on the other hand, was jittery from the inaction. His need for the extraordinary denied relaxation and calm. Something was going on somewhere, and he damn well wanted to find it.

Owen's knees twitched back and forth as he stared wide-eyed at his glass. Every few seconds he would flick the rim and wait for the resonating *ping* to trail off. Suddenly he leaned forward. "Ever any fights around here?"

"Yup," Pint said. "Right on Anson. The Cat's Paw. Folks fight they niggers there against one another. Lots a gambling too."

Owen clapped together his hands. "That's what I'm looking for. Hey, Cannon, you want to come with me and check it out? We don't have to stay long. Just watch one or two guys get knocked out."

John found the idea of forced combat appalling. "No. I shall stay here and wait."

"You sure?" Owen said, already up with a foot toward the door. "Then I'll be back in less than an hour. James, Pint, I'll see you gents later."

The sailors nodded, and Owen left the bar. When committed to a course of action, he wasted no time.

Three drinks later, Owen was still not back, and John was telling them the one about the milkman from Jersey who entered his horse in the New York mayoral race.

"You see," John explained, "he got three hundred folks to sign a petition to put Ole Dobbin on the ballot . . . apparently some folks thought he was a Swede."

John thought it was pretty funny, but the sailors didn't seem to get it the first time, so he told it again. His head was hurting a little. It felt better if he rested his chin on his hand and closed his eyes for a minute.

Another drink helped, too. He paid for the round but had Pint go get the drinks. That seemed fair enough. He was going to tell them the one about the one-armed fiddler, but he needed to rest a little bit first, because the way the fiddler passed the hat was really very funny, and you had to tell it just right. . . .

• • •

"He asleep?" Pint asked, staring at the motionless Yankee.

"Think so. He ain't opened his eyes for about ten minutes."

"What was it he was trying ta talk about just 'fore that?"

"Couldn't tell ya. Something about needing a bow and a hat, I think. Couldn't but understand a few words of it on account of the slurring."

Pint laughed. "He sorta speak crazy anyway. Even sober. Like he was up'n raised in a library or something."

"Yeah. And he sure thought fiddle playing was funny." He reached across and picked up John's glass, then swallowed the last sip. "You think he's got any money?"

"Probably. He's wearing a suit. Why, you wanna rob him?"

"Why not? He ain't got no more stories in him, and he ain't buying no mo' drinks."

"Hey, I know. We could take him outside, rob him, then throw him in the Cooper."

James smiled. "It'd wake him up. That's for sure."

"Yeah. And he's so sauced he'll probably think he just stumbled in on his own."

The two men stood and walked behind John, who sat slumped, breathing heavily.

"Poke him," James instructed. "See if he wakes up."

Pint did just that, eliciting no more than a slight twitch from John. He was out.

"Help me get him up," Pint said. "We can get the money out-side."

They lifted him and carried him toward the door, dragging him out to the delight of many sailors present.

Once back on Elliott Street, they propped him against a building and proceeded to rifle through his pockets.

"Hey," Pint said in a whisper. "What if he wakes up? From what that little Irish guy was saying, this guy can fight pretty good."

"Naw. A crock a shit, that was. Ain't no man can fight off ten or twelve folks with bats. I's guessing that it wasn't more than three."

"Yeah. But we is only two."

"Look at him, though. Even if he do come to, he ain't in no condition to fight. He's drunk as a skunk."

They went back to the pockets, searching thoroughly, eventually winding up with a total of three dollars and some change. The watch chain was caught on his belt somehow and wouldn't come loose. They then perched his arms over their shoulders and carried him back up Elliott, toward the wharves. Toward the Cooper River.

As they reached the East Bay, both men panting from the additional weight, they turned right. They were less than fifty yards from the river. A stocky man walked out from under an awning and into their path, whistling an atonal tune. He stopped just in front of them, his pockmarked face and red hair highlighted by the light from the wharves.

"Where y'all going?" he asked.

"Ain't no business of yours," Pint replied.

From beneath his topcoat came the unmistakable click of a hammer cocking. "I said, where are y'all headed with that man?"

"Just fixing to toss him in the Cooper. Give him a bath, that's all."

The man chuckled. "I got a better idea. A way to get that Yankee out of our hair for good." He paused.

"Yeah," James said. "What's that?"

"There's a ship just over yonder. The *Albatross*. Leaves at first light for Hispaniola. I'd say that it's one passenger short."

The sailors laughed.

"He'd sure be in for a surprise in the morning," Pint said.

The pockmarked man turned around, facing the docked ships. "Then follow me. I know the watchman. The Yank is in for a heck of a journey. And it's an awful long way to swim back."

The two sailors slowly followed, carrying John Sharp toward the sea.

TEN

The hollow and heavy sound of quick feet on stairs awoke him. He kept his eyes clamped shut. He could swear that the bed was actually moving. John vowed with certainty that he would never drink again.

He rubbed his sandy tongue against the roof of his mouth in search of moisture. He swallowed nothing. A nascent headache, just a second ago subtle, steeled into a crippling wound. Still, he kept his eyes shut. He knew that if he opened them, it would only get worse.

He knew that this was not his room at McClellan's. That in itself brought a shiver. He also did not remember leaving the bar last night, or what he might have done subsequently, after the demon in the jug took over his body. The accumulation of thoughts was so harrowing that he cloaked himself in ignorance, keeping his eyes closed as his brain rocked against the sides of his head.

The door slammed open, and John shot to a sitting position, adjusting his vision to the meager light around the man who just entered.

"Get up!" the man yelled, his loud, tinny voice like an untuned horn. "On deck. See Mr. Fetzer."

John squinted at the laconic man, a sailor. The confusion grew. "On deck? Where am I?"

"The *Albatross*. Now hurry up." He slammed the door behind him.

John hunched over, resting his elbows on his knees and cradling his head in his hands. He was on a ship. How in the name of heaven did he get on a ship?

He looked around the cabin. These were not passengers quarters. A pair of bunks lined two walls with but three feet between them. It smelled as if someone had been cleaning fish on the floor. He rocked to his feet, braced himself just long enough to assuage the dizziness, then broke for the door.

A beam of light offered direction down a dank hallway to a flight of rickety steps. The motion of the ship was now unmistakable, the slight sway beneath his feet no longer attributable to a hangover. He stumbled up the stairs toward the light.

Emerging, he saw that he was mid-deck aboard a schooner, a seventy- or eighty-footer built for speed and open water. Anxiety turned to outright panic as he looked to his right. There sat Charleston, the peninsula a half inch high on the horizon, its only identifiable features gray towers of smoke.

The realization that this was not a fishing vessel heightened John's sense of urgency. He had to get off now! He looked up and down the ship for men of importance, seeing no one but sailors busy in their duties. He yelled to a man who hurried past, lugging a thick rope over a dipped shoulder.

"Mr. Fetzer?"

The man raised his unused arm and waved it to the rear of the ship. John hustled in that direction, just short of a run, dashing over and around crates and jagged obstacles. Not a sailor reacted to his urgency with anything beyond a scowl, and answers to his repeated inquiries after Mr. Fetzer were universal—imprecise gestures toward the ship's stern.

Out of breath from frantic concern, John finally found Fetzer leaning against the side of the ship, talking with a man who appeared by dress to be the ship's captain. Dusting both arms down the side of his bedraggled coat, he composed himself and approached the two men.

"Mr. Fetzer, my name is John Sharp. There has been a terrible mistake."

The captain took a step away, then stared out to sea with the men at his back.

Fetzer made a hard lunge at John, well invading his personal space, then sneered. "Wait over there," he ordered through bared, yellow-stained teeth. "I'll deal with you in a minute."

John's urgency forced an attempt to clarify. "But, sir, I do not think . . ."

"Shut up," he barked, a sneer curling his lips. He was a mean-looking man, sun-beaten and scarred, with a widow's peak so pronounced it appeared fiendish. "Wait over there, or I'll have you cleaning the bilges."

John, shaken, retreated a few steps under Fetzer's glare. Once satisfied there would be no further interruption, the man turned back to the captain, and the two resumed their discussion, apparently unaware that a dreadful error was now compounded by their inaction. Each second took John farther from Charleston.

The sun was still low in the sky, but growing in intensity. It reflected off the water and the stark white sails that hung from the twin sixty-foot masts and the jib line. The light felt as if it was burning straight through to the back of John's head. He raised a hand to block it and peeked back at the two men, who carried on with no immediacy, no sign of concern. John wondered if a screaming fit would get their attention.

"Batten the sails!" a voice shouted, sending sailors scampering up the masts with short pieces of wood.

John squinted up and saw another man perched at the top of the foresail on a precariously narrow board—the lookout. He hoped he was looking for a route into the nearest port. Savannah, perhaps. That would work. He could catch the next train back to Charleston.

He shut his eyes against the sun and inched back toward Fetzer and the captain, hoping to filter their conversation from the surrounding shouts of sailors.

"We must be careful entering port from the west," Fetzer said. "The *Adelaide* went down there not six months ago. Her masts could rip through our hull in seconds."

"Aye," the captain responded. "Chart a course in from the east. I've heard reports that there's been unusually rough weather in the islands for this time of year. I don't want ta take any chances."

The islands? Well, John did not want to take any chances either, but if an island port was the alternative, that strip of land to starboard was looking pretty good right now. He walked to the rail and tried to estimate the distance. The sight made him quickly abandon the thought of trying to swim it. Not in the Atlantic Ocean. He had not swum in years, and never such a distance. It was a gamble he was unwilling to take.

The men finished their discussion. The captain walked toward John, then past him, his eye drifting to him only momentarily. His gruff appearance did not invite a plea. John returned his attention to Fetzer, who seemed to have forgotten him. The man removed a knife and a piece of wood from his pocket and began to whittle.

John's need to rectify the situation was paramount, and he waited for no invitation from Fetzer to approach.

"Sir," he voiced in an agitated tone. "I apologize for whatever inconvenience. However, there has been an egregious error. I am not supposed to be on this ship."

Fetzer shaved three curls of wood from the stick. Seconds passed. "Indeed. You're most certainly not supposed to be here." His attention returned to the stick. He added a few notches.

"Well, then, there has to—"

"We don't think too kindly of stowaways aboard this ship."

"Stowaway? I most certainly am not. Sir, I assure you, the last place that I presently wish to be is aboard your ship."

Fetzer alternated his attention between his carving and the ship's wake. "And yet here you are. So tell me then, if not a stowaway, how d'ya manage to find your way aboard?"

John exhaled, reticent to reveal his ignorance. "Unfortunately, I do not know the answer to your question. By mistake or treachery, someone placed me here after I had consumed a bit much of the local brew. But again, I pledge that I had no intention to stow away."

Fetzer stopped his whittling for a moment and gestured toward John with the tip of his knife. He did not appear to have heard a word John said. "You running from the law?"

"The law?" he repeated, floored. "No. Of course not. As I stated, I—"

"Just trying to figure why you're so intent on getting to Hispaniola." The headache returned in force.

Fetzer continued. "You've got a lover down there, perhaps?"

"A lover in *Hispaniola*? Why, that is absolutely absurd." He paused, befuddled by the question and the man's blockishness. "Let me attempt to explain. I have no desire to go to Hispaniola. In fact, I do not wish to go anywhere but back to Charleston. I am not in trouble with the law, I have no *friends* in the islands, nor do I wish an apprenticeship as a seaman. All I want to do is to get off this boat at the nearest accessible location. That is it. Now, how can I do that?"

Fetzer smiled. A smile that made one wish he had never done so. "Impossible. We stop for no port before Hispaniola."

Nausea twisted his gut, forcing him to wait as it settled. Then he spoke softly, almost in a whisper. "Certainly there must be some other option. A quick stop in Savannah. Or a barrier island. If nothing else, just get me closer to shore so that I might swim in. Please, there must be some way I can get off this boat without traveling all the way to the Caribbean."

Fetzer answered immediately, eliminating any suggestion that he may have pondered an alternative. "Nope. Ain't got time for a stop. Even a short one. Got a schedule to keep."

John dug his hands in his pockets in search of money, anything that might help to alter Fetzer's resolution. He found a solitary dime. Out of options, he resorted to an arrogant tone. "Then, perhaps I shall take my case before the captain."

Fetzer turned and spat over the side. "Not advisable. Cap'n hates stowaways worse than anyone. You go talk to him, and you'll likely spend the trip to Hispaniola in irons belowdecks."

John's head dropped. "Then it is hopeless."

"Gettin' off the ship? Yup."

John leaned on the rail, bracing himself, his knees suddenly weak. "There's also the issue of work."

His head snapped back up. "Work?"

"Well, this trip ain't free. Gotta pay your way somehow. If you ain't got no money, then you tender it with labor. What is it you can do?"

Disbelieving, he answered. "I am a writer."

Fetzer snickered. "Nope. Ain't got no use for that. Can you sew?"

"I suppose," he replied in a beaten, lethargic voice.

"Very well. Then we'll get you started on mending sails. After you finish that, we'll move you up ta something more useful. Hell, maybe a month from now you'll be pulling the night watch."

Each word from Fetzer's mouth was like another jab to the stomach. Yet there was one more question that he had to have answered. "How long will this trip last in its entirety?"

"Depends on the winds. I's guessing, though, that the *Albatross* will be back in Charleston in two and a ha' months."

"Two and a half months." He mouthed the words silently.

Fetzer's hideous smile returned. "That's for the *Albatross*. How you get back is up to you. Once we're in Hispaniola, you're on your own."

"You mean that I cannot return on this ship?"

"Nope. Told ya 'fore, cap'n doesn't look too highly on stowaways. You'll have ta find another ship back." He began to walk off. "I'll have Garceau find you and bring you the sails. Then you can get to work."

His departure left John perfectly despondent. It was too painful to watch Charleston disappear, a city he thought he would never miss. Instead, he let his mind go numb and looked to the open sea.

John sat with his back to a crate as he unskillfully manipulated a large needle in and out of a thick cotton sail. Despite the pain it brought, he was unable to stop his mind from leaping from one dismal thought to the next. He cursed himself for his impetuous decision to visit the wharves, even after being warned. Then he derided himself for his unreserved consumption. Each of the events that had contributed to his present state of vagabondage were given adequate attention, followed by an intense and amplified round of self-denunciation.

Soon his thoughts began to drift from his own plight to the impact of his actions on others. He pictured Owen, distraught, sharing a teary pint in a dingy tavern while composing his penny-press epitaph.

"Reporter Disappears in South's City of Sin!" "New Yorker Last Seen in Bar below Bordello!"

He saw a perplexed innkeeper, McClellan, unsure what to do with his personal effects, and his editor, impatiently stalking the *Herald* offices, cursing his hasty decision to send such a green reporter to cover something so important. His job was assuredly lost.

This assignment had been an opportunity to cover an important story, to establish himself as a top reporter, to bring honor to the family name . . . Now, his parents would think him dead.

Every thought brought fresh torture. Each augmented his headache, an affliction born of liquor and a possible concussion but acerbated by circumstance. He did best to focus on the work, to block thought with it—counting stitches, rethreading the needle, counting again, faster.

The sun was nearly satisfied, perched just beneath its zenith, scorching those bold enough to creep from beneath the sail's shadow. John remained by the crate, his legs extended into the light, the needle still tucked between his thumb and index finger. He was fast asleep.

Fetzer shoved the sole of his shoe into John's arm. "Good Lord. You certainly are useless, ain't ya?"

John spent a second or two regaining his bearings. He quickly retracted his baking legs and glanced up at the face. Fetzer's features were hidden by glare. "I apologize. I must have drifted off a moment ago."

Fetzer crouched down, his smile wide, somehow less sinister. "You really don't know nothing about ships, do ya?"

The question seemed to invite a sarcastic response, but the search for something glib was too taxing. "No."

"We've been tacking for the last half hour. Slowing down as we got nearer to land."

"You don't mean . . ."

John pounced up with the prospect not fully digested, then spun around so quickly he banged his knee against the corner of the crate. He never felt the pain. There, not two hundred yards away, was land. A glorious grassy neck at the confluence of a tributary, so beautiful and so close he could make out the yellow clumps of dandelions.

"Aha!" he shouted, an exclamation of discovery and rapture.

Fetzer began to laugh along with John. "You was really ready to travel all the way to Hispaniola and back. Why, that's rich."

John kept his eyes trained on the shore, his smile not wilting. "Then you had this stop planned all along?"

"Aye," he said, slapping John robustly on the back. "Had to stop off and deliver supplies to someone here 'fore we made our way on."

John was too consumed with elation to even feign outrage.

"Dropping anchor!" a sailor boomed.

"There's a dinghy set to row in and drop some stuff. You're welcome to ride along. Unless, of course, you're intent on going on." He chuckled.

"No," John said, kicking the partially mended sail off his feet. "Here seems just fine."

John was the last to be loaded on the small rowboat. He sat braced on the lip of the bow, fighting for room with two large supply boxes at his back. As the oarsman pushed off from the *Albatross*, John looked back at Fetzer. He leaned over the side, still smiling, the shadow from his widow's peak painting an arrow across his forehead.

"Hey, Fetzer!" he yelled. "You know that you are a scoundrel."

"Aye," he replied, nodding along. "They'll put it on my gravestone." With that, he turned and walked away, his shoulders bouncing up and down in laughter.

They rowed around the neck and entered the tributary, a slow, narrow river that took a lazy bend around a small bluff where an unsure cedar angled unnaturally out over the water. Just beyond it was a dock, their apparent destination.

Five men stood at the dock's edge: a white and four Negroes. As they rowed close, the sailor behind John threw him a line of rope.

"Toss that so they can tie us off."

John did so, hoisting the line to a black man who leaned out well beyond the dock's edge. After the boat was secured, the black man took his place beside the others, and the white man stepped forward. He was a stocky, redheaded man with a pock-scarred face. He smiled and stuck out his hand.

"Let me help you up, sir."

John grasped his hand and pulled himself onto sure footing.

"All's well I hope, Mr. Sharp."

John gazed down at the short man, confused. "Yes," he answered. "How—"

The man had turned back toward the slaves. "All right, boys, we need to unload all of this, quick-time. We got another boat full after this one." He looked back at John, apparently surprised he was still there. "Oh, sir, Mr. Breckenridge is waiting for you just a few feet from the dock."

John nodded as if this was something to be expected, then turned slowly to the land.

Breckenridge stood about a hundred feet away in the shade. He was a young man, no older than his mid-twenties. He was also strikingly good-looking—blond, tall and slender, blessed with ideal proportions. His relaxed tan suit and straw hat suggested a forgotten cool. Breckenridge had the gift of perfect stillness, a self-sufficiency that required no shift of weight, no flexing of the hand atop the brass handle of his cane, not even a blink. Indeed, if not for the gentle flapping of his pants as they were cajoled by a sea breeze, John would have confused his presence as rendered and his backdrop as canvas. As John approached, the man's lips curved in a temperate smile.

John slowed his pace, granting himself the extra time to collect his wits and digest the circumstances. The effort was fruitless. John felt bedraggled, befuddled, and entirely out of his element.

The stranger took a half step forward and extended his hand. "Mr. Sharp, it is a pleasure to make your acquaintance. I am Tyler Breckenridge." His voice, in two sentences, vindicated the southern dialect. His pronunciation was free of artifice or twang, consonants and vowels softened to a fluid lilt.

Later, John would try to recall exactly what had transpired in their first meeting—Breckenridge's comments, his own questions, the southerner's specific responses. In truth, most of the discussion was formal, sparse exchanges amid long periods of silence. As often as John replayed their conversations in his mind, he was never sure that he understood the man.

John began by shaking the offered hand. "A pleasure, Mr. Breckenridge."

"Undoubtedly your morning has been a harrowing one. You are all right, though, I hope."

"Yes," John answered, his voice slow with uncertainty. "I am fine. But it does appear, Mr. Breckenridge, that you have me at somewhat of a disadvantage. For it seems that you were made aware of an arrival that I had no intention of making."

"That is true," Breckenridge responded, using an agreeable tone that indicated his comfort with an upper hand. "Please, join me in my carriage. I will explain everything on the way to the plantation house."

John stood still, put off by the lack of a direct response. "While I am sure that you have a lovely plantation, it is very important that I return to Charleston as soon as possible. So, if you could direct me on the best possible route, I would greatly appreciate it."

Tyler Breckenridge regarded John quietly for a moment. "Rest assured that I have no intention of keeping you from any event of importance that you may have in Charleston. The most direct route on foot could prove rather arduous." He nodded toward a dense thicket. "However, if you will accompany me back to my home, I can arrange adequate transportation for you there." The voice was firm but friendly. "If you please." He turned to the side and directed an arm toward a gravel path.

"Very well," John answered with a dubious smile. "I would be in your debt."

They walked slowly and silently up the gravel path until they reached an elegant enclosed carriage. A black servant stood at attention beside the door. The servant opened the door for John, bowing slightly, then assisted Mr. Breckenridge, taking his cane. John looked at the cane, the accessory of the southern gentleman. It was of beautifully carved wood with a fine patina. It looked old.

"Back to Willowby."

"Very good, sir."

John settled into the leather seat opposite Tyler Breckenridge. After ordering the carriage away with a gentle tap on the wood, the planter placed his hands in his lap and looked out of his window with an expression of unfaltering assurance. As the path became smooth and the carriage gained momentum, John felt the welcome breeze against his damp forehead. It was the best his head had felt all day.

He glanced briefly at Breckenridge. The man didn't appear to perspire. No need to suggest the cabbage leaf trick to him; he obviously knew all about it. In fact, he acted like he knew a lot about everything. That was the problem.

"So tell me, Mr. Sharp, how do you find Charleston since your arrival?"

John returned a polite smile, his most earnest attempt at mimicking his host's polish.

It is a sinful city with weapon-toting outlaws as its citizens. Since my arrival, I have been threatened, attacked, and kidnapped. There seems not to be an ounce of normalcy within its territorial boundaries.

"It is fine, thank you. Perfectly pleasant."

The planter responded with a single nod, then turned his gaze back outside the window. After a moment, he reached into his breast pocket and pulled out a silver cigar case. With a simple gesture in John's direction, he wordlessly offered him a smoke.

"No, thank you." John checked his pocket watch as Breckenridge withdrew a tobacco pouch and cherry pipe from his breast pocket. It was just after noon. "I do not wish to sound ungrateful, sir, but could you tell me how long it will take to reach your plantation?"

"We are on the property now. It is about twenty minutes to the house." He filled the pipe. "I suppose that it seems quite a world apart from New York City. Charleston, I mean. It would take a certain amount of time to adjust from one lifestyle to the other." He glanced briefly at John and began to light the pipe.

John's heart beat faster, and his face took on a light pink. He was entirely sated with this childish game, and could play genteel no longer. He adopted an intentionally counterfeit smile and locked eyes. "How do you know where I am from, Mr. Breckenridge?"

Breckenridge took no rush to answer. Eventually, he nonchalantly shrugged his shoulders. "I tend to know most of what goes on in Charleston. Most of the comings and goings." His mouth twitched a bit at one corner. "Your presence, Mr. Sharp, was a bit less than covert."

John dropped his eyes to the floor, then quickly out his own window. "It was not my goal to be covert," he said, somewhat defensively.

"Oh, please, take no offense, Mr. Sharp. I meant only that any New

Yorker is recognizable as not being local. I would guess that it was the same for me when I visited New York. I spent the better part of a summer there in '46. A magnificent city, it truly is. Yet there is something about it that you never get to know." He drew on the pipe, seeming to savor the fine tobacco. "Do you find it that way as well, Mr. Sharp?"

John looked back at Breckenridge's face. The man was obviously playing with him, but the face reflected only civility. His short hair, conservative clothing, and even features seemed well suited to the apparently staid personality. Even his blond mustache was subtle. It was the first case John remembered where the southern mustache did not overpower all else.

"Yes," John responded. "To some extent I think that is the case. New York is ever changing. There is a fever to build more and more. Bigger and more magnificent."

Tyler Breckenridge thought for a moment. "Yes, a fever. I think that is well put. I wonder if I would even recognize it anymore." He stared unfocused at the carriage wall until a memory triggered a slight smile. "I resided in a home uptown, on Fourteenth Street. I used to make it a practice to take a daily walk, which usually culminated at Union Square. I enjoyed the lovely fountain, I suppose. I began to notice that every day, right at ten in the morning, a man entered the park walking a pack of six dogs. Large dogs. Retrievers, which proceeded to drag him about at their will. The incongruity was that the man's face was so terribly dour, his attire so formal. He wore impeccable formal attire." He chuckled and again drew on the pipe, watching the smoke as he exhaled. "I remember that I found the sight so peculiar that I made an inquiry. In fact he was a butler. For the Higginbotham family, if I remember correctly. Are you familiar with the name, Mr. Sharp?"

"Yes. They amassed a real estate fortune."

"Indeed, that does strike a chord. Regardless, I could not help but be enamored with the sight. I began to time my daily walk so that I might intercept them. Six dogs." He laughed. "The poor man was helpless." He stopped for a moment. "I think that it impressed upon me the nature of northern society." He was now looking at John, directly in the eyes, his face unreadable. John looked back but said nothing. One corner of Breckenridge's mouth twitched. "Nonetheless, 'tis amazing that it is the little things we remember, is it not?"

John hummed in agreement and was quiet for a moment. Then he smiled with just the corner of his mouth, like Breckenridge. "You may wish to avoid making assumptions based on the Higginbothams, however. These are people who hired a nanny and kept her in their employ for two years even though they were childless, simply because all of their friends had nannies."

Breckenridge flashed a quick smile. He leaned forward a little and looked at John as if he expected him to continue. When John did not, the planter leaned back and relaxed, his expression pleasant but contemplative. They rode in silence for a good five minutes.

John felt that he was pretty good at reading people, but he had to admit that Breckenridge had him stumped. The man was reserved, but not shy. He did not appear to enjoy social interaction for its own sake, but, John guessed he could talk and mingle without effort if it suited his purpose. Right now, easing John's mind was apparently not high on his list of priorities.

As the minutes passed, John attempted to piece together Breckenridge's role in his present situation. The peculiar thing was that he felt Breckenridge was deceiving him—notwithstanding the fact that he hadn't actually told him anything. And Breckenridge's failure to be forthcoming with explanations bothered him considerably. Now that he had apparently clammed up after a brief but amiable exchange, John found the planter's continued silence particularly galling. Perhaps, as a wealthy man, Breckenridge was accustomed to having his own way locally. But John was not part of his realm of influence, and he did not intend to fall into whatever role Breckenridge had in mind.

The planter appeared to notice the growing tension in John's posture, the clenching and unclenching of John's hands. He again offered him a cigar. John refused. John's frustration finally forced him to surrender the charade of indifference.

"Sir, there is an issue that can no longer be neglected. The fact that you knew of my arrival at the dock today shows some sort of complicity on your part. I would appreciate an explanation."

"Yes," he nodded, lighting the pipe. "I was hoping to share the story with you over lunch." He waved his hand gently before him. "In more welcoming surroundings. However, I understand your urgency. I am certain that in your position, I would feel the same.

"Then, I suppose I shall begin with where I first saw you, Mr. Sharp, so that you might ascertain all of the details. I spotted you yesterday, outside the courthouse, after the trial had ended. I did not need much help. You were propped up on a gas lamp, well above the crowd that had gathered to hear Geoffrey Bainbridge's obnoxious speech. As I remember it, you were wearing a black wool suit." He exhaled out the window. "That, in itself, draws an eye in the South. A suit that black in the dead of summer."

"Yes, I am aware that my wardrobe was ill adapted. Please continue."

"Certainly. As I am sure you recognized, the situation after the speech became dangerous. It was not part of my plan to continue watching you. In fact, I lost sight of you for a considerable amount of time. But then, you again came to my attention as events deteriorated. It seemed you were being dragged into the crowd as they set upon the wharves." His face grew grave. "I cannot imagine how harrowing that must have been. You disappeared completely for a time, and then my man Rogers caught sight of you in a doorway beside the Regan Bakery. You were badly shaken, as I remember. We were both preparing to come to your assistance when a man, your friend I assume, arrived to help." He stopped for a moment, took two or three puffs, then resumed. "It was at this point that I made a decision for which I hope you will forgive me. I asked my man Rogers, the man who assisted you out of the boat at the dock, to follow you." Breckenridge stopped and let the thought settle.

"As a spy?"

His light laugh, without words, dismissed the statement as frivolity. "No, no. Of course not. Merely to make sure that you would be all right. As it turned out, I think it was a wise decision. Later in the evening, Rogers followed you and your friend as you ventured down to Elliott Street." He opened his eyes wide and further softened his melancholy drawl. "I do wish that someone had warned you about the taverns by the wharves. They are entirely unfit for a gentleman like yourself. Nonetheless, Rogers became concerned when your friend later left the establishment alone." He emptied the pipe. "As it turned out, you emerged about an hour later. From Rogers's description, I would assume that you have no memory of this."

"None," John said in whispered embarrassment.

"Oh, Mr. Sharp, do not be ashamed of that. At some point almost every southerner has lost a battle with moonshine. It is simply a part of life."

"Yes," John replied, lifting his head. "I am quite happy, then, to have that part of life at my heels."

Breckenridge smiled. "Yes, quite. So, as I said, you left the tavern a time later. With you were a band of sailors. A large group of six or seven who proceeded to act very indecently." He sighed. "Even to speak of such a thing invites distaste. However, I suppose that I must. Initially, they just robbed you. However, when they picked you up and began to carry you toward the Cooper River, Rogers, understandably, became quite concerned. He followed closely, and when they began weighing down your clothing in the hope of drowning you, he made the bold move to intervene. Since he was physically no match for the men, Rogers was forced to take alternative measures. He proposed instead that they throw you aboard the *Albatross*, a ship bound for Hispaniola, knowing full well that that ship had to first make a stop to deliver me some supplies. He conveniently withheld that fact from the rogues. I don't know if it was Rogers's power of persuasion or the fact that he carried a pistol, but it worked." He stopped and slowly shook his head. "Quite quick thinking, I must admit. From there, Mr. Sharp, I assume your memory takes over. You found yourself this morning aboard that ship. And presently, here you are." His face went soft with modesty—mock or sincere, John could not tell.

John Sharp sat quiet for a time, attempting to fully grasp the peculiar predicament just explained. His contemplation only seemed to invite more questions. "Mr. Breckenridge, did the man, Rogers, say if he knew what the reason was behind the sailor's actions? Why they were so eager to do away with me?"

"No. He did not say. I would not put much thought into that, however. For I am certain that you most likely did not precipitate their violation by anything other than your defenselessness. Sailors are an unruly lot. And typically their mischief is not governed by premeditation. More likely, by drunken spontaneity."

John nodded as he listened. The explanation seemed to work as well as any. He straightened up a little. "Mr. Breckenridge, I must apologize for my rudeness. Your action . . . your man Rogers's actions on my behalf, now explained, were entirely commendable. My frustration was due to my lack of information. Please accept my apology as well as my gratitude."

Tyler Breckenridge replied in an easy voice that suggested the apology was gratuitous. "Please, Mr. Sharp, think nothing of it. It is you who was placed in the uncomfortable situation. I am glad to assist in fixing it."

John watched as Breckenridge's attention returned to the passing scenery. Though his posture was composed, he looked perfectly relaxed. Only the eyes moved.

John's mind began to work again. With the most pressing question answered, new ones began to arise. John looked again at the planter. Though distant, and possibly preoccupied, Breckenridge's manner with John did not come across as aloof or patronizing. Nevertheless, John recalled the name as that of one of the most powerful families in Charleston. Why would this man, who seemed to radiate passivity, go out of his way on John's behalf? It was very strange. What interest could Breckenridge possibly have in an inappropriately dressed young man from New York City?

"Why, Mr. Breckenridge?" John asked abruptly, yet with a light tone. "Why would you make such an effort to come to my aid?"

The planter hesitated as his gaze became fixed. Then he turned to John as if interrupted from another conversation. "Why?" he repeated.

The question brought more silence and what appeared to John as unanticipated introspection. It truly seemed as if he did not immediately know the answer.

Suddenly Breckenridge's eyes regained focus and he looked to John with an odd little half smile. "Well, I would s'pose that it was simply concern, Mr. Sharp. For your well-being."

Of all that Breckenridge had told him thus far, this statement, oddly, carried the greatest ring of truth. John blushed without knowing why. "Thank you again."

This time Tyler Breckenridge did not dismiss the gratitude, but rather accepted it with a light nod. He relit his pipe and returned his attention to the sights outside of his window.

Another five minutes passed before the carriage made a right turn. The change in direction breathed life to the quiet carriage as Tyler again smiled at John.

"We are just about at the house. This road leads up to it."

"Excellent," John answered, quite excited to catch sight of his first plantation.

Large trees, apparent through both windows, lined the road and restrained his curiosity. The branches of one oak blended into the arms of the next, leaving only rare glimpses of open sun-soaked green. Only John's sense of social decorum quelled the childish desire to spring forward and stick his head out of the window. That constraint dwindled each time the road took a dip and the uneven coach rocked forward, enticingly close to offering a view.

Fortunately, Tyler interrupted the internal dispute. "After we get to the house, please use everything at your disposal in order to freshen up. I cannot imagine how eager you must be to do so after the unfortunate conditions you have faced."

John's earlier occupation with important matters had diverted attention from his physical discomfort and appearance. Now, as they approached the plantation house, John became acutely aware of his state. Scattered stubborn patches of sawdust and chalk marred the pants and sleeves of his suit. His hands and fingernails were filthy. As to his face and hair . . . Well, the lack of a mirror offered no peace, for John's rich imagination supplied the image of a seedy, stubble-faced refugee from a bar fight. And he smelled. Of that he was certain. He could now notice it himself. No wonder Breckenridge had spent the entire trip with his face to the window.

Breckenridge seemed to sense his fresh discomfort and readily changed subjects. "After you have taken care of what you need, perhaps you could join me in the garden for a spot of lunch. Then we can see about getting you back to Charleston."

"Very well," John replied. "I am again in your debt."

As the carriage made a slow turn onto the final drive, an escort of three giggling black children scampered up beside John's window. They began to run at the side, their pace picking up and fading as each scoured the interior with playful eyes. The boys' panting produced amplified bursts of laughter, charging the air with the unmistakable sound of juvenile fun. They soon slowed and waved the carriage on with animated arms that flapped overhead like wheat in a windstorm. John found himself waving back with a face-wide smile.

The boys' disappearance hardly removed the element of motion. In fact, the capacious lawn was alive with activity. Ahead, scores of slaves mingled about, all busy in some way or another. Something about the scene jarred him, for it was nothing like what he expected.

He paused to consider the discrepancy between his preconception and this reality. The conclusion was simple, but profound. In theoretical discussions, the literal and figurative description of slavery as a black-and-white issue had caused John to dilute all phases of color from his mind's image. He envisioned slaves as part of a grainy daguerreotype—emotionless, silent, and monochromatic. Yet here was the stark rebuttal. Vibrant shades littered the lawn, injecting the environment with a pulse of liveliness. The bright yellow scarf worn by a woman carrying a jug contrasted with the face below it. Water blue overalls draped on a lean, fit man had white handkerchiefs blooming from the front and back pockets like ripening buds. There were cream dresses, and pink hats, and smiling maroon cheeks. There was a glimpse of a glimmering silver earring, a blanched white apron, and twisting red suspenders on a man who swung a scythe. The entire complement invoked beauty.

A hollow guilt interrupted his thoughts. How could he allow himself to be so taken with this scene?

He did not try to actually answer the question, but instead avoided serious contemplation so that he could stay focused on the unfamiliar sight. Guilt simply remained an intrusive penance.

"Mr. Sharp, you will have to excuse the present state of Willowby. You see, we are in the stages of preparation for an annual party. This year it falls on Monday. That may explain why things appear in such chaos."

"On the contrary, Mr. Breckenridge, I find the level of activity quite exciting."

The response appeared to please the planter, who reacted with a tight smile and minute nod.

His explanation helped to clarify some of what John saw. There were numerous crates and tables littering the lawn in no semblance of order. A somewhat surreal set included a large deserted box with a brass candelabra perched atop, standing just next to an elegant settee. Men moved about, shuttling back and forth furniture and equipment, hesitating only long enough for a quick swipe of the arm across a sweaty brow. The women, for the most part, planted. A great many knelt along the drive and walkway, their skirts fanned open like a field of poppies, planting purple, white, and pink petunias. Farther along, more women worked potting begonias in stone and ceramic planters.

The sounds contributed to the surprising atmosphere. Behind the shouted orders there was laughter, and beneath the scattered voices was a low, upbeat hum. Altogether, the buzz was excitement.

The carriage slowed to a stop, and John's door was opened. An older black man in formal livery stood with his hand extended. He dipped his head just a fraction and spoke crisply, his pronunciation extremely acute, each word a performance.

"Welcome ta Willowby, sir."

"Thank you."

He turned his head to Breckenridge. "Welcome home, sir."

John grasped his hand and exited. He now paused for his first unobstructed view of the mansion. After everything amazing he had seen on the grounds, it was exactly what he expected it to be. A magnificent structure. A large, white plantation house that rose two stories with a columned portico at its center.

Tyler walked up to his side. "If you would excuse me for just a moment, there is something that I must attend to. Jenkins here will see to your needs."

As Breckenridge walked away, John fought to swallow his awe and better grasp the surroundings. Jenkins waited patiently, just a few steps away. His face was warm and accommodating. His expression invited questions from a man naturally inclined to ask them.

"Jenkins, I was wondering, is the plantation always like this? Always this . . . happy?"

Jenkins shook his head and laughed. "No, sir. Not this good-natured. We're having a party. Folks 'round here get real excited about it. It's the biggest of the year. Everyone takes a certain pride in it. That's why it's the best in all the low country. Better than the Farmer or the Williams. Even better than the Campbell."

A tall man walking past, carrying a box, took the opportunity to eavesdrop and add an opinion. "Campbell ain't nothing. They done gone and ran outta the booze. What kinda party that supposed ta be?"

"Enough from you," Jenkins snapped. "That's none a your business, either way." Jenkins looked straight ahead, making up for the man's interruption with increased formality. After a moment, a small smile returned and he spoke out of the corner of his mouth. "They didn't run out of *all* liquor at the Campbell. Just gin and bourbon."

John smiled back, then returned his attention to the house.

Tyler Breckenridge, who had walked away soundlessly, now appeared to weight his steps as he approached. "Have you been to a country home before, Mr. Sharp?"

"A plantation home? No."

"Do not leave me in suspense," he said in a tone that indicated none. "What is your impression?"

"It is everything that I imagined."

Tyler paused to mull over the statement, then nodded. "That, then, is good. Because intelligent men have splendid imaginations." He looked John in the eye for a moment. "But I'm sure your tolerance is wearing quite thin. Jenkins will show you around and get you anything you need."

Jenkins walked forward, ahead of John. "Just this way, sir."

John stopped at the doorway and turned. His reason for doing so became irrelevant, for it was instantly forgotten. For a split second, before the curtain of genteel civility was again in its place, John caught Breckenridge's unguarded look. Then both men assumed faint smiles as John turned again toward the house. But John had seen his reflection defined in the southerner's eyes. He was prey.

ELEVEN

Until the most recent national disruption, Charleston and the South Carolina low country had retained a reputation of whispered envy throughout the Union. Even the punctilious New York elite pronounced the city's name cautiously, as if speaking of a more gifted sibling. Of course, when generalizing about any city, one tends to marginalize the average and evoke the exceptional. And although they constituted but a small percentage of the population, none outdazzled the wealthy planters of the lowlands of Carolina. The concept of Divine Right—elsewhere an anachronism, a casualty of the Revolution—lived and breathed here in the environs of Charleston.

It was therefore ironic that John Sharp, who had experienced the privations of the Five Points and continuous trials since his arrival in Charleston, had yet to experience such a level of discomfort as that which he now faced in the home of Tyler Breckenridge. For not since childhood had he been naked in any one's company but his own.

He swayed his knees back and forth apprehensively, sending small waves patting into the side of the porcelain tub. Every minute he would peek behind him, just over his shoulder, fixing on the man who stood at attention beside the door. He was young and black and at all times frozen, with only a white towel over his right arm interrupting the dark suit. Each time John looked at him, his eyes were up and forward, never so impolite as to steal a glance. And still, each time John turned the young slave made an assumption based on the redness of the face in his peripheral vision.

"Mo' cool water, sir?"

"No, thank you," John answered, turning back around. "I am comfortable."

He had been in the bathtub for what felt like an eternity, yet he had been unable to develop a plausible diversion that would allow him to extricate himself with no audience.

He was clean. His fingers looked like prunes, and the water was getting cold. He cleared his throat. "I am going to get up now."

"Yessir," the slave answered, his voice confused. The man might as well inform him of his next planned breath.

John rose shakily, his chin raised high in faux pride. Before even taking a step, he was enveloped in the soft terry cloth of the towel. Blessedly, he was allowed to pat himself dry before he was escorted to an accompanying bedroom.

Prior to the bath, Jenkins had insisted that John be measured. " 'Tis Mr. Breckenridge's wish that you do so," he told him. Now Jenkins stood before him, his right arm straight out to the side, holding a fine suit of clothes.

" 'Tis the best we could do on the short notice. Hemmed the pant legs and the sleeves. T'won't be no perfect fit, but should carry you through the day just fine."

"Thank you," John said, enamored by the outfit. "I'm sure it will be excellent."

Minutes later John stood before a full-length mirror as Jenkins dressed him in the jacket. The attendant smoothed the shoulders and tugged lightly on the sleeves.

The slave smiled. "Must admit. You do look fine and proper."

John grinned as he studied himself in the mirror. It truly was a magnificent suit, a light cream garment with a subtle yellow vest. Even more amazing was the feel. The light linen felt soft on the skin, and its looseness allowed for pleasant circulation.

Jenkins handed him a straw hat with a cream band that matched the suit. "If you're ready, sir, Mr. Breckenridge is a waiting in the garden."

He stole a few more seconds at the mirror before he acknowledged the statement with a slight nod. "Yes. Let us go."

At the East Side of the mansion, a thick row of hedges marked the perimeter of a garden. John walked just behind Jenkins, outside the hedges, until the black man stopped and ushered him forward with an extended arm. As he continued alone, he saw Tyler Breckenridge standing beside the garden entrance, hands clasped at his back. He was looking off in the distance, a purposeful gaze akin to a captain's survey from the bridge of his ship.

As John walked up beside Breckenridge, the planter displayed a southern gentleman's reflex—a slow, smooth turn that implied an inherent knowledge of presence. His eyes dipped to the visitor's outfit, and he flashed a smile.

"The clothes suit you, Mr. Sharp."

John reflexively looked down at himself and smiled. "Thank you, sir. I am much more comfortable. I hope the alterations did not damage them permanently."

"Please, do not concern yourself with that."

There was a sound of paws running on gravel, and a golden retriever suddenly materialized at Breckenridge's side. The dog stopped abruptly and sat at attention, eyes glued on the planter, tail thumping vigorously. Breckenridge bent to pat the head and scratch behind an ear.

"This is Duke."

As if to acknowledge the introduction, the dog stood up and bumped a cold nose against John's hand.

"When he is not chasing squirrels, he ensures that I do not lack for companionship." Breckenridge straightened, glanced about, then turned back to John. "Mr. Sharp, would you care to accompany me on a walk? It will allow time for our lunch to be set up in the garden."

"Certainly."

"Let's take a drink with us." Breckenridge raised his hand in a simple gesture. A servant appeared almost as quickly as the dog. "I will have a rye whiskey. And for you, Mr. Sharp?"

"Bourbon, please."

Breckenridge smiled at the visitor as the servant hurried away. "Your acclimation here seems quite swift."

John commented on the beauty of the grounds, and as Breckenridge followed with a brief dissertation on ornamental grafting, the servant reappeared with their drinks—a good three inches of amber liquid in each glass.

John found himself thinking that it was impossible to get service like that in New York. Then the horror of his own thought struck him. The bath attendant, the valet, the servant with the drinks—all of them were the *property* of Tyler Breckenridge. In this orderly world where each soft-spoken wish was quickly fulfilled by seemingly eager staff, the staff were not eager. They were enslaved.

John glanced up and found Breckenridge looking at him. He had little doubt that the planter had read his expression and therefore his thoughts.

"Shall we walk, then?"

As they left the garden, Breckenridge walked to a wall and picked up a shotgun. He carried it casually in the crook of his right arm like a country gentleman on a shooting party. John stopped in his tracks and eyed the weapon.

The planter noticed John's hesitation. "We get vipers down here from time to time. Only way to deal with them."

Breckenridge began to walk, but John wasn't following. A dozen thoughts raced through his mind, topped by the realization that no one knew he was here except for Breckenridge and the people he owned.

He noticed John was not following. "You needn't worry about the snakes. As long as you make plenty of noise, they get out of your way."

John took a hesitant step forward, and the men locked eyes. Breckenridge was unreadable. Then John saw a little twitch at the corner of his mouth. "I'll walk a step or two ahead of you," he said. "In case this thing goes off accidentally."

They walked up a steady incline of freshly cut grass. The blades emitted a sweet smell as they were displaced, leaving only a faint outline of green on the edge of their shoes.

"This spot has seen human habitation for a long time." Breckenridge's gesture encompassed the house and the high ground around them. "My great-grandfather built our home not quite a century ago on the ruins of a house of considerable size. It had been destroyed by fire. Indians, I'm told." He pointed to the left. "That line of oak trees is at least a hundred and fifty years old. Note their uniform size and spacing. They were planted deliberately, probably by the first of the white settlers. Before that, the Creek lived here."

"Do you ever find any arrowheads?"

He nodded. "The children bring them to me when they find them. I have quite a collection in my study. It also includes stone axes and some pottery. I'll show it to you."

As the men reached the peak of the hill, both stopped and looked down before them. There, the land dipped down into a small, unspoiled valley with tall grass, dandelions, and wild flowers rising up to the height of a knee. At the low point was a good-size pond gated by a ring of tremendous willow trees, their limp branches just tickling the water's surface.

Breckenridge pointed to the trees. "The inspiration for Willowby."

They began to descend the hill, walking on a narrow path cut through the tall grass. Breckenridge, with his eyes forward, spoke with an appropriate tranquillity.

"My great-grandfather planted the area near the pond around the time he built the house. And, as it was for my father and grandfather, it is my favorite place to come and sit. I believe it is because of the seclusion. Isolation is nice from time to time."

John smiled and nodded. "Do your parents still live here as well?"

"No," he answered, retaining a soft but emotionless voice. "They have both passed. My father four years ago, when I was twenty. And my mother just last summer."

"I am terribly sorry."

Breckenridge nodded.

"Mrs. Breckenridge, is she . . ."

Tyler turned to him and smiled. "No. There is no Mrs. Breckenridge. I have not as yet had that honor."

John was confused. "But you mentioned children."

"I meant the plantation children."

"Then do you live here at Willowby alone?"

"Hardly." He chuckled. "Presently my sister Clio and our cousin, Mary Ellen Parker, stay here at the house. As does my uncle, Jackson Breckenridge. But you see, Mr. Sharp, at any time the list of those living here can change. Family members tend to come and go at their whim."

As the men continued to walk, John looked about for evidence of cultivation. No fields were visible. "What is it you grow here at Willowby, sir?"

"Sea cotton."

John nodded. "It does seem that everyone is growing cotton now. The world has proven to have an immense appetite for it."

Tyler answered quickly. "Sea cotton is quite different from most cotton being grown. It is much more durable, yet has a softer feel. It tends to be used in fine clothing and things of that nature. In fact, much of our market is in Europe."

"Oh, I see," John said, swallowing his impropriety. "That sounds quite different from normal cotton."

Duke had been conducting an inspection of their route, sometimes trotting before them, sometimes lagging behind. While he had now taken up a position just ahead and to the left of Breckenridge, his interest seemed focused on a clump of rocks about twenty feet downhill and just off the path.

Breckenridge stopped. "Don't move." He handed John his drink and nodded toward the rocks. His voice was low but conversational. "On top. Just to the left." John saw the head of a large spotted snake.

The next events happened in a matter of seconds. The snake

moved, and the dog leaped forward across the path. Breckenridge brought the shotgun up in one motion to little more than waist high and fired in advance of the dog. The dog had the snake in its jaws an instant after the gun fired, giving it a fierce shake, snapping its neck. The dog would have killed it instantly if it weren't already missing its head.

"Looks like a big one," Breckenridge said, taking his drink back from John. "Almost five feet."

John was still stunned. "Is it poisonous?"

"Indeed. It's a copperhead." He walked over and moved it with his boot.

"Very impressive," John commented, eyeing the shotgun.

"Yes," Breckenridge said, looking at the dog. "Duke just doesn't like snakes. I wish he wouldn't do that, though. I'm afraid he'll get bitten one of these days." He sighed. "I guess it doesn't pay to worry about it."

They approached the pond and an old stone bench, swallowed in the shade of the enormous trees. As the men sat, the dog took off around the pond's edge, scaring imaginary game with spirited lunges into the reeds. The men sipped their drinks in silence for a while, staring at the placid surface.

A nearby plop in the water set free a gentle set of ripples.

John looked at Breckenridge. "Are there a great many fish in your pond?"

"Yes," he said. "The pond is spring fed. There's a fair amount of sunfish and bream."

John unconsciously tucked in his legs at the next thought. "And alligators?"

Tyler looked at John with amusement. "No, Mr. Sharp. No alligators."

John straightened his legs and smiled. "That's good."

After a minute, Breckenridge leaned forward, dropping his shoulders a bit. He appeared to be choosing his words carefully. "It is such a shame that your first view of Charleston should be now, amid all the unpleasantness. She is normally such a fine city, with much to see and many warm faces, yet you have seen only the worst. You must bear in mind, you have come during a rare and unfortunate time of local discord. Do not be took quick to form a judgment." He looked at John, openly appraising him. "But no. You seem a more worldly man than that."

John bowed lightly. "Indeed, Mr. Breckenridge, I try not to form my opinions in haste. However, I must disagree with you on one point. The disquiet I have seen over the last few days seems anything but local. The crowd that gathered beside the courthouse yesterday seemed quite receptive to the speaker's ideas on secession. I do not know of a more national issue than that."

Breckenridge nodded. "I concede that secession is indeed a national issue. However, Mr. Sharp, you witnessed a rabble, responding to an issue as rabble would—with simplified slogans and violence. Charleston society does not all agree with the crowd you witnessed. I would ask that you consider your perspective when reviewing southern politics. Do not paint us with too broad a brush."

"Meaning?"

He considered for a moment. "Let us say you are viewing a painting from across a room of a girl in a white dress. When you look at the painting up close, you see that her dress isn't white at all, but a mixture of many colors. The people of Charleston and South Carolina are like that. We are not a faceless mob, but individuals of varying backgrounds and objectives."

John nodded. "I would ask that you consider, sir, that perception also may be distorted from too close a vantage point. When your eyes are several inches from the canvas, you see brush strokes and individual dabs of color, but you may not recognize what the picture represents."

The planter looked at John and chuckled. "Touché, Mr. Sharp. Perspective must be balanced. I believe I would enjoy discussing actual art with you sometime." He took another sip of his drink, and his tone grew serious again. "At the risk of trying your patience, I feel the need to emphasize to you that the incident you were caught up in yesterday is not the real Charleston."

"Perhaps," John responded. "But the event, the riot, happened. And a similar event nearly occurred at the same location the preceding day. It may not have been representative, but it was *real*."

"I don't dispute that. But I think if we are not careful, our response to events such as these may have significance that transcends the events themselves." Breckenridge looked up to the sky for a moment, then back at John. He smiled. "I mentioned before my stay in New York City. As we both know, New York can be a dangerous place. Fights and riots are all too common. Yet they do not define what is New York." He paused and took out his pipe. "Take the Astor Place incident, for example."

Breckenridge's sudden mention of Astor Place took John by surprise. He knew he must have reacted physically—a flinch or a slight flush—because Breckenridge paused for an instant before continuing.

"A group of low-class working men marched on a theater of the rich. The violence escalated from there, until scores of men were shot and killed. Now, some thought it possible that a war would break out in the city. The signs were certainly all there." He lit a match and paused to light the pipe. "But here we are, some time later, and normalcy has returned. Each side refrained from engaging in actions that would inflame the other. The conflict did not escalate. Men of reason prevailed.

"At the present time, what is most important is that certain people—men without prejudice—understand what is going on before acting on any impulsive gambit by those who don't fathom the consequences." He looked out over the pond. "You see, Mr. Sharp, I think constructive change is accomplished from bold claims followed by limited actions."

John paused for a moment, studying the comment. "Yes. But there is a caveat to your theory. If action is never taken, if the change goes unaccomplished, bold actions by others may precipitate a revolution."

Breckenridge glanced at him briefly. John could not be certain, but he thought he detected a trace of a smile.

On the slow walk back toward the house, John felt a twinge of discomfort at not revealing his occupation at the outset of the conversation. "Mr. Breckenridge, before, you made mention of the uncharacteristic glimpses I had seen of Charleston. The unrest, so to speak. But I think it is important that you understand something about me. That unrest is the reason I've come to Charleston. You see, I'm a reporter. With the *New York Tribune.*"

"Then you came here with the reporter who was killed in the accident?"

"No, actually. I came later, after my paper received word of his death."

Breckenridge nodded gravely. "Please accept my condolences. It must be difficult to have to take over for a colleague under such circumstances. And it left you so little time to prepare for the trial." He paused. "But then I'm sure your colleague cabled his progress to your editor. Reporters check in, don't they, when they are away on assignment?"

It was not the question itself but rather Breckenridge's deportment that seemed odd. The planter did not glance back at John as he had throughout their conversation. Instead he looked away, focusing on Duke's progress up the path. He seemed to be avoiding eye contact.

"He cabled." John paused for the space of several strides before he continued. "But, of course, such communications are necessarily brief."

"Of course," Breckenridge replied, still watching the dog.

John allowed several minutes of silence before returning to an earlier point. "You mentioned the trial. What is your opinion of it?"

He took a few steps before answering. "It is unfortunate."

Breckenridge's response did not surprise him. In spite of the property issues involved, he did not seem the type to be calling for the man's blood.

"Do you think that a guilty verdict is certain? And if so, could you speculate on the sentence?"

The planter's lips tightened for a moment. "I cannot provide you with concrete information on this matter. I am not in a position to second-guess the judge."

John recognized that he had run into a brick wall with that line of questioning. He decided to backtrack, and go at it from a different angle.

"Very well. Then what is your opinion of Darcy Nance's decision to accept defense from a northern lawyer? Do you think it will greatly harm his chances of an acquittal?"

Breckenridge took a deep breath. "Darcy Calhoun is a man of limited intellect. That is the way God made him, and therefore you will hear no ridicule or censure of Darcy from me. I believe he didn't know what he was doing when he accepted the service of that northern lawyer." He stopped walking and turned to John. His face was utterly devoid of emotion, and he spoke in a soft voice with little inflection. "The northern lawyer, however, invites contempt. He does not come to Charleston to provide expert defense within the framework of our legal system. Rather, he comes here to further his political agenda. I find this more than despicable. I consider it criminal."

He fixed John with a direct gaze. "Now perhaps you will allow me to ask you several questions of a sensitive nature." He did not wait for John's assent. "Just how powerful is abolitionist sentiment in the North? Congress appears to be polarized along geographic lines. But the people of New York—your readers—are they united on this issue?"

"Mr. Breckenridge, the only defining quality of New York politics is the absence of consensus. As I have walked the streets of Charleston, each demonstration I have seen seemed linked thematically to the others. There seems to be a prevalent point of view. It could not be further from the situation in New York, where each rowdy exhibition requires an investigation just to pinpoint who, exactly, is the aggrieved party. There are Unionists, separatists, free-soilers, and abolitionists. There are also quite many who care little for national politics in general—those who gravitate toward social issues, such as those defined by class or nationality. The only issue that seems to unite all these discordant voices is the southern threat of secession."

John took a sip of his bourbon. "Earlier you insinuated that the secessionists were not so many as the demonstrations seemed to indicate. I can assure you, the percentage of northern abolitionists pales in comparison. They are a very vocal minority."

Both men stood silent for a moment. "There is one other thing, however," John continued. "Another issue that is quickly hardening northern ire."

"What is that?"

"The actions being taken under the auspices of the Fugitive Slave

Act." He paused. "Outside the courthouse yesterday, I heard a man, one you called a rabble-rouser, draw a parallel between the South and the patriots of the Revolution. On this point, I think he was entirely incorrect. I feel that the same wrongs that the colonists claimed are much more analogous with northern grievances than those of the South. You see, a major complaint of the revolutionaries was the invasion of their homes by soldiers of the crown. Many feel it is quite similar to the way the South presently wields the power of the slave laws. According to the southern interpretation, those laws give bounty hunters the right to charge into the homes of innocent and unsuspecting citizens at any time, often armed, in search of an escaped slave." John paused and looked at the planter directly. "For every door you kick open in your search, you create a town full of enemies."

"An excellent point, Mr. Sharp. And exactly the reason why it is integral that men like us continue our civil discussions."

They took lunch in the rose garden beneath a circular stained glass window that was part of a small chapel annexed to the house. According to Breckenridge, his great-grandfather, John Tyler Breckenridge, had built it for a Catholic wife he adored who then died young. Subsequent Breckenridges worshipped the Protestant God. The chapel was illuminated from within, and dapples of colored light fell onto the settings of fine china and the white linen cloth.

The food was simple rather than opulent—a selection of cold smoked meats and cheeses, fresh fruits, preserves, and unusual breads and crackers.

"They're called benne wafers," Tyler said of John's favorite. "The slaves say they brought the seeds from Africa. They cultivate them here in their gardens and use them in a variety of dishes. You may have heard them called sesame seeds."

. . . And there was more whiskey. Each man had his own crystal decanter. John's hangover seemed to wane with each additional sip.

They didn't talk much during lunch. John was famished. It was all he could do to restrain himself and eat slowly. Breckenridge seemed pleased that John was enjoying the food, but he ate little himself, preferring to sit back with his pipe and rye.

"We'll arrange transportation for you back to Charleston later this afternoon. If you have time, I can offer you a brief tour of the plantation before you go."

"I would be most interested in seeing it," John responded sincerely. "And I regret that I must inconvenience you for a ride back to the city. I know that you and your staff have other matters to attend to. I will admit, however, that I am concerned about several people who will be worried that I have gone missing."

"If you refer to Mr. Conway, feel no distress. He has been informed of your whereabouts, as has the keeper of your boardinghouse, Mr. McClellan. Rogers left word there early this morn before returning to Willowby."

John felt relieved and off-balance at the same time. There was certainly nothing improper in Breckenridge or his man's actions in notifying John's innkeeper and his friend of his safety. Yet that such a detail should have been covered under such chaotic circumstances, that Breckenridge's grasp of the matter included the names of the parties involved, spoke of a level of control that John found unnerving.

The planter made another subtle summoning gesture, and a servant appeared immediately. "Simon, tell Miriam that our guest is quite fond of her benne wafers and seed bread. See if she has some more for us."

John protested. "Oh, no, thank you. I couldn't possibly eat any more."

Breckenridge again spoke to the servant. "Then send someone to fetch Solomon. Ask him to have Thunder and Tulip saddled, and to meet us at the north field." He turned back to John. "Darcy Calhoun is also quite fond of our cook's wafers and seed bread. When Miriam traded our pecans for Darcy's berries and crab apples, she always sent along a tin of wafers."

"You know Darcy?" John was incredulous.

"To a point," he responded slowly. "Little more than just to nod to. His cabin is but three miles from the western line of our property. Over by Cowford."

The thought occurred to John that his presence here was indeed fortuitous. While his initial desire upon arrival had been to return to

Charleston as soon as possible, he now wished that he had more time here—to get a firsthand view of southern plantation life, to see Darcy Nance's cabin, and to interview those who knew him. The question was, how could he finagle an invitation to stay here an extra day without appearing crass?

The men walked through a peach orchard, then a pecan grove, carrying their drinks. Breckenridge also carried his loaded shotgun in the crook of his arm.

"Are there more snakes out this way?"

"Not to speak of." The laconic response offered no explanation for the weapon. He glanced at John and added dryly, "No alligators either."

It occurred to John that the ubiquitous gun offered protection from a different threat. He recalled the paranoia among the white population of Charleston, the result of past slave uprisings, real and imagined. Breckenridge and his man at the dock had been the only whites he had seen since his arrival at Willowby. He thought a direct approach to the issue might be the best one, but chose his next words carefully.

"Sir, I do not wish to take advantage of your courtesy and hospitality. But, in light of our earlier dialogue, there are several sensitive questions I would like to ask you."

Breckenridge stopped walking and looked John in the eye. "Mr. Sharp, because you are a native of New York, I can make inferences concerning your political positions on certain issues. I am also familiar with the editorial positions of the *New York Tribune*." He weighted his next words. "I will not debate the ethical aspects of slavery with you." He paused. "That said, I will attempt to answer your questions to the best of my ability with the understanding that you will not quote me directly or name me as a source in print. I will show you as much of Willowby as you care to see. I will also allow you to speak with whomever you wish."

"That is more than fair." They again began to walk. "Since my arrival in Charleston, the most striking aspect of the city has been the fear displayed by the citizens. It is palpable and omnipresent. The white citizens are terrified that the blacks will rise up against them.

The blacks are afraid that the whites suspect them; they are afraid they will become targets of an inquisition."

Breckenridge nodded. "Your assessment is correct."

"Then how real *is* the threat of a black uprising? Is there truly something to fear?"

He considered for a moment. "I do not think that a general uprising of any size falls within the realm of possibility. Isolated incidents can always occur, of course, such as the one in Habersham County. These are normally attributable to very specific altercations among individuals. So, while small-scale incidents are always possible, I do not think the current level of fear in Charleston is justified.

"As for myself, I do not perceive that I am a target, though, as I said, random incidents are always possible. Your experience at the courthouse is one such example. Here at Willowby, however, there is no cause for concern. Most of our people were born here. Some came to us through marriage. The few that I purchased outright were men of specialized skills. I knew their previous owners and their backgrounds."

John nodded. "Before coming to Charleston, I was made aware of an incident that happened some time ago. There was apparently an aborted uprising led by a free black man named Denmark Vesey." Breckenridge reacted to the name. "Is it possible that the memory of that incident continues to influence relations between blacks and whites even today?"

Breckenridge looked past John. "Yes. The ghost of Denmark Vesey still walks among us."

"So the threat was real."

Breckenridge looked back at John and gave just the slightest of smiles. "I will tell you what I know of the Vesey uprising. I was born in 1826, and the incident occurred in '22, so this is all hearsay." Breckenridge took another sip of his whiskey. "The prevailing story was that Vesey recruited over a thousand blacks, some slaves from town and others from surrounding plantations. The plan was to set fire to Charleston, kill the whites, and commandeer ships in the harbor and sail to Haiti.

"The conspiracy was compromised before it could be implemented.

Vesey and five leading cohorts were tried and hanged. Subsequently, over thirty more blacks were executed.

"The mayor of Charleston presided over the court at the time. The proceedings were conducted in secret. My grandfather was to have served on the panel, but illness prevented him from doing so. I know that he later questioned the court's findings, as did the governor. The issue was raised that the mayor was using the situation for his own political purposes. My grandfather and the mayor never spoke again."

Breckenridge gave a little shrug as he looked at John. "I do not know what really happened. I do not think we'll ever know. . . ." He raised an eyebrow. "My source for most of this information, by the way, is Joshua Mannion, editor of the *Charleston Gazette*. He will be out here for the party on the fourth. It is a shame you have to get back to town. I would have liked for you to meet him. Mr. Alford, the prosecutor in the trial, will be here as well."

John started to speak, but bit back his words. He could think of no comment that did not sound like a blatant request for an invitation. Fortunately, the change in surroundings now forced him to redirect his attention.

The groves of trees had now ended, and the men stood in full sunlight. About thirty yards beyond them, on the other side of the thick grassy border, the cultivated fields began. John stepped out onto the brown earth, his feet leading him forward without thought. Then he stopped. As he stood in the cotton field, his back to the buildings at the plantation's hub, his foremost impression was of lines—the longest lines he had ever seen. John stood on the soft ground between rows of cotton and stretched his arms out to each side, shoulder high. As he sighted off his fingertips, first one side, then the other, the lines seemed to go on forever, the converging *V*'s meeting in the lost focus of the great distance. Before him the green rows of cotton became endless marching ranks, then corduroy, then solid green to the horizon.

Breckenridge stood a step behind, gracefully silent as he allowed the northerner a moment of survey.

John turned to him with an unabashed smile. His only recourse was understatement. "It is vast!"

Breckenridge smiled back. "You should see the fields when the plants are fully mature and the cotton is ripe." He borrowed John's style. "It is pretty."

There was a sound of approaching hooves, and a black man astride a gray horse emerged from a trail in the trees about a hundred yards away. He led two other horses. The man was well built, about forty, with a deep weather-beaten face and shrewd eyes. He wore a long-sleeved white cotton shirt of good quality and a straw hat.

"Excellent," Breckenridge stated. "Here comes Solomon, our overseer. While you are about the grounds, Solomon will be able to help you in any manner."

The statement perplexed him. "Your overseer? But he is black."

"Yes," Breckenridge responded simply. "Quite."

"But I was of the idea that the position of overseer was reserved for a white man."

Tyler nodded at the assumption. "You see, Mr. Sharp, it is as we had mentioned before. Not all things are what they are said to be."

The man stopped a few yards away, dismounted, and removed his hat.

"Solomon, this is Mr. Sharp. He is from New York City, and he's interested in seeing how our plantation operates. He will be looking 'round, and he has my permission to speak with any of our people."

Solomon looked at John and dipped his head. "Sir." He looked back at the planter. "Yessir, Mr. Breckenridge."

"Now, what is our carriage situation? We need to see about getting Mr. Sharp back to Charleston later this afternoon."

Solomon momentarily seemed to be at a loss. "I'm afraid I just sent yo' carriage over to the Witherspoons, and the other ain't back from the city just yet. That would mean getting Mr. Sharp on the road pretty late." Solomon gave John an apologetic look.

John looked at Breckenridge. "I really don't want to inconvenience you. And I have been thinking. I really would like to see Darcy Nance's cabin and talk to some of the people in Cowford who knew him. Perhaps I could find lodging in Cowford for the night, then catch a ride back to the city sometime tomorrow."

Breckenridge and Solomon chuckled and exchanged a look. "You will understand why we are amused when you see Cowford, Mr. Sharp." He turned to Solomon. "Excuse us for a moment."

Solomon made busy with the horses as Breckenridge put a hand on John's shoulder and ushered him a few feet away. He still had an amused expression as he looked John in the eye. "There won't be a thing happening in town concerning the trial this weekend, and we would be pleased to have you stay at Willowby through the weekend for the party. It would be no inconvenience; rather, it would be my pleasure. I would look forward to conversing with you at great length, and I'm sure my guests will offer some opinions you would not hear in New York. We'll see that you are back in town early Tuesday morn. Are you up for it?"

"Why . . . yes," John stammered. He actually blushed a bit. "If you're sure . . . I mean, you know the status of my wardrobe."

"We'll get my valet to work on that. It is hardly a problem."

"Until next week," John replied, smiling, "when you discover that all your favorite pants are a good three inches above your ankles."

While Breckenridge provided instruction to Solomon, John walked over to inspect the horses. One was a mammoth animal, a beautiful black stallion with a well-brushed coat that glowed in the afternoon sun. The horse had an attitude—he arched his neck and eyed John with an air of open superiority. The other was a docile sorrel mare preoccupied with munching clover.

"Which one's mine?" John asked brightly as Breckenridge approached.

The planter walked up to the stallion and mounted, calling out, "Tulip is a very docile horse. You should have no problem with her."

Breckenridge showed John the church his father had built for the slaves a quarter century ago. It was not a grand structure by any means, but it was obviously well maintained by the parishioners. The planter seemed proud of it.

He was, very obviously, proud of all that he showed John in his quiet, understated way. They toured the carpentry shop, the dairy, and took the "upwind" path around the hog pen and poultry yard. They now rode along a good-size field of beans and cabbage.

"Is the plantation here self-sufficient?"

"No. We are far from it, but the meat and dairy we produce here helps to offset the price of feeding so many."

"How many?"

"Nearly two hundred. And since we do not grow a substantial food crop, we must import tons annually. We require significant amounts of flour, corn, and rice. But, of course, everyone grows rice around here, so we can buy it quite cheaply. The fruit and vegetables cost, though. I provide the seed for those who want to tend their own gardens. They keep what they grow. It provides variety, and if they have a good crop, they can sell some back for a small profit." He turned and looked at John. "I'm going to insert an editorial comment here, Mr. Sharp. Contrary to what the *abolitionists* would argue, it would make no sense to treat our workers like dogs. Making sure they have good food, clothing, and quarter is my main responsibility, since they supply my livelihood. The stereotypical portrait of malnourished, mistreated workers would not only be inhumane, it would make for poor business."

His choice of terms did not escape John's ear. Breckenridge rarely used the term *slave*. Rather, he called them servants, workers, or his people. The reporter in him made John wonder whom the planter was trying to fool.

Smoke trailed upward from a copse of trees just ahead, and with it came the faint smell of hickory. The rhythmic clang of hammers on metal announced the presence of the smithy.

"Next, I'll be showing you one of my favorite projects," Breckenridge said. "I started it when I took over four years ago."

A new brick outbuilding with its tall chimney stood in the clearing just past the trees. In front of it, in the shade of a large oak, three shirtless black men worked over an open hearth. They pounded and folded the red-hot metal, then plunged it into the water bath, raising clouds of steam.

"Is it common for a plantation to have its own smithy?"

"Not on this scale. Some of my neighbors can do simple repairs, but they send their serious jobs here. Many of the plantations operate some sort of specialty labor. About twenty miles from here, at the Wilkes plantation, they have a tannery. The Spekes, just to the south of us, have a cooper."

Breckenridge gestured toward the oldest of the men. "These men are craftsmen. I came across Johnson in town several years ago. He was being underutilized, so I brought him here and put him in charge." He pointed to an intricate wrought-iron gate that leaned against the building. "That is his design. These men built the railing over the balcony at the house, as well as the fence that borders the garden."

"It is fine work," John observed.

Breckenridge nodded. "In just these few years they have established a fine reputation. Johnson is the most sought-after smith in the area, including Charleston. He is often contracted to different clients for weeks at a time."

"Then he is allowed to leave the plantation?"

"Of course, Mr. Sharp. This is not a prison. Johnson will often go and work at a private residence. While there, his boarding is part of the payment, but he brings in considerable income."

"That sounds like a favorable business equation for you."

"Yes. But Johnson receives a percentage also. He does well, I assure you."

The men were working with varying sizes of metal. Each hammer blow rang with a different pitch. Soon the blows fell into a noticeable rhythm. The pounding beat entranced John, as did the shower of sparks from each swing. John could understand why Breckenridge liked to watch the blacksmiths work.

John inhaled deeply. "What is the purpose of the hickory?"

"It adds flavor."

Breckenridge looked past John's quizzical expression and raised his voice a bit. "Johnson, what is for suppa' tonight?"

The man set down his hammer and walked to the far side of the hearth. He smiled wide, showing just a smattering of teeth, then picked something up with a gloved hand. "Rabbit," he exclaimed, raising the roasting by the legs. "More than enough if y'all is wishing to join us."

"You're tempting us," Tyler replied. "But you know Miriam. She'll pout for days if we don't do justice to her dinner. You men enjoy your suppa'."

After a moment, John felt and heard the thud of approaching hooves. As he turned, the man Solomon rode quickly up to them.

"I'm sorry to bother you, sir, but Master Jackson is looking fo' ya. Said you was to meet this afternoon."

Breckenridge pursed his lips. "Yes." A faint sigh seemed to accompany the word. "Well, Mr. Sharp, it seems our tour has come to an end. Of course, you are more than welcome to ride about on your own. See and talk to whomever you wish."

John had hoped for this opportunity. "You mentioned that Darcy Nance's home was in the area. Perhaps this would be a good time to ride over that way."

Tyler cocked his head and pinpointed the sun. "I would think the morning might be a better time. 'Tis beginning to get late, and the woods between Willowby and Darcy Calhoun's home are rather thick. It is not the place one unfamiliar with the geography would want to find himself at dusk."

"Still, I'd like to give it a try," John persisted.

Breckenridge pursed his lips and looked to his overseer. "Solomon, where are you headed from here?"

"I was just going to make sure that the bridge support was repaired ova' by the North Creek."

"Perhaps Mr. Sharp could ride with you partway, and you could show him where the trail veers off toward Mr. Calhoun's place."

"Certainly, sir."

Breckenridge turned back to John. "Once you get to the trail, follow it west until you reach a wide stream. Simply walk north beside the stream for about a mile. Mr. Calhoun's cottage will be the first you come to."

John nodded. "I'm sure that I will find it."

Breckenridge looped the reins tightly around one hand, initiating impatient high steps from Thunder. "Dinner tonight will be at nine. I would be pleased if you could join us."

"I look forward to it."

"Very well. Then, until dinner . . ." He kicked a heel to the horse's side, which was obviously the invitation Thunder had hoped for all afternoon. The animal broke into a fevered charge that took him from sight in seconds.

John nodded to Solomon and put a boot into Tulip. The animal blew a heavy gust from her nose and leaned to the west, taking them forward at a characteristically southern speed.

John took his leave of Solomon at the point where a narrow dirt track headed westward into the brush. In spite of his assertion to the contrary, John never would have found the track in the first place without assistance. Staying with the path, which disappeared at regular intervals only to reappear heading in a nonwesterly direction, taxed John's navigational skills to the utmost. He was soon ready to concede that he was no Kit Carson, but he hated to give Breckenridge the satisfaction.

John spoke aloud in an exaggerated drawl. "Ain't much figuring that you was a horseman, so I corralled ya this here ride Tulip. She's nice and docile, just perfect fo' a man from the big city. Don't get lost now, ya hear?"

He finally let out a huff of surrender. He turned Tulip around and gave her a swat. "Home, Tulip." He hoped she knew where home was.

After he emerged from the woods, John headed in the general direction of the smoke from the smithy. A small black boy of about six appeared from behind a row of shrubbery bordering a fence. He seemed to be headed in the same general direction. The boy marched along with a sense of purpose and soon overtook them.

"Hello, sir."

"Where are you going?" he called after him.

"I's going to see the fight."

"Are some boys fighting?"

"Not boys. Men. They's fixing to."

"They are going to have a fistfight?"

The boy looked at John as if he considered him a bit slow. "No, they use long sticks. Big knives. They poke with 'em." The boy made an imaginary thrust and grunted for emphasis.

"Hold on a minute." John dismounted from Tulip and looped the reins through the fence. "Some men are going to fight with knives?"

"Yes, sir."

"How do you know?"

"I sees 'em getting ready before. Over behind the smithy. They was getting the knives sharp."

"They were sharpening knives to fight?" John asked incredulously. "Other black men?"

"Naw. Massa Breckenridge. You sure take some explaining."

"Does anyone else know about this?"

"Most folks know they is doing it."

"You better take me there."

"Well, all right. But you mustn't tell. I ain't supposed to watch."

The boy chose a vantage point behind the wall of a small shed. There was a space between two boards, and they had a clear view of the blacksmiths' shop.

John heard voices, that of Breckenridge and another man. John was about to step forward when the man came into view. He was tall, white, and in his mid-forties, with a patrician face and proud demeanor. He wore a padded vest and carried a fencing foil, which he whipped in several sharp arcs.

"I know you prefer saber, Tyler, but Ratcliffe is still working on mine. The balance isn't right."

Breckenridge was now in view. He wore a vest and carried a foil also. He raised the tip of his foil in salute. "So you're leaving for Savannah tonight?" he asked.

"That's right. I can't say I'm up for dinner with a Yankee reporter anyway."

"And you won't be back for the party?"

John didn't hear the response. The men began a series of choreographed lunges and parries. Judging from his pedantic tone, the older man was the master, but Breckenridge appeared to be his match.

"I sure hope you know what you're doing. This thing with the Yank could blow up in your face."

"I know exactly what I'm doing!" As if to prove it, Breckenridge scored a hit just to the left of the man's breastbone.

"Touché. You concern me sometimes, Tyler. You know your father thought—"

Breckenridge looped his foil around his opponent's in a move that appeared to involve only the wrist. The older man's foil went flying.

Breckenridge's face was a mask, his voice cold. "You may wish to avoid this topic when I am armed."

Long after the conversation had changed, the prickles on the back of John's neck remained. Eventually, he left his vantage point and went to collect Tulip. He had no idea of what to make of the conversation between Breckenridge and the man he assumed was his uncle. More to the point, he had no idea what to make of Breckenridge.

He had been receiving contradictory messages from the planter since their first encounter. At times John had the feeling that the man liked him; that he was eager for an exchange of ideas. At other times he wondered if it was all a charade; if he was simply Breckenridge's pawn in a game he didn't understand. The overheard conversation supported the latter theory.

John assessed his position. He was a weekend guest at a magnificent plantation with license to observe and interview. He would have access to Darcy Calhoun's hometown and to the Charleston aristocracy at the party. John decided that if Breckenridge was using him for some purpose, he was perfectly capable of using Breckenridge as well. He knew that Simpson would have approved.

John employed the same approach with each of the slaves he met on his ride back toward the house. He introduced himself as a newspaper reporter from New York City and a weekend guest of Mr. Breckenridge. He asked them what it was like to work at Willowby.

Almost to a man, they told him that Willowby was the finest plantation in all of South Carolina. Since everyone John interviewed had been born there and had no basis for comparison, he considered this an obvious tribute to Breckenridge's public relations expertise. But unless the planter was also conducting a school for actors, the slaves seemed quite sincere in their pride in the plantation and their respect for their master.

John approached a group of older women who sat in the shade, shelling peas. They returned his greeting politely and nodded to a spot for him to sit, but showed no inclination to rise or interrupt their work. They worked quite quickly as they conversed among themselves, almost as if competing with one another to fill their baskets. John wondered what incentive they had to hurry, and asked them.

"Well, the massa don't put up with no nonsense," the oldest woman answered. "And Solomon always says to us, 'Work hard and work smart.' "

"What does that mean?"

"That means we don't waste nothing. 'Specially time." The woman laughed at John's quizzical look and pointed to her basket. "When this one here is full, I's done for the day. Not like these slowpokes." She gestured to her friends, who laughed at the insult. "Then, I's headed down to the creek to do me some fishing."

As John reviewed his notes, he concluded that the consensus about Breckenridge and Solomon was that they were demanding but not unkind. There were rumors that Breckenridge had eyes on the back of his head and that he never slept. And most seemed to think that his horse was possessed by the devil.

John now approached a small village of wooden cottages— slave quarters. He slapped the reins to Tulip's neck and cajoled her forward. The collection of uniform huts were laid out in the shape of a triangle. He entered at the blunt end, opposite the apex.

The nature of the housing took him by surprise. While the construction of the homes was similar—rectangular, sloping roofs, with a small pancless window at the front—each boasted of its diversity through subtle additions. Some had brightly colored drapes, others homemade shutters, others dangling chimes now mute in the still heat. A worn shirt was pinned to the door of one house, presumably to dry it. There was a wooden box of planted pink flowers beside one door. Another bore a holiday decoration of sorts; scraps of colored cloth formed a flag with four blue stars and an assortment of red and white stripes. Crosses of all sizes were everywhere; some on doors, some above them, and one forming a frame inside the window.

At the center of the triangle, well away from the homes, was an open common area. Benches sat beside a circle of stones, where a tar-black residue told of past fires. John dismounted and hitched Tulip, then walked forward to the hearth. He stopped and closed his eyes, hoping to reincarnate the ghosts of whispered boyhood tales. He tried to imagine the rituals that clung to exotic fireside scenes: the pounding of animal-skin drums, the chants and wails of an incoherent tongue, a wild Saint Vitus' dance born of the soul. He thought of all things savage; a word conjured because it was the opposite of what white men perceived themselves to be—civilized. He tried hard to tap into the memories of this hearth. The dancing, the chanting, the music. But none lived. It was just a campfire sight, surrounded by poor people's homes.

"Hello there, young massa."

John turned to see two ancient-looking black women sitting on a bench in the shade in front of a cabin.

"Good afternoon," he called back as he walked toward them.

"You see, Sissy, I told you it was Massa Tyler all grown up."

"No, Buella, it ain't. It's another gentleman."

John offered a hand to the woman who called to him. "I'm John Sharp, from New York City."

"Well, of course ya is looking sharp," the woman said, shaking his hand. "You was always the handsomest child. And so good-natured. Didn't I tell you he was a sweet boy, Sissy?"

Sissy rolled her eyes and looked at John. She tapped her fingers to the side of her head.

"How come you don't come to see me no more, Massa Tyler? You know I love ta sing those old songs with ya." She turned to the other woman. "He can sing like an angel, Sissy. Didn't I tell ya that?"

"This ain't Massa Tyler," Sissy said firmly. "He was here last week. He brought you a tin of that candy you like from Charleston."

"That wasn't my young massa." Buella stuck out her lip. "That was *Massa* Breckenridge. His daddy."

A coarse cough from one of the huts drew John's attention. He excused himself from the women. Seconds later the door was opened, propped against the foot of a young white woman who looked out toward the commons. She looked at John.

"Pardon me, sir," she called. She peeked forward. Her face was flushed and her dark blond hair done up in braids, leaving a few damp, wayward strands curled against her cheeks. She was pretty in a quiet way. "What luck that I saw you. Could you help me, please?"

"Yes, of course." He walked forward quickly.

Layers of petticoats fanned out the skirt of her gray dress. She wore a white apron atop it, tied tightly about a slender waist. She offered a pleasant smile.

"Ever so sorry to bother you. The woman inside the hut has been awfully sick. It is hot, and the air in the cabin has become quite stale. I thought it best if she sat outside for a time."

She met his eyes directly; hers were a soft cornflower blue. "If you wouldn't mind carrying a chair out here into the shade, I'd be ever so grateful."

"Certainly, miss," John replied. "I'm happy to help."

Another deep-chested cough resonated inside the hut. Its violence forced a pause.

"What is wrong with her?" he asked.

"The croup," she responded, leading him forward. "But don't worry. She is convalescing. There is no danger of you catching it."

They walked inside, where an older black woman lay on a pallet. The young woman pointed John to a chair in the corner while she leaned beside the bed, placing an arm beneath the frail woman's shoulders.

"Let's get you up, Betty. You'll be much more comfortable outside."

"Yes, miss," she said hoarsely. "Thank ya, miss."

John carried the chair to a spot beside a fig tree. She assisted Betty into the seat and softly rubbed her hand across her back.

"The fresh air will have you up in no time," she soothed.

"Yes, miss. I's feeling better already."

"Jimmy should be back soon with your suppa'. He can help you inside when you're ready."

John walked beside the young lady as she returned to the hut. There she gathered a white bonnet and a small wicker basket. After tying the bonnet's ribbon beneath her chin, she looked up at John, smiling.

"Thank you so much for your help."

"It was really no trouble."

She took a panoramic glance out behind him. "Did you ride out here all alone?"

"Yes, but I'm on my way back to the house now."

"Well, then," she said with a gentle smile, "perhaps you would accompany me."

"I would be honored." He eyed his mount. "That is, if I can distract Tulip from her meal of daisies."

"Just whisper 'oat bin' in her ear," she said with a laugh. "It gets a rise out of her every time."

He extended his arm, and she floated her hand atop it. The touch was satin. Then they walked, trailing Tulip behind them.

The young lady had a way of turning her body, a soft swivel of the hips that allowed her arm to rest immobile on his. She would glance at his face, then away as the look was returned. "So then, you are the northern reporter come to visit."

Surprised, he answered, "Yes. My name is John Sharp."

"Well then, Mr. Sharp, it is a pleasure to meet you." She whisked her eyes across his body. "Indeed, it seems you share my brother's sartorial taste."

"Your brother?" He paused for the length of two steps. "Then you are . . ."

"Clio Breckenridge."

His left arm, the arm beneath her's, clenched. He stared hard at her, his surprise overcoming his manners. "Forgive me, for—" He stopped and looked down, unsure of the reason for initiating an apology. "It is a strange but beautiful name. Clio."

She answered in a light sigh, a sort of whimsical hum. "My brother jokes that it was my parent's way of ensuring that I grew up oft spoken to. It has always brought considerable discussion, my name. I know of no other with it."

"Are you named after Cleopatra, then?"

"No. Clio was the Greek muse of history. My parents were especially fond of the classics." She paused and smiled. "Of course, my brother somehow escaped their Hellenistic passion. I guess it's because so many people give their black boys mythological names. But I've often liked to imagine that they would rather have named him Homer or Heracles, instead of something so plain as Tyler."

John laughed aloud at the thought. Then he looked down to her, and she up at him. This time the eyes and smiles held. Abruptly, beneath the weight of her unabashed eyes, John remembered his wound—the black and purple bruise surrounding the gash beside his right eye. She seemed centered on it.

A flood of self-consciousness caused John to break the look. *She must think me a barbarian.* He turned his head off to the side, focusing just above a tree line to their west.

"A writer then, are you?" she asked as they turned on to a wide dirt path.

He turned back just enough to offer his profile, the bruise still hidden. "Yes. For a newspaper in New York."

"Quite thrilling, I'd imagine. To be witness to so much." The words came across sincere.

"Yes. At times it can be quite fascinating."

"I assume I know what brought you to Charleston. But tell me, Mr. Sharp, how have you found your way here to Willowby?"

"Your brother, as a matter of fact. He helped to extricate me from quite an undesirable predicament."

"I see." Just as she began to ask another question, her mouth twitched as she noticed John's distant focus. "Mr. Sharp, are you anticipating a glorious Carolina sunset, or is there some other action taking place over there?"

He snapped back around, finding her barely suppressing her amusement. "I . . . I don't . . ."

There was a moment of pause as she studied his face. "It certainly must have been quite painful. A wound like that."

"Yes, miss. I failed to dodge a flying brick at the courthouse."

"My goodness, sir. It seems like you have a knack for finding yourself in harrowing circumstances."

They cleared a rise in the land and saw before them the sparkling white of the plantation house. In honor of pleasant company, they mutually slowed their step.

"Will you be with us for dinner?" she inquired.

"Yes, miss. As a matter of fact, your brother was gracious enough to invite me to stay for the entire weekend."

"Is that so?" she said, her voice soft. "How wonderful. So you will be here for Monday's party." He nodded. "Tell me, Mr. Sharp, have you ever been to a country party here in Carolina?"

"No."

She smiled. "Then it should suit your taste for danger. There is seldom as harrowing an experience as one's initial foray into low-country society."

He raised his good eyebrow. "And tell me, what is it that they throw *here*?"

"Barbs, accusations, and denunciations." She patted his arm lightly with her hand. "Not to worry though. I can tutor you on everything you will need ta know. . . ."

The sun began to dip behind the trees off to the west, and John and Clio walked along at a dilatory pace. The temperature began to drop, and a soft breeze began to blow from the east. It ferried the sweet smell of flowers and cooking fires. John smiled as he walked. There was no tension here, none of the feeling of grime that clung to a large city. He looked to the seductive backdrop of the plantation home and savored the company of a beautiful young lady. John found himself thinking that life could take some interesting turns—not all of them for the worse.

TWELVE

V ery good," John's mother had told him as she slid her chair forward and gracefully took her seat at the table. "This time you didn't bounce it off the back of my knees."

John had been eight years old. Mother had been beautiful then— her hair elegantly coiffed and her face unlined and carefree. This had been his first dinner in the dining room—a milestone of sorts—even if Mother had been his only dining companion.

John normally took his supper early in the nursery, as was the custom. But he liked to lurk in the alcove at the top of the stairs as the guests arrived in dinner jackets and a rustle of bright silks. He sometimes fell asleep there, listening to the clink of cutlery, the hum of conversation, and the gentle laughter that filtered up from the dining room. In his mind, the conversations were always brilliant and the women always beautiful.

As time passed and Father was away more often, Mother invited him to dine with her quite frequently. Formal table manners soon became second nature. Dinner conversation had been another matter.

"Never discuss business or politics at the table," Mother informed him.

So from an early age, their discussions focused on books. Later, John went away to prep school, and even on his visits home, conversation was confined to literature and his studies. (Events more than a generation old were acceptable topics because they had moved from "politics" to "history.")

John considered it regrettable, however, that neither his mother nor his banker father had ever included him in discussions of business, for this, rather than the words of Thomas Paine or Voltaire, had materially changed his life. The whispers of scandal, of lost fortune, had come first from others. When the family-owned bank failed during John's first year at Yale, his visions of the future ended abruptly.

So John was never a participant in the ephemeral dinner parties with fine wine, beautiful women, and elegant repartee that he had imagined as a child. He had never honed his social skills among the New York elite, and certainly not among the famed elite in Charleston. Now, as he looked up from the glitter of silver on damask placemats into the candlelit faces of the Breckenridge household, John desperately hoped that they wanted to talk about books.

The four of them sat at a rectangular table so polished that the reflection from the chandelier above appeared as the centerpiece. Breckenridge sat at the head of the table, with Clio as hostess at the opposite end. John sat to her right, with the Breckenridges' young cousin, Mary Ellen Parker, across from him.

Breckenridge had offered brief introductions earlier in the drawing room. Mary Ellen, a girl in her early teens, eyed John with interest, offering a well-practiced smile of submission when he glanced in her direction. She had crystalline blond hair pulled back from her face with cloisonné combs before falling to her shoulders in neat ringlets. Her face was pale but lively, and her youthful expression hinted of constant amusement.

John's eyes were drawn to Clio. She had dressed for candlelight. Her hair was also swept up and back, settling in soft curls at the nape of her neck. She wore a simple silver chain about her throat with a stone the color of seawater. The stone and her pale blue dress enhanced the soft blue of her eyes.

"Clio, you mentioned earlier that you and Mr. Sharp had already met," Breckenridge said, inviting elaboration.

"Yes, we enjoyed one another's company on the walk back from the cabins." She offered John a discreet smile.

"With no chaperone?" Mary Ellen emoted with shock.

Clio scorned her with a glance. "You hush."

The young cousin looked at John; first at his hands, then lifting her gaze to his face. "Tell me, Mr. Sharp," she asked directly, "are you a married man?"

"No, miss. Not as yet."

She turned back to Clio, her bearing noticeably more assured. "Well, then, had it been me, I would have required a chaperone."

"That is because you are only fourteen," Clio answered authoritatively. "Besides, Mr. Sharp is here because he is a guest of your cousin."

"Indeed," Breckenridge stated. He turned to John. "We are pleased that you are able to join us. Do you find your room satisfactory?" The last inquiry was delivered with a level tone and a straight face.

"Yes," John responded in kind. "I find the equine motif quite charming. The South has obviously produced some fine horses"—John paused slightly—"if one judges by your paintings and lithographs. The portraits of Sir Charles and Sir Henry are certainly a tribute to southern Thoroughbred breeding."

Breckenridge cracked a smile, then beckoned a servant with a nod. The man approached and placed a large tureen in front of the host. As Breckenridge ladled the clear soup first for John, then the others, Mary Ellen continued her appraisal of John.

"How do you and Mr. Sharp know each other?" she asked her cousin. "Is he a friend from college, or do you know his family in New York?"

"Actually, I first encountered Mr. Sharp yesterday in Charleston."

"And thought he would enhance our holiday gathering, no doubt."

Clio spoke quickly and with enough enthusiasm that she appeared to blush a little after the comment. She gave John a shy look, then glanced down at her hands, then back to his face with a hesitant smile.

Their shared glances did not slip past the attentive eyes of Mary Ellen Parker. The young lady, assuredly possessed by a wicked motive of disclosure, opened her mouth just wide enough to allow the prelude of a gasp.

The servant removed the soup course, replacing it with deviled crab with lemon butter. Another man followed him, removing the existing glasses of wine and pouring from a new bottle.

Clio looked to John with the pleasant bearing of a hostess. " 'Tis rare that we have a guest from as far away as New York, Mr. Sharp. Please tell us what you think of your first visit to South Carolina."

"I have never seen anything like Willowby, Miss Breckenridge. I am impressed by the exceptional beauty of your home and its grounds." He looked at her directly, lowering his voice a little as if he were speaking just to her. "The greens here are different—there is more of the light yellow-green of new growth—and there are so many flowers. As a city dweller, I am accustomed to narrow streets and vertical towers. Here, your fields seem to go on forever."

Clio smiled with obvious pride and answered in a soft tone, "You paint a lovely picture, Mr. Sharp." She glanced over at her cousin and raised her voice a little. "Don't you think so, Mary Ellen?"

"Mm-hmm," she replied, eyeing her plate. Selection of her next bite was apparently more interesting to her than comparative geography.

"As for Charleston itself," John continued, "I think I might describe my experience there as one of . . . unending excitement."

An instant after releasing the words, John recoiled at his own lack of sensitivity. Just days ago he had used the same word in the same context—with a man who had just witnessed a grotesque hanging. Now, as the seconds passed in silence, John felt as if he had trivialized the local problems by describing them as if they were entertainment.

"Not exciting, so to speak. But . . ."

"I take your meaning," Breckenridge said. "Excitement can arise from a variety of circumstances, not all of them pleasant. If one can maintain a certain detachment from events, they can be quite stimulating." He took a slow sip of wine. "It must be quite a life that you lead, Mr. Sharp, as a reporter. Always finding yourself in situations of excitement."

Mary Ellen placed her fork beside her plate and looked at John with renewed interest.

The main entrée came next. It was pheasant, covered in a citrus glaze and laid atop a bed of rice. John smiled as he savored a bite, happily conjuring the image of Owen Conway at McClellan's pine dinner table, suffering through yet another boiled potato.

"How is the pheasant, Mr. Sharp?" Breckenridge asked.

"It is excellent, thank you. Quite a departure from the fare I had become accustomed to in the city."

"Mine is gamey," Mary Ellen professed, her face pursed by the affront. Neither Clio nor Breckenridge paid her any mind. She then looked to the servant. "Miller, tell Cook that the pheasant she prepared is quite gamey, so she will know better in the future."

"Yes, miss," the man said and excused himself.

After dinner, a servant produced a silver tea service and a plate of small cakes. As Clio poured each of them a cup of the jasmine-scented liquid, the servant circulated with attractive servings of fresh pineapple. John could not believe his eyes. His mother had ordered some once for a special party and had let him taste it in the kitchen. The flavor was incredible.

"You haven't learned to grow pineapple locally?" John asked.

"Oh, no," Clio replied. "They are imported. But they have become quite popular in Charleston of late." She nodded toward the tray of cakes. "Miriam made the little round ones for you to try because you liked her benne wafers," she said to John. "These are quite different. They are flavored with lemon and cardamom seed. They also complement the pineapple well."

He tried one. "They're wonderful. I've never tasted anything like them."

"I'll let Miriam know."

"I think she used too many seeds this time," Mary Ellen observed dryly, before peeking over her teacup to engage John's attention. "Please, Mr. Sharp, tell us something about New York ladies."

John smiled, recalling Owen's description of redheaded women with bollard-like legs. He decided to pocket that metaphor. "I think they are much the same everywhere," he started. Mary Ellen's obvious disappointment caused him to modify his response. "But I am a poor person to ask. You see, the majority of my time with women lately has been spent among prostitutes."

The table went silent as the three listeners desperately avoided each other's eyes. Finally, peering back at John with a grand smile, Mary Ellen answered, "How ghastly!"

John only then realized the context of his comment and turned a bright pink. He could not bring himself to look at the women. Breckenridge started to speak, then flashed his half smile instead. The look he gave John implied that he would have to bail himself out of this one. John finally stammered an answer. "I was not soliciting their services, of course. Just speaking to them for the sake of an interview."

Clio screened her laugh behind her white linen napkin, but the slight quivering of her body was unconcealable. Mary Ellen seemed to be enjoying her cousin's loss of composure as much as the garish turn in John's complexion. Tyler, however, summoned his grace, and offered the Yankee a reassuring smile.

"Of course we understand what ya mean, John. I am sure that it is simply a hazard that accompanies your work." As John nodded back, his eyes affixed tightly to the coruscating reflection on the table, Tyler looked to his young cousin. "So tell us, Mary Ellen, what have you been up to today?"

She clasped her hands at the edge of the table like a student, and spoke sarcastically. "Oh, it was truly a thrilling day. Just this morning I got to assist Clio on her rounds to the stray cottages near Cowford. Of course, she made me change my clothes twice before we left. As if what I wear makes a bit of difference to these people."

"Actually, it does," Tyler stated. He nodded to Clio, who turned to the girl.

"It is a fine line, Mary Ellen," she said. "They know we can afford to dress well. It is respectful if we wear nice clothes to pay them a visit.

It lets them know that they are important enough to dress up for. But we mustn't be ostentatious either. We are not doing this to show them up."

"Well, it's good that I was properly attired for a truly stimulating morning. How exciting it was to hear old Mrs. Comstock speak in detail of her problems with rheumatism and warts. Or to listen to the gastric concerns of Mr. Heinlin." She paused and expanded her artificial smile. "Truly, my only concern after a day as exhilarating as today is that my diary may not have enough pages to recount it entirely."

"Really, Cousin," Clio said. "At least you must be excited about the upcoming party."

"Why should I be? At it, I will be forced into spending time with those juvenile boys and their immature antics. I swear, if Thomas Cantrell drags me outside one more time so that I might revel in his marksmanship, I think I just might die. As if watching someone shoot a gun at a distant tree impresses me."

Clio, perhaps recalling her own past experiences, laughed sympathetically. "Surely it is not all that bad."

"If that is what you think, then I shall be sure to summon you when Thomas Cantrell begins polishing his weapons."

After a moment's pause, Tyler straightened in his chair. "Well, ladies, I think it is about time to conclude our dinner."

"But it's still early," Mary Ellen protested. "I would love to hear some tales from Mr. Sharp—of *crime* and *prostitution.*"

"I'm sure you would," Tyler said with a quirk of a smile as he pushed back his chair. "But not tonight, Mary Ellen. Mr. Sharp has had an extremely long day, and before he retires, I would like to speak with him in the study." He looked to the reporter. "That is, if you are up for it, John."

"Of course."

"Then we shall bid you ladies good night."

As the cousins departed arm-in-arm, John was able to overhear Mary Ellen's comment from the doorway.

"His wound makes him ever so exciting, doesn't it, cousin?"

"Shh." Clio laughed softly.

• • •

The study, a small cozy room hidden behind a large double door, smelled of leather, tobacco, and old books. John sat on a small sofa, and Tyler, after pouring them each a brandy, sat across from him in a tall leather chair.

"Your family is delightful," John said.

"Thank you. I do believe that Mary Ellen is quite taken with you." He paused. "As is Clio." He swirled his glass with an imperceptible motion of the hand, then looked to John with surprising familiarity. "I can tell you that the position of helping to raise two young ladies has not been an easy task, John. I am no longer just brother or cousin. But neither am I their father. Since the death of our parents, I have been forced to assume a more formal role—that of a guardian. I fear that it is something I was not altogether cut out for."

John looked at Breckenridge. Because of his demeanor and level of responsibility, it was easy to forget how young the man was. With the confession, John felt a sudden empathy.

"I know that having to assume such a role would terrify me. But you certainly seem to be doing a fine job."

Breckenridge rested his head against the back of his chair. "Thank you. I must say, the most difficult task of late has been dealing with Clio's potential suitors. Now that she has turned nineteen, we are under increasing pressure from the family to arrange her engagement. The boys I grew up with, my college friends, indeed all of my unattached contemporaries, treat me with the cautious courtesy of a prospective father-in-law. It makes me feel ages older."

"And how does Clio feel about this?" John inquired with more than feigned interest.

"I think that we have narrowed the field to several mutually agreeable candidates, but I fear that my sister may be resisting on my account." Tyler paused for a sip of his brandy, and John raised an eyebrow. "She believes I would be unable to look after everything here at Willowby without her help."

"I am surprised, then, that your family isn't pressuring *you* to marry." John wished he could recapture his words the minute he uttered them.

Breckenridge gave a quick smile. "Oh, they are. But they're also learning that I'll do things in my own time and my own way." There was an edge to Tyler's voice with the last statement, and John recalled the scene he had witnessed between Tyler and his uncle. John guessed that the relatives were learning quite quickly not to engage in a contest of will with Tyler Breckenridge.

Tyler straightened a little in his chair and eyed John's half-empty brandy snifter. "Are you tired?"

John smiled. "I'm feeling rather mellow, actually."

Breckenridge took a long, silent breath. "I was meaning to ask you about something. Earlier, when I mentioned the riot at Astor Place, I could not help but notice your response. Were you there?"

John swirled the brandy and watched it sheet on the sides of the glass. "Yes. I was."

Breckenridge used a gentle tone. "Will you speak of it?"

John looked at the planter. He was not sure why he wanted to tell him the story. He had been asked the question countless times over the last year, by curious young boys and hardened old men. He sometimes spoke of it when asked, but never told the story exactly the same way twice. Unlike other stories, where the event erodes with repetition, where passion dissipates beneath description, Astor Place would not scab. The images would not conform to memorized passages or even to John's written word.

John ferried the glass of brandy to his lips and took a long sip. "People called it an actors' dispute." He shook his head dismissively. "But that was merely the catalyst. You see, two Shakespearean actors with equally unsavory opinions of each other took every available opportunity to assail the other's character and talent. Edwin Forrest, an American, tended to appeal to the lower classes, while William Macready, an Englishman, was quite popular among the rich." John's voice became quieter. "I don't think either man had a notion of what their invective would awaken.

"In early May, Macready began performing at the Astor Place Opera House, a grand and opulent venue well beyond the means of the average New Yorker. While the poor were not technically prohibited from attending, both price and society tended to keep them away. From the inside at least. But as Macready took to the stage to perform the first night, he was met with catcalls and rotten tomatoes from a few of his detractors who had managed entrance, and vengeful shouts from countless others gathered outside. Needless to say, he did not perform."

John took a sip of brandy. "One would have hoped that was the end of it, but Macready had a stubborn streak—a trait more born of arrogance than determination. It was made known that he was again to take the stage, again at Astor Place. The date set for the performance was May the tenth.

"I still worked for the *Intruder* at the time. As such, it was impossible for me not to notice the blatant aggression simmering throughout the poorer sections of town. The performance was taken as an affront, and it didn't take long for the rabble-rousers to further antagonize the angry. Captain Isiah Rynders, the undisputed chief of the Five Points gangs and an avowed Anglophobe, issued handbills throughout the city urging people to defend the country against the foreign insult. His lieutenants, men with names like Dirty Face Jack and Country McCleester, further disseminated the malicious message through every bar, brothel, and tenement, many churches, and some schools.

"The mob that arrived at Astor Place was later estimated to be between ten and fifteen thousand people." John shrugged. "Having arrived very early, I was near the front of it, and no number does it justice, for there seemed no end to the crowd."

He paused for a moment. "Pride," he muttered with distaste. "It was pride that turned Astor Place from a demonstration into a war, pride that coaxed those with tickets to still attend, pride that brought Macready back to the stage amid such tumult." He finished the brandy in one swallow. "When news filtered outside that Macready was indeed performing, fury spread like a windblown flame. Men began to hurl bricks toward the windows, shattering them, showering shards upon the patrons inside. Each success galvanized dozens more, until the dark sky filled with the hail of projectiles. It felt somehow medieval." He took a deep breath. "Then it got worse.

"Men attempted to set the building on fire. It caught in some places, but never spread. Meanwhile, the police, hopelessly outnumbered, attempted to restore order. As they confronted the rioters, *they* became the new target. From where I was, on top of a brick embankment seventy or eighty feet from the opera house, I saw one officer, unconscious, being pulled into the melee. Individuals emerged from the mob to assault him, then melted back into the anonymity of the mass. Those who dragged him looked and behaved like animals. No one action killed him, but when they had finished, they left behind a body, not a human being.

"Then the Seventh Regiment arrived and formed a line between the crowd and the theater. The noise was so loud that I couldn't hear the orders. When the soldiers raised their rifles, I expected a warning volley, nothing more."

John's voice carried fresh emotion. He spoke as if relaying the news on that very night. "*They fired into the crowd.* Some at point-blank range. The people . . . some dropped immediately." He let one hand fall against his thigh with a thud. "Others staggered back, causing a stampede. And the soldiers kept firing. A bullet hit a few feet below me on the embankment. I was too shocked to even move at first. But then . . . but then things became even more surreal. With the crowd in full retreat, and men lying before them dead and dying, the soldiers charged. They charged as if after a hated enemy, as if it were not fellow citizens but an army to be eviscerated." He paused. "I do not pretend to know of war, Mr. Breckenridge. I have never fought in nor reported on a battle. But I have no doubt that this was far harsher than any skirmish or assault. For soldiers, along with advanced weapons, carry will with them into battle. The crowd had neither weapons nor will. They were not killed, but slaughtered."

He still stared down at his empty glass. "As I jumped down from the embankment, I saw the carnage. Men, boys, mutilated or bleeding. Others dead. The crowd was no friend to itself either, trampling those too weak or too unfortunate to stay erect. Twenty-three dead," he whispered. "Almost two hundred wounded. My words do not give horror its due."

Breckenridge looked away. "I understand now," he said softly.

John's eyes found focus. "I normally am able to block it out, but sometimes I feel guilty for having been there."

"Why?"

"Because I benefited from it. It was my article in the *Intruder* on Astor Place that caught the attention of the *Tribune*'s editor. It seems my close vantage was as profitable as it was dangerous."

"I see." The planter nodded slowly. "So what did you write? Surely every paper in the city described the event. What made yours different?"

John locked eyes. "Most played up the irony of a trivial issue turned deadly, but it was no actors' dispute gone crazy. Such anger and such response cannot be explained so simply. No, trivial issues sometimes expose major grievances. They can be the spark that ignites the tinder. That was what happened at Astor Place. It was not the fans of one actor against the other. It was the poor against the rich, outright class warfare, more equivalent to the storming of the Bastille than the thoughtless actions of the unruly."

"And the rich could afford no flashpoint like the Bastille," Breckenridge responded. "No revolution to undermine their order. That is why the soldiers attacked."

John nodded. "And that is what I wrote."

After several moments Tyler leaned forward and poured John more brandy. He looked at John appraisingly. "I would like to qualify a statement I made to you earlier this afternoon."

John cocked his head.

"You asked me about Darcy Calhoun," Tyler continued. "I implied that I barely knew him." He paused for a moment as if choosing his words. "While it is true that our personal contact has been limited, I actually know him quite well."

John leaned forward. "You can tell me something of his character, then?"

Breckenridge nodded slowly. "Yes. And something of his background. Darcy Calhoun is a good man. He is a hard worker, primarily a subsistence farmer, who grows a small field of cotton for a modest surplus. He is also extremely religious. In fact, from what I have heard, he devotes the majority of his free time to helping the local reverend."

"Is he married?"

"No. Nor does he have any family in the area. He moved here with his parents around ten years ago, but his folks have long since passed.

He spends most of his time alone, not bothering a soul. I truly believe he enjoys the solitude, though, were you to run into him, he'd have nothing but a wide smile and friendly word."

"He hardly sounds a criminal."

"Nor do I think him to be. You see, John, men who are . . . less intelligent, like Darcy Calhoun, often don't grasp the idea of repercussions. They act only in the moment. I am quite confident that Darcy did not look beyond the action to see all the trouble it would bring to him."

"I do not see then why there is so little compassion. Why does the public rush to convict him?"

"Because they feel powerless, John," he responded. "And because they do not know him." Tyler paused for a moment. "Allow me to tell you a story about Darcy Calhoun. It happened about four years ago, in the springtime, just as the cotton was about to be planted. One of my men, Devon Tull, was helping him get his land ready, and he witnessed it."

"Why was Devon helping Darcy?"

"At times of planting and harvesting, I will often lend out some men to help the local growers with their crops. You see, it is too costly for them to hire someone full time, but too much work for one individual in the busy weeks. It is simply the neighborly thing to do." Tyler arose and retrieved a pipe and tobacco from a desk drawer before continuing. "So, it was springtime, and that particular year we had received excessive rain. The stream beside Darcy's home was swollen and impassable."

Breckenridge paused to fill his pipe. "Before I go any further, an important side note you must understand is Darcy Calhoun's compassion for animals. He has two dogs that he adores, animals that travel with him everywhere. And some years ago, when there was a crop failure, my mother gave him a young pig because she was worried that Darcy wasn't getting enough to eat. He named it, and raised it as a pet. I also suspect that a few chickens he kept lived unusually long lives."

John smiled, and Tyler continued. "The two men were working the land when they heard a kind of scream; a nightmarish sound that Devon could only describe as something ungodly. They both rushed immediately to the stream. What they saw when they got there was a mule, struggling as if caught on something beneath the surface. It seems a man had made the hasty decision to cross the animal a few hundred yards upstream, but the current was much too strong. So here, before Darcy's cabin, the animal lay entangled in its harness, lashing at the water, fighting to keep its head above the surface.

"Devon, understandably, hesitated by the shore. I cannot stress to you enough, John, the danger of the situation. But Darcy Calhoun did not even pause. He just jumped right in." Tyler stopped briefly, as if to pay respect to the feat with a moment of silence. "He disappeared beneath the water, and Devon ran back to the house to gather some rope. When he returned, the animal was giving up, its head just bobbing at the surface, and Darcy was nowhere in sight.

"Then, to hear Devon tell it, Darcy came bursting up out of the water with the end of the harness in his hand. Devon threw him the rope and helped to guide Darcy and the mule to a shallow bank. It was then that Devon saw what had happened to Darcy. He had been caught by a hoof, and his stomach had been sliced open clear up to his ribs. The doctor didn't think he would survive it. It was a good month before Darcy was up and around again. . . . All of that to save a mule that wasn't even his."

John summoned to mind the simple man standing before the court in Charleston, hunched a little as the catcalls rained down on him from above. He reconciled the image with the softhearted animal lover who had risked his life on impulse. He didn't really need Tyler's words of summation to complete the picture.

"So you see, John, if a runaway happened on Darcy Calhoun's land, well, I just figure that Darcy . . . well, he jumped right in. Never bothering to think of the consequences."

John was not sure what caused him to awaken. All he knew was that it was pitch-dark, and he didn't know where he was. He felt that he had been asleep for some time. The bed didn't seem to be moving, thank God. Awareness came slowly—of soft sheets, curtains fluttering in a faint breeze, a scent of lavender from the pillow—ah, the plantation.

Then he was aware of footfall in the hallway, the intermittent click of an animal's nails on hardwood and the heavier sound of boots on carpet. The steps stopped outside his door. Then silence. John lay motionless, listening, and eventually became aware that he was holding his breath. He heard the scraping sound of a match being struck, then several breaths later, detected the smell of tobacco smoke. He lay with all senses trained in the direction of the door for what seemed like several minutes. Then a board creaked and the boots began to walk away down the hall, followed by the staccato click of the animal.

"The massa neva' sleeps."

What is it that never sleeps? The primitive part of John's brain was telling him that something was wrong. Something wasn't adding up. And because it was in these dark hours of the morning, when small pains become illness and all troubles are magnified, suddenly nothing was adding up.

Why was he a guest on this plantation? Why would a man like Breckenridge give him the time of day? And who exactly was he? The man could sit as still as stone, then strike like a snake. He was so very reasonable, yet John thought him capable of lying without compunction. He was a gracious host, a loving guardian to his sister and niece . . . and he was utterly ruthless. He was twenty-four going on forty. So why did he like him?

John resolved never to let his guard down with this man, never for a moment. . . . Then it was daylight.

THIRTEEN

◠

John stepped outside into the yawn of a Carolina morning. The dewy grass slipped gently beneath his shoes as he descended from the front porch onto the lawn. The front of the house was calm today; the scene lacked the activity and the obstacles that had enlivened yesterday's arrival. The only sounds were birdsong and the hum of the summer cicadas. He rubbed his eyes and took a deep breath, happy in the moment of serenity.

John brushed his hands down the body of a light brown suit, one of three tailored outfits he had found this morning hanging in his closet. His own ill-suited clothing had gone missing, sparing him an unwanted decision. An air-light, comfortable, and attractive suit was his only option.

He walked along the side of the house, outside the row of hedges that fenced the rose garden. As he reached the path at the garden's entrance, he glanced inside and saw Clio Breckenridge, her back to him as she tended the flowers. He walked up behind her, then paused as she pulled her arm back abruptly from a stem. She delivered a delicate sigh as she removed a gardening glove and raised her pricked finger to her lips.

"Good morning, Miss Breckenridge," he said, removing his hat.

She dropped her hand and turned. "Oh, good morning, Mr. Sharp," she answered sweetly, still pressing together her thumb and index finger. "Did you have a good night's rest?"

"Yes, thank you. I couldn't help but see what just happened. Are you all right?" He walked forward, pulling a handkerchief from his pocket.

"Oh, of course." She looked down uncertainly, staring for a moment at her hand. She reached forward and allowed John to wrap the handkerchief around her finger. "It is really nothing. In fact, it happens so often that I am surprised I can still even feel it."

"Why do you do it, then?"

She smiled, turning back toward the roses, her skirt fanning eloquently in response. "You see, Mr. Sharp, one must be fastidious with roses such as these." She reached in and removed a small yellow-and-black-speckled leaf, then dropped it into the pocket of her apron. "If not properly monitored, this black spot can kill the bushes. Besides, the leaves make them much less attractive."

"Why don't you have a . . . servant do it instead?"

"Because I enjoy tending them, of course. Mother loved the roses too, you see. She started teaching me to care for them when I was a little girl."

"Would it distract you if we talked while you work?"

"Not at all, Mr. Sharp." She smiled as she replaced her glove and resumed her activity. "So tell me, what is it that you have planned for today?"

"I intend to visit Cowford. I hope to speak with some of the residents regarding Mr. Calhoun." He drew a long breath. "Do you think they will be receptive?"

"Truly, I do not know. I know this might seem strange, but people just don't talk about it out here. There has been barely a whisper of it since the news initially spread throughout the area. I think people are . . . Well, I think they are somewhat embarrassed by it. As if it reflects somehow on them as well."

"Why would that be?"

"Because, as reclusive as the man may have been, he was still a member of the community. And there is a certain unquestioned trust that accompanies that. So, perhaps it is that they feel a mixture of betrayal and guilt."

"Do you feel that way also?"

"Absolutely not," she answered in an even tone. "Each man makes his own decisions, right or wrong. I take no responsibility for them, whether they be to run off and fight in Texas or to help assist a fugitive slave." She paused. "For me, community identity only extends to a certain point."

"Did you ever meet him?"

"Yes. And he always seemed a simple, good man, which is why this is all very sad." She shook her head a little. "He was always so very self-conscious if Tyler and I stopped by that Tyler suggested we leave the poor man in peace. Instead, we had our people check on him periodically and sent things to him that way."

She moved on to another rosebush, and John shifted the conversation. "So tell me, what must *you* do today?"

"Well, since it is Sunday, the first thing I will do is go to church." She gave him a look, a playful glance that chided him for his own forgotten piety. "But after that, I will be entirely consumed with the final preparations for tomorrow's party."

"Is there really much left to do?"

"Unfortunately, yes. The remaining chores are all relatively minor—seemingly simple tasks that are more time-consuming than difficult. But, as my mother always professed, it is the simple things that make a party elegant. They are the things the guests remember."

Clio looked back at the roses. "So tell me, Mr. Sharp, which are your favorites?"

John considered for a moment. "I think I'm partial to the deep red ones."

Clio carefully cut several teacup-size blooms and placed them in her basket. "I'll have these sent up to your room. But now, I think it's about time to get ready for church."

• • •

Later that morning, John attended service with the Breckenridge family. Trapped inside the oppressively hot family chapel, he endured a lengthy dissertation from Reverend Mimms on the parallel between the pagan idols of the Old Testament—Baal, Dagon, and the Golden Calf—and the evils of contemporary society. The sermon struck him more as a divine test of man's patience than any sort of self-applicable lesson. Mercy came a full hour and a half after the introit.

Before Tyler left to make his rounds on the plantation, he supplied John with directions to Cowford as well as a reliable mount. After barely surviving a scourge of swarming mosquitoes, John rode into the town at the height of midday.

Cowford struck him as an accident. It was a town built at the intersection of two country roads and founded, perhaps, in anticipation of trade routes that never materialized. The woodframe buildings seemed huddled together for support. Few had ever known a coat of whitewash, and those that had were now faded to drab. Almost half of the town's windows were boarded up, and the remainder peered from behind a coat of dust with a look of desolation. Time, it seemed, now lurked patiently, ready to overcome the last holdouts.

John tied his horse to the only visible hitching post, just outside the general store. Over the next hour, he worked his way from one end of town to the other, braving sagging stoops and porches to pound on rickety doors. He asked the townsfolk about their neighbor, Darcy Nance Calhoun, but most had little to say. Anger at Darcy or suspicion of John's profession formed a barrier—John was barely able to coax a few comments.

"He's a damn scoundrel," Mr. McGee had professed, his lip quivering. "What he gone and done proves he was never worth a salt anyways."

Mrs. Toth was a bit more sympathetic. "I'm just glad his mother ain't alive to see it. She was a good woman. Agreeable and hardworking. All this would just have killed her."

John did glean bits of hard information from among the residents' stock answers. Darcy was generally liked, if seen as a bit slow and helpless. He handed out jars of preserves during the holidays and gave the children candies when he had them. Several commented on his voracious appetite. He was rarely seen without a strap of jerky or an apple at hand, and the owner of the general store mentioned he ate nearly twice as much as any other man in town.

John also managed to get directions to Darcy's church, just a half mile from the center of town.

There was no sign marking the small church, just a raised cross above an arched door. John walked through the open door into a cramped room where a lectern stood midway between an altar and four rows of pews. John guessed that a well-attended service might hold no more than thirty parishioners.

A young man wearing a religious collar and a suit of good quality emerged from the sacristy door at the rear. He held a broom.

"Reverend Rose?"

"Yes," the man answered, lengthening the word in uncertainty.

John looked at him. His boyish face was adorned with precisely manicured muttonchops. John, who had not expected to encounter a reverend no older than himself, offered a friendly smile. "My name is John Sharp. I'm a reporter visiting from New York. Could you perhaps spare a moment?"

"You wish to speak about Darcy Calhoun." As John nodded, the reverend rested his hands at the top of the broom handle and explained his conclusion dryly. "It was not hard to guess. What else would lead a man from New York here to Cowford?" He looked around him, as if the confines of the room spoke to his point.

"Will you talk with me then?"

As John stepped forward, the reverend glanced down at the broom, then propped it in a corner. "I s'pose. But this will have to be quick. I have another service in Bensonville later this afternoon."

John sat in the first pew as Reverend Rose began collecting hymnals. "Can you tell me anything about Darcy Calhoun as a man?"

"What have you heard?" The question implied impatience, the desire to avoid covering old ground.

"Not very much. So far as I can tell, he lived a simple life with few intimate friends. He had a love for animals and food. He was a hard worker. He was kind to his neighbors. And he was deeply religious."

As John finished, there was no break in the reverend's activity or any sort of acknowledgment. John filled the silence by adding, "And I heard that he was . . . well, less than smart."

The reverend straightened; the last point seemed the only one of sufficient interest to trigger a response. "No, Darcy was certainly no scholar. He couldn't read and, outside of his name, couldn't write either." He placed a stack of hymnals in one of the two boxes on the first pew. "But he wasn't stupid. I'd be hard-pressed to find a member of any of my congregations who had a better knowledge of the Scripture."

"Memorized? But how?"

"Devotion," he replied. His tone implied that it was a quality John might lack. "Whenever I read a passage that moved Darcy, he would ask that I teach it to him. I would repeat the text over and over until he was able to recite it himself. He often committed the short passages to memory in one visit. Some of the longer ones could take weeks. But he was truly committed. Entirely devoted."

"Do you remember any of his favorite passages?"

Reverend Rose lost focus and smiled. "As I recall, he was particularly fond of the Psalms."

"Can you tell me anything else about him? You are the only one to perceive that he wasn't dim-witted."

Reverend Rose nodded slowly, his eyes downcast in thought. "Darcy had an adaptable quality that was really quite remarkable. He seemed to recognize his deficiencies and find a way to work around them. He tended a fine garden, and although his cotton field was small, he usually brought in a good crop."

"So he was somewhat of a green thumb."

"Yes. But his versatility stretched beyond farming. He devised quite an interesting trick for understanding directions. You see, when his garden produced a surplus, he would sometimes travel to some of the more distant towns in order to sell it. Since I travel throughout a wide area in my ministry, he would oft come ask me how to get to Pekin. Or Hampshire. When he asked, he brought with him a few strands of string. As I explained the route—for example, following the right fork in the road as it split—he would tie one piece of string to the other, knotting in the direction which he should take." The Reverend mimicked the action with his fingers. "He had a whole number of symbols that he devised. Two short knots indicated a stream. Three knots for a hill. His speed and dexterity in making these maps was really quite amazing."

"It does sound rather ingenious."

"Yes. As I said, Darcy was not stupid." Reverend Rose had now picked up the last of the altar cloths. "Well, then . . ." His tone implied the end of the interview. He began to walk amid the pews, collecting Bibles.

"Sir, might I ask you one final question?"

"Go on," he muttered without looking.

John knew his question was a delicate one. He stood up and began to assist by gathering Bibles from his own pew. "Do you think that there was something in Mr. Calhoun's religious beliefs that caused him to act the way he did? In the supposed crime?"

Reverend Rose stood up straight, balancing the stack of books against his chest. His voice was caustic. "I wonder if the same question is asked every time a northern man commits a crime. Somehow, I think not. You know, Mr. Sharp, your motives are entirely transparent. If I gave you an affirmative response, your story could be packaged perfectly."

"I am sorry, then, that I have to disappoint you, sir. For Darcy's crime was not motivated by the church's teachings, but by a moment of weakness in which he succumbed to bad judgment." The growing flush on the reverend's cheeks reflected his passion. "If you believe anything else, then you are only fooling yourself. For here in South Carolina, *our* religion is compatible with *our* way of life."

John paused, allowing the reverend a moment of composure. "I beg your pardon, sir, for upsetting you. And I thank you for your time." John picked up the box of Bibles, silently asking where they should be set.

"If you would be so kind as to put them in the wagon just outside on the street."

John Sharp nodded and left the church.

After placing the Bibles in the rear of the cart, John turned to walk away. The reverend's call surprised him.

"Mr. Sharp, could ya wait for a moment, please?"

"Of course," he replied, walking back toward the wagon.

"If you might indulge me with a question of my own?" He paused, then fixed John with a hard gaze. "Why are you doing it, Mr. Sharp?"

"Sir?"

His voice was less aggressive, but still cold. "I do not understand your interest, nor what you may hope to accomplish. This story you are covering, it is not of some New Yorker being subjected to southern law. There is no grave injustice here." He looked up at the sky and drew a breath. "Darcy, he is a South Carolinian. He is a part of our society, and is bound by our laws. The nature of your purpose here stumps me."

John recognized that something deeper than his question had caused the reverend's agitation. He opted for a direct response, but kept his voice level, emulating Breckenridge's manner by keeping emotion out of the equation.

"I will explain my question," he said softly. "Many churches in the North preach that slavery is wrong. Darcy's action upholds rather than violates the northern churches' concept of what is right."

Reverend Rose interrupted. "But what they in the North perceive as wrong is entirely legal here—was legal even in biblical times. Here slavery is not against the law. But divesting a man of his property is. And breaking the law is wrong."

"As you stated yourself, laws vary from state to state. Do you suggest, then, that morality is relative?"

The reverend's voice quivered. "What are you implying? What are you trying to do here?"

John continued to speak softly. "I am not implying anything. I am trying to uncover the truth of the matter."

"What is truth?" His tone was exasperated. He turned back toward the wagon, then froze abruptly. "John 18:38," he whispered. Then, without turning, he mounted the wagon.

With Cowford at his back, John reached into his saddlebag and pulled out the map showing directions to the home of Darcy Calhoun, supposedly two miles distant. The map proved useless almost immediately. The vague and bucolic instructions had John scrutinizing every tree he passed as a potential landmark. Beside an *X* on the map were the words "Follow the path that lies just beyond the mossy oak." The problem was, John had seen a number of oaks, was unsure how to interpret what constituted a "mossy" one, and had found nary a path since he started. He longed for the luxury of street signs.

Fortunately, John's horse was thirsty. It led him to a stream, and through the trees he made out a small cabin on a rise with cleared land behind it. He rotated the map, and the details seemed to fit.

John heard a sharp bark, then another slightly weaker in pitch, and soon two dogs were barreling down the bank toward him. They were homely mongrels, but well fed and obviously friendly. John's horse gave them a cursory glance, then ignored them.

He rode up to the cabin, dismounted, and tied the horse to a nearby sapling. He paused to pet the dogs, then began to walk around the home, hoping for confirmation. At the side he found a sizable garden, and beyond that, what seemed to him a considerable cotton field. A thin black man who was working the field with a hoe had apparently been alerted to John's presence by the dogs. John called out a greeting.

The man dropped the hoe and walked swiftly toward him, his right arm emerging from his pants pocket with a document he waved before him.

"Got my paper right here, sir," he called as he approached.

"Paper?"

"Yessir." He stopped just in front of John and handed him the sheet. "My letta from Mr. Breckenridge saying I's supposed ta be here. You look there. Got his sign and all right there at the bottom."

John could see why the slave was impressed with the importance of the paper. It was of high quality, and the precision of the script would put most documents of state to shame.

The man's finger ran along the line of text as if leading John through it. Then he tapped the signature for emphasis. The note read, "Josey of Willowby Plantation is working the Calhoun land under my authority. T. Breckenridge."

John handed it back immediately. "I do not question that you are supposed to be here."

The black man folded the paper and stuffed it back in his pocket. "No matta, then. What can I do for ya, sir?"

"This is Darcy Calhoun's land," John confirmed.

"Yessir. Mr. Breckenridge is having me tend to it till he comes back." He started to reach for the note again.

John waved his hand and shook his head. "Then you live at Willowby?"

"Yessir. I just come out here in the afternoons. Make sure everything is looked afta." Josey added with a smile, "I gets to pick the ripe vegetables for myself for doing the watering on Sunday."

John surveyed the land around him, making a slow point turn. The size of the lot seemed an extraordinary task for one man to manage. Tyler Breckenridge's comment about the need for additional help at the times of planting and harvest was now entirely clear.

"Anything else you'll be a-needing me for, sir?"

"No," John answered. "Thank you for your help."

"No botha, sir," he replied, then returned to the field. The dogs bounded after him playfully.

John walked back to the front of the cabin. The building was reasonably well built. A brick fireplace rose up beside the slanted shake roof, and a covered front porch stuck out a comfortable length from the home itself. A raccoon pelt was stretched and nailed to the wall just beside the front door, and a few feet farther down a washboard rested on the rim of a water-filled barrel. The only other feature was a slew of mud-dried footprints tromped chaotically atop one another.

He opened the door and walked inside. There was an austerity to the two-room cabin that bordered on spartan. The table in the front room sat attended by two chairs; one, with a flowered seat cushion, might have belonged to Darcy's late mother. The empty chairs gave the cabin a sad, abandoned feel. There was a hutch, a fireplace, and an ancient but well-kept firearm mounted on the wall, but nothing more. No amenities, no luxuries.

The back room, a bedroom, was small and dark, even in the daytime. Beside the bed was a dresser with a washbasin and towel on top.

A small cross hung off-center on the wall opposite the door. The bed was made, the towel folded neatly.

The aspect John found most surprising about the home was its comparative neatness, especially considering the pastoral setting. There was little dust, no clutter, no sight of trash. The only jarring elements were the numerous muddy tracks that littered the floorboards throughout the . . .

John felt a weight in the pit of his stomach, a feeling he had commonly battled at crime scenes in New York. The footprints told the story—a frozen witness of the felony itself. The tracks ranged in size, the imprints left by a number of different men. He counted as many as six unique sets of prints.

But the most disturbing tracks were of those alone in the corner by the table—bare, unshod prints, discernible by the toes. The parade of mud led toward it, that spot in the corner, and John could almost see the convergence of men around the quivering slave.

He returned outside, back to the porch, still transfixed by the hardened imprints. Beside a ridge of caked dirt there was a speckle of white. John hunched down and flicked away crumbling clumps of mud, tugging from beneath it several lines of interconnected string. One of Darcy's maps, indecipherable in his hands as nothing more than limp strands. As he spread it across the floor of the porch, though, its features became readable. Knots at the root of each divergent string spoke of direction, while clumps of knots told of landmarks. It was, as the reverend suggested, quite an amazing idea from a universally belittled mind.

"What the heck ya doing here?!" a distant voice yelled out.

John leaped to his feet and stuffed the string into his pocket as he looked about. He saw no form to accompany the voice. He descended the steps and heard a mumble of words coming from the field. As he approached, the slave was again away from his hoe, speaking at a distance to a white man as he flapped the paper at his side. John walked toward them.

". . . 'Cause Mr. Breckenridge done told me to, sir," the slave stated.

"Can't see as why," the short man slurred, a shotgun pitched against his shoulder. "Alls know he ain't a-coming back."

"Well, all the same," the slave replied with a shrug of the shoulder.

That seemed to be the end of their conversation, and John walked quickly to intercept the traveler before he departed.

"Excuse me," he said at a fast step. "A moment, please."

The man, now but a few paces away, turned toward him. His nose had been broken on more than one occasion, improperly repaired, and left to look like a jagged prominence on the face of a cliff. He snuck his words past an inflated cheek of tobacco. "Who the heck is you?"

"My name is John Sharp. I am visiting from New York. Staying at Willowby."

He nodded slowly, a dullardly, drawn-out rock of the head. "And?"

"And I was wondering, did you know Darcy Calhoun?"

The man squinted from beneath the short brim of his porkpie hat. "Knew him much as a man knows the dirt." He stomped his foot twice. "It's there. Wasn't much friendly with him, if that's what ya mean."

"May I speak with you about him for a moment?"

The man stood frozen for a moment; the fabric from his worn cotton clothes was wrinkled and loose at the joints. "I's kinda in a rush. Got someplace I gotta get."

John glanced back at the horse. It was well secured and grazing contentedly. "Could I walk with you, then?"

After a moment of contemplation, he nodded. "I s'pose."

John stuck forward his arm and shook hands firmly. The man then loosed an arcing line of brown spit over the connection. John recoiled and said dryly, "I do appreciate your time."

The man brushed it away. "Ain't no botha. Beauregard Throckmorton's the name. Done lived in this neck of the woods all my life."

The name, aristocratic in all but the pronunciation, brought a smile to John's lips. Beauregard leaned to the ground and picked up two dead ducks by their necks, slinging them over the shoulder opposite the rifle. A fifteen-inch bowie knife hung from the scabbard on his belt. They walked off into the Carolina woods with Beauregard Throckmorton armed to the teeth, and John Sharp harboring the uncomfortable feeling they were off to join a skirmish.

Rapidly falling behind the spry native, John attempted to lasso Beauregard with a question. "Where are you heading?"

" 'Bout three miles up from here. At the Wilcox land. Folks is gathering for a party there. Should be pretty wild. Tonight there's gonna be music and dancing, a big ol' feast, and I even heard Ryan Wilcox got his hands on some of that forty-rod whiskey."

"What is that?"

He whoomped a vulgar laugh that sent the nearby birds to flight. "That there is whiskey so strong that once ya drink it, ya feel like your head is forty rod lengths from your body."

"How delightful." John's mouth unwittingly curved. "But it is Sunday."

"Uh-huh. All the best parties is on Sunday." Beauregard looked at John, his eyes never fastening on one spot for more than a second. "You can come if ya want. Ya see, I'm a pretty big man 'round here. Lived in this neck of the woods all my life. So, if I says you is all right, then ain't no one gonna up and botha ya. So, if ya want, you can come along."

"I'm truly tempted," John replied. "But I'm already promised for dinner."

Beauregard shrugged, then ducked beneath a low vine. "No problem. It's gonna be you who's missing out. The party should be going till well in the morn. Food and drink and women." He hummed an anticipatory laugh.

"I suppose it makes Monday's work nearly unbearable. These common Sunday night parties."

Beauregard's face twisted in puzzlement. "Work?" He returned to a grin before imparting his simple wisdom. "Work is for fools and slaves. Us Throckmorton men is like the Breckenridge and the Campbell. No proper man 'round here works."

"And how is it that you survive?"

"Like every Throckmorton man has for generations. Hunting and fishing. Every once in a while taking odd jobs." He laughed. "For us Throckmorton men, working runs against our character. That's what Daddy always said." The regal sentiment was followed by a protracted line of spit, some of which clung to the whiskers on his chin.

John waited a few moments, respectfully ensuring that Beauregard had concluded his explanation of the family creed, before returning to the matter of interest. "Could we speak about Darcy Calhoun?"

"Sure. What is it you's wanting ta know?"

"Anything at all you could tell me about him. The kind of man he was."

"He was always kind of strange. You know, a little off. 'Twas like that since he moved 'round here—since 'bout ten years ago, I'd guess. He ain't never fit in. Never really had no friends. Some of the boys used to pick on him when they got liquored, 'cause he wasn't the sort for fighting back. Yeah, they messed with him early on."

Beauregard pointed them toward a trail, then continued. "I'd guess you'd say it got worse for him after his momma passed. Ya see, when she was still alive, it wasn't uncommon that you came across Darcy at a picnic or a party. I think she'd always drag him along, hoping that one day he'd fit in more normal like. Maybe someday find him a wife." He clicked his tongue and shook his head at the thought's absurdity. "But afta' she died, ya never much saw him no more. Not unless you happened across him in town or on his land."

They reached an open clearing, where John was happy to again travel fully upright and without fear of being impaled on a pointed branch.

"So tell me," Beauregard began, "what is it that has ya so interested in Darcy anyways?"

"I work for a newspaper, and I am writing a story that involves Mr. Calhoun."

"Oh," he voiced, stretching the exclamation out in interest. "You's a storyteller."

"Well, yes. I suppose."

Beauregard Throckmorton's expression resembled a child's bewilderment. "Why would ya wanna tell a story 'bout Darcy? It'll go and put folks to sleep faster than foxglove and laudanum."

"The interest, to a high degree, involves his crime."

"I see," he responded, somewhat dubiously.

"Now, about the—"

"Ya know, there's a lot of real interesting stuff that goes on 'round these parts. The kind of stuff good for stories."

The man's eyes rebounded from sight to sight. John felt as if he could almost see the wheels turning as Beauregard's mind searched for a story-worthy peculiarity. He decided a preemptive question was in order.

"What did you think when you heard of Darcy's crime?"

It took a moment for Beauregard to digest the question. "Oh, his hiding that nigger. Well, I thought that was 'bout the dumbest thing I ever heard. Even coming from Darcy as it was."

"Dumb in the sense that he was bound to be caught?"

"Sure," he answered. "But even dumber in the sense that he was passing up on a sure reward. Folks will pay twenty or twenty-five dollars if ya catch a runaway. I's even heard of a man getting forty fo' catching a whole family. Darcy done passed up on sure money. And all he had to do was turn the nigger in." He spit down at the ground. "Heck, if I'd have known there was a runaway in these parts, I'd have been out looking myself. And instead, Darcy set to hiding him. I tell ya, it's the dumbest thing I eva' heard."

Beauregard looked at the sky and scratched his whiskers. "On the line of that storytelling we was talking on before, I bet ya didn't know that you's in the proximity of *the* Miles O'Brien farm."

"No," John answered in an ignorance extending beyond geography.

"That there is where they unearthed the potato that was the spitting image of Senator John C. Calhoun himself. Saw it with my own two eyes, I did. 'Twas big news 'round here. So much so that they rounded them up a delegation of folks, and they took the potato to Columbia, where the senator was giving him a speech. Heard he took one look at it and turned white. The man was speechless. Then he sorta stumbled over his words and said that he ain't never seen a potato that looked more like him. Not in all his life. Quite a story, huh? Got dozens of 'em. I'll remember me a few more once I get some liquor in me at the Wilcox. You coming?"

John was as sure as God made little green apples that he wasn't wanting to go to the Wilcox party. He shook his head no. "I really must be getting back. I left my horse tied up back there, and I'm already promised for dinner."

"I'd give ya an invite for next week, but I'll be pulling my shift of wearing the blue."

"What do you mean?"

"Me and the Farnsworth boys got called up for the militia. Taking our turn in Charleston."

"How long will you need to serve?"

"Just ten days."

John figured that was about as much as the unsuspecting population of Charleston would be able to handle.

Back at Willowby, before dinner, Tyler had inquired politely about John's visit to Cowford and Darcy's cabin.

"I hope you didn't have any trouble finding it."

"No. The 'mossy oak' on the map was a dead giveaway." John felt he was mastering the art of Breckenridge-like responses. The secret was in the inscrutable delivery—expression and inflection could offer no clue.

"I assume you ran into my man Josey?"

"Yes, he was busy tending the fields. Everything seems to be in order there. Undisturbed. I had wanted to see how Darcy lived. Now I know."

"Did you encounter anyone of interest?"

John named the Cowford residents he had met and interviewed, but Tyler's attention seemed to wander. He was preoccupied during dinner as well.

Although plans called for an early night because of the party the following day, the ladies prepared a game of whist after dinner. The Breckenridges proved to be cutthroat card players, particularly the ladies. John suspected they used conversational diversions to impair their opponents' concentration. John kept his wits about him, however, and luck was on his side. He took more than his fair share of tricks, and his partnerships emerged victorious. By the end of the evening, Clio and Mary Ellen were demanding a rematch.

"With the party tomorrow night, that will have to wait until we get back to Charleston," Tyler remarked. He noted John fidgeting with his pocket as they rose to bid the ladies good night.

"Have you been hiding an ace in there?" he asked dryly.

John withdrew his hand, and with it the piece of knotted string he had retrieved from Darcy's cabin.

Tyler glanced at it, then looked John in the eye. "I get it. You've been using that to count cards."

FOURTEEN

John heard a gentle knock as soon as he had began to stir about his room. He hastily pulled on a long robe, then walked over to unlock the door. The robe was obviously Tyler's, because it trailed on the floor behind John as if he was mounting the dais for his coronation.

Ellis, the young manservant who had apparently been assigned to him, offered a cheerful greeting. "Happy Independence Day, sir." Curtains were opened, flooding the room with light.

While John partook of his breakfast tray of coffee, fruit, and biscuits on a small table adorned with a vase of Clio's red roses, Ellis delivered John's freshly polished shoes and hung his cleaned suit from the preceding day in the closet. He laid out a handsome tan ensemble.

"Will this do for ya, sir?"

With John's reply in the affirmative, the man withdrew, then reappeared after John had dressed.

At John's request, Ellis showed him to a quiet upstairs parlor where he could work on his notes away from the bustle of party preparations.

"Just don't tell Massa Breckenridge we put you in here," he said in a conspiratorial tone as he nodded toward the room. "The massa ain't crazy 'bout the portrait."

John nodded. "One other thing. I had something in the pocket of the suit I wore yesterday—the one you just returned. It was made out of string. I can't seem to find it. Could you check for me, please?"

Ellis's brow knotted. "String, sir? I will ask about it, sir."

The parlor had been a lady's room. Lace curtains provided the backdrop for bright floral upholstery and graceful light-toned woods. A collection of porcelain figurines and delicate blown glass decorated the tables and the top of a small bookshelf of leather-bound classics in Greek and Latin. A book of botanical watercolors sat open on the coffee table as if in use just moments ago. John noticed a cane resting in a stand beside the sofa. It had an L-shaped handle inset with rose-colored cloisonné. It was a practical appliance rather than an accessory.

The portrait to which Ellis had referred graced the wall above a French mantelpiece. It was of Breckenridge, and could not have been more than a few years old. As John regarded the portrait, he wondered at first why Breckenridge disliked it. It was an excellent likeness of a worthy subject. Breckenridge stood relaxed beside a pillar of Willowby's south portico—handsome in a wheat-colored suit, one hand resting on the wrought-iron gate. His expression was pleasant, if unsmiling.

It would have been no strain for Breckenridge to pose for the portrait. From what John knew of him, there would have been no restlessness, no fidgeting in position. Yet the man appeared frozen in time like a wasp trapped in amber.

There was an unsettling quality to the eyes. The serious, slightly sad look the artist depicted was almost right—but not. When Breckenridge was not addressing someone directly, his eyes were always moving. Like the driver of a carriage on a busy street, he was constantly evaluating, aware of the position of all around him, and as a consequence, consummately aware of his own position. Here the eyes were frozen; unable to assess, unable to control, helpless against the passage of time.

• • •

John spent several quiet hours compiling the detailed notes of his interviews and impressions from the preceding two days. His notes fell roughly into two categories under the headings "Darcy Nance" and "Breckenridge."

In spite of the fact that John had only observed Darcy for a few minutes in the formal setting of the courtroom, he felt that his picture of the man was falling into place. It was a reflected image, of course— accounts from the eyes of others. But what had the poet Burns said? "O wad some Power the giftie gie us, to see oursels as ithers see us!" John nevertheless resolved to try for an interview. Maybe he could use his connection with Breckenridge to secure one. Right now, anything seemed possible.

As John reviewed his notes on his conversations with Breckenridge and his observations of Willowby, he could only shake his head. As opposed to Darcy, he had spent hours with this man. Yet he still had no idea of what to make of him. He looked again at the portrait, at the eyes. They seemed to be looking back at him from the instant the artist had committed to their capture. John wondered what he was thinking, then stopped as he began to feel the goose bumps.

A time later, John descended the stairs into a controlled commotion— the fleet but mannerly steps of passing servants whose steady mien showed a task-centered resolve. All were dressed formally, surprising given the hour, outfitted in starched white shirts and midnight black jackets. As they walked, each stride was answered by the tap of shoe on hardwood and the settling of a crisp pleat. The scene bordered upon surreal, and it seemed easy to imagine majestic formality being no farther than a room away.

John stood at the base of the stairs, watching the servants as they passed, their quick smiles displaying as much pride as courtesy. The hour no longer seemed in question. He guessed the sight would have been the same four hours earlier as it was now. Their party was upon them; the fact that they were working was irrelevant, for they were part of a performance. This was opening night. John guessed that they had dressed for their roles at daybreak.

He walked across the hall into the large parlor and saw Clio Breckenridge speaking with a manservant. John stopped a distance away, beside a table, and feigned interest in the floral display as they conversed.

"You see, the garlands are not intended to *festoon* from the balcony." She stretched the word and made a U shape with her hand. "Rather, they are to dip just slightly." She spoke more quickly than usual, not impolite, but hastened by pressure. "Do you understand?"

"Yes, miss."

"Then see to it, please."

As the servant walked off, John approached. "Good day, Miss Breckenridge."

"Oh, good day, Mr. Sharp." Her response was distant, lost somewhere between thoughts of ornamentation and impending arrivals.

As he drew within a few steps, he watched her eyes, lost in thought. "Is everything going all right?" he asked.

She flashed him a smile. "Oh, yes. Things have just managed to become a bit hectic." She used both hands to pull her hair back at the sides, then took a deep breath. "I do apologize that you have to see the house like this—in such chaos."

"I find the sense of anticipation rather exciting, actually."

"I am glad to hear it."

"Are you overseeing the preparations alone?"

"Oh, no. Mary Ellen is presently monitoring the kitchen. Considering the experience of our staff, I am sure she is trying their patience to the utmost." She laughed. "Most of the servants overseeing matters have done many parties in the past. They have a good idea of what must be done."

"And what of the host?"

"Tyler? He's off inspecting the plantation, of course. His lack of involvement on the day of parties is so common it's tradition. In fact, I would be surprised to even catch a glimpse of him before five o'clock." She smiled. "It is actually a blessing that Tyler does not fancy himself as helpful. Certain tasks should be left in the capable hands of the ladies."

Her eyes were moving again, and John prepared to leave her to the arrangements. "If I might ask you a question? I know this might seem terribly insignificant with your countless concerns, but I made the mistake of leaving something in the pants pocket of yesterday's outfit. Do you know whom I might see about its retrieval?"

She hummed for a moment. "If it was washed, there is a good chance it is lost. But, regardless, I'll check with Jenkins."

"Thank you."

She started to turn away, then stopped. "I may not be able to see you before the party, but Ellis will be able to fill you in on anything you need to know." She paused and flashed a coquettish smile. "I hope you will not fill your dance card too quickly this evening. I'm counting on you to rescue me from too many dances with our more elderly guests."

John subconsciously lowered his head a little. "I do not mean to disappoint you, but . . ." His throat clenched, and the sentence dangled.

Clio cocked her head, as if puzzled, then blurted with humor, "You can't dance!"

John shook his head and raised a palm in negation. "Yes, I can. I can waltz with the best of them," he stammered. "At least, I think I can. I'm just not sure about the local steps."

Clio flashed an impish grin and retreated hastily to the hallway door. She scanned the foyer. "Daisy! And Elijah! Come here, please."

A very pretty teenage black girl in a fine black dress and lacy white cap entered carrying an arrangement of lilies. "Do you want these in here, Miss Clio?"

"You can set them over there." She gestured vaguely at an end table. "Ah, Elijah. Please take a break and help us out."

An elderly, dignified black man entered and nodded gravely.

"We're going to teach Mr. Sharp the Carolina reel."

Elijah, who had certainly not danced the Carolina reel in his lifetime, looked totally nonplussed as he advanced to the center of the room. Daisy looked at John and stifled a giggle.

Clio dragged two armless chairs from a table and a writing desk and set them facing each other about eight feet apart. "These are the Carutherses," she intoned seriously. "Mr. Sharp, Elijah, you line up on either side of Mr. Caruthers. Daisy, you can stand opposite Elijah. Yes, you get to be a girl this time—but you are still going to have to lead.

"This dance is in four-four time at a lively pace. One-two-three-four. One-two-three-four," she clapped, singing the beat to a tune. "First, honor your partner. I mean bow to your partner. Then bow to your corners . . . Now we will swing our corners."

Clio skipped toward Elijah, who also advanced on the diagonal. Clio rotated Elijah as if he were an armchair on coasters and sent him back to his "home" position. Daisy then skipped forward and twirled John, with authority. She had obviously done this before.

"Now we repeat the same swing with the left hand." Both girls were humming and clapping now, and Elijah was rolling smoothly. "Now both hands."

That maneuver completed, Clio took both of John's hands in hers as Daisy continued to clap. "Now, partner, we are going to slide to the end of the row and back."

"Slide? On what?"

Daisy nearly doubled over.

"On the balls of your feet," said Clio, hopping and dragging the trailing foot.

"Men actually do this?" John asked. Elijah shot him an understanding look.

"Yes," Clio assured him. "But not like their feet are encased in cement."

They "slid" to the end of the row and back.

"Now, we separate and march around the other couples to the end of the line . . . No, John. Perhaps march was the wrong word. This isn't the militia drilling on the public green. Skip! . . . Now, we form an arch with our hands, and the other couples, including the Carutherses—use your imagination here—pass under . . . See, we are now at the opposite end of the line and the Caruthers become the lead couple. Now, lets do it again."

Clio and Daisy sang and clapped while John and Elijah stoically performed their maneuvers. John noticed that Clio's eyes had begun to sparkle, and her cheeks were flushed with color. He actually found himself skipping a bit.

Satisfied that John had assimilated a basic understanding of the Carolina reel, Clio released a disappointed Daisy and a grateful Elijah to their previous activities.

"Now let's try out that waltz." Clio held out her right hand and draped the left over the arm of an imaginary dance partner. "One-two-three, one-two-three . . ." She swayed and turned grandly. "Are we talking about the same dance?"

Not hardly. The box waltz John had performed with another recalcitrant freshman at prep school had been a kind of Puritan gavotte compared to the graceful, sweeping dance Clio was demonstrating. But John was no coward. He stepped forward and took her hand, resting the other on her slender waist.

She placed her left hand over his and pressed it firmly against her waist. "Hold me tighter, or it tickles." She moved her hand to his shoulder but did not make eye contact. "One-two-three. One-two-three . . . ," she began to sing softly.

At some point John stopped worrying about where he placed his feet. Or about counting. Or when to turn. Those things seemed to happen by themselves. Instead, he was aware of the shadow of her lashes on her cheek, soft breaths through parted lips, and the way his hand felt as he held her. He forced himself to keep his breathing steady.

"One-two-three, one-two-three . . ." Her singing trailed off. They danced a moment in silence, then slowly came to a stop.

Clio looked up at him. Her eyes were too bright and too dark at the same time, and her breaths were quick and uneven. A look of understanding passed between them—of vulnerability and power.

Clio cleared her throat and gave a low chuckle. "There is nothing wrong with your waltz, Mr. Sharp." She turned and walked to the door. "I'll see you tonight at the party."

FIFTEEN

⌒

It began by the pond, stirring the tips of willow wands to paint patterns on the water's glassy surface. It left branches swaying as it moved on to the meadow grass, lifting dandelion fluff like soap bubbles up the hill toward the cooking sheds. It fanned mesquite embers and set the game hens to sizzling on the spits, the juices dripping and sending up frequent puffs of smoke. The glossy-faced chefs sighed, closing their eyes and feeling the cool against their faces, inhaling the aroma of the roasting meat before it swept past them to the white tents on the lawn by the house. Chandeliers of strung seashells, paper thin, rustled and tinkled while the gossamer tent curtains lifted and swirled, making faint blue shadows on the flagstone walks. A lace valence fluttered above open French doors, and a wispy blond ringlet brushed a fair powdered cheek. Clio Breckenridge smiled.

John Sharp was halfway across the room, enraptured. His eyes would not have left her smile had her entire aspect not demanded it. The framing was perfect. The summer evening light through the French doors provided a glowing background for her alone, as if she were some mythological being visiting the mere mortals assembled in the dimmer world of the parlor. The dress was angelic white with a shimmer of beadwork at the sleeves and waist before flaring into a full hooped skirt. She wore pearl earrings in the shape of teardrops, and the twin strands of pearls about her neck were joined at the side with a diamond clasp. It looked as if she had captured a star.

John stood at the far corner of the parlor with three middle-aged guests introduced to him by Tyler Breckenridge. They, like most their age, gracefully bowed to the younger generation by living at the party's perimeter—a factor that forced the young reporter to lift himself ever so slightly on the balls of his feet. After a brief exchange of small talk, Mrs. Batt, the plump wife of the plumper gentleman next to her, leaned toward John and offered a dry observation.

"I see you are taken with the local architecture. Tell me, Mr. Sharp, do they have French windows where you are from?"

A smile met John as he turned back around. "Yes, ma'am, we do," he answered sheepishly. "But fenestration of all types has always fascinated me."

"I see," she said, craning momentarily back toward Clio, her subtle grin intact. She then tucked her arm inside John's and turned him slightly. "However, regardless the amount of interest, one should not strain so hard. It's bad for the eyes."

She shuttled John back a few feet to a strategic spot amid the volley of conversation. Mr. Gotter, a tall and refined man with a mustache that curled into an upward spiral, courteously briefed John on topic.

"Mr. Batt and I were just speaking about John Fremont's book— the tale that recounts his and Kit Carson's exploits in mapping the West. Tell us, Mr. Sharp, have you yet had the opportunity to read it?"

"Indeed, I have. I found it gripping. It's like there's another world just beyond us. The Great Basin and Rocky Mountains promise dangers and marvels we have yet to imagine."

Gotter flashed a smile of mutual interest. "Tell me, have you heard the rumor that the two were preparing for another expedition?"

"They say at my paper that it is no longer rumor. Supposedly they are outfitting for it now. My only regret is that we shall have to wait years before finding out more of their adventures." He took a drink of his bourbon. "But I believe that if they are again so successful, their names will have a place in history, as well as greatly further the dream of Manifest Destiny."

"Poppycock!" Mr. Batt exclaimed, a shot traced by a light rain of saliva. His voice was so loud John could feel others in the room turn toward them. "Mere Yankee propaganda, is all that is."

John, slightly startled, turned toward the portly man. Never, he thought, had formal attire appeared so ill adapted to the human frame. His shirt bloused awkwardly at his midsection, tucked tightly at one spot, billowing loosely at the next. His cummerbund tilted upward while his bow tie sagged, a sight that hinted the two articles hoped to eventually meet. Batt lifted his glass from a resting spot on the upper ridge of his belly and downed the remaining sips.

"Excuse me?" John said softly, balancing his tone to that of Batt's outburst.

His wife's scowl of censure was totally lost on Batt. He continued vociferously. "Manifest Destiny ain't nothing but a tool of Yankee tyranny. It's just an excuse, that's all that is. An excuse to soak up more land and carve it into states bent on nothing but furthering Yankee policies and annihilating the South." He took a breath and ushered the empty glass to his lips, staring with confusion at finding it dry.

Mr. Gotter stood still, at a loss for words. John Sharp did not.

"But, sir, that is not entirely accurate. The fate of the new lands has not yet been decided. And, under the spirit of the Missouri Compromise, it would be logical to assume that neither region, the North or the South, would gain enough states to manipulate the Congress. So, no matter how much land is acquired, it is really of no more advantage to one side than it is to the other."

"Compromise, you say? You go tell the Texans about your compromise. You tell them why the land they were promised ain't theirs no more. Why, the *Union* now says that land is for a new state—a state that's gonna bow down to whatever the North tells them to do. That ain't compromise, it's just plain thievery."

"The New Mexico Territory?" John questioned. "It would most likely enter as a slave state, or, at the least, one whose political affiliation is left to the vote of its residents."

"In which case the Yanks would move in enough squatters so that it was called New Wisconsin before it was called New Mexico. No, if you ask me, the Texans are justified in whatever actions they take to get back their land. The sooner they go ahead and cross the Pecos River to run off those troops, the better for us all. The government won't listen to reason, so maybe they should hear the rifle."

John's pitch dropped, his words weighted. "That act would probably lead to war."

Batt looked at John as if they, themselves, were formalizing the declaration and said sternly, "So be it."

John found himself considering the irony of Batt's position. The man's untempered anger would not move him a mile carrying pack and rifle. It would not see him through one bivouacked night, nor would it provide courage in the face of an enemy company. But it would not have to. John regarded the heavy man, now sweating profusely, whose ire seemed indefatigable. It is the old who want war, he thought, for they do not have to fight it.

"It looks as if you need a drink, Mr. Batt," Tyler Breckenridge said mildly, appearing from nowhere. "Allow me to have someone bring you over another."

Breckenridge, whose arrival was anything but chance, suggested just the opposite by his manner. He appeared casual, an unteachable skill when wearing formal attire. As he conversed with the group, the party felt intimate. There were no generalized comments, no routine questions, nothing impersonal. Mrs. Batt blushed as he detailed her prizewinning garden, Gotter stood a little taller as his host quoted one of his witty observations, and Mr. Batt chuckled as Breckenridge recounted how he had picked four straight winners in the spring stakes races.

"I am so pleased you all will be sharing this evening with us," he said, taking a step back. "Mr. Sharp, would you mind coming with me? There is someone I would like you to meet."

John agreed and bid leave. As the two men drifted back into the party, John gave Breckenridge a dry smile.

"I see you open your festivities here with fireworks."

Breckenridge traveled a nod to a guest as he passed, then answered in a level tone. "Yes, Mr. Batt can be quite spirited at times. I do hope that he wasn't too much for you."

"Of course not. He was merely a bit louder than I expected. But nothing—" The realization was swift. Tyler was too adroit to commit a gaffe by putting political antagonists next to one another. Not unless he intended to. John's voice was free of question as he muttered, "You knew that would happen."

Breckenridge continued his slow walk, but now focused on John. "You wanted unvarnished opinion, didn't you?" He did the half smile. Without whispering, his voice became quieter. "But yes, it wasn't hard to guess that Batt would be cantankerous. In order to cope with the outfit, the man has been drinking since ten this morning."

John laughed well, his mirth dissolving into the wash of party chatter.

"Now, let's see if we can find you someone a bit more congenial," Tyler said, ushering him toward the group near the piano. "Mrs. Livingston has three marriageable daughters. She should do nicely."

Above the parlor, three grand chandeliers were already lit, adding a yellow twinkle to the pale pink of the dwindling daylight. Countless dangling pieces of crystal amplified the candlelight, projecting a soft, dappled pattern on the walls and guests, augmenting the set's natural beauty—a beauty of white and light.

"So tell us, what are the parties like in New York?" a teenage girl asked excitedly.

Her friend interrupted immediately. "Yes, and what are the ladies wearing?"

"Are the buildings as tall as they really say?" another inquired, her porcelain face tilted upward.

"Is it true that northern ladies travel to Europe to find their husbands?"

It had been ten minutes since Mary Ellen Parker had stolen John from a polite, though rather dull, conversation with a couple oddly preoccupied with the topic of disease. She escorted him to the study, where they were met by five of her friends, a lively group that surrounded him in an ever-contracting semicircle. Since then the questions had flown faster than thought. One-word answers were common, sentences a rarity.

"You are all being silly," Mary Ellen lectured, looping her left arm inside John's right. "Mr. Sharp is unconcerned with such trivial things. As a reporter, he deals with much more serious topics. Like crime and murder. Even *prostitution*."

A response of shivered breaths met the description, as if the news was borne on a cold draft.

One girl placed her hand on her bare upper chest and spoke with dramatic concern. "Isn't your work terribly dangerous?"

Before John answered, he looked past the girls to the study door. Two boys, the same boys present since his arrival, paced the area like sentries, their poisonous stares more potent with each pass.

"Dangerous? It can be. But one takes precautions to decrease the chance."

A young lady leaned in and asked in a daring whisper, "Are the slums as bad as they are said to be?"

He whispered back darkly, "Worse," shivering the audience once again.

"And the prostitutes," another began, blushing so floridly one might have thought her likely to faint from her own question. "Are they everywhere?"

"In some districts they are said to outnumber even the rats."

As mumbled giggles sneaked past gloved hands, one young lady stated, "I find it impossible to imagine."

"Many curious New Yorkers have chosen to bypass imagination. Of late, it has become fashionable for the rich, themselves, to go slumming."

After the word was mischievously repeated, Mary Ellen squeezed tightly on John's arm. "What exactly is it?"

"Well, a group will visit a slum such as the Five Points. There, they will have a tour of the area, taking in the sights and sounds of the streets, witnessing the tenement houses, speaking with some of the less haggard residents. Oftentimes they will have their servants prepare a picnic lunch, which they will dine upon in the same manner as if they were visiting a park or zoo."

"But are they not accosted?"

"The rich pay well for their protection. They are always accompanied by guards—typically policemen—who ensure their safety. I have heard of no assaults or robberies on these outings."

"Remarkable." They sighed, looking at one another nervously, as if they had just been offered a tour of their own.

"But Mr. Sharp is much more courageous than that," Mary Ellen announced, again squeezing his arm. "He ventures without protection. That bruise by his eye is proof. He received it after being hit in the head with a brick during a near riot." She paused and allowed the sympathetic sighs to wilt. "Mr. Sharp is quite drawn to danger. Why, if there *is* a war, I would guess him to be reporting on it from the front lines. Isn't that right, John?"

"Let us hope it does not come to that."

"Indeed," one young lady agreed. "I'm sick to death of hearing all this war talk. It's as if the men and boys can speak of nothing else."

"Better just to have it over with," another chimed. "I have heard that if it does happen, it will only last a month or two. Better to hurry it along."

"Either way," Mary Ellen said, "just so long as things return to normal."

Reinforcements arrived outside the study, more boys with loaded glances. John thought it best to antagonize them no further.

"Ladies, it has been a pleasure, but I really must be getting back to the other room."

"Yes, yes," one said. "But first, tell us once again of the ladies."

"And the parties."

As a guest among strangers, John was powerless over his own movement. He was handed from one conversation to the next, steered by a simple introduction with no more volition than drifting jetsam. The current deposited him before a relatively young planter by the name of Kenneth Brent, who sported a pompadour, long, manicured fingernails, and a diamond ring on his little finger. He had apparently been sharpening his tongue in preparation for the eventual encounter. A third party, Mr. William Howery, was the innocent bystander.

Brent opened. "What does your family plant, Mr. Sharp?"

"They do not plant anything, sir. I am from New York City."

"I beg your pardon. I assumed, as you are a guest of Mr. Breckenridge, that your family were landed people."

"I am sorry to disappoint you. What do you plant, Mr. Brent?"

"Sea cotton."

"Oh, I understand that it is particularly soft and durable. Where is your market?"

"Primarily London and New York."

"Yes. I expect that New York's sophisticated markets would demand a quality product. Have you ever been there to see the end result?"

"I have no desire to. I'm afraid coal fumes and crowded tenements do not appeal to me. And neither do the politics of the locals."

"What politics are those?"

"Extremist politics. Don't pretend not to understand me, Mr. Sharp. Mr. Breckenridge indicated that we do not have to treat you with kid gloves. Surely you are aware that New York was the only state carried by that avowed abolitionist, Martin Van Buren, in the last presidential election."

"Yes, they did back Van Buren. And you were a supporter of John C. Calhoun, I assume?"

"I'm proud to say I was, God rest his soul."

"Most in the North viewed his politics as equally radical, I assure you."

Mr. Howery's voice was baritone, and in that octave the drawl was heavy. On their initial walk, Clio had described the accent as "more rice than cotton" and best facilitated by a translator. "Tell us, Mr. Sharp," he began, "how do most in the North view the president and his policies?"

"I believe that most recognize that President Taylor was a general, and that he continues to govern like one. His lack of diplomacy, as well as the perception that he refuses to hear certain voices of opposition, have left him rather unpopular."

Brent nodded. "At least we agree on that. Know this, if he does not quickly tame his treacherous tongue toward half the states he claims to captain, then, I assure you, he shan't captain them much longer."

"I wonder if you hint at his recent threat to hang Jefferson Davis if he continued to speak of secession?"

"I do not hint."

John decided it best not to point out that President Taylor's stand against Davis was one of his few popular policies among New Yorkers.

Howery's deep drawl offered moderation. "Regardless of one's opinion on the matter, I think we all might agree that now is an important time to speak cautiously, civilly. I pray that our president soon comes to that understanding and tames his rhetoric."

Brent smiled without amusement. "Well, if he does not, if he tries to follow up on his tough talk with action, he may be in for a surprise. For we are not buying what he is selling. He may have snuck those troops past the Texans, but our eyes are wide open down here in South Carolina, and we are ready for him."

There was a momentary silence, and Howery appeared to blanch. "Well now, Mr. Brent, I did not intend my statement to raise your ire. I just think that both sides should take a quiet look at what they have in common."

Brent appeared to ignore Howery as he leaned in toward John. Their eyes locked. "Come to think of it, Mr. Sharp, South Carolina and New York may *not* be all that different. In fact, I believe we share a certain pragmatism. Your decision to vote for Van Buren illustrates the death of compromise from your citizens, for we both know his election would have brought immediate secession. And we here are also sick of that word—compromise. Perhaps both of our states grasp the inevitable." He stuck out his hand and gripped John's firmly. He kept his voice low. "At least you and I *know* we are enemies." He released his grip. "But now, if you would excuse me, there are others here I must visit with. Good evening, Mr. Sharp."

"Mr. Brent."

"Mr. Sharp!"

John felt a tug at his sleeve and turned to glimpse a white-gloved hand disappearing back through a potted palm. He pulled aside a frond and met the shining eyes of Clio Breckenridge.

"Come around the screen," she whispered, casting a conspiratorial glance to his right.

A four-panel painted screen and several large plants hid a service door from the room full of guests. Silent servants passed back and forth from behind it with trays of drinks and canapés. John ducked back to find an amused Clio.

"How are you enjoying the party?" she whispered like an excited child.

"I'm enjoying it just fine," he responded, laughing.

She slipped an arm through his, pulling him closer, and they both looked out at the room through the palm.

The parlor and the hall were now filled with sparkling people. Notes from a piano rose and fell over the continuous hum of conversation and periodic bursts of gentle laughter. The scene was everything John had dreamed of from his childhood perch at the top of the stairs, with an added element of excitement he never would have guessed.

"Why the secrecy?" he whispered back.

"I'm hiding from my suitors." She was leaning lightly against him so that the servants could get by. She smelled like flowers. "And I wanted to talk with you. Without being the center of attention."

Huddled beside him, Clio now rested both of her hands on his forearm. Their conversation came in whispered phrases—with pauses for the rise of music and the passage of servants.

"Are the guests treating you well? Are my friends and neighbors minding their manners?"

John chuckled. "I have heard a few spirited points of view, but people have been polite enough. I will admit, though, that I feel a little bit like Duke."

Clio raised an eyebrow. "Like Tyler's dog?"

"When I was taking the tour the other day with your brother, we crossed a pasture of your dairy cows. Ostensibly, they kept on doing what cows do." John gestured toward the guests. "Munching, drinking, socializing in little cow groups—but meanwhile, every eye was tracking Duke."

Clio flashed a coy smile. "You are most definitely being watched, Mr. Sharp."

"Do New Yorkers in South Carolina really stand out so?"

"This particular New Yorker does."

John gave her a quizzical look.

"Well, for half of our guests, the reason is really quite simple." Clio paused as if she had just imparted the clue that explained all.

"Don't keep me in suspense," John prodded.

"In case you haven't noticed, you are easy on the eyes, Mr. Sharp." Clio looked up to the ceiling as if admiring the crown molding, while John felt his cheeks grow unnaturally warm.

Clio looked back at him playfully and lowered her whisper so that he would have to lean closer to catch her words. ". . . And the other half's trying to figure out what on earth you're doing here."

John laughed and shook his head. "I'm kind of confused myself. I'll bet it's really a puzzle to them. Quite vexing."

"Yes, but these people love puzzles. Half of their waking hours are spent trying to uncover each others' secrets."

"And how successful are they? Do all here know the secrets of everyone else?"

"All but Tyler's and mine." Several servants passed with trays while John thought that one over. Clio continued. "Our circle in Charleston and here in the country is quite small. People talk. . . . When I was younger, Tyler told me that I could listen to gossip all I liked, but I should be cautious about spreading it. So I try to use knowledge of others' affairs in a constructive way. As a good hostess, I must make guests comfortable in my home—steer conversations away from topics that might disturb them."

"Political topics?" he asked.

"More like things of a personal nature—errant relatives, poor harvests. Several men here have had poor harvests of late. We avoid talk of crop failure to spare them embarrassment. But everyone has secrets that are far from secret."

"So you find the secrets useful," John commented.

"My brother says that all knowledge is useful, whether one chooses to use it or not. If you know facts about someone, they explain his motivations—why he behaves the way he does, how he may behave in the—"

Clio pulled back immediately from the plants, tugging John back to the wall beside the servants' door. John looked through the fronds and saw Tyler Breckenridge standing no more than ten feet away. As one hand squeezed John's arm, Clio caught John's eye and raised an index finger to her lips.

After a moment, John dipped his head behind her ear and whispered, "And what is your secret, miss?"

John heard her breath catch as Tyler moved away. Clio raised her face to John's and gave a breathy laugh. "You should know, sir."

John delayed his departure after Clio exited from behind the screen. As he prepared to emerge, two gentlemen paused with their backs to him, blocking his escape.

"It has to be an embarrassment for Tyler."

"I should think so, happening right here on his doorstep."

"Particularly after Tyler befriended him and all," the first man added. "It reflects badly."

"Well, Tyler's making a public show of urging restraint, but I think he secretly hopes the man gets what he deserves. I'd say that Tyler would as soon see him hang as anyone."

It was that magical time just past sunset when colors intensify before fading to gray. Dinner was served under the large white tents set up on the lawn. Illuminated as they were by candlelight from within, the tents glowed like a string of paper lanterns. A few gauze panels were tied back to facilitate the circulation of air and servants, but most were left to billow like curtains in the gentle breeze from the sea.

John sipped clear ruby consommé from a silver spoon and marveled at the beauty of the young ladies as the candlelight painted their faces yellow-gold. They dined on shrimp and scallops baked in seashells, followed leisurely by roasted game hens and rich medallions of beef. By the time the cheeses and brandied fruits appeared, night's shadows flickered outside the tents' walls, imparting an intimacy to those cosseted within.

The diners talked of little things—of feathered hats and fast horses, of menageries and carousels and concerts in the park—and the wine made everyone terribly witty. Then the gentlemen excused themselves for brandy and cigars on the terrace, while the ladies stayed behind for cakes and sweet tea.

"Mr. Sharp," a mousy voice called from a step behind. "A moment, please."

John, on his way to the terrace, turned to find Mr. Joshua Mannion, the chief editor of the *Charleston Gazette*. They had been introduced to one another just before dinner. Mr. Mannion was quite diminutive, gaunt as a matter of fact, with his collar fallen and bunched at the bottom of his reedy neck, and both sad, slumping shoulders disappearing beneath the wide cut of his tuxedo.

"Of course, Mr. Mannion. I had hoped that we might speak." John made a motion toward the house, but Mannion stood firm.

"Perhaps we might rather stroll," he recommended, using one hand to battle the loose rim of his wire glasses. "I believe there is enough light left. The walk will afford us some privacy."

"Certainly." John followed him along the path that led toward the Willowby pond at a leisurely pace.

"So tell me, how have you found the party in general?" Mannion asked. "Are the guests treating you well?"

"Oh, yes," John answered. "Most have been quite kind."

"Is that right?" Mannion responded, balancing amusement with skepticism over the next few steps. "It might interest you to know that you and your presence here have become popular topics over the last days in Charleston. Most are aware of the death of your colleague and that you were endangered as well in that altercation by the courthouse." Mannion readjusted his eyeglasses and noticed John's expression fall. "I am sorry. I did not mean to trouble you."

"Of course not. It is only that I would rather report on news than be it."

Mannion's entire body nodded. "I understand. However, it is a price we sometimes pay when we venture into . . . foreign territory at a time of crisis." He removed his glasses and fiddled with them as he spoke. "In '42, I was a reporter sent to Philadelphia to study northern opinion on the annexation of Texas. As you know, the abolitionists and many others were staunchly against it, rightly figuring that Texas would enter the Union as a slave state. Somehow, the reputation that I wrote for the largest paper in Charleston preceded me, and at every gathering I attended I was met by—" He paused and smiled. "Let's just say that they were a bit vociferous with their arguments." He wiped his brow and put on his glasses. "Do you know why they acted that way, Mr. Sharp? It was because of my perceived influence." He stopped walking and turned to John. "That is why Mr. Batt erupted into his political tirade earlier this afternoon, as most likely did Mr. Brent, though he holds his liquor considerably better. You see, they know whom you write for, and they believe that by acting more stridently, they might somehow influence you, and in a grander sense, New York opinion. Or"—he paused—"they may simply wish to scare you." He chuckled. "I think, Mr. Sharp, that you are both more powerful than you know"—he waved a hand toward the plantation house—"and less powerful than they believe. If you come to grasp that, you will be a better reporter for it." He again began to stroll toward the pond. "Now tell me, what questions do you have for me?"

"Mr. Mannion, I had hoped that we might speak about Darcy Calhoun's trial. Why doesn't the *Gazette* report on it?"

"Report on what? Nothing has happened over the last few weeks. We reported Mr. Calhoun's arrest when it happened, we reported the hiatus, and we shall report the outcome at the time it is announced. Everything in between is merely speculation."

"But what of its effects on Charleston? What of the near riot outside the courthouse just the other day? What of the vigilantism? And the lynchings?"

"Now you begin to blur the issues. I understand that you have not been in Charleston that long, and hence, you judge the tumult as attributable to a primary source—Darcy Calhoun. That could not be further from the truth. Charleston's unrest arises from a combination of events and the suddenness of their onset. These events, more than Darcy's trial, have produced what you've seen. Darcy would not even be a story here if the abolitionists were not making a big deal about it in the North."

"Then what about the fires?"

They stopped on a level patch fifty feet from the pond, and Mannion took a deep breath. "The fires." He exhaled. "We have a different approach to reporting crime down here than journalists have in New York—a different perspective. So please bear with me for a moment.

"By our standards, crime reporting in New York is sensationalized. Your papers seek to excite and titillate the reader. Eventually, the public becomes desensitized, and shock is replaced by a simple desire for lurid gossip. Do the stories actually frighten anymore? Hardly. No more than a ghost story might, or a tale of pirates."

He raised a finger. "Now let me explain to you why it would not work here. It is not because southerners would not read it. I assure you, were a scandal sheet allowed to exist in Charleston, almost everyone would get his hands on a copy. No, Mr. Sharp, the reason is a simple one—danger. Let me put it to you this way. How much empathy exists for the victims of those crimes in New York? The ones you write about? When a prostitute is murdered, do you think the average woman feels a greater sense of danger? When rival gangs kill off one another in the Bowery, do those not in the gangs worry a great deal more? When a drunk is murdered in the Five Points, does a banker look up in his mansion and sigh, 'There but for the grace of God go I?' Of course not. Because there is distance. Safety.

"Now let me answer your question about the fires and your soon-to-come follow-up on the uprising—they are one and the same after all. The fires and the revolt threaten everyone who lives in Charleston. There is no distance from it, only a common knowledge that we all live amid that danger." He paused for effect. "Here in Charleston, as many blacks inhabit the city as whites. They live in our houses, cook our meals, and tuck our children into bed."

Mannion looked back at John, his face barely discernible in the darkness. "Do you know what might happen if we were to continuously write about revolt or arson, Mr. Sharp? Reaction. Violent reaction to unimaginable worry. By writing those stories, we would contaminate the city with panic." He paused a moment. "Believe me. There is enough innate fear right now without the press fanning the flames."

A moment later, at Mannion's suggestion, they began to walk back toward the party.

"If you would allow me one more question," John stated. "I was sent here, among other reasons, to get a sense of the public's proclivity toward war. By a graceful stroke of luck, I have been able to discuss this issue with the planters, and I feel I have a general understanding of their views. Their anger toward the national government is quite clear. As slaveholders they are attempting to look after their own interests. But what of the general public? Was the incident at the courthouse representative? Are they, too, so bellicose?"

Mannion's eyes lifted from his feet to the now shimmering white plantation home. "Your research on that issue need go no further, Mr. Sharp. A relatively small percentage of Charlestonians own slaves. Yet, the greatest percentage of the wealth is concentrated in the hands of those with large slaveholdings—they are the ones with the true power." He took two steps. "So, does it really matter what the general public thinks?"

John's tone was deep. "No, on a decision-making level, I suppose not."

"Please also bear in mind, Mr. Sharp, that there are also men with conciliatory opinions at the party tonight. You just won't hear their voices, because that is not the message they want you to take home."

"But the anti-Unionists *do* currently carry the popular voice?"

"Yes," he hummed. "At the present time."

As they approached the house, Mannion put his hand on John's forearm and held it tightly.

"Mr. Sharp, I hope that I might offer you a crucial piece of advice."

"Of course, sir."

He pursed his lips and paused a long time before he spoke. "If something happens in the upcoming days, some major event that transcends all you have so far witnessed, please heed this warning. Leave Charleston immediately. Duty may tempt you to remain, but in a city out of control neither your newspaper, nor Tyler Breckenridge, can protect you."

John stammered as Mannion's hand slowly released his arm. "But, sir—"

Mannion raised his palm. "Mr. Sharp, I can truly say no more."

John was amazed as he followed the pull of the music from the lawn to the terrace. During dinner, anonymous workers had transformed adjoining high-ceilinged parlors into one grand room. Enormous chandeliers had been lowered and lighted, furniture and rugs removed, and the string ensemble that had provided subtle background music during dinner now filled the room with rich sound. It washed over everyone, sweeping the pretty ladies in swirling silks with their gentlemen onto the dance floor, stirring patriarchs and dowagers in their wake. Even the silent servants seemed to sway in time as they moved through the eddies at the room's periphery with their trays of drinks and sugared almonds.

Tyler Breckenridge danced every waltz with the most graceful girl in the room and every reel with the most charming. John wasn't sure how he managed it, as the girls could be thin, plump, plain, or shy. It didn't matter; when they danced with him, they smiled and blushed and believed.

John followed Breckenridge's lead and was quick to find spots on the dance cards of Mary Ellen's friends, who seemed inordinately concerned with his enjoyment of the party—his being a stranger and all. John was quick to note that this afforded him the opportunity to sharpen his skills with those who were not yet connoisseurs of dancing. He found himself rewarded with approving smiles from Clio.

It may have been the wine or his early success with the waltz that drove John to secure a partner for the upcoming reel. His sense of irony led him to select Mrs. Caruthers, a nervous, myopic woman with a pronounced overbite. As they assumed a position at the head of the line, he flashed a smile at Clio, one couple down. Her eyes were wide with horror.

John gave her a look of reassurance and honored Mrs. Caruthers with a sweeping bow. He then honored his corner, a pert little matron in a fetching fuchsia gown, and began to skip toward her. But she was otherwise occupied, executing a graceful pirouette guided by her partner. John looked hastily back at Mrs. Caruthers. She was rotating—suspended between lines like a trapeze artist waiting for her swing to return, her mole-like eyes darting about in confusion.

John felt a shove to his posterior and hurried back to retrieve his partner from limbo. Meanwhile, Clio and her partner brushed past him into the lead position.

"Watch us," she mouthed.

Over Mrs. Caruthers's shoulder, John could see Daisy in her lacy white cap against the far wall, trying to hide her laughter behind her hand.

"I don't think anyone noticed," John declared to Clio after the reel had disbanded and each sipped a punch by the patio doors.

Clio blinked at him mildly. "You're probably right," she replied, proving she could lie with a straight face. "And least of all Mrs. Caruthers."

"Well, maybe Daisy noticed. She seemed to be laughing pretty hard."

"Daisy doesn't miss a thing," Clio answered, casting an amused glance at her maid. "After the party she will describe the happenings with enough detail to make your editor weep."

The band began to play the introductory chords of a waltz. Clio closed her eyes for a moment, swaying just a little to the tune. "Who is your partner for this dance?" she asked.

John consulted the card in his cuff and began to glance around the room. "Blond hair and two strands of pearls—Miss Elizabeth Anne Carlborg."

"Ah, one of Mary Ellen's friends. You will not find her, Mr. Sharp. Unfortunately, she and several of her coterie partook of the wrong punch bowl. Elizabeth Anne is presently unwell."

John feigned a look of distress. "Whatever shall I do?"

"I happen to be free," Clio remarked with a veiled glance, before investigating the pattern on her punch cup.

John took the cup from her hand, his hand remaining on hers a moment longer than the transfer required. "Would you do me the honor?"

"Only if you promise not to put me in a spin and then go skipping off toward that doxy Mrs. Prescott."

"The one with the bright pink dress?"

"The very one."

"Not a chance," John whispered and pulled her toward him in a graceful turn.

The waltz was to be John and Clio's only dance as partners all evening. Clio's obligation as hostess required a diverse dance card, and John played the responsible bachelor by entertaining a variety of ladies. Their meetings as "corners" in the reels, however, were peppered with whispered witticisms, and John knew that the frequency of such encounters could not be a matter of chance—he wondered if Clio played chess.

John kept a wary eye on the array of gentlemen who claimed Clio for each dance. At first he tried to rationalize his jealousy of all men under sixty by mentally cataloging their faults. Eventually he gave up and escaped to the terrace, where he diverted his attention by trying to light his new pipe, a gift from Breckenridge.

John's concern over Mannion's cryptic warning led him to seek out Brett Alford, chief prosecutor of the Calhoun case. It was immediately apparent that he should have found the man earlier, for Mr. Alford was now well beyond lucid. He had a florid complexion, puffy eyes, and a network of tiny lines on his nose and cheeks—obvious clues to his friendship with alcohol. Alford had already put away a large glass of scotch in the short time since he had joined Tyler and John in the study.

Despite both subtle and overt attempts to steer the discussion toward Darcy Nance Calhoun, the prosecutor remained loquacious on the subjects of parties and women, but laconic on matters of substance.

John awaited an opportunity, the long tip of the glass to Alford's lip, then fired again. "Might we speak on the Calhoun trial?" he asked, hoping the long pause would this time force acknowledgment.

Alford lowered his glass and quickly scanned the room. He

searched as if another topic hid beside the bookshelf or behind the desk. A nod from Tyler refocused him.

"Work." He sighed, chasing the expletive with more liquor. "It follows me like a shadow. Would you not both rather talk of Miss Green's provocative dress? Or, or, the sweet mulberry wine they are now making on the Eustis farm?" He found an unreceptive audience. "Very well, then," came a deflated response. "What do you wish to know?"

"Do you consider the conviction a certainty?"

"Like sunrise and sunset. Or a moonshine hangover. Hell, the man got caught in the act, then went out and confessed to doing it. There ain't much more of a sure thing than that. Why, it's hardly worthy of my time and effort."

"Then what do you expect from the defense?"

"Well, I know Mr. Smith, his previous lawyer, was planning on arguing that Darcy just didn't know any better. That he didn't know that runaway was a slave." He shrugged and laughed again. "It'd take a hefty couple gallons of that mulberry wine for me ta start believing a story like that. But, I suppose that would have been as good a defense as any. As futile as any."

"But isn't it a possibility?" John asked. "By all accounts, Darcy Calhoun is slow. Could he just have been confused?"

Alford stood up from the sofa, surprising John with sure balance in the face of heavy drunkenness. "Mr. Sharp, there is stupid, and then there's *stupid*." He waved his half-full glass wildly around him, greatly threatening the carpet. "If a man comes across a bedraggled-looking nigger in a place he ain't never been seen before, I'd think he'd have a pretty good idea that nigger was a fugitive, wouldn't you?"

John walked back to the corner, refilling his own glass with bourbon. He talked to Alford without looking. "What, then, do you expect from his *new* representation?"

"The Yank lawyer? Why, I expect he'll most likely defend abolition instead of his client. He'll come down carrying his cause and some nifty words, contending that Darcy is innocent 'cause slavery is the real evil." The glass again spun on a carousel of drunkenness. "That *Darcy's* the only innocent man in all of Carolina. But I tell you, Mr.

Sharp, he's got about as good a chance winning on those grounds as a blind man has at a poker table. And it'll get Darcy to the gallows before the first evening supper."

Alford now moved to within steps of the door, humming to Breckenridge again of young women and dancing. Tyler held an eye on each man.

"Have you met him?" John called out, interrupting Alford's descriptive fantasy. "Darcy Calhoun?"

Alford rolled his eyes as he turned back toward John. "No. Nor do I have to."

John stepped toward them. "But what danger exists in finding out if a man is less culpable than you think? What if he really is so naive to have committed a crime without understanding the consequences? What if his simplicity stretches only to God and his garden, and does not grasp the politicization of this issue? The law can have compassion in that case, can it not?"

Alford snickered as he looked at Breckenridge. "Passionate, isn't he?" He looked back at John. "You are a young man, so that passion can be forgiven. But let me explain to you a point you seem not to understand. The law is merely an extension of the peoples' will. And there is not a man in all the South who does not want to see Darcy punished for what he's done. Therefore, if they have no compassion, then why should I?"

John shot a look to Breckenridge, but the planter's face reflected nothing. He turned back to the prosecutor. At that moment, he recalled the conference between the prosecutors' bench and the mayor in the courtroom. "Is it the people who wish to see him punished, or the politicians who wish to make an example of him? I assume the decision to seek the death penalty came from higher up than the prosecutor's office. Who did it come from, Mr. Alford?"

Alford looked at Breckenridge. "There is a limit to what I'll take from a reporter, even with fine scotch and jubilant surroundings." He looked back at John. "My advice to you is to take this all a little less seriously. A few months from now, the name Darcy Calhoun will mean nothing to anyone—nothing more memorable than a hiccup in a long night of drinking." The sound of distant laughter took his attention away from the study. "Now, if you gentlemen will excuse me."

Alford left, and Breckenridge moved to retrieve his own drink from his desk. John stood still, his eyes unfocused, latched to nothing.

He spoke more to himself than Breckenridge. "Let him not quit his belief that a popgun is a popgun, though the ancient and honorable of the world know it to be the crack of doom."

"Yes," Tyler responded over his shoulder. "But I have always thought Emerson to be a bit too dour."

John found Clio looking distraught near the French doors to the patio.

"They aren't eating the cake."

Indeed, the two-tiered sheet cake, adorned with white roses and a stirring rendition of "Old Glory" in buttercream icing, had been largely ignored by the party's guests. Except for a few missing pieces at the periphery, the theme remained largely intact.

"Won't you have a piece of cake, sir?" A benevolent-looking black woman offered a china dessert plate to John as he approached. "It is our governor's wife's recipe—the best in Carolina."

John took a bite and agreed. "It's just about the best anywhere."

"Well this icing surely won't hold up overnight," Clio remarked. "We had better circulate the cake on trays." She made a summoning gesture and two servants were dispatched with the offering among the guests. John observed that they weren't getting many takers.

"Perhaps we should scour the veranda for potential cake eaters," John suggested to Clio. She gave him a look. "Come on, it's a beautiful night."

Clio smiled and took John's arm. As they stepped onto the patio, she called back over her shoulder, "Better tell them the governor's wife made it herself."

John led Clio away from the house to the edge of the patio, where flagstones met soft waves of grass. An ancient oak spread octopus arms in a dark silhouette to their right. The sky above was clear.

"Look at the stars," John exclaimed softly.

The night sky was dramatic at Willowby. Almost directly overhead, the Milky Way spilled diagonally through the Summer Triangle in a blaze of glory undiminished by gaslights or the haze of factories.

Clio's chin tilted upward. "Do you know any of their names?" Even though no one was near, her voice was hushed, as if they were in church. "My father used to talk about the constellations when I was little. I'm afraid I don't remember how to find them."

"I'm better with the winter sky," he replied, "but I know the major stars in the Summer Triangle. . . . See those three bright ones? The brightest, over there, is Vega. It is in the constellation Lyra, the lyre." John pointed. Clio stepped closer to sight along his arm. "And down over there is Altair," he continued. "It is in Aquila, the eagle."

"Where?" she asked, looking in vain for an eagle pattern in the stars. She leaned back a little, her back to John, resting her head against his shoulder. He slipped an arm around her waist.

"I could never figure that one out myself," he confessed. "Now there is Deneb. It is in Cygnus, the swan." Her hair felt soft against his cheek. "See that cross? There is the body . . . and the wings. I seem to recall that the myth involved a tragic romance between a mortal girl and Zeus. She was turned into a swan."

Clio replied. "I guess that's better than the one who was turned into a cow."

Then they were silent for a while, looking at the stars, listening to the sound of crickets as the party faded behind them.

"What is they looking at?" It was a child's loud whisper, originating from somewhere among the branches of the oak.

"Shhh!" The chorus came from several directions.

"But I want ta see it, too." The whisper was louder, petulant.

"Is that you, Millie?" Clio asked. "What on earth are you doing up at this hour? Your momma will be livid."

A clump of leaves moved aside to reveal a wide-eyed five-year-old black girl. She was nestled in the crook of a branch with an older sibling.

"Please, don't tell Momma, Miss Clio. We just wanted ta see the dancing."

"How many of you are up there?"

There was a round of, "I am, Miss Clio," in a variety of pitches from various parts of the tree.

"Sounds like about a dozen." John laughed.

"Y'all better get down now. Don't you know that it's after midnight?"

An assortment of black children in a variety of sizes descended from the tree. They hung together in a loose gaggle, alternately hiding behind each other and jockeying for a better view.

"You sure do look pretty, Miss Clio," offered an astute boy of about seven.

"All sparkly," another added. There was another round of agreement.

John leaned close to Clio's ear. "I think we have flushed out our quarry."

Clio raised an eyebrow.

"Cake eaters," John whispered.

Clio flashed him a big smile. She turned back to the children. "Mr. Sharp has a very interesting idea. Why don't you all sit down quietly, and we'll see if he has a surprise." She turned to John. "Tell Naomi to give you the entire top layer and a knife. Nobody is going to eat a bite of that blooming flag, anyway."

John and Clio perched on a stone bench with the cake between them, while the children fanned out around them on the grass. John's second piece of cake, served without the benefit of silver or china and accompanied by a litany of happy noises, tasted even better than the first. The governor's wife had done herself proud.

When they had finished, Clio divided the rest of the cake on napkins for the children to take home and offered the stern admonition that further consumption that night would result in tummy aches. The assembly slowly and reluctantly began to depart.

John reached over and took Clio's hand. "This has been a fascinating evening." Oddly, the statement encompassed the party in its entirety, with all of its jarring contradictions.

"Is that your new beau, Miss Clio?" asked one little girl as she backed slowly away. "He's real pretty too."

"I like him better than the others," Millie offered. There was a general round of agreement.

"Good night, all," Clio said firmly. She shook her head and smiled at John as they rose to return to the party. "I'm sorry about that. They're just children."

Instead of the direct route across the patio, John and Clio walked slowly to the house along a hedge-lined walkway to a side porch.

"Before we go inside, Mr. Sharp, I would like to rid my shoe of a pebble. The dancing slippers were obviously not intended for outdoor wear."

"May I assist you in some way?" John asked.

Clio laughed. "By averting your eyes while I go to that bench over there and remove it. I will rejoin you shortly."

John had waited but a moment when the sound of footfall accompanied by male voices drifted from the walkway on the other side of the hedge. The footsteps stopped just short of the entry to the veranda, and John heard the scrape and flare of a match, followed by the aroma of pipe tobacco.

"Where are they meeting?" Kenneth Brent, the man with whom he conversed earlier, was speaking in low tones.

"In Nashville, I believe."

John thought he recognized the second voice as belonging to George Campbell, who had been seated across from him at dinner. He heard the flare of a second match.

"And who is attending?"

"Just about everybody. Well, maybe not our northern neighbors, considering what's on the table."

"Well, they could always invite Delaware," Brent responded with a laugh. "They are always threatening to quit over something or other, aren't they?"

John was so focused on the conversation that he was startled by the nearby rustle of Clio's skirt. Her glance conveyed surprise and disapproval.

"Well, Mr. Sharp, I believe I have solved that problem." She spoke in a manner that announced their presence.

John knew he should have announced himself sooner, and the look the men gave him as they stepped onto the porch implied exactly that.

"Lovely party. Lovely night," Campbell said, directing his remarks primarily toward Clio. "If you are taking the air, we can move along." Campbell gestured with his pipe. Brent simply regarded John coldly.

"Oh, no problem," Clio replied cheerfully. "We were just heading inside." She extended her arm to John. "Shall we?"

Both men were silent as the couple entered the house.

The hour was late, and the steady trickle of departing guests left only a few behind. For those remaining the energy was gone—already spent on dances and revelry and food and spirits. Most of those remaining sat, while John stood at the wall in the parlor, offering a nod and smile to those leaving.

Initially, he passed off the young men's glares as mere posturing— a sophomoric way to impress one another, if no one else. He guessed them to be in their late teens, an age at which immaturity still prohibited them from concealing their feelings; an age where the face is still the mirror of emotion. As they walked toward him, he was sincerely glad for that. At least he knew motive from the outset.

The taller boy stopped just before John, while the other stood a step behind his shoulder. Both were handsome, thin, and blond, though each wore his formal attire like a burden.

"Mr. Sharp," the tall boy said roughly. "I am Ryan Hedgecoth, and this is my brother Luke."

"Gentlemen."

Ryan spoke through his teeth. "I wish to inform you that you are a liar, sir." He paused for dramatic effect, but seemed a little confused when John just looked at him without speaking. He decided to go on. "I heard you talking with Mr. Cochran right after the Independence Day toast. You said something about a 'common bond' when we threw out the British . . . That's hogwash, sir!"

"Hogwash!" the boy behind him echoed between hiccups.

John looked at them calmly. "Perhaps you would like to fill me in on why you think so."

Ryan swayed from foot to foot. "It's hogwash 'cause your words entirely miss the point of Independence Day. Men from Carolina and Virginia did not fight for you, or any other Yankee. They fought so that we *here* would be able to do what we wanted in this country, without being ordered around by some faraway tyrant. *That's* what the old Swamp Fox fought for. And that's what we're ready to fight for again." His brother nodded emphatically as Ryan Hedgecoth caught his breath.

"It is sad that you are so eager to fight men you do not know."

"I know enough," he snapped. "I know their aims. Tell me, Mr. Sharp, if the North and South go their separate ways, if we secede, will the Yanks come down here and try to stop us?"

"I'd wager they would."

"Then my desire to fight is really a desire to defend. To kill the aggressors. To grind them into the dust."

John laughed a bit at the statement—rehearsed, it seemed. "So you both have fought in wars, have you? You're certain of your superiority because of your past experiences in battle?" He swung his eyes back and forth between the boys. "It is imprudent to underestimate those you intend to fight."

Ryan crossed his arms and smiled. "Do you know what all southern boys do when they're young? They hunt, and shoot, and fight. Constantly. We are well practiced with all types of guns and knives, and can kill a man with our own hands." He paused. "And what is it that northern boys do in their youth? They take apprenticeships in factories or industrial shops. They learn to become cobblers or haberdashers." He shook his head arrogantly. "One will be an army of fighters, the other of shopkeepers."

"With age you may come to understand the point you, yourself, just made. For while you are off fighting and hunting, what do you think those boys are busy making in the factories and industrial shops?" He allowed the point a moment to settle. "There is more to war than just men and grit, Mr. Hedgecoth. An unsupplied army, history has shown, is a paper force."

"Papers!" the older Hedgecoth spat, apparently missing the point. "You come down here with such arrogance—"

"Making eyes at our girls," Luke interjected.

"—invading our territory," Ryan resumed. "Well, don't be surprised if we smash ya like the maggots you are."

"Yeah," Luke joined in between hiccups. "All eight—or eighty of ya . . . Every last one!"

John smiled. "Seems like that many, does it?"

"Don't laugh at us, 'cause you're gonna be the first to go, you lily-livered bastard."

"Ryan! That is *more* than enough!" The words came from Tyler Breckenridge, whose own angered charge left the Hedgecoth brothers cowering. There was palpable fury in his expression. "You disrespect me and every other guest here by speaking in such a juvenile manner. Your bellicose threats are an affront to civilized company." He looked hard at both of them. "Now, go find your father. Tell him exactly what you said. Explain to him how you have disgraced yourselves in my home by insulting my guest."

In an instant, the boys were transformed from righteous defenders of the South to socially inept teenage boys. They walked slowly away, slumped at the shoulders.

"Do forgive me, John. I did not expect anything like that out of those two."

"Don't apologize, Tyler. It was youthful spirit . . . and alcohol talking. But it did help me to realize something."

"What is that?"

"Earlier I made the assumption that it is the old who want war, since they are excused from fighting it. I see now that I was wrong. The young down here surely echo their beliefs."

"Not all," Breckenridge answered.

John stood on the second-floor balcony watching the carriages depart. The string of carriage lights formed a graceful S-curve across the lawn until it disappeared onto the tree-lined drive.

Breckenridge, having just provided instructions to a coachman, stood about thirty feet away on the other side of an oleander hedge that bordered the house. He stopped to light his pipe, watching the departing lights.

There was a sound of heavy footsteps on the porch below, then the sound of male voices, low but discernible.

"I can't understand why we are staying the night here." The voice was young and angry. It sounded like one of the Hedgecoths.

"I'll tell you exactly why we are staying." The voice belonged to an older man. "The three of us have had more than enough to drink, and so has your mother. The woman can barely stand up. And she refuses to ride anywhere. She fears it might further rattle her stomach."

"I told you what Tyler said to us. He defended that Yankee reporter as if he was kin. Made us both look stupid."

"Damn right," came another young voice. "Makes ya wonder who he is siding with."

"Keep your voices down. You both talk too much."

"Well, why did he invite him here in the first place? It's like having a Yank spy in our own backyard."

"He might have done it to keep an eye on him." The older man paused. "I doubt it's because he agrees with his politics. But I'll be damned if I can figure out what Tyler has in mind for him."

"Well, Miss Clio sure seemed interested in him. It was like she was going through the motions with everyone else. Think Tyler's trying to arrange a Yankee husband?"

The older man laughed. "Miss Clio is just a year older than you are, Ryan. The Yank is a new face, and he dresses well; she may just like the look of him. But remember, he is just a reporter; the Breckenridges have money. . . . No, what concerns me is Tyler's role in arranging more important things. Lord knows the Breckenridges have been running things in these parts for a long time. It's just that some folks here and in Charleston think Tyler's overstepping a bit, trying to pull the strings at too young an age."

"Well, he sure has the money to pull whatever strings he wants." It sounded like the older of the two boys.

"The thing about money, and influence for that matter," the old man said, "is that those who have a lot of it, have a lot to lose. Some folks will bear watching over the next few weeks. . . . But now, let's go back inside. I need to check on your mother."

The footsteps walked back across the porch, and a door closed.

John had been watching Breckenridge throughout the conversation, illuminated as he was by the light from the upstairs window. He had stood motionless as usual, face impassive. Now, his shoulders seemed to slump a little, a sign of fatigue. The mask dropped, and for the first time since John had met him, the man looked old for his age.

John prepared to step back out of Breckenridge's line of sight, but just then he looked straight up at John—obviously aware of his presence. The eyes held John's for a long moment, and John felt a chill that the night air did not warrant. It was some time before John realized what he had read in Tyler's eyes.

SIXTEEN

@

John stood outside the Charleston telegraph office where the carriage from Willowby had dropped him a few minutes earlier at his request. There was a sea breeze in Charleston this morning, and the semitropical port-city smells that had plagued him upon his arrival were liberally diminished. He began the short walk to the boardinghouse carrying the light valise that his valet had packed for him at the plantation. It contained his old clothes and some borrowed items better suited to the climate.

John had walked but a few yards when an open carriage stopped beside him.

"Good morning, Mr. Sharp. May we offer you a ride somewhere?" It was George Campbell and his wife. Judging from his tone and relatively benign expression, Campbell had recovered from any pique resulting from the eavesdropping incident the previous evening. John was nevertheless uncomfortable, for the substance of his wire to Haggerty had been a suggestion for research into the meeting of southern states in Nashville.

He assumed an affable tone. "Good morning, sir. Good morning,

Mrs. Campbell." John touched his hat. He recalled that the man was inordinately proud of his stable. "That is an exceptionally fine pair of Morgans," he remarked, nodding toward the team.

"They are only five years old," Campbell said with the trace of a smile. "And smarter than horses have a right to be."

"Now, George, don't get started," his wife cut in. "Won't you join us, Mr. Sharp?"

John declined the invitation. He still wasn't comfortable with Campbell, and he wasn't sure it would do to have the carriage pull up at McClellan's boardinghouse. As the carriage pulled away, he found himself humming a tune—a waltz from the party. He thought to himself that after all of the evening's contradictory events, it was the upbeat tune that stayed in his mind.

He marveled that he felt as good as he did. He had consumed prodigious quantities of bourbon last night, followed by very little sleep. Yet today he experienced only a mild insouciance, reflected in his easy pace through the city.

He paused to allow a wagonload of laborers to pass. They were an exceptionally muscular crew, and judging by the sledges and picks stacked at the rear of the cart, they were headed out to work at the seawall down at the East Bay. The men looked bored and sleepy. One of them covered a yawn as he passed. It made John yawn, too.

John opened the door to his room and smiled. Owen Conway, clad in a bunched circus of long underwear, lay facedown on the bed, snoring. John slammed the door and watched the body stir just slightly.

Owen moaned and spoke into the pillow. "Mr. McClellan, I already told you, I can't eat breakfast because of my digestive disorder."

John laughed. "It's near time for lunch, you lazy braggart."

Owen rolled over, squinting and puzzled. With realization came a gleeful smile. "Hey, sport," he said, raspy but enthused. "What in the hell have you been up to?"

John chuckled. "It is a rather long and detailed story."

It took a moment for his eyes to focus. "And what in the hell are you wearing? You look like Bonnie Prince Charlie."

John blushed a bit at his beige suit. "My clothes were ruined a time back. These are their replacement."

"I swear, you're a tailor's worst nightmare. But I must say, this one's hardly the fig leaf forced upon Adam." Owen sat forward and massaged his hangover with both hands. "You know, you had me worried senseless the other night. I was up till morn trying to find you. Until the letter came, that is." He stood up with a look of disappointment. "If you were planning on going out to some plantation, you could have told me, John. I don't see why you had to just up and go."

"Owen, I assure you, it was unplanned. And even if I *had* known, it would have been impossible to tell you." John rolled his eyes at the memory. "I was incapacitated."

Owen nodded, but the gesture was still one of uncertainty. "Yeah, I guess it wasn't the smartest idea to take you out drinking. Not after you'd been plunked on the head like that."

John smiled. "Get dressed so we can go to lunch. I'll explain everything there."

"Your treat?" Owen asked, his expression again playful.

"Of course. That is, unless your digestive disorder prohibits it."

Owen rhythmically slapped his stomach. "It is no lie. I merely left out that McClellan's cooking is the cause of the malady." Owen began solving the puzzle of the location of his discarded clothes. He looked back to John after a moment, a wrinkled shirt in one hand, his balled-up pants in the other. "Don't think that just because you've been gone, Old Owen here hasn't been working. In fact, I've uncovered a story bigger than anything yet. Something that will totally obscure that Darcy Calhoun and his runaway slave."

"What?"

Owen walked to the dresser, opened a drawer, and removed an item wrapped in paper. He handed it to John.

As John unwrapped it, he found a fine silver lighter. He stared at it for a moment. "A lighter?"

Owen nodded vigorously, his cheeks stretched back from the smile.

John stared at it again. "Has it to do with the fires?" he asked dubiously.

"No, no," Owen scoffed. He walked to John and flipped the lighter over in his hands. "Look at the letters."

John read the engraved monogram. "J.L.A."

"Uh-huh," Owen replied, his grin returned.

"Is this supposed to mean something to me?"

Owen showed a child's impatience. "J.L.A. James Lancaster Aubry."

John paused. "The dandy we saw that day in the courtroom?"

"The very one."

"You stole his lighter?"

"Of course not. I bought it." He hesitated as if to heighten the suspense. "From a whorehouse on Charlotte Street."

John began to laugh. "This is what you think will turn the Calhoun trial into second-page news?"

Owen snatched the lighter from John's hands. "Just because it isn't your scoop doesn't mean you have to belittle it."

"I'm sorry, Owen. I just don't see how Aubry's lighter turning up at a brothel is such news."

"Well, it didn't walk there."

"I assumed not."

"And I'd say the shocking sexual habits of a member of the Charleston elite are far from the triviality you're implying."

"So he's a frequent customer?"

"Used to be." Owen drew nearer to John and dropped his voice. "Till he met up with that troublesome Frenchman, Louis Veneri."

John's jaw dropped. "He has syphilis?"

Owen beamed. "That's the rumor. Folks say that's why he wears all them beige and gold suits. On account of the heavy mercury treatment and the way it's put the shine to his skin."

"Do you have any proof?"

"Not as yet." Owen adopted a cunning look. "But I hear that if you talk to him long enough, he'll start babbling like a buffoon." He tapped a finger to his temple. "Not quite all there anymore. Figure I'll see if there's any truth to it."

"But why would he talk to you in the first place?"

"I just told you, the guy's off his rocker. Hell, he thought you were a priest, remember? Maybe I'll put on a big hat and tell him I'm the pope."

John stifled a laugh. "Come on and get dressed. I'm hungry. You can tell me more about it at lunch."

John's distinguished palate suffered through bites of oversalted ham and watery rice as they sat at a pine table in the Hamlet Inn. Owen did not allow the chewing of food to slow his questions.

"So you're telling me you were rescued from a band of murderous sailors by a servant of this guy, Breckenridge. Then he put you on a ship that dropped you off just miles from his plantation, where you were then invited to stay during the holiday weekend." His incredulity was apparent even through the slur of a mouthful.

"Yes. That is just about it."

"And why would he do this? Why would this rich, powerful southerner take it upon himself to protect the interests of a slanderous Yank?"

"He never explained it fully, but I believe it sprang from some sense of civic responsibility. More a protection of Charleston's reputation than my own."

Owen responded with a mouth full of rice. "So protecting John Sharp is now part of the Charleston City charter. At this rate, they're gonna name streets after you before you leave town."

"Hardly, Owen."

Owen waved his spoon at John as he swallowed. "So this plantation you were at. Tell me about it."

"It was impressively large and apparently very prosperous, with perhaps a couple hundred slaves."

"Any signs of forced miscegenation?"

"No," John shot back, appalled.

"What about beatings? Did you get to see anyone flogged?"

"Of course not."

"You make it seem like it doesn't happen. But it's going on somewhere. Hell, I've seen blacks in New York whose backs are so torn up from the lash that they look like washboards. Somebody had to do that."

"I am sure it has happened somewhere. But certainly not with the people I've met. These people are businessmen. What good would it do them to wound their own labor?"

Owen shrugged it off and returned to his lunch. "So what all did you do while you were out there? Just sit on the porch and sip lemonade while all the happy slaves played ring-around-the-rosy?"

John pushed away his half-eaten plate and swallowed a sip of ale. "No. I was quite busy, actually. I had full access to the plantation and saw the operation. More important, it happens that Darcy Nance hails from the same area—just a few miles away, as a matter of fact. So, I had the opportunity to visit his cabin as well as interview a number of his neighbors."

"And what did you discover? Is the poor fool as guilty as they say?"

"It seems so, yes. But from all I've heard the man sounds absolutely harmless."

"You mean stupid."

"Not entirely. He certainly does not have a scientific mind, but he is creative in other ways. He also has a firm command of the Scriptures. More so than anyone else in the congregation, according to his reverend."

Owen swallowed an overstuffed bite and smiled without humor. "He's gonna need it."

Owen Conway reclined back in his chair after finishing the meal. He brandished a toothpick and set about that daunting task while seeking to fill in the gaps in John's account of his trip.

"So, you meet any ladies out there? The ones in their full skirts and tight corsets?"

"Yes. I met a few."

"Any of them delightfully unladylike?"

"Your soul is truly without hope," John answered, smiling behind his mug of ale.

"Yeah, I should have known better. You're the Puritan, right?"

"I am hardly a Puritan." Perhaps it was pride, or the need to invalidate Owen's assumptions that caused John to blurt, "I did meet a young lady, and I rather think she likes me."

Owen lowered the toothpick. "Well, I'll be. You do have it in you, Mr. John Sharp, no matter how well you hide it." He leaned forward. "Tell me, who is she? Does she have a proud figure?"

John leaned back cavalierly. "Her name is Clio, and she is quite comely."

"She is the only daughter of neglecting parents, then. Or a widow perhaps."

"No. She is Clio Breckenridge. Younger sister to the man I spoke of before."

"Whoa," Owen responded. "You do have nerve, John. There is no doubt of that. 'Cause if Old Tyler Boy finds out, you'll be the one strapped to the whipping post." His laugh returned. "These folks think we Yanks are corrupting enough without us soiling the honor of their young women."

John buried his face in the mug of ale and finished it off.

He spent the next few minutes dodging intimate insinuations and double entendres, leaving the aftertaste of regret more palpable than food or liquor. He cut off one of Owen's lurid interrogatories in hope of changing the subject.

"The holiday party at Willowby was quite amazing."

"Well? Tell me of it."

"There was music and dancing—ballroom dancing that filled a great hall with spectacular women and their partners. And each food was a delicacy. There was shrimp served in seashells, and beef that nearly melted in your mouth, and strawberries dipped in chocolate." John laughed as Owen pushed away his plate in disgust. "And they had every type of liquor imaginable. You, in fact, would certainly have enjoyed it. For, I believe there were a number of men who could even outdrink you."

"Now you're just being rude. No blueblood can outdrink Owen Conway. Not on his best day."

"Regardless, it was as majestic a night as I have ever had. I also had a chance to speak with some of the planters and other prominent men of the area."

Owen nodded. "So tell me, these important men that Breck wanted you to meet, how did they treat you? What did they have to say?"

"They were cool but civil, for the most part. They seemed intent upon impressing me with the direness of the situation."

"Did they speak of war?"

"Some. Some used it as a threat; others alluded to it as a consequence to be avoided."

"Did they try to win you over with persuasive arguments?"

"Breckenridge did." John laughed. "But most of them were just polite while they told me how bad things were."

Owen was quiet for a time, drinking his ale and glancing about the inn. Then he leaned forward. "Look, I know that of the two of us, I am more easygoing and you more prone to thoughts of conspiracy. But something isn't right about all this. Something just isn't right."

"What do you mean?"

His face showed mild concern. "It doesn't make any sense, John. That the only option to protect you from bloodthirsty sailors was to put you on a ship that just so happened to be bound for his plantation." He shrugged. "You think that sounds normal?"

"I still see no reason he would have to lie about it."

"Okay, then. Say it was just altruism. Then why in the world would the man wish you to stay the entire weekend at his home? Why wouldn't he just provide you with transportation back to Charleston? The idea of having a snooping Yank reporter around doesn't strike me as one many of these rich sorts would find agreeable. Talk about a skunk at a garden party!"

John hesitated. "Perhaps Breckenridge was curious about what I had learned in Charleston and what I intended to write."

"That seems reasonable. But why the entire weekend, then? Why not just ride back to Charleston with you and talk along the way?"

"I don't know," John answered with annoyance. A reporter did not like to be questioned when he did not have the answers. "But whatever the reason, the action hardly seems malevolent."

"Or so it would appear. You said before that this man Breckenridge thought it worthwhile for you to speak with these influential men at the party. Men who later came across as somewhat hostile, right? A bunch of anti-Unionists. Why in the hell would he do that?"

John masked his inkling of suspicion with a calm tone. "Maybe he wanted me to see the true state of affairs down here so I might report that to the North."

"But to what end?" Owen took a deep breath. "John, you work for the *Tribune,* and that makes you the most influential of the reporters here in Charleston. And you still think it an accident that one of the most powerful men in Carolina happened across your path through blind luck? Powerful men have motives for nearly everything they do. You need to figure out his."

John took a sip of his replenished ale. "I think you are blowing this out of proportion, Owen. I really do."

Owen shrugged. "While I hate to remind you, but you are the *second* reporter from the *Tribune* sent here to Charleston. The first wound up dead."

"Owen!" John looked at the other reporter with incredulity. "You and Woodridge both assured me that Simpson's death was an accident."

"By itself it appeared to be. But after this thing with Breckenridge—" Owen suddenly slapped his hand on the table. His smile was huge. "I've got it."

"Got what?"

"You know, back in New York, I was covering a story once about a real lowlife who ran a couple factories in Manhattan. Word was that the guy treated his workers worse than dogs—making kids work all day, seven a week, underfed and underpaid. A couple of them, rumor had it, had died right there in his shops." He took a sip. "So imagine my surprise when I get in contact with the guy and he tells me he's happy to give me a tour. Sure thing, showed up the next day and he was there to greet me at the door. He took me on a tour of the factory, let me talk to the workers, he even joked and kidded with some of 'em like they were family. Sure, the place was no utopia, but I had seen far, far worse."

"What's your point?"

Owen laughed. "My point is that two months later the cops got inside his other two factories and shut them down for the very reasons I cited. 'Hellholes,' a couple cops called them. Worst places they had ever seen." Owen smiled. "So I'm wondering, while Breck showed you the utopian side of his plantation, what the hell was he trying to hide? What *didn't* he want you to see?"

John considered Owen's question. With the free access he had been given at the plantation, Owen's scenario seemed unlikely. And information on the meeting in Nashville, his potential scoop, had been gleaned only because of his presence at the party.

Then John suppressed a shiver in the dank heat of the Hamlet Inn. "Owen, on the walk over here, you said that nothing of significance had happened in Charleston while I was away."

"Nothing did. It was rather dull, as a matter of fact."

"You're certain. Nothing you perhaps missed or slept through?"

"Of course not." His eyes widened. "Wait a minute, you think whatever he was trying to keep you from was happening here? In Charleston?"

"Perhaps. If your hypothesis is correct." He sat quietly, mulling over countless questions. "A desire to keep me away from the city," he whispered. Suddenly, his head shot up.

"What? What is it, John?"

He leaned in, his voice tense but quiet. "At the party, the editor of the *Charleston Gazette* hinted to me of some significant event that might soon take place. He was entirely vague, but he warned me that if it did happen, I should leave the city immediately. It would be far too dangerous for me to remain. At the time, I thought it was in regard to the trial—what would happen to the city if Darcy Calhoun was acquitted. But now—"

"Well, what do you think it concerns?"

"I do not know. But I cannot help but wonder if that was the reason for keeping me on the plantation." John looked down at the table, his thoughts wild. "Owen, think again. Were there any rumors or whispers that you heard that you may have forgotten? Anything at all?"

"The rumors were nothing extraordinary. Mere threats to march a mob to the jail at Fort Moultrie in search of Darcy Nance."

John shook his head. "No. Those aren't new. I've heard them since my arrival." He put his head back down, staring at the table.

Owen twisted his lip as he spoke again. "Of course, I could be wrong about this whole thing with Breck. After all, nothing *did* happen while you were away. Maybe it was all innocent."

"Heck, Owen, make up your damn mind."

"Truth is, I just don't know, John. Stuff sounds fishy, but there's no proof to back it up. I'm just saying that you should be careful. Especially with this Breck guy. Something about him rubs me the wrong way."

"But you've never even met him." John paused. "Look, Owen, you've got me jumping at shadows here. I have to trust my gut about Breckenridge. In spite of the apparent contradictions, I think he is a good man."

Owen nodded. "Well, anytime you run into that many contradictions, you've got to think something's wrong with your assumptions. The guy just doesn't add up."

Upon his return to McClellan's after lunch, John sat at his desk by the window reviewing copies of the *Gazette* and other papers he had picked up from a stack in the front room downstairs. Today's front page item reported that the president was sick with a stomach ailment after eating bad fruit. The story referenced a page-four column under the byline of a "Mrs. Pruitt" on safe food storage and preparation during the summer months. Another lead story told of a riled Texan who had taken a potshot at the courier of a federal cavalry unit. Whether he had missed through accident or design was a matter for debate. There was also advance buildup for the Breckenridge holiday party, including a lengthy guest list. But, as expected, there were no reports of fires or civil unrest in Charleston.

John's thoughts were interrupted by a gentle knock at his door.

"Come in."

The door creaked open slowly, and Samuel peeked in.

"All right if I come inside, Mr. Sharp?"

"Of course, Samuel. How have you been?"

Judging by the boy's wide grin and proud stance, Samuel Grass had been well. "Oh, I's been fine, sir. Got me good and rested while you was off out in the country. Hope ya don't mind, but I's stopped by here to find out when you's be back." He tucked his shoulders back and his face became serious. "Ya see, I's ready to get reporting again. Help ya with what you need. Whatever you be wanting, I'll look into it fo' ya." He reached into his pocket. "Even got me this little piece of chalk. Figure if there's anything you be needing me ta keep a tally of, like before with the fires, I can use this to make a mark."

John smiled at the boy. "You're getting to be a heck of a good reporter, Samuel. But unfortunately, with the trial not set to begin until Friday, there is little I can have you do without causing suspicion."

Samuel's head tilted down, and his posture sagged.

John stood up and studied the boy for a moment. "But perhaps I was hasty in dismissing your assistance. In fact, there is something that I need for background in my articles. It is quite important, though, and will require extreme diligence. Do you think you might be up for it?"

The boy stood erect. "Oh, yessir. Anything, sir."

"Well, I do need to know the exact number of churches here in Charleston, both white and black. But accuracy is critical here, Samuel. If you count wrong and I report it, it would look unprofessional."

"I won't be letting ya down, sir. I'll use the chalk, just like I said. That way there won't be no forgetting."

"Excellent," John said with a pleased smile. "And remember, Samuel. Same rules as before. Don't let on to anyone what you are doing."

The boy seemed pleased at the added element of secrecy. "Of course, Mr. Sharp. Ain't nothing for you to worry 'bout."

Not five minutes had passed when John was interrupted by another knock at his door. It was McClellan, the innkeeper.

"I didn't see ya come back, Mr. Sharp. I was out back at the cooking shed." He wiped his glistening face on his sleeve. "I heard the boy leaving, though, and he told me you were here. You must be an important man, getting invited out to the Breckenridge plantation and all."

"I hope my absence didn't inconvenience you, Mr. McClellan."

"Not at all. A man came by and told me where you was gonna be. He came by again about an hour ago."

"Who was he? What did he look like?"

"Don't know his name, but I think he works for Mr. Breckenridge. Nice enough fella, but not a looker, if you know what I mean." McClellan reached into his pocket and withdrew an envelope. "He left this for ya."

Owen picked that moment to open his door and poke his head into the hallway. "So who's it from?" he asked impertinently.

John stayed silent. He waited until McClellan had departed, then broke the wax seal and unfolded the heavy bond. The note was short and to the point.

John,
   The favor you requested has been arranged. Arrive at 141 Franklin Street at ten o'clock tonight.
      Regards,
         T. B.

"So?" Owen repeated more urgently.

John remained stoic, unsure of how to react. As Owen pressed again, he looked up and answered quietly. "I am to meet with Darcy Calhoun. Tonight."

Queen Street was dark. Nearby windows hoarded their light behind tightly drawn curtains. Blocks ahead, a lone gaslight cast a narrow luminescent path over the brick street like moonlight on water. The pedestrians they encountered were backlit—faceless in the shadows. It was impossible to see if their eyes took note of John or not, but he imagined that they did. Conversations stopped as he and Owen approached. Carriages slowed ominously before speeding up or turning. And one particular carriage passed them more than once.

"I truly hope we won't have to run," Owen commented with sufficient volume to be heard for half a block. "McClellan's boiled potatoes are still sitting in my stomach like a lead weight."

"There won't be any running. And there won't be any fighting either, Owen. Don't think that your continuous expressions of concern for my well-being in any way fool me. I know very well why you have come along. And it is not to thwart a potential ambush."

"You wound me, John. I have no desire to meet this character, Darcy. My readers would not rush to buy the jailhouse ramblings of an imbecile. And if none of this strikes you as odd . . . or sinister . . . then I'm surprised you've lasted as long as you have."

John forced a smile to hide his unease. "What could be sinister about this? We are in a good neighborhood surrounded by a number of people. This is not Paradise Alley."

"The better it was. At least there you know what to expect." He looked around. "It doesn't feel right, John. And your blind faith in this man Breckenridge is equally disturbing. I tell you, I expect a pack of bandits at this address more than I do Darcy Nance." He pulled back his jacket to expose his waist. Sticking up over his belt was the handle of a blade. "Perhaps you should carry this."

John shook his head. "Put away your knife, Owen. We won't need it." He walked a couple more steps. "And it's hardly blind faith."

Number 141 Franklin Street was by appearances just another residence. As the men approached, a fine carriage slowed and stopped just ahead of them. The driver climbed down without a glance in their direction and walked forward to check the horses. He knelt beside the lead animal, lifting a foreleg to inspect the hoof. As he turned his head, the light fell on his face; the pocked scars and red hair were unmistakable.

John walked swiftly toward him with Owen a step behind. "You are Breckenridge's man, are you not?"

He stood up and looked past John. "Who's he?"

"He is Mr. Conway, my associate. I can vouch for him."

The man paused for only a moment. "Very well. Get in quickly."

They did so, then watched as the driver lowered the shades, covering both windows.

"You see," John said with a bit of triumph as the carriage started forward. "I told you there was nothing to worry about."

Owen smiled. "Right." There was no sound beyond that of the wheels and hooves on brick. "Except you have no damned idea where they are taking us."

Approximately ten minutes later, the carriage slowed to a stop and the men heard the driver dismount. It was quiet except for the flapping of canvas in the wind and the tolling of a distant harbor buoy. The air smelled of salt and seaweed.

Owen leaned in with gallows humor. "If they offer you a blindfold, don't take it. Nothing good ever happens to people who wear blind-folds."

"Do shut up, Owen."

The carriage door swung open. "Follow me."

It was an odd place. A peninsula on the peninsula, a stretch of land as wide as two roads that stuck out from the rest of Charleston like a wayward piece of a jigsaw puzzle. At the tip of the land, with the Ashley River nibbling on three sides, a plain brick building stood next to a rundown warehouse. The driver walked toward the brick structure.

"Perhaps this is where they feed us to the alligators," Owen whispered.

"Don't joke. I don't like alligators."

Breckenridge's man led them to a door on the side of the building. He rapped twice. A burly, balding man with a beard answered the door suspiciously, speaking through a half-foot crack.

"You said there'd only be one."

"Now there's two."

"And Mr. Breckenridge is aware of this?"

The man nodded, then turned to John. "I'll pull around the warehouse. I'll wait for you until you come out." He walked back toward the carriage.

The door swung open, and John and Owen entered a large, dimly lit room. It was bare except for a desk and chair facing out from one wall and a rough wood bench along another. It had the smell of dust and abandonment.

"What is this place?" Owen asked.

The man answered sharply, each word an inconvenience. "Water-front lockup. It's the old holding cell for seamen."

"And you are . . . ?" John followed.

The man walked to one of the two interior doors. "Wait here."

Moments later, a different man emerged. He was younger and per-sonable, with a clean-shaven face and pleasant expression.

"Hello, gentlemen." He extended his hand to John, then Owen.

"My name is Michael Allen, and I am assistant to the mayor," he explained. "My duties are varied. I shall show you to Mr. Calhoun in a moment. First, we must discuss a critical point—one that must not be compromised. You can neither speak nor write of this place until the trial is over. Otherwise, men's lives will be in jeopardy."

"Yes, of course," they answered.

"Very well. Then follow me."

They walked to the heavier door, which had a narrow slit of a window at eye level, and waited as Allen inserted a key. It swung open with a pealing creak of neglect to reveal a narrow hallway with a concrete floor and stone walls stained with mildew. Allen's lantern led them to a second door of thick oak, which also purred as it rode its hinges. The small anteroom and the cell beyond it were illuminated by a single lantern that hung from a bracket on the wall outside the cell.

The cell was a good size, maybe ten by twelve feet, with a single barred window just below the high ceiling. It was obviously meant to accommodate several prisoners. Tonight it held only one.

"Mr. Calhoun, you have some visitors." Allen unlocked the cell door and left it open. He turned to John. "When you're finished, knock on the oak door and I will let you out."

John nodded, then stepped inside the cell.

"Y'all my lawyers? My new rep-re-sentation?"

Darcy Nance Calhoun stood before his cot. He looked much different from the man in courtroom. His wiry frame now slumped at the joints, a manifestation of weariness one could only imagine. His brow seemed more deeply furrowed and the lines on his face more pronounced, whether from care or the sharp shadows cast by the lantern. Without breaking his gaze, he licked his palm and began to pat at cowlicks scattered across his head. As his hand dropped, the rebellious hairs again broke free.

"No, we are not your lawyers. Mr. Calhoun, I am John Sharp, and this is Owen Conway. We are newspaper reporters from New York City. We have both been—"

"New York City, huh? That's an awful far-off place. Y'all travel all the way here by coach?"

"No," John answered. "By train. On the railway."

Darcy Calhoun laughed. "Ya know, I've never before even seen no train. Heard one a couple of times. Off when I was delivering my food crop up near Hampshire—heard it loud and clear. Ya see, a track runs past not a mile from there." He shook his head and smiled. "Sounded like a thousand horses on some sort of stampede." His eyes grew wide. "What's it like ta ride on one? Is it so loud you can hardly bear it?"

"No," John responded, a bit taken aback. "It is not that loud once you're inside."

"Uncomfortable as sin, though," Owen remarked.

Darcy nodded slowly. "So what was it again that ya wanted?"

"Well, Mr. Conway and I are both reporters here to cover your trial. We had hoped you might speak with us."

Darcy suddenly looked downward. His forehead again wrinkled tightly. "Were y'all at the court the other day? The day I was there?"

"Yes," John answered.

He winced, then shook his head quickly back and forth. "Wasn't right what they done. It wasn't right what they called me."

John thought for a moment. "A criminal?"

The brow again tightened. "Naw. Calling me by my middle name. Darcy *Nance* Calhoun. Ain't nobody called me that. Not even my folks. Some middle names just ain't meant ta be said." He took a long, deep breath and sighed. "A man should be called what he wants to be called. No matta the circumstances."

John shot a glance back at Owen, who looked equally bewildered. He then pulled a small paper bag from his coat pocket and handed it to Darcy. "These are for you."

He stared at the bag dubiously. "What is it?"

"They're butterscotches. Mr. Koch, from the general store in Cowford, told me you were quite fond of them."

Darcy smiled, his face relaxed for the first time. He quickly unwrapped a candy and popped it into his mouth. It rattled against his teeth as he spoke. "That's awful kind of you, sir. Don't much get any sweets in here." He glanced briefly around the cell. "But I'm not minding my manners," he said, looking a bit embarrassed. "I've not asked ya to sit." He gestured to the chair beside John. "Sorry there isn't but one." He looked toward Owen. "You's welcome to sit on the cot."

Owen took a step back and leaned against the wall. "This'll do just fine. I've been sitting all day."

Darcy sat down on the cot himself as John took his chair. "So what's yo' names again?"

"I am John Sharp, and that is Owen Conway."

"Mr. Sharp and Mr. Conroy—the train travelers. That's how I'll remember yous." His face pursed as he sucked hard on the butterscotch. "So, Mr. Sharp, how was it that ya came across Mr. Koch? He ain't in town, is he?"

"No. I visited Cowford, Mr. Calhoun. I visited so that I might find out as much as possible about you."

Darcy replied. "Such an interesting topic, is I? Gotta tell ya, Mr. Sharp, ain't much interesting 'bout me. Not much you'll find of interest in Cowford, neither." He smiled. "If you'd have come here first, I'd have told you and saved ya a lot of time." He smacked his candy. "But tell me, who'd ya see out there?"

John hummed. "I met a few of the residents. I spoke with Reverend Rose. And I also got a chance to visit your home. You'd be—"

Darcy lurched forward suddenly. "You see my dogs? Is they all right?"

"Yes, they are fine." As John stopped, Darcy's face begged for further reassurance. "They are being looked after by one of the slaves from the Breckenridge plantation—the same man who continues to tend to your land. He takes them home with him at night, then back to your property during the day. They both seemed quite healthy and playful."

Darcy leaned back and fiddled with his hands. The relief on his face was obvious. "Can't tell ya how worried I's been on account of 'em. The little one, Sara, she can't sleep 'cept beside me in the bed. And Dusty, the other one, why he's as finicky an eating dog as I's ever seen. Being without 'em has been like . . . Well, I's just been so worried."

John's voice was comforting. "They are both fine. I assure you."

Darcy swallowed the painful relief with glassy eyes. He cleared his throat. "So, you's been out to my land, huh?"

"Yes, and as I said, it—"

"You know the little one, Sara, she oft whimpers in the night. Like she's dreaming a bad dream. Her paws twitch a little like she's running. Now, I don't know if no dog can dream or not, but she sure acts like it. Normally, once I shake her, she settles down. I hope me being gone ain't making it worse." After a period of silence, Darcy again looked at the reporters. "So how'd my cabin look?"

"It looked . . . fine. Of course, I had never seen it before, but—"

"No one's been inside, has they?"

John spoke sheepishly. "I have, as a matter of fact. Though I can tell you, it was only for a matter of seconds."

Darcy became serious. "Well, what'd you see?"

"Nothing particularly odd. It did not look as if anything had been touched since . . . Well, since you left it."

"And folks haven't looted it or stole nothing, has they? No robberies or nothing?"

"It did not appear so, no."

He smiled. "Thank the Lord. I ain't got much, but I'd just as soon hold on to the little."

"Of course." John opened his notebook. "Now, Mr. Calhoun, if it's all right with you, I'd like to ask you a few questions." John watched as Darcy nodded. "How old are you?"

Darcy squinted. "And this is for a newspaper, huh? From what folks told me, all they was filled with was harvest predictions and advertisements."

"Well, in New York they cover a bit more. There are stories about what is going on in the city, and also around the country. People there are interested in what is happening in Charleston right now."

Darcy nodded. "Oh, I see." He paused. "I's thirty-two, I think. But there may've been one year I counted twice." He smiled. "But age don't seem to matter much unless you's real young or real old. So thirty-two is fine by me." John's smile coaxed a laugh from Darcy, an abrupt cough of a laugh. He leaned forward a little. "So how old is you, Mr. Sharp? And you too, Mr. Conroy?"

Owen did not correct him. "I'm twenty-five."

"I'm twenty-two," John responded.

"A bunch of spring chickens, that's what we is," Darcy laughed. "My grandpa—his name was Otis—that used to always be what he said to people. He lived to be seventy-eight, ya see, and no matta how old someone was, as long as they was younger than him, Grandpa Otis would call him a spring chicken. Drove Mr. Nelms, the local butcher, near mad, being that he was sixty-something hisself. He didn't seem to like it when Grandpa Otis called him no spring chicken." Darcy laughed. "I can sort of understand why, too. Mr. Nelms done looked like a crotchety old rooster if I eva saw one."

Owen's laugh increased Darcy's smile.

"How long have you lived in the area near Cowford, Mr. Calhoun?" John asked.

He began to slowly scratch his stubbly cheek. "Long time, now. Since a couple of years 'fore Momma passed, I guess."

"About ten years, would you say?"

"Sounds 'bout right."

John's face was now serious. "And had you ever been arrested before?"

"Heavens no," he answered. " 'Fore this, I's not exactly sure I knew what it fully meant. What with the jailing and the trial and the like. No, sir, it's been such a horror that I can't imagine no man would do it more than just the once."

"So did you do it? Did you do what they charge?"

There was no hesitation, just a drop in tone. "Yeah, I helped that man."

"Why?"

He drew a breath. "Frankly, 'cause I ain't know I was breaking the law. Not 'fore it was too late to do nothing 'bout it. You see, I ain't no quick thinker. All that happened was that I seen a man who needed help, and I helped him. I didn't stop to think of laws or courts or nothing."

John leaned forward. "Will you tell me of it? How the incident happened?"

There was no gaiety in his smile. "It's funny, ya know. I ain't one good at remembering—not a couple days back, let alone weeks. But that day sticks tight in my thoughts." His stare drifted to the moonlit window. "I remember I was coming back up to the house to fetch me some water. 'Twas late in the day, and it was raining a bit, but I remember figuring I still had a couple hours left of light. Enough time to clear me at least two more rows 'fore supper. As I was standing on the porch, I heard a sorta ruckus coming from the woods—the woods to the southwest, just beyond the creek."

"What sort of ruckus?"

"Well it sorta sounded like a wild pig, 'cept it was moving too fast. You know, the sound of twigs and branches breaking. And the birds was flying off, too. So I start ta take me a couple of steps toward it, on account of curiosity, when all of a sudden a Negro man breaks through into the clearing. When he saw me he just stopped. He was frozen-like, 'cept for his chest was heaving. And then he just stares at me. He didn't look evil or nothing, just scared. His arms was all torn up, probably on account of all the branches being broke, and his shirt was clear ripped to shreds. He just looked sump'n awful."

"What did you say to him? Or he to you?"

"Neither one of us said nothing. After a minute or two, I just sorta waved my arm so he'd know it was all right to come up by the cabin. As he starts ta walking t'ward me, I could see his limping. That's when I saw he ain't have no shoes on. One of his feet, I can't remember which, had a gash in it the length of two fingers. The bleeding would've been worse, 'cept for both feet was caked in mud."

"So that is when you brought him inside?"

"Uh-huh. Gave him a damp cloth so he might clean out the wound. It wasn't but a few seconds later that I heard the men coming."

"Were they shouting?"

"No. You could hear the dogs first. And they was hounds, you could tell by their yelps. Soon afta' that I start to feel the horses shake the ground just a portion. Enough ta know they was getting close."

John locked eyes. "Surely *then* you must have sensed he was a fugitive."

Darcy looked down at his hands. He seemed a bit embarrassed. "Can't remember thinking that, no. Can't remember thinking much at all. I just kind of stood there."

"Did the man, the slave, say anything? Did he react at all to the search party?"

Darcy adopted that same humorless smile. "Ya know, it's funny. I don't think he or I said no words to the other. We just sort of stayed quiet. Like that might make it go away."

John nodded. "How did they find him?"

"A man called from outside, a man on horseback. He asked if anyone's home. That's when I walked out on the porch ta meet him. He asked me then, had I seen a nigga run through there—the nigga they was chasing. I told him I hadn't." He paused, looking from wall to wall, as if solace lay somewhere else.

John spoke calmly, intent on not embarrassing him again. "Why not just tell him then? You must have guessed there was at least a chance they might catch you."

He thought for a moment, then strained a scared smile. "Ya know, Mr. Sharp, I done thought about that a lot. And every time I do, I just think about a time when I was little—when I was still school taught." He paused for a moment. "Well, this one day I broke my chalkboard, one of them little ones every kid had." He held up his hands, forming a small square. "It was really an accident. It slipped from my hands when I wasn't paying attention. Split in two right there on the floor. Well, I tried ta hide it, on account of how 'spensive they was, and so as ta not take a whooping. Hid it right inside my school desk, figuring I could just hold the pieces together in class until I could save up enough ta buy a new one." He exhaled. "But the next day, my teacher, she come up ta me with her hands behind her back and she says, 'Darcy, did you break your chalkboard?' And ya know, I just knew she was holding the broke pieces behind her back, but I said no. I said I hadn't." He swallowed. "I know it ain't a real good answer to your question— the question of why—but it's the same way I felt when that man asked me 'bout the Negro."

John waited a moment, waited again for Darcy's eyes to lift. "How did the man on horseback figure it out?"

"Well, at first when I told him, he seemed contented. He starts to looking off in the woods again. But then another rider come up beside him, and he starts to looking at the porch. Guess I hadn't noticed when the Negro was on the way in that his bare prints was all over the steps. That and some blood. And, since I was wearing me my working boots . . ." He shrugged. "I s'pose the one man figured it then, 'cause he took a bugle off his saddle and starts ta play it. That called all of 'em over—five or six, I think. One of the men, he tied my hands in rope, while the rest set to searching the cabin." He shook his head. "Didn't take 'em long. They came out carrying the Negro in not but a minute, all of 'em whooming and laughing and the like."

"Was he struggling? The Negro?"

Darcy began to shake his knees back and forth. His voice fell to a whisper. "No. Either he ain't have no strength left, or he knew he wasn't gonna win. He was crying though. And he had his mouth wide open, like he was yawning or sump'n. But ain't a word come out. Not a sound."

John had scribbled a line or two in his notebook, but for the most part he just listened. Owen was silent throughout the story. Only an occasional shift of position even reminded John that he was there.

"And since then you have been in custody," John said solemnly.

"Yessir. I done put my head down and woke up in some manner of cell every day since. That don't really leave no time for anything but thinking—sump'n I ain't never been no good at. But maybe that's what they want. As part of the punishing, I mean." Darcy took out another butterscotch and popped it in his mouth.

"Mr. Calhoun, in the description you just gave, you do, in essence, admit to doing what they are charging you with. So I wonder, why did you not plead guilty?"

He looked squarely at John. " 'Cause I don't think I is. They said what they is trying me for is helping out a slave. But I didn't know that man from Adam. I ain't never set my eyes on him before. So how's I to know who he is or what he's doing? Even my old lawyer, Mr. Smith, he says it's probably true." During the pause, Darcy's face went sad. He spoke in a mumble. "He says I just might be that stupid."

Owen nearly growled. "Only an ignorant man tells another that he is stupid."

Darcy looked up to Owen with a wan smile. "Thank ya, sir." He turned back to John. "But there's another reason, too. Another reason I ain't saying that I's guilty. And that's 'cause my old lawyer, Mr. Smith, he says that the punishment will be the same whether I say it or not. So why not go to trial and see. Maybe the judge will believe me. Anyway, Mr. Smith, he says that's my only chance, if the judge thinks I'm . . ." His voice trailed off, but he did not flinch at the implication.

John spoke to fill the silence. "I certainly understand why you did not want this man, Smith, to be your lawyer. But why not choose another lawyer from Charleston? Why pick a man who may use you to further his political agenda?"

Darcy's brow furrowed, and his voice sounded confused. "Well Mr. Smith says that the other man *wants* ta help me. That he *wants* ta work with me. If that's the case, I'd rather have a man's help who's willing. Not one who looks at me like I's the devil himself." The butterscotch rattled against his teeth. "And also, Mr. Smith says the new lawyer has to listen to what I say. That he can't make me say nothing that I don't wanna. That's true, right?"

"That's right. He's not supposed to put words in your mouth. But I must warn you that he might try." John paused to allow the point to settle. "Mr. Calhoun. Darcy. Because of all this, because of what you did, there will be certain people in the North who will look at you and this case as a symbol for the abolitionist cause. They might describe you as a man who stood up against slavery. What do you think of that?"

He laughed. "A symbol, eh? My old reverend, Reverend Parker, he used ta say, 'Just 'cause a man steps in a puddle don't mean he's no rainmaker.' " He shrugged. "I told ya how it happened. It truly wasn't nothing that should make people think I's someone I ain't. I ain't no symbol, that's for sure."

"Then what do you think of slavery?"

"It is what it is. Been around since I was a boy, so I don't really know nothing different. I heard that up North the Negroes are the same as the whites. I imagine that'd be sump'n to see." He paused. "But as for me personally, I don't think I could ever do it. Have slaves, I mean. I ain't real good at telling folks what to do or ordering 'em around. It just ain't me."

John closed his notebook and leaned forward. "I have just one more question, Darcy. Are you sorry for doing it?"

The man looked calm in reflection. "There ain't no sin in helping a man. Even the Bible says that 'to him that is afflicted, pity should be showed.' So for that I won't apologize. But if ya ask me if I had it to do over again, if I would do the same . . . Well, on that, I just ain't sure."

John stood up. "Darcy, thank you for speaking so openly with us. I want you to know that when I write my story about you and about the trial, I will treat you fairly." He shook Darcy's hand.

"Oh, I know that. I can tell by looking at ya that you's a fair man, Mr. Sharp. And meeting with you, the *train traveler*, has been my pleasure." He laughed. "You too, Mr. Conroy." He stared at Owen with a sly smile. "You sure don't say much, do ya, Mr. Conroy?"

"You and Mr. Sharp seemed to be talking all right."

"Oh, that's quite all right. My momma used ta say when I was a boy that I should always look out for the quiet folk. 'They's smart,' she'd say. And ya know why?" He pointed to his ear. " 'Cause they's listening."

Owen smiled and shook his hand. "I do hope we meet again."

"Me too. Don't oft get ta talk to folks no more. Mr. Allen, he stops in from time to time. And they let me see a reverend once. But it do get lonely. That's why it's been so nice talking to y'all." He leaned over and picked up the paper bag. "Would you like ta take a couple of candies with ya? I couldn't eat all of these without my teeth falling out."

"Oh, no," John answered. "Mrs. McGee intended those for you. She would want you to have them."

John and Owen walked out of the cell and knocked on the large oak door. Darcy stood beside his cot, his face illuminated by the lantern. "God bless ya both," he said with a wave.

"You too," John answered. He forced a smile.

As they walked away from the lockup, they heard the sound of the carriage pulling out from behind the warehouse. As they walked toward the beaten track, John turned to Owen. "I know I told you to let me ask the questions, but I hardly expected that."

"What?"

"You. You were as quiet as a mouse."

Owen's face remained steadfast. "It was your interview, and you seemed to be doing a good enough job. I just didn't feel the need to add anything."

"All right. Then what else is bothering you?" Owen didn't answer. "What?" John repeated insistently.

Owen stopped walking. "I just didn't expect to like the son of a bitch. That's all." Owen shook his head, then walked ahead quickly toward the carriage.

SEVENTEEN

Samuel Grass tapped on John's door at ten in the morning, sharp. He entered wearing a proud look of accomplishment.

"Did like ya asked, Mr. Sharp. Counted me up all the churches in town, white and black."

"Excellent. And you're sure you didn't miss any?"

"Yessir. Unless they's hiding one somewhere, I got 'em all. Went up and down every street. Twice a couple of times just to make sure."

"Good work, Samuel. So what was the total?"

"Counted fifteen white and sixteen black." The boy's brow tightened. "Except, there's one black church I ain't sure 'bout. Used ta be a church. I know that. But this time, when I went by, there was a couple boards over the door. I didn't count it on account of the boards."

"I think you're correct, Samuel. It sounds as if they closed."

"Yessir. I'd have thought that too, 'cept for all the men inside. Sure sounded like they was having a meeting."

"A church meeting?"

"Don't know what other kind. Black folks ain't allowed to get together in groups except for church meetings. So, I just figured that must be what it was."

John nodded. "Where was this church?"

"Ain't too far from here. Just a few blocks yonder, over on London Avenue."

"Perhaps I'll check it out. Accuracy is important, after all." John walked over to his desk and wrote the numbers Samuel had given him in his notebook. "You've saved me an incredible amount of time, Samuel. And you're sure no one noticed you, right?"

"Oh, yessir. I was real careful on that, just like you said."

"Good, good." John walked over to his dresser and fetched the boy a quarter. "You did good work for me. Right now, I have some errands to run. But check back later, and I'll see if I have any more reporting for you to do."

"Yessir. I's good and ready if ya need me." The boy's fist squeezed the quarter, and he smiled wide. "I'll check back with you later."

The abandoned church on London Avenue appeared unremarkable at first glance. Its long body was sandwiched between a black mortuary and a woodworking shop in a neighborhood of run-down businesses and black homes. Boards covered the windows, and someone had nailed a plank across the front door that bore a wooden cross as a lintel and a drift of sand at the sill. The other black churches John had seen in Charleston were well tended; this one obviously no longer had an active congregation. There was not a soul in sight. John was at a loss to understand why Samuel had mentioned it at all.

John was ready to dismiss the former church from his mind and continue on his way when he remembered a key fact about children. They take shortcuts—through alleys, backyards, and corridors between homes. Samuel had probably not approached the building from the street.

John ducked into a narrow passage west of the mortuary and walked the hundred-foot length of the building. He now began to hear sounds of activity—the bumps and scrapes of crates on gravel, and the mumbled exchanges of workmen. He selected a hidden vantage point in the shadow of a fig tree at the corner of the mortuary and watched for several minutes. He began to feel a tightening in his stomach. Something was wrong here.

About a dozen black men were unloading crates from two wagons and moving them into the old church building. The crates were fairly uniform, a good ten feet long, and heavy enough to require the efforts of two men. There was a furtive quality to the enterprise. The men handled the crates with quiet deliberation and spoke in low tones. John would have suspected a theft in progress were the men not moving crates into the building, rather than out.

The reporter strained with limited success to hear what the workers were saying. While John could distinguish individual words, the grammar and syntax were alien. The laborers were speaking a dialect reserved for each other—not for white men. Oddly, the soft, fluid quality reminded him of the Breckenridges' speech.

What content he could understand did not, however. The men called each other "Nigga" and "Hoss" as they cursed and grunted with effort. The skinny one said, "My Sara says I's gonna make her a widow with this business."

"Ain't that the truth," said another.

A third said, "Jist don't be talking 'bout it."

John felt the bite of mosquitoes and the sticky sap from the fig tree on his face and neck, but dared not move. It looked like Owen was right. Some Charleston blacks were obviously up to something—in a city where they risked the workhouse or even a noose.

A sharp cry and the crash of a crate falling made John jump. One of the workmen had lost his grip, and a crate fell from the level of the wagon bed to the ground, bursting open. Rifles spilled out into the dust.

"For the love of God," John breathed.

Jebediah Jones. He's raising an army. Blacks had weapons here in the heart of Charleston. The words of Joshua Mannion, the local editor, flashed through his mind. "In a city out of control, neither your newspaper nor Tyler Breckenridge can protect you."

John stood frozen. The men stood perfectly still also, staring at the weapons.

A voice from the building hissed. "You gonna just stand there looking at 'em? Get 'em back in the box." A burly white man stepped from the back door of the old church. He shook his head. "They ain't loaded, so they ain't gonna bite you. Now get moving." He turned to someone inside. "When the other shipment comes in tomorrow, take it all down to the Winchester warehouse."

John slipped away, back along the mortuary wall to the front of the building. He was sweaty, sticky, and confused. So the church was now a warehouse, and white supervisors had blacks doing the heavy work, unloading crates of guns. No conspiracy here. Things in this city could go from normal to crazy then back again in the space of half an hour. Well, Owen might be right about one thing. It could just be the heat . . . Or maybe the ghost of Denmark Vesey.

John's sense of relief rode on the back of a soft ocean breeze that now blew into the lowlands of Carolina. That measure of comfort seemed to lift the pervasive melancholy that hung over the city as well. Life in Charleston moved faster. Pedestrians and wagons clipped about the bustling market with more urgency, children ran about the streets brazen with indiscretion, and even the indigenous molasses drawl seemed to roll off the tongue more fluidly. John smiled, observing the correlation between temperature and activity. Forty more degrees, he thought. If the temperature dropped that much, the residents might then begin to resemble New Yorkers.

He felt a tap on his shoulder. "Hope you haven't been waiting long, sport." Owen wore his usual smile. "I got kind of caught up. I was supposed to meet with this militia fellow, but he never showed." He shrugged. "Anyway, where do you want to eat?"

They began to walk down the East Bay. "Actually, I was only waiting to tell you that I couldn't make lunch. I am going to the Breckenridge mansion."

"Jesus, John. You and this Tyler guy act like long-lost kin." He shook his head. "So, what is it today? A visit from the governor, perhaps? Or has he set up a meeting with that fellow that orchestrated the uprising? That Jebediah Jones?"

John shuddered a little. The recent scare was not quite erased from his mind. "If you must know, I am not going there to meet with *Mr.* Breckenridge."

Owen offered a sly smile. "Well, that explains why you're wearing your high-society suit. So that you can take the day off to cavort with your new lady friend. And while I suspect that those boys back at the *Tribune* wouldn't approve, I am entirely for it."

"Heck, what else am I supposed to do? I certainly cannot make this trial start any sooner. Nor can I make the lawyer's train travel any faster. And I've about run out of locals who will admit that they knew Darcy Calhoun."

"Hey, sport, you're preaching to the choir here. I just told you I was all for it." He slapped John across the back. "Besides, with the way things have dried up here over the last few days, your story is the best thing I've got going." Owen swept his hand across the sky as if polishing a headline. " 'Prominent Belle and Yank Reporter Caught in Lurid Affair.' " He laughed. "Or, if things really heat up, 'Yank Reporter Shot in Duel by Lover's Angry Brother.' I like the second one better. It has more spice. What about you?"

John couldn't help but smile. "You're acting like a voyeur. It is hardly an affair."

"Call it what you will. Just remember to tell Old Owen all of the intimate details. I'll come up with the appropriate verbiage."

They turned on Water Street, now only a stone's throw from the tip of the peninsula. "You know what is rather odd?" Owen continued. "The way that the locals have clammed up over the last few days. When I said a minute ago that your story was the only promising lead that I had, I was only half kidding. People have stopped talking with me. Even the drunks and the sailors aren't saying much."

"Maybe they have nothing to say."

"That's normally when drunks and sailors talk the most. That's when they spill their guts with tall tales and rumors. But I'm not getting any of that. Most won't even speak with me. The sudden distrust, it's really strange."

"Do you think it might have to do with the trial? Darcy's decision to use a northern lawyer?"

"I'd have thought so, but that's not when they quit talking. I was still getting good leads until the day before yesterday. And damned if I can figure out why."

"I wouldn't worry about it. Anger, more than alcohol, seems to loosen their tongues. I think that as we get closer to the trial, that will become apparent."

Owen shoved both of his hands in his pockets and nodded. "You're probably right. It sure was the case with those chaps at breakfast this morning. Berating a man like that when he has fallen ill hardly seems sporting. Especially when you consider that the man is our president."

"I have heard much stronger denunciations of President Taylor than that down here. I think a case of food poisoning would be almost preferable to the kind of reception he could expect on a visit to Charleston. These people perceive him as the fourth horseman of the apocalypse."

They stopped in front of a narrow but exquisite three-story mansion. The white of the small columns supporting the porch and second-story piazza gleamed of fresh paint, and the faint smell of turpentine wafted to them at the head of a breeze. From the porch, a symphony of wind chimes began to tinkle above a rustling of potted palms. A black man working above on the piazza relaxed a moment to savor the breeze before returning to the redundant task of polishing already immaculate windows.

"I believe this is the place," John said.

"Yeah, a real rat's nest. I don't know how you'll cope."

"With true diligence." He began to walk toward the house. "I'll see you back at McClellan's."

"Yeah," Owen answered over his shoulder. "Perhaps we can get some dinner."

John was greeted at the door and informed that Miss Breckenridge awaited him in the garden. As he walked through the French doors to the garden, the view was enchanting. Though not particularly grand in size, the garden intoxicated the eyes with every imaginable shade of color. The landscaping was perfectly imperfect, casting the yellows and purples, whites and reds, against one another like overlapping flags. A herringbone brick walk guided his view toward the center-piece—a sprawling ancient oak that drenched half the backyard in a blanket of shade. Around the garden's perimeter ran a wall of fine brickwork, and atop that, a lattice hung with ripening grapes.

Clio appeared from behind the oak, as if waiting offstage until the beauty of this setting could be fully appreciated. She wore a white dress and a bonnet with peach-colored flowers. "Do you like it?" she asked sweetly.

"It is magnificent. The flowers and the color . . . I can say without question it is the loveliest garden I have ever seen."

His answer pleased her. She walked toward him with a simple smile and looped her arm through his. "Horticulture was my mother's passion. We have many varieties that are quite rare in this part of the world." She gestured toward some blooms of deep indigo. "She kept detailed notes on every species in the garden. She made me learn their names—*in Latin.*"

"Oh, really." John gave her a look of mock apprehension.

She squeezed his arm. "Don't worry. This lecture tour shouldn't take more than an hour."

They began to stroll leisurely, following the path of bricks, immersed in the shade. Clio still carried a parasol on her shoulder.

"So, Mr. Sharp, what is it you would like to do today?"

He smiled. "My knowledge of Charleston has been confined to the courthouse and a tavern or two. I rather hoped that you might make a suggestion."

"Very well. Since the weather is so pleasant, I took the liberty of packing a picnic lunch. There is a place called Fox Hall Gardens that is perfect for such occasions."

"That sounds excellent."

"It is really quite a shame that your trip here did not coincide with the social season. Between February and May, there are ever so many activities to enjoy—parties and races and all sorts of events. But now, because of the heat, we are reduced to only garden walks and evening concerts."

"I am not disappointed. Those activities would be a distraction from the pleasure of the company. I think a park sounds perfect."

She looked down to cover her smile. Then she removed her arm from his and walked a few feet away, stopping beside a rather odd-looking apparatus. It somewhat resembled a bench, consisting of a long piece of wood supported by two knee-high blocks on the ends. But the piece of wood for sitting was made of cedar and appeared somewhat flimsy, and there was no back for support. Clio stood next to it, eager to be asked.

"What is it? Some sort of bench?"

She shrugged coyly. "Not exactly. It is a joggling board."

"What is its purpose?"

"Well, children use it as a springboard. They jump up and down on it, then go flying off." Her quick glances to the back of the house and her mischievous expression were puzzling.

"Are you suggesting that I try it? For if I'd have known, I would have dressed—"

"It has other uses." She sat down as if riding sidesaddle. She looked back at the oak, whispering back. "Courters also find it helpful." She found John with the corner of her eye and pointed. "Sit."

He sat at the opposite end from her, ten feet away. She kept her glance elsewhere and said not a word. John spoke dryly. "I would guess the courting process is a rather slow one if this is considered helpful. I, for one, would much prefer a shorter joggling board."

She looked back to him, her eyes laughing. "Bounce."

"Excuse me?"

"Bounce. Up and down, like this."

She began to do just that, gaining momentum until each bounce lifted her partially from the board. John, once over the paralysis of shock, joined in with enthusiasm. Gravity then took over. The bounces brought them toward one another, the creak of the wood drowned out by the volume of their laughter. They were five feet away. Then three. At the point John guessed two more bounces would land her in his arms, a woman's voice bellowed out from the house.

"That's far enough, Miss Clio. You stop just there."

John's shift in direction defied physics. He bounced almost back to the end of the board upon hearing the order. Clio just sighed as she turned back to the middle-aged black woman in the doorway.

"Yes, Da," she called out.

"Now yo' picnic basket is all packed up. You two come inside so you can get on your way." She closed the door, but her eyes lingered.

John stood up. "Who was that?"

Clio picked up her parasol and stood as well. "That's my Da. My mammy from when I was a girl. She still keeps a watchful eye."

"And has the ability to make me again feel thirteen." He smiled past the embarrassment.

She walked toward him, twirling the parasol, allowing each step to take her to the tops of her toes. She leaned in to whisper without stopping. "Oh, Mr. Sharp, you got much farther than you would have at thirteen."

Fox Hall Gardens was a place of gazebos and pergolas and a pond with pink flamingos. Music from a brass band filtered through the trees from a flag-draped pavilion. Swings hung from the branches of grand magnolias, and one could hear squeals of delight from the young ladies as they clung to the bars of the merry-go-round with gloved hands.

Clio selected a spot beneath an oak in sight of the pond. Then John and Clio set off to explore, while two servants laid out their picnic.

They found strange and wonderful things. A young man was cranking an instrument called a hurdy-gurdy while his younger sisters harmonized a melancholy tune. A man with a cape was making flowers and doves appear from under his top hat. And then there was a very pretty young woman with a German-like accent who attracted quite a crowd, mostly gentlemen, as she walked barefoot on a rope stretched between two trees, a good five feet off the ground. She had a full skirt and petticoats and a parasol, and one could see a good six inches of shapely leg above the ankle. Clio tugged at John's arm to suggest that it was time for lunch.

Clio and John sat on cushions beside a low table set with china, flowers, and a spread of cold roast chicken, soft cheeses, and crusty bread.

"There is no milk on the menu today," Clio remarked, "in deference to our suffering president."

"That is the most sympathetic reference to President Taylor that I have heard down here. Most call him insufferable. I read that he is still indisposed, but I thought it was because of bad fruit."

"Oh, dear," she said with distress as she uncovered a bowl of fresh berries.

John shrugged. "I say we eat them anyway."

They ate the berries as they drank white wine, and John refilled their glasses. The setting, the wine, and the company produced lively conversation and laughter.

Clio set down her glass and pointed to an area behind her. "You know, when I was a girl, they used to have elephants just over there."

"To ride?"

"Do not be profane, John. A lady would not think of such a thing."

He laughed. "So why are they no longer there?"

"I am not exactly sure why. They bring in different animals from time to time, but I think it's too expensive to keep them here for long." Her posture slackened. "Over the last years, the number of people of means has dropped considerably in the lowlands. Or at least, those concerned with civic improvements and the arts. Politics and war seem to be the only suitable topics of conversation now. I, for one, can not think of a more crude replacement." She paused for a moment, then looked up cheerfully. "But they do still shoot off fireworks here. Of course, they don't do it if it has been dry for days, but if we get a good rain while you are here, perhaps we can watch them."

"I would like that very much." John reached over and picked up a peach-colored rose petal that had fallen to the tablecloth and rubbed it gently between his fingers. He looked about him at the park. He had never felt so content. "This is a pretty place. Not just the park; I mean Charleston."

"And what of New York?" she asked. "Where would you take me if I ever visited there?"

John stopped for a moment to consider. P. T. Barnum and his American Museum seemed totally inappropriate. And oddly, at that moment, John could not think of a single thing about the New York he knew that seemed suitable for the girl.

She prompted him. "Are there parks? I hear there are tall build-ings."

"The buildings are tall. But they are, well, functional." He fur-rowed his brow. "And the parks are not as nice as this."

She tilted her head a little. "What is it that you like about it?"

"Well, they are planning to make one." John was still back on the parks. "There is a large forested parcel just north of the city that they hope to turn into a grand park—a central park. The city will grow up around it."

"Well, that sounds promising."

John smiled a little, took a sip of wine, and looked at her. "I guess that's what I like about it. The promise. You see, as the city grows, so does the imagination. New streets spring up daily, and down those streets a thousand new ideas. Perhaps it's something in the air we all breathe, perhaps it's in the poison belched from the factories and pulp mills, but we all have it. That need to outdo the man before, to make the advances of the last decade seem ancient in the next." He leaned forward. "There is talk of building a crystal palace, a grand building made entirely of glass, where they will show off exhibits from every country in the world. And the idea of an elevated railway—one where the train will travel *above* the street—is constantly discussed." Clio's eyes brightened, sparked by the excitement in his voice. "Two years ago, I sat in the wire office on Printing House Row and heard reports on the Mexican War almost as it unfolded. Ten minutes after a battle ended over a thousand miles away, I knew details and information previously reserved for a general. Such a thing would have been un-fathomable twenty years ago."

They both looked up as an unmistakable silhouette appeared in the unshaded grass near the old oak.

"Why, hello, Brother," Clio chimed.

John turned and immediately arose. Breckenridge was a few feet away, dressed impeccably in a light brown suit, with a cane tucked beneath his arm.

"Hello, Tyler. Will you join us?"

"For a moment."

"What brings you here today, Brother?"

"The same reason as you, I would guess. To enjoy the weather. I thought a stroll might serve me well." As he spoke, he looked off in the distance. "Tell me, John, did everything go well last night?"

"Yes, and I cannot thank you enough." He paused. "But I would imagine my continued appreciation is beginning to wear old."

Breckenridge looked to him. "Nothing could be further from the truth. All that you have asked I have been happy to provide. Friends do that."

The word was not lost on John. He affected nonchalance, nodding slightly.

Clio sensed something in Tyler's demeanor and made a sudden, offhanded excuse. "Would you both pardon me? I have to attend to . . . things."

"Of course," they said in turn.

John offered her his hand, and she arose gracefully. As she walked toward the pavilion, the men began a slow walk across the grass.

Tyler looked only forward. "His lawyers arrived today. Late this morning."

"Was there any trouble?"

"No. It was planned so there wouldn't be. But, since they arrived on time, the trial *will* begin on Friday."

John nodded. "Has Darcy met with them yet?"

"As we speak, I believe." His gaze fell from the horizon to the grass. "These lawyers have me concerned, John. A man I know well was part of their escort, and he spoke with Mr. Coulter at length. He described him as a raving ideologue—a man here to represent the abolitionist cause rather than Darcy Calhoun. I'm sure you can imagine what the reaction to such a defense would be, both in the courtroom *and* the streets. I fear that under those conditions, I would be unable to . . ." He drew a long breath. "I fear that then the judge would dismiss talk of leniency. Only the harshest penalty would placate the angry."

"But when I spoke with him, Darcy seemed to understand that the lawyers must adopt his version of the defense. He is not an abolitionist, and I do not believe he wishes in any way to be associated with that cause. Coulter must abide by that."

"Yes, but the unsophisticated are the most susceptible to coercion. Darcy makes an inviting target. And make no mistake, John, this lawyer's victory would come in convincing Darcy he's something he isn't. To him, the verdict is of secondary importance."

John nodded. "Let us hope, then, that Darcy is able to understand that."

They stopped walking and faced one another. Tyler's tone was serious. "Do you plan to meet with him again?"

"I did not know it was possible."

"I have instructed the men watching him that you are allowed to see him whenever you wish. I only ask that you travel there covertly."

John thought it a rather odd thing to grant. His questions pertaining to the crime had already been answered, and he had intended no follow-up visit. "Thank you," he muttered, a bit confused.

"If you do speak again, I hope you would impress on him that he need be only responsible for his own testimony, nothing that the lawyer says. Just tell him to be honest with his words and to watch out for their tricks."

"If I speak with him, I will mention it."

"Good," Tyler said with a slight smile. They began to walk back toward the oak. "So what did you think of him?"

"I rather liked him. There is a simplicity about him that is entirely disarming. And the fact that he is not overly . . . sharp, makes his story strangely believable."

"I felt the same way upon hearing it. I believe that is why I am so concerned."

They walked for a time in silence, nearing the oak. "There is something that I still wonder," John said, "and I don't think Darcy could even answer it. It is an entirely hypothetical question, but I wonder if he would have helped that man if he *had known* he was a slave."

"Tell me, John. Did Darcy, at any time during your meeting, behave like a man who felt he'd made a terrible mistake?"

John shook his head. "No."

"Well, then, I believe you have your answer."

Breckenridge turned away, off to his right. "Ah, Clio, you are back," he called at her approach. "I shall leave you two to enjoy the rest of the afternoon. John, perhaps you might like to join us for dinner at the house?"

"I should like that very much," he answered.

"Let us say seven-thirty then."

John had been back in his room at McClellan's but a short time when the thump of quick feet up the rickety boardinghouse steps drew his attention. They pounded down the hallway to his room, and his door slammed open.

Owen's breathing was heavy. "Thank God you're here. I was afraid I'd have to scour the town, maybe break up your little soirée."

John paid little attention to the drama of Owen's entrance. He raised an eyebrow. "Did you find another lighter?"

"This is monumental," Owen snapped. He took off his jacket and flung it on the bed. The typical joy was estranged from his excitement. "Something damned sinister is going on here."

"What is it?" John now gave the Irishman his full attention.

Owen took a deep breath and stared silently for a moment, shuffling from foot to foot. "John, I write for the *Police Gazette*. Scandal, corruption, nothing too serious, nothing too deep. I came down here to cover a hanging, not a trial.

"I want you to know that I didn't lie to you—before, when you asked me right after you got back from the plantation if anything had happened while you were gone."

"Tell me what's going on, Owen."

Owen exhaled. "When the trial was postponed, I began to look for another story. I started looking into the fires. There's such a mystery down here about who's doing it, I figured it would be an interesting investigation. So I went to a lot of the burned buildings and asked questions where I could. I talked to people about who they thought was doing it, if anyone at all."

"Yes," John agreed, "I started a similar investigation of my own."

"Well, there were no new fires while you were away, and the story seemed to be getting cold. But about an hour ago I came to a realization." Owen leaned forward, and his words spilled out quickly. "Would it surprise you to learn, John, that in every fire that occurred in the last month, only once did more than one building burn, and in that case the second fire was put out immediately? *John, the fires never spread.*"

John furrowed his brow in disbelief. "That seems impossible. Especially with the close proximity of the buildings."

"Exactly. The only way it would be possible was if the fire company was in on it. If they *knew* where the fires were going to be set."

"And that would mean . . ." John's words trailed off as their eyes locked.

"A conspiracy," Owen said with a trace of his old smile.

John looked skeptical. "You're sure about this? I mean, you're absolutely sure?"

"About only one building each time? Very sure. I've just come from looking at them."

John shrugged. "But why? I mean, to what end? Why would people in authority intentionally set fire to their own city?"

"I'm damned if I know."

John felt the color rise in his cheeks, and it wasn't purely from the excitement of an interesting lead. If Owen's information was correct, this was a scoop he should have uncovered himself. This was a major story, and he had delegated the legwork to an eleven-year-old boy. Because he had not seen the fires firsthand, he had missed an interesting clue. The racial tension in Charleston and Samuel's report that no black homes had burned had fostered the assumption that the fires had racial overtones. Owen's information suggested other possibilities, perhaps one as simple as an arsonist on the fire department, but potentially something more sinister.

"Owen, what can you tell me about the nature of the buildings that have burned? I understand that none of them were owned by blacks."

"I didn't know that. I just know that the buildings were either vacant or businesses. Do you think that someone is trying to deliberately increase tension between blacks and whites?"

John shrugged. "It could be as simple as the fact that someone was always home at the black-owned houses. It could also be that the buildings aren't locally owned. Perhaps they are tied to northern interests. Right now I don't know what to think. There are some people that might provide some answers, though. One is Prescott Woodridge, the reporter from Boston you introduced me to on my first night here. He has been to Charleston before and might give us some perspective. Then there is Breckenridge. I'm supposed to have dinner with him tonight. I could feel him out on the subject."

Owen looked dubious. "I agree about bringing Woodridge in on this, but I don't trust Breckenridge."

"I wouldn't tell him what we know," John answered. "I would ask him questions and see how he responds. I'd like to think we have a pretty good rapport. Hopefully, he would be fairly open with me at this point."

Owen nodded. "Well, I guess I could start by trying to track down Woodridge. I've seen him a couple of times at the bars."

"I'll do the same thing before I leave for dinner. I'll check the places I've seen him. I agreed to interview Darcy again tomorrow morning."

Owen raised an eyebrow in question.

"I want to try and find out if he likes his new lawyers," he responded. "But let's meet here tomorrow around two unless we turn up something sooner."

The tavern was as dark now as when John had visited one week ago; darker even, because of his eyes' adjustment to the daylight outside. He stood still near the entrance, waiting for the blur of shapes to become the detail of faces. As they did, he saw no one familiar.

He walked past the trestle tables at the front, past the smell of roasting meat and spilled beer. But he did not find Woodridge at the back either. As he considered where else he might look for the man, he became overtly aware of three men coming toward him; three men of physical diversity but sharing one disturbing similarity. They all wore the blue jackets of the militia.

The tallest man, the man in the middle, stepped too close to John for his comfort. He appraised John slowly, looking him up and down, stopping for an uncomfortable pause when he reached the face.

"I know who you are," the man said atonally. He ran his tongue over his mustache, salvaging the remnants off his last sip of ale. "You may look a mite bit prettier, but I still know who ya are."

John took a half step back and smiled. "Then I fear you have me at a loss, sir. For I have no idea who *you* are."

The man nodded. "Didn't figure that ya would. But we all know what ya done." He elbowed the man next to him, who nodded in agreement. "You was outside the courthouse after the trial. Ain't that right?"

"Yes," John answered slowly.

"Then you's the one that pulled Chester Dalton outta that crowd afta' he got himself into all that trouble. Ain't ya?"

The statement brought a measure of relief. "Yes, I was."

The man twisted his lip and nodded. "I figured I was right when I saw ya walk in here." He took a deep breath. "Now I know you's a Yank, but what ya done was right. And right is right, no matter where ya hail from. So me and the boys here would appreciate it if you'd let us buy ya a drink."

John nodded. "Of course. It would be my pleasure."

He joined the three militiamen at their table and thanked them again as a glass of ale slid his way. "How is Mr. Dalton? Has he recovered?"

The large man, now introduced as Buster, responded. "Yeah, he's all right. They let him out of his duties. Let him go home."

"What about the rest of you? How much longer until you get to go home?"

The small stocky man named Wiggins smiled. "Not but another six days. Can't wait, neither. I'm damn sick of wearing this jacket, having people yelling at ya, throwing things at ya. It wasn't so bad when we was quartered over by Sullivans Island. No one's out there ta bother ya. But here in Charleston . . . phew." He took down half his ale in one sip. "I's darn ready ta leave."

"Amen," Buster echoed. The third man, Hoot, said nothing. He had yet to do anything but stare.

"Why were you out on Sullivans Island?"

"Not on it. Just in that neck of the woods." He corrected himself. "More like neck of the beach. Fort Moultrie's up that way."

"We was drilling," Wiggins joined in. "They've been rotating folks from here to there and back again. Keeps us on our toes, they say." He shrugged.

"So there are militia there now?"

"Yup," Buster answered. "Some are out at Sumter, too. Fort there ain't finished, but there's room for a bivouac and room to drill. Heck, what ya see here in the city ain't but scratching the surface."

"Will they all be here in town for the trial?"

The tall man shrugged. "That's the plan, I guess. In case sump'n happens, the more help the better."

"I'd imagine it's been quite hectic. Even worse because of the fires." John looked hard at the men for any kind of reaction, any hint of discomfort. He was disappointed to find none.

"Yeah," Buster agreed. "But since they bumped up the number of us in town, ya ain't seen no flames. What's it been, Wigs, four or five days?"

"At least."

"Yeah. So like I said, the more help the better."

John took his final sip. "Thank you all for the drink."

Buster nodded. "Thanks for giving us sump'n we can rib Chester about for the next few years. Saved by a Yank. He may never live that down."

John shook their hands. "I enjoyed speaking with you." He looked at Hoot, an apparent mute. "And sharing a drink with you."

"Ah, don't worry 'bout Hoot," Wiggins said with a chuckle. "He don't talk much. Thinks he's better than the rest of us just 'cause he gets two dollars more a month for being artillery."

Wiggins and Buster laughed, while Hoot remained silent.

John arrived at the Breckenridge mansion at a quarter after seven for dinner. He was escorted to the bar, where he fixed himself a tall drink and sipped it as he stared out a window into the garden.

John knew he would probably have to wait until after dinner to speak alone with Tyler. He couldn't decide how much to tell him of what he had learned about the fires. John planned to test his response to several questions, then decide.

For a few moments, John paid no attention as the bells began to toll. He had grown immune to their perpetual announcement of time. It was not until he heard the sound of running above him, the stomps of hurried feet on the second floor, that he realized they were ringing at the wrong time and with a difference. The tolling was louder. More urgent. It was an alarm.

Two servants rushed down the stairs, one after the other. The first ran through the foyer and out the front door without breaking stride. The second, a neatly dressed black man, stopped as he caught sight of John, and in a somewhat surreal maintenance of station, tugged to straighten his jacket as he captured his breath.

"It's a fire, sir," he intoned calmly. After John nodded, the man walked crisply in the direction of the kitchen.

Clio appeared on the landing a second later. Her cheeks were flushed, her words fast and loud as they battled against the continued tolling. "Have you seen it?"

John walked quickly toward the stairs. "The fire? No."

She began to descend, her hand white as she clutched the banister. "It is just awful. Just terrible."

John took her hand for the last two steps and could feel it tremble. "I am sure the fire department will have it under control in no time," he said.

"I saw it from my window," she continued as if not hearing John. "A thick cloud of smoke off to the south. It is big. And with the wind blowing the way it is . . ." She put her hand to her chest and breathed deeply. "Where is Tyler?"

"I have not seen him."

"Scipio!" she called to the vacant rooms.

The man appeared a second later. "Yes, Miss Clio."

"Where is my brother?"

"He ain't come home just yet."

She sighed a determined breath. "Scipio, round up all the men. Gather the buckets and start filling them from the pump in the garden. You know what to do. Go now, quickly."

"Yes, miss."

"Is the fire really that close?" John asked, suddenly tense.

Her eyes, wide with fear, focused briefly on him. "This is a small peninsula, Mr. Sharp. And the wind is blowing in this direction."

The two of them hurried outside. Clio lifted her skirt with both hands to lengthen her steps. They stopped on the sidewalk, congregating with countless others who were similarly pulled from their homes. Their worried faces craned upward in unison as their eyes followed the column of gray smoke, smoke that billowed up in surges as if fanned by unseen bellows.

"It seems to be coming from the warehouses along the Ashley," Clio said, looking upward at the smoke.

"They would be empty this time of year, right?"

"Yes, most storage does not begin until the end of summer. But—"

Tyler appeared from behind them. Clio turned and hugged him. "Oh, Tyler." She composed herself and swallowed. "I have instructed the men to fill all the buckets. They are doing it as we speak."

"Good," he said, holding her hand, his other arm around her shoulders. "But I'm sure it won't be necessary. You go inside now. Calm the servants, particularly Birdie and Da. You know how they get when there's a fire. Tell them dinner will be a bit later."

The reassurance and the soft grip of his hand appeared to bring solace. She squared her shoulders with determination. "Of course, Brother."

"I am going to head down there," Tyler said with a nod toward the fire. "I told Rogers to hitch up the wagon and load some buckets. He is bringing it around now."

"Be careful." Her voice was urgent.

"Of course." He managed a smile.

John waited until she was out of earshot, watching as the smoke thickened. "Why is this fire so dangerous?"

Tyler was less reassuring after his sister's departure. "The warehouses are quite large and made entirely of wood—they are tinderboxes. And with the winds blowing the way they are, the chance of a spark crossing the street to the homes on Rutledge is quite high."

"And then?"

Tyler took out his handkerchief and wiped the back of his neck. "There is no significant break between the homes and this section of town; if the blaze gets too large, we are all in danger."

A wagon rounded the corner, and was pulled to a halt beside them. Rogers shouted down from the driver's seat. "It is *yo'* warehouse, sir!"

Tyler jumped up next to Rogers, and John did not wait to be asked. He climbed into the back, stepped over buckets, and sat down on a small box, then braced himself as the horses broke with a violent jerk. As he was jostled about, the streets passed in a blur. Only the growing plume of smoke stayed steady.

The Breckenridge warehouse came into view as the wagon turned on to Rutledge Street. As they drew closer, John could see flames visible at the roofline on the north side of the building and at the south side of the adjacent warehouse. A collection of about forty men, white and black, were pumping water into troughs and running back and forth with buckets. More were converging on the site.

Breckenridge watched intently, then shook his head. "It's too far gone. We'll have to wet down the south end and see if we can keep it from spreading to the homes."

As the wagon lurched to a halt, Tyler jumped down and dispatched Rogers to organize the bucket brigade. He engaged in an animated conversation with two black men who immediately ran up to him. Tyler yelled back to John. "At least there's no one inside, thank God."

John now realized that Breckenridge's passivity had been an illusion. The coiled spring was released. The planter stripped off his jacket and worked harder and faster than the others, filling and passing buckets, shouting orders, organizing men with poles to push in a wall about to collapse.

Breckenridge glanced back at the south end of the building and reacted with surprise. One of the doors farthest from the fire was open, and smoke poured out.

"He didn't go in there, did he, Gabe?!" Breckenridge yelled to an older black man.

"Yes, sir. Jimmy said *yo'* new equipment is down at this end! He thinks he can get to it!"

Breckenridge muttered an oath. He grabbed his coat and soaked it in the trough, then strode toward the open door.

"You're not going in there?" John shouted to him, starting forward.

If Breckenridge heard him, he did not answer. He stopped just short of the door and peered into the smoke. "Jimmy, get the hell out of there!"

There was a sharp crack inside, followed by the crash of falling wood. Breckenridge sprang forward through the door.

John took off after Rogers and Gabe, who also sprinted toward the building. They almost collided with a young black man who was forcibly ejected through the door. Breckenridge was right behind him. He grabbed the young man by the collar of his still-smoking shirt and jerked him farther away. He threw his coat over the man's shoulders.

The young man was coughing, and tears were streaming down his face from the smoke. Breckenridge was livid. "Jimmy, if you ever disobey me like that again, you will be back at Willowby digging ditches so fast your head will spin."

Something caught Tyler's attention on the horizon behind Jimmy. John followed his gaze—it was a second column of light gray smoke, well across town. The plume was in the direction of the bell tower where John had earlier spotted the descending workman.

Breckenridge looked quickly about. John could see the alarm in his eyes. He yelled for Rogers, who came toward him at a run.

"Take the wagon and get up to Elliot Street. Fast!" The planter spoke through clenched teeth. "You tell them I said to get that fire wagon *here*. Immediately!"

The fire engine eventually arrived, and the fire was confined to the two warehouses. John observed the men's furtive glances at Breckenridge and overheard their mutterings that the fire engine had been slow in coming. The plume across town had disappeared some time ago.

Breckenridge's face was grim as he walked among men with blistered, bleeding hands and soot-stained faces. He approached each group and thanked them for their help in fighting the fire. He came to

John last. Tyler's hair was soaking wet, and his face streaked with black.

"John, I would be much obliged if you would let them know at the house that things are all right here. Get something to eat, but tell them not to expect me. I will be here for a while."

As John left, he saw Tyler striding purposefully toward a lone man in a fireman's uniform; one with gold braid on the cap.

EIGHTEEN

⌒

Darcy Calhoun sat on his cot with one leg tucked against his chest and the other on the floor. He smiled wide as he sucked on a warm peanut shell.

"How d'ya know I liked boiled peanuts, John?" he slurred, wiping his fingers across his moist lips.

"It was just a lucky guess."

The look on Darcy's face justified the visit. Initially, he had decided against coming. John thought that seeing Darcy again would only increase his own frustration over the trial, with no useful benefit. But Darcy's response served to thaw John's anger. Twice he had narrowly averted hugs, and Darcy's smile was all but permanent.

"I just can't believe what a run of luck I's had. First, you stop by for a friendly visit. Then my lawyers come yesterday, and they's real nice too. And look, here ya is back again." He started to laugh. "Heck, I figure I'm gonna have ta ask 'em for some curtains for that window up there on account of all the company."

John smiled. "So you like your lawyers?"

Darcy's fingers fumbled for another peanut. "Oh, yeah. They was real decent. They asked me much of the same questions you did. Stuff about how it happened and how I got caught. I think they stayed a bit more than an hour."

"Did they talk about your strategy for the trial? What things you would say in court?"

"Not really. They's supposed ta come back later today, so maybe we'll talk about it then. I ain't worried, though. They said they was confident, and they seemed real smart about it."

John kept his tone conversational. "Some people are concerned that these lawyers might try to use you; to put words in your mouth that you really don't mean. They think you need to be very careful."

Darcy furrowed his brow, but just for a moment. "Nah, they don't seem like that. Besides, it wouldn't really matter anyways. Once I swear on the Good Book, I gotta tell the truth. Ain't matter what I was asked or who was doing the asking." He shrugged. "I can't lie about it."

John watched him silently for a moment. The man was utterly consumed and pleased with the bag in his lap. "Are you nervous about the trial?"

He popped a shell into his cheek and smiled uneasily. "A little bit. My lawyer, he wants me ta wear a suit. They done measured me yesterday and everything. I'm sorta worried 'bout how it'll make me look. I ain't never wore nothing like that before." His finger probed the peanut bag, and his manner relaxed. "But I'm glad it starts tomorrow. I want all this ta be over so I can go home."

"I can only imagine," John offered sympathetically. "Will you go back to your cabin near Cowford?"

Darcy looked puzzled by the question. "Of course."

"I just thought you might move somewhere else. Maybe back to where you grew up."

"To North Carolina? Why would I do that?"

John spoke slowly, crafting his words with care. "I thought that your neighbors might turn out to be less than hospitable because of the misunderstanding." In truth, he was much less worried about the neighbors than he was about area vigilantes unfamiliar with Darcy's shortcomings.

He nodded slowly. "I thought about that. Can't imagine that they's gonna throw me a party or nothing." He snickered. "But, they's never did 'fore neither. And that's where my land is—my cabin, my crops, my garden. Can't rightly be leaving all that, even if folks is a matter more persnickety." He looked back down at the peanuts. "Besides, if I was gonna go somewhere, it wouldn't be back ta North Carolina. Sweared the day I left that I wasn't coming back."

"Why?"

"On account of what folks said about me. The way they's treated me. Folks is stubborn, John. The Bible, it tells 'em to forgive, but most don't. The grudges, they only get worse."

John sat forward. "What grudge did they hold against you?"

His answer was matter-of-fact. "They says I was a nigga lover. That I wasn't fit ta be 'round other white folk."

John's eyes widened. "Darcy, you weren't caught doing this before?"

He laughed halfheartedly. "Heavens no. I was just a boy back then." He looked up after a moment and realized John expected more. His forehead crinkled. "It's sorta a long story. I mean, if ya wanna understand what really happened."

"Please."

He took a deep breath. "Well, I growed up in Jasper County, kind of near Durham. Born and raised there, right in the heart of tobacco country. Our cabin, though, it wasn't really near nothing. It was a few miles to the nearest town, and the only other cabin 'round there belonged to the O'Malleys. And they was all grown. So, except for school, I was ofttimes alone as a boy. Ya see, I ain't had no brothers or sisters, and my folks was most times busy working. My father, he'd sometimes have me help him with the land. But normally, afta an hour or so, he'd catch me doing something wrong." He smiled. "He'd start ta yelling and cursing, and his face and neck would puff up and turn red. Momma says he looked like a cornered animal when he got like that." The smile faded. "Then he'd just tell me ta go help my momma. It was kind of funny, really, watching him get like that. All but the cussing, I guess.

"My momma, she didn't really have much use for me 'round the house, so she'd always smile and say, 'Go off and do what boys do.' So that's what I did. I went fishing and exploring, sometimes walking all morn to find a spot I ain't neva seen before. I happened 'cross a bear den once. I set up a trap ta try and catch it, you know, putting leaves and twigs over a dug-up hole so that it might fall in." He laughed. "Stayed all night and the bear never came home. Good thing, too. 'Cause if he'd have stepped in that shallow hole, there'd a been a riled bear and a small boy with a fishing rod, face ta face." He laughed even harder. "And I'd have bet on the bear."

He took a moment to compose himself. "But anyways, this one day I was fishing a creek a ways north of our land when this Negro boy come up behind me. He was 'bout my age, a little bigger though, and he tells me ta give him the pole. The fishing pole. Well, of course, I says no. I told him it was my daddy's fishing pole and I wasn't giving it ta no one. Then he just starts ta laughing. He says he ain't wanna steal it, he just wants to show me what I's doing wrong. He tells me his name is Bristol, and then he says there ain't no dog fast enough ta catch him and ain't no fish slippery enough ta get away." Darcy smiled again. "I remember that so well 'cause he'd say it most every time I saw him. 'Ain't no dog fast enough ta catch me, and ain't no fish slippery enough ta get away.' He was right 'bout the fishing, though, that's for sure.

"See, it turns out that Bristol was a slave on the Menard plantation, but 'cause he wasn't yet of a working age, he got ta go where he wanted afta he finished his chores. So me and him got ta be friends. For a time we was always together. We'd go fishing most every morn and trouble-making the rest of the day. Truth be told, most of the troublemaking was his thinking. He'd normally have ta butter me a little ta get me ta come along. I always did, though. Every single time."

Darcy muffled an excited laugh, a child's laugh. "This one time, he tells me he has this hankering for some crab apples. Well, I know the only place 'round us with crab apples was old Mr. Hannety's, and it was known he didn't take kindly ta trespassing. 'Specially not from no kids like us. I tried and tried ta talk Bristol out of it, telling him there was some really easy places we could get our hands on some figs. He wouldn't hear none of it, though. He was stubborn like that, always saying he *had* to do this or that. There was just no talking him out of it."

Darcy's voice fell to a hush. "So, we crept up on old Mr. Hannety's crab apple trees, real quiet like. I was ta be the one ta climb up and get 'em, while Bristol was the lookout. I told him that we should just take the ones that'd already fallen to the ground, but he says no. He says all the best ones is still on the tree. So I climb up there, doing my darnedest not ta shake the leaves too heavy. But afta I tossed down a couple dozen, my foot got caught on sump'n and sent me tumbling faster than an elephant from an eagle's nest. I hit the ground hard, gashing the heck outta my leg and stirring such a ruckus that old Mr. Hannety comes storming from his cabin like a house on fire. He starts ta yelling for us ta stop there, but when I look up ta see where Bristol's at, he's already gone." He clapped once and began to chuckle. "I don't know if there was no dog fast enough to catch him, but old Mr. Hannety sure wasn't. He ain't never even saw him.

"Of course, I took a beating out of it. Mr. Hannety done walked me all the way home with my ear 'tween his fingers and saw that I was punished. I limped for a while, too, on account of the gash I got from the fall. But the next day, Bristol shows up outside my cabin with a smile you could shove a pie through. And you know what he's carrying? A basket chock-full of crab apples—twice more than we'd picked the afternoon before. I tell ya, John, those were some of the best tasting things I eva done ate." Darcy grew quiet for a minute, smiling as he stared blankly at the wall.

"So that is why they called you a nigger lover? That's why they chastised you? Because your best friend was black?"

"Oh, no, John. That wasn't it at all. Lots of folks is friendly with blacks when they's children. Folks don't care much 'bout that. No, I didn't get on their bad side till later, well after me and Bristol grew apart." His eyes moved quickly as he devised how best to continue. They went still as he began to talk again. "After a couple years of being friends, Bristol got to the age where he was expected ta work on the plantation. Seeing him got ta be rare. On occasion, I'd take half my day's catch and sneak it ova to the slave huts at night, splitting up the fish just like we'd always done. But after a while, I started ta notice that my coming was making him sad. I don't think it was personal or nothing, I just think it reminded him too strong of how things used ta be. Of all the fishing and the troublemaking. So, soon after, I just stopped coming. After that, I rarely saw Bristol at all. Maybe once or twice when he'd run errands into town. We didn't say much, though. Just sort of smiled and said hi."

Darcy paused for a moment, then looked up at John. " 'Round about when I was twelve or thirteen, during my last year of schooling, some of the boys 'round my age took ta picking on me here and there. It wasn't nothing too serious—they'd sorta make fun of my stutter in school and sometimes a couple of 'em would pound me on my way home. Just the stuff that boys always do at that age, I guess. Well, this one day in the spring, two of 'em had waited for me on the road that led out of town. I wasn't up for running that day, don't know as ta why, so I just kind of took 'em head-on. They starts ta beat on me pretty good, then. The one of 'em, Jim, he was 'bout the strongest kid in town and he was really letting me have it. Then, all of a sudden, a third guy jumps on the pile. My eyes was shut by then, so I just figured it was another boy from school eager to get his licks in, but soon the pounding on me just stops. I look up and what do I see, but Bristol, beating on the both of 'em. The one boy, I can't remember his name, well he jist runs off. But Jim, he couldn't get away from Bristol, not for a while. Not till Bristol had punched out most of his teeth and bloodied him sump'n awful. In the end, I was the one who had ta pull Bristol off that boy. Then we's both ran away, back up the road, laughing and giggling like we's eight again." His smile passed quickly.

"Except it didn't turn out ta be funny. The boy, Jim, he needed sutures, and his family went and raised Cain over the fact that it was a Negro that done it. They went to his owner, Mr. Menard, and insisted that Bristol be punished proper for putting his hands on a white boy. They neva did care that Bristol wasn't the one who went and started it. Neva even bothered ta ask, or to concern themselves with my black eye or split lip. But Mr. Menard didn't have no choice, I guess. So Bristol got a lashing. Ten strokes on the back, I was told. Now, I has heard of far worse lashings than that, but with Bristol, sump'n just didn't go right. The wound, it got infected, or else he came down with something, 'cause a week later he was still abed. Couldn't walk, let alone work. 'Round then, I snuck onto the land ta pay him a visit. I even brought him a few crab apples—picked, not off the ground." Darcy winced. "When I saw him, he ain't look so good. He was laying on his front and his voice was soft. We didn't talk that much. I told him about how our favorite fishing creek had begun to dry up and how I was looking for a new one. I remember he told me that once he got betta, he'd sneak off a day and help me find one with even more fish, twice as many as the last." He smiled. "That made me happy. I remember that. Just as I was going ta leave, Bristol turns his head to the door and he says, 'Darcy, what d'ya know 'bout me?' Well, I sorta laughed and I told him, 'There ain't no dog fast enough ta catch ya, and ain't no fish slippery enough ta get away.' He smiled, and then I told him what a good friend he was." He sighed. "I was always glad I done that. Told him, I mean. I think he knew anyway, though. I think he knew."

Darcy's voice was level. "Bristol died two days later. The only reason I heard people give was 'complications.' Afta the funeral, his folks buried him under a big ol' tree near the back of the plantation. I always thought Bristol would get a kick out of that—the way he liked climbing like he did." A smile passed over his face. "In fact, when my time come, I'd like ta be buried like that, too. Under a tree. Something peaceful about it."

Darcy waited a moment, then continued. "Anyway, afta that's when folks start ta giving me a hard time. Calling me a nigga lover and saying I's the cause of Bristol's death. Hearing it stung real bad for a while, but as the years passed, it just started ta make me mad. That's the reason I was so happy ta get away from there. And that's why I ain't neva going back."

John sat still, at a loss for words. A mumbled, "I'm sorry," initiated another period of silence. Finally, seconds after Darcy again picked up the bag of peanuts, John had a question. "Darcy, do you think what you did to help that slave at your cabin was in some way related to your feelings about Bristol?"

His brow furrowed for a moment, then he began to laugh. "Oh, John, you's gone and figured that my thinking runs akin to yours. That just ain't the case. Like I told ya before, I wasn't thinking 'bout nothing when that man came running out of the woods. Not Bristol, not morals, not nothing. And that's the God's honest truth."

John nodded. "Of course." He stood after a moment. "Well, Darcy, it has been a—"

"You're not leaving just yet, is ya, John?" His features drooped.

"I suppose I can stay a little longer if you like."

Darcy beamed. "How 'bout if ya tell me some of your stories. Being a reporter like ya is, I'm sure ya got some good ones."

"Let me think a moment," John responded. Most of his barroom tales seemed somehow inappropriate. He settled on a true story he had heard as a child. He told Darcy about Governor Dewitt Clinton and the building of the Erie Canal. Darcy hooked his hands under his knees and rocked back and forth as he listened to John's description of the size of the project—the amount of digging to be done. He seemed to enjoy the fact that the barges were pulled by mules that walked a towpath beside the water. He liked the songs the mule drivers sang.

After John finished, Darcy responded. "I tell ya what, John, ya tell a good story. You seem ta be one heck of a reporter."

"That's not really reporting, Darcy. I didn't dig up the information. I'm just passing on stories I heard." He smiled. "Just because I stepped in a couple puddles doesn't mean I'm a rainmaker."

Darcy's laugh filled the cell. As John stood to leave, Darcy walked over and patted him on the shoulder. The men shook hands. As John was going to pound the heavy wood door to notify Michael Allen of his departure, he stopped. He turned back to Darcy, who stood smiling, leaned against the bars.

"Darcy, the time you saved that animal, the mule that was caught in the current near your cabin, why did you do it?"

Darcy's smile turned sly. "Thought you'd have guessed by now, John. I didn't think about it," he said with a shrug. "I just did it."

John smiled back. "I'll see you at the trial tomorrow, Darcy."

• • •

Later, John was back in his room at McClellan's, staring out the window toward a barren alley just below. As if in a trance, he watched an animated piece of windblown trash float from wall to street to wall like an errant butterfly. He was unaware of Owen's approach until he heard a sharp rap on the door.

"I've been looking for you." Owen's face was haggard, his movements jerky, like a drinker coping with forced abstinence. "You know about the two other fires last night?"

John nodded. "I was at the warehouse fire down on Rutledge. It was Breckenridge's warehouse."

"Did you talk to him about it?"

"No. There was too much going on."

"Well, I was out combing the bars for Woodridge. I got to the fire on Elliot Street when it was all but out. The engine had already left for the warehouses. Mine was a vacant building. There was very little danger."

"I'm not surprised. It was right there by the firehouse."

Owen shook his head. "It was nowhere near the firehouse." He looked at John pointedly. "The firehouse was in your direction, over on King Street."

John walked quickly to the desk and flipped open his notebook to his first day in Charleston—to his first encounter with a militiaman outside a burned house. John had written in the margin, "Firehouse—King Street."

John sat down heavily in his chair, his eyes unfocused on the wall.

"What is it?" Owen asked. "John?"

John slowly turned back to the other New Yorker. "Breckenridge knew."

Owen stared at him without speaking.

"Breckenridge looked upset when he saw the second fire. He sent his man to get the fire engine. I thought he was sending him to the firehouse, but he was sending him to the other fire. Breckenridge knew the engine would be there."

Owen spoke cautiously. "Do you think he figured this out? Like we did?"

"I don't know."

"John, I'm not rubbing your nose in this, but I told you that guy doesn't add up. Whatever is happening, he could be a part of it. What do you think he is trying to do?"

"What are any of these people trying to do? My God. What is going on here?"

John picked up his notebook again and opened it to the first pages. "Bear with me, Owen. I've got to try to make some sense of this. I just want to review the facts of what has been happening here—without the local commentary."

John skimmed through his notes, reading some passages aloud. "First it's about racial tension, lynchings . . . Then it's about too many suspicious fires . . . Militia everywhere . . . There is civil unrest over the trial . . . Again the fires—no black homes burned . . . At the party, most are polite but bellicose . . . Back in town, more militia . . . too many militia . . . Fires again—only one building burns each time . . . Blacks are loading munitions for white foremen at an abandoned black church—Winchester warehouse . . ." John paused. "When I think about it now, the oddity wasn't that blacks were involved in the loading. It was the location. Why would white men store guns in a black neighborhood?" John breathed deeply. "It looks like things are building to a hell of a confrontation here. Someone is orchestrating it, but to what purpose?"

There was a tap at the door, and both men froze.

"Yes," John called out.

"It's me, Mr. Sharp," Samuel's voice responded.

John opened the door. The boy was wearing a broad smile.

"I's got me some new scoop for ya, sir," Samuel said proudly. Then his face fell as he spotted Owen.

Owen glanced at John. "I need to get my notebook from my room. I'll be back in a minute."

Samuel waited until John's door closed and Owen's door opened and closed across the hall. "Do ya know about the warehouse fire off Rutledge, and the building up on Elliot?" the boy asked in an excited whisper.

"Yes, Samuel. I was at the warehouse fire myself."

"Oh." The boy looked mildly disappointed, then brightened. "Well, I did mo' reporting than that.

"Your first day in town, ya asked me 'bout the fire that happened three days before. Well, I did some checking, and figured out which one it was. We already counted it, but it was the one next to Bryce's Feed Store—just a few blocks from here."

"That's very good, Samuel," John said with sincerity. "That gives me the last piece of information that I need on the fires—the missing piece to the puzzle." He reached into his pocket and pulled out a dime for the smiling boy. "The fire assignment is over now. Well done. No more counting; this has to remain a secret. Understand?"

The boy nodded.

Owen's door opened and closed, and Samuel moved toward the door, pocketing the dime as Owen reentered the room.

"Let me know if you be needing anything, sir." The boy looked like he wished he could stay longer, but he nodded politely and backed out of the room.

"You start your stringers kind of young, don't you?" Owen remarked.

John ignored him. "I've been thinking. I'm going to take a look at the Winchester warehouse. A weapons shipment is to be delivered there today. The whole thing seems a little odd. Want to come along?"

"Actually, I have a lead of my own that I want to check out."

John raised an eyebrow.

"I'll let you know if it amounts to anything," Owen said.

John wore his tailored beige suit and carried the accompanying straw-ribboned hat at his side as he walked along the East Bay beside the wharves. The Winchester warehouse was just ahead, the only one with any visible activity. Blacks were moving crates, like those John had seen the previous day, from the warehouse to covered wagons lined up along the dock. Apparently, the shipment wasn't remaining at Winchester's long. It was headed somewhere else. Armed militia stood guard at barricades that cordoned off the dock from the others. This group of militia had a military bearing; unlike many of their cohorts around town, they looked like they meant business.

John walked with exaggerated slowness as he approached the wagons at the end of the wharf. Maintain a southern speed, he thought. Walk deliberately, move deliberately, and by all means, talk like there are a few marbles in your mouth.

Thirty feet from the makeshift barricade, he was noticed. He saw a dozen uniformed men turn to watch him. One militia sergeant moved quickly to intercept his path halfway down the dock. The man's expression—his pursed lips and steel eyes—was in itself a sober warning.

"Stop there, sir," he called out. "This area's off-limits." He stopped five feet from John, blocking any advancement.

"That right?" John drawled affably. "So what's this hullabaloo all about?"

"Sorry, sir, can't tell ya that." He swung his rifle off his shoulder and held it diagonally across his chest. It was intended as a threat. "I need you to leave the area now, sir."

John looked over the militiaman's shoulder. He could count eleven wagons. They were pulled in tight and close, conserving space for more to come. The canvas covering the wagons had been pulled tight, completely covering the cargo. Several wagons blocked his view of the men doing the loading.

"*Now*, sir!" The order rang in his ears.

John smiled and leaned in to whisper. "Now you can tell me. Is this Montgomery's art collection? I had heard he'd planned ta ship it all north. I never had no idea, though, that ol' Monty had him this much."

The man's hand crept up the butt of his rifle toward the hammer. "Now I warned ya twice," he snarled. "If you don't leave now, I'm running ya in for trespassing."

A wagon began to pull out of the way, and John could now see the loading in progress. It wasn't just crates of rifles this time. It looked like gunpowder.

John smiled and took a step back just as reinforcements approached. "All right, all right. Just wanted to find out if Monty's Peale portrait was to be shipped too. I've been trying to buy it for years. Good day, then." He tipped his hat, then turned and walked languidly toward the street.

"Who was that?" a voice asked from behind.

"I don't know. Wanted to know if this was artwork or something. Not a real sharp one, you could tell. Probably just some planter's idiot brother."

The other man laughed.

Back in John's room, the two reporters compared notes.

"So how many wagons did you see?" Owen asked.

"There were at least eleven. The fully loaded ones were covered with canvas."

"What makes you think it isn't just new rifles for the militia?" Owen chuckled. "Have you seen some of their weapons? Some look like they saw action against the redcoats."

"It's the way they're acting," John responded. "If it's just guns so the militia can keep the peace, why hide them in an abandoned black church? And why have an edgy unit guarding them at the docks?" John paused and looked hard at Owen. "And not one of them was smoking."

Owen gave a low whistle. "It *is* gunpowder, then. Do you have any clue yet of what they are up to?"

John shook his head. "I just can't put the pieces together."

"Well, I guess I have another piece to add to the puzzle." He flashed a sheepish grin. "I have to admit that I eavesdropped. I overheard that little black kid telling you the location of the fire that occurred the day Simpson died.

"I already knew where he was killed," Owen continued. "Actually, it was about six blocks from your warehouse. I talked to a shop owner, a fellow by the name of Lloyd who sells saddles and tack. He saw it all happen in front of his store. There was something strange about the whole thing, John."

"Do you think it wasn't an accident?"

"No. It still seems pretty clear that it was. The odd thing is that Simpson was *not* running toward the fire."

"He wasn't?"

"No. In fact the man said he seemed oblivious to it. He came running off the jetty and cut right across in front of the horses pulling the wagon."

John frowned. "Was there any activity on the jetty? Did he say if anything was going on back there?"

"He told me those wharves are pretty much vacant this time of year. No one's back there. Lloyd's partner saw the whole thing, too. I wanted to talk to him also, but he was out. Maybe I'll try again tomorrow if there's time before the trial."

John stood silent for a moment, then shook his head slowly. "I wonder where he was going."

Several hours later, John could not get Simpson's death out of his mind. He walked down to the stretch of wharves and warehouses by the Ashley River, and managed to locate the saddle shop. It was already dinner hour, however, and he found it closed. He walked behind the business to the wharf-lined finger of land that Simpson had apparently visited before the turmoil of the fire. Owen was right—the area looked deserted. The only warehouse, Sandman's Storage, was locked. John peeked in through a window, and it appeared to be empty.

The jetty did provide a good view of Charleston and its harbor, however. Up the shoreline, John could make out the lockup where Darcy was being held. About six blocks in the other direction, men were still working down on the dock by Winchester's warehouse.

John moved back behind the cover of Sandman's Storage. He had not changed clothes since morning, and there was always a chance that one of the militia on the loading dock might spot him and recognize him. He sat quietly and looked out toward the barrier islands. They wrapped around Charleston's harbor like a closing jaw. Sullivans Island, which housed the federal compliment at Fort Moultrie, lay to one side, Morris Island to the other. In the middle was Fort Sumter, still under construction, standing on a shoal at the harbor's entrance. It was little more than a blur on the horizon, but John thought he could still make out the mast of a ship moored there.

John's militia buddies from the bar had told him that some of them were encamped out there.

John suddenly felt an eerie stirring in the pit of his stomach. Why drill or billet men on Sumter? Why not just march them someplace and forgo the trouble of transporting them by ship? . . . Unless there was a reason someone wanted the militia on an island in the middle of Charleston Harbor.

John looked at Sullivans Island, then Fort Sumter, then back again. He felt the hairs prickle on the back of his neck. He suddenly understood why Simpson had no interest in chasing down a fire.

He emerged from behind the cover of Sandman's Storage and began to walk purposefully back toward town. His heart pounded as if he were running, but he dare not do that. Not too fast, he told himself. There was no cover, and he did not want to attract the notice of the militia of the Winchester dock.

He heard a call behind him that could have been a seabird, followed by a sound that was definitely not a seabird—*footsteps*. First they matched his pace . . . then faster, breaking into a run.

John looked back over his shoulder, his pace quickening. Then he stopped and made a long exhale. "Owen."

"Jesus, John, you're a hard man to track down."

"What are you doing out here?" John asked, exasperated.

"Probably the same thing as you."

"Look. We've got to leave this place." John glanced toward the Winchester dock. The militia had halted their activity and appeared to be looking at them. John slapped Owen on the shoulder in a show of camaraderie. "Act nonchalant," he instructed. "We've got to talk, but right now, I'm worried about that group watching over there."

"What is it, for God's sake?"

"I think I know what Simpson saw that made him run." John started to walk again slowly. "Don't look, but what do you know about those islands back there?"

Owen looked anyway. "You've got Sullivans and Morris Islands on each side, and they're building Fort Sumter at that spot out there in the middle."

John looked Owen full in the eyes. "Some militia bought me a drink in a bar yesterday. One of them said they had been drilling out on Sullivans Island and at Fort Sumter. It seems that there are a lot more militia than what we have seen here in town. They keep rotating them in and out so none of the same ones are here too long. And there's something else." John's voice took on a flat quality. "The man said his buddy was in artillery." He paused. "Owen, if these people are here for guard duty during the trial or as a deterrent to the fires, then why do they need artillery? We have a police force here that is acting like an army."

Owen stood silently, looking back at Sullivans Island. "I kept hearing rumors," he said after a minute. "You know, the kind you catch wind of in a bar late at night when everyone's had a few too many. Some folks said they heard that people were going to head out to Fort Moultrie and bust Darcy Nance out—give him a quick taste of justice." He paused. "I didn't pay much attention because I knew Darcy wasn't at Fort Moultrie. I didn't think it was worth following up."

"Owen, maybe that's what they wanted us to think and why they consented to our interview with Darcy. We both know now that the only damned attraction at that fort is the presence of federal troops."

The men sat in silence.

"I wonder how many are out there," John said under his breath.

"Somebody said there were eighty—including the marching band. I only remember, because I figured it wasn't enough if they were guarding Darcy."

Eighty. John remembered the blurted boast from Luke Hedgecoth at the party. He remembered Tyler's anger and the admonition, "Go tell your father exactly what you said."

The reporters were back on Castle Street. The militia could not see them now. Yet John had the feeling he'd been watched since the moment he returned to Charleston.

The men walked slowly back toward the boardinghouse. John glanced at Owen. The loquacious Irishman had gone silent. Instead, he was biting his lips and pulling at the threads of his frayed cuffs.

"Owen, do you know what will happen if they attack Fort Moultrie?"

It was a rhetorical question, the consequences obvious.

Owen waited before answering. When he spoke, his tone affected nonchalance. "We'll be on the wrong damn side of the chessboard, that's for sure."

They ate a dinner of fried pork and greens at a local tavern across the street from McClellan's.

Owen spoke to John from behind a newspaper. "Get ready for today's front-page news from the *Charleston Gazette*. 'President Still Sick with Food Poisoning.' "

John pushed his plate away. "I know how he feels."

Owen peered over the paper. "Hey, how long does something like that last? Food poisoning?"

"I don't know. Three, four days. He should be fine tomorrow."

"Not if he hears about this." Owen tapped the paper on his leg as he spoke. "John, I'm kind of wondering about something. Shouldn't we tell someone about this? Maybe send a wire back to New York about what we've seen and heard."

"I already thought about that. I don't think it's a good idea. After all, what evidence do we have? Too many militia in town? Nobody would believe us. They'd think we'd spent too much time in the sun."

"But we could try."

John paused. "Then there's the other side of it. What happens if folks here become aware of our suspicion? If we tried to send that wire, the local telegrapher might put it through or he might not. But he'd certainly alert the authorities. I mean, if Woodridge doesn't trust them with his dispatches about the trial, can you imagine how they might react to this? It could force their hand—make them move things forward. No, Owen, I think it best if we just wait a while longer and try to get something a little more solid."

The two men sat in silence for a few minutes.

"Shoot," Owen exclaimed suddenly. "The trial, Darcy's trial, it is nothing but a farce. Nothing but a smokescreen."

"What are you talking about?"

"Think about it, John. It's the perfect ruse to draw attention away from what's really happening."

John hunched a little, slightly annoyed, his tone dismissive. "You forget the main player in your ruse, Owen. Darcy Calhoun is hardly capable of such an act. He committed the alleged crime, I have no doubt of that."

"Of course he did. That's not what I'm suggesting." He smiled wide. "But they could have had this trial a month ago. It would have been open-and-shut. Instead they turn it into a public spectacle. What better cover for an attack than that?"

John shook his head. "You're forgetting a major point. By turning it into a spectacle, they also drew us here. The press. Yankee reporters. It would be rather brazen to invite enemy lookouts into your camp as you prepare for a sneak attack."

"I already thought of that. And *you* are forgetting the one key to the whole equation."

"What is that?"

"The militia." He paused for effect. "How else could they have built up such a formidable force here in Charleston without arousing suspicion? The trial calls for it, to maintain order. But no one else seems to notice or care that their numbers are growing every day." He took a sip of his beer, then spoke quickly. "What if there were no trial? How would they hide a military buildup? Lots of northerners do business down here. Believe me, plenty of them would have noticed troops converging on the city. You don't think they would have wired home and raised the alarm? Compared to that situation, a few reporters are nothing to worry about. We are a mild annoyance, that's all." His voice was becoming more excited. "The trial is the perfect alibi, the perfect cover. It keeps us occupied while they move to attack the fort right under our noses."

John sat silently for a moment, looking down at the table. "I don't know, Owen. I think the fires and the militia buildup are definitely tied together. That was my initial reaction when I arrived; then I became distracted by the racial tension. But the trial as a cover? My gut reaction is that the trial has a different significance altogether."

John tossed some coins on the table, and the two men rose to leave.

"So what's our next step?" Owen asked.

"We need to look for additional corroboration. I was thinking of talking with Breckenridge, and maybe Mannion, the editor of the *Gazette*."

Owen shook his head. "I don't think that's a real good idea. We don't know where they stand on this. It wouldn't be smart to tip our hand and let them know we're on to something."

"I won't give away what I know. I just want to feel them out. Both men are in a position to be aware of what's going on, and neither would approve. I'm certain of that."

"Hey there! Irish fella!"

An older man approached them as they mounted the steps to McClellan's porch. He addressed Owen. "You're the police reporter, aren't ya?"

"The *Police Gazette*, yes," Owen responded slowly. He looked hard at the man in the fading light. "You're Mr. Lloyd from the saddle shop." Owen smiled and gestured to John. "This is my colleague, John Sharp. He was a friend of Mr. Simpson, the man who was killed."

"Terribly sorry for your loss," the man said. "It's a shame to die like that, so far from home. Terrible accident."

"You were there when he died?" John asked. At Lloyd's nod, John continued. "Did he say anything?"

"I'm afraid not," the shopkeeper responded. "He was hurt too bad. He did look aware, though, for a minute. And he kind of smiled." He gave John a reassuring look. "He had time to make peace with his Maker."

"Thank you."

John was phrasing his next question when Lloyd extended a small appointment book. "Fella who works with me found this in the street later that afternoon. I remembered it afta you came by." He nodded to Owen. "When you said the man's name was Simpson, I put two and two together." He pointed to the letter *S* embossed in the leather.

"I'm much obliged to you, sir. May I buy you a drink for your trouble?"

"No, no," Lloyd responded shaking his head. "I was coming this way to visit my brother." He looked back at Owen. "Remembered you was staying at McClellan's." He tipped his cap. "Evening now, gentlemen."

John moved to McClellan's porch, where a patch of lamplight fell on the railing, and began to quickly leaf through the book.

"What do you see?" Owen asked.

"March, April. . . ." John hummed as he flipped though. "Ah, here it is. Charleston." John studied the entries, attempting to decipher Simpson's shorthand. He reached the final page of appointments, and felt a wave of nausea as he read the last entry. *No. It couldn't be.* He read it again.

> *Tues. 3 PM—T. B.*
> *Jetty—Castle Street*

John shot up and tore down the street.

"John!" Owen yelled. "What is it?"

"Mr. Lloyd," John called out from half a block away. "Wait a moment, sir." He covered the ground between them at a sprint, and upon reaching him, did not pause to catch his breath. "Mr. Lloyd, I have a very important question. Tyler Breckenridge. Was he there at the accident?"

"As a matter of fact, yes," the man said, nodding. "He came a running and sent for the doctor. He seemed real sorry that yo' friend didn't make it."

"I'm sorry, sir. Mr. Breckenridge is not at home."

The servant's tone conveyed sincere regret, though both men knew the statement was not to be taken literally. The low rumble of conversation and the play of shadows on the drawn curtains of Tyler's study left little doubt that the man was indeed at home, and with considerable company.

John kept his voice cordial. "Please let him know that John Sharp called, and that I hope we can meet at his earliest convenience. It is a matter of importance."

John left his card on the silver tray provided by the servant, then descended the porch steps and began to walk up the block.

John wanted to yell in frustration. In his agitated state, he had not considered the possibility that Tyler might not be available. John was desperate for answers; the only one in a position to provide them was Tyler Breckenridge.

John had to believe deep down that Tyler was an honorable man. Early suspicions of the planter had been gradually replaced by a growing respect in the course of his stay at Willowby. By the time he returned to Charleston, John was rather in awe of the man, and flattered that Tyler treated him as a friend.

But chance remarks by others left no doubt that Tyler was a manipulator. Could he also be a traitor? He had failed to mention his appointment with Simpson and his presence at Simpson's death. To his chagrin, John recalled that Tyler had actually questioned him at their first meeting concerning Simpson's cables home.

Owen, on the other hand, was convinced of Tyler's duplicity. He wanted to accompany John to the Breckenridge mansion and call the man out. But John had insisted upon coming alone. This was not to be a confrontation. If there was a reasonable explanation for the meeting with Simpson, John hoped to hear it; for he still needed Tyler as a confidant and ally in the matter of the conspiracy. With the planter's connections, John had no doubt that he could get to the bottom of it, and find the necessary corroboration.

He reached the end of the block and turned the corner. He could see the carriages and horses waiting at the rear of the Breckenridge home. The carriage lamps were lit, and the drivers and groomsmen were with the horses, not settled in clusters with drink or dice. That meant that the guests could be leaving soon. John decided to find a spot among the carriage houses and wait.

It was not long before the liverymen began to stir, and John guessed that they would begin bringing the carriages around. To his surprise, a servant unlocked the garden gate, and guests began to exit through the rear door.

John moved to a vantage point that allowed a view of Breckenridge's back porch. Departing guests were backlit and featureless as they emerged from the doorway, but as they passed the lamp near the steps, John had a brief glimpse of their faces.

They departed in groups of two or three. The men had a secretive air, similar to the denizens of late meetings at Tammany Hall. John recognized many of them from the courthouse and the party. Aubry came out, his suit and skin shiny in the lamplight, followed by George Campbell. Mannion from the *Gazette* was there. He hurried away quickly without talking to the others.

Michael Allen accompanied the mayor. The mayor stopped at the steps, then walked back alone toward a tall man who stood in the shadows near the doorway. The lamplight danced across blond hair. *Breckenridge.* The planter's face was obscured. The old man put a hand on Breckenridge's shoulder, and the two of them descended the steps together. Whatever Tyler said made the mayor laugh.

The next man to leave looked vaguely familiar. John could not place him from his glimpse of the face. Then he put on his hat. John felt a weight in his chest as the insignia glinted gold in the light.

"The militia's colonel." John exhaled the words under his breath. The man had been the commanding officer at the courthouse the day of his arrival.

The final guests filtered through the doorway, and all was quiet as the last of the carriages rolled away. John lost track of Breckenridge. Then he heard the low, amiable rumble of conversation and the flare of a match. Breckenridge stood on the porch lighting his pipe, his face intermittently lit by the pulsing glow of the puffs. Another man stood conversing with him, but John could not see who he was. Tyler extended his arm, and the men shook hands. Then the guest turned and descended the steps. He wore a fire chief's uniform—the same man who had remained behind with Tyler after the warehouse fire.

The click of hooves on cobblestone died away. John sat very still as he watched the planter smoking on the porch. At one point, John felt that the man was looking directly at him, but he knew that was impossible, since he was totally in shadow.

Breckenridge turned as a servant opened the back door and extended a small silver tray. Tyler removed a white calling card, then stiffened. He reacted physically, as if muttering an oath, and glanced quickly up and down the street. Then he tapped out the contents of his pipe, and strode into the house. The slave closed the door quietly behind them.

John stood alone, leaning on the Battery wall. White Point Gardens was behind him. The light from the mansions of the East Bay reflected on the water. He shut out all sound but the lapping of the waves against the seawall and the tolling of the harbor buoy. He had been standing there for a long time. His throat still felt tight, and his mouth tasted like metal, but his anger was reduced to a smolder now, and he began to feel capable of organized thought.

He realized that if he was going to be an effective reporter for the balance of his stay in Charleston, he would have to clear his head of the anger that had overpowered his ability to think clearly. And he had to understand it to get it under control.

Breckenridge had deceived him. But men had lied to him before. Reporters faced that all the time. The lies did not explain his anger.

No. Breckenridge had gone farther than that. He had offered John the benefits associated with the goodwill of a wealthy man. When it came right down to it, John had been bribed—with a weekend of a lifestyle he envied, with the "loan" of fine suits Breckenridge could never wear again, and with free access to influential men who would have never otherwise granted him an interview. And John had taken the bait, and the bourbon, and the benne wafers. He had been thoroughly seduced.

Then there was the friendship aspect. Breckenridge had said, "Friends do that," when John had expressed his gratitude for the interview with Darcy. Friends did not . . .

Darcy. John felt the sweat turn cold on his forehead. What kind of game had Breckenridge been playing with Darcy? Breckenridge was a slave owner—a man who had the most to lose from acts such as Darcy's. Yet he had spoken of him with compassion, arranged for John to visit his cabin, and arranged exclusive interviews, *twice.* John did not buy into Owen's theory that Darcy's trial was a smokescreen to cover the militia buildup. But it certainly looked like Breckenridge had used the poor man to divert John's attention from whatever the hell that meeting had been about.

John now felt an instant of perfect clarity. He suddenly understood why Mr. Batt was willing to fight for the Texans, and why the Hedgecoths were ready to slaughter New Yorkers and Ohioans. For at that particular moment, John felt he could shoot Tyler Breckenridge with no qualms whatsoever.

NINETEEN

⌒

Owen Conway walked up behind the bench where John sat along the East Bay. He also set his eyes on the distant wharf, where a tall-masted vessel now rocked at anchor.

"I see they're getting reading to load a ship," he said, unsurprised.

John did not turn. "Yeah. It's called the *Port Royal*."

Owen sat down beside him. "How long ago did it get here?"

He answered through a fog. "Just before dawn."

"Well, it's not like it's unexpected. They weren't lining up those wagons for a parade."

"I know."

Owen brought his eyes back to his companion. "Jesus, John, you look like hell. Did you get any sleep last night?"

"Maybe an hour. Maybe two."

"Well, here, I brought you this." Owen handed him a hot cup of coffee. "I made it Irish. Thought you could use it."

John blew the steam off the top and took a sip. "I'm much obliged."

He looked back to the wharf. "Have they moved anything on board yet?"

"No, not yet. They're still waiting."

"So, I'd figure that tonight's the night, huh? I mean, it would seem strategic to move that as quickly as possible."

"You would think," he whispered distantly.

"I'm telling you, John, you've got to stop beating yourself up over this Breckenridge thing. So the guy's a con artist. That's hardly your fault."

"I should have known better. I should not have let myself become so absorbed in his world. I feel a fool."

"You're looking at it all wrong. Whatever his motives were, they failed. You didn't miss anything in Charleston while you were away, and you still discovered their plot *before* it went forward."

"It could have gone right by me, Owen, I was so caught up in his world. Your suspicion of Breckenridge and your initial discovery about the fires brought it all together."

He waved a hand in the air. "You'd have gotten to the bottom of it without me. I'm sure of it. And look at what you gained out of the shenanigan. You got to hobnob with some of the conspirators. Plus, you got to meet with Darcy Calhoun." He continued. "I tell you what, this Breckenridge may have set out to use you, but from where I'm sitting, he's the one who got taken. You're not just aware of the operation. Thanks to him, you know who the players are and how their minds work. You ought to send him a thank-you note."

"You're right about that." He pointed a hand toward the far dock. "If this goes forward, I'll send him a little note via the *New York Tribune*. I'll make him and his cohorts infamous."

"That's the spirit," he announced. "But I'd still pocket that ire till you got well out of town. This Breckenridge guy, you're going to have to see him at some point. Maybe even today at the trial. I don't think it'd be smart to confront him. He could be dangerous."

"What, then, do you propose that I do? Talk with him as if I'm still ignorant of his duplicity? I don't think I could pull it off. I'm no actor."

"You better learn quickly, then. 'Cause if this guy knows you're hiding something, he's likely to lock you up. Or worse." His smile easily dispatched the gravity. "If you see him again, just tell him you aren't feeling well, or that you are worried about Darcy. Whatever, just so long as he doesn't catch on to our secret." Owen stared back toward the wharf for a moment. "Anyway, there's no use sitting here waiting for the pot to boil. You should go back to McClellan's and freshen up a bit before the trial. If anything happens, we'll hear about it."

John began a low nod. "Yes, I suppose you're right. They still have to load the ship, and they probably won't attack in daylight."

Darcy Calhoun's lawyer, Mr. Malcolm Coulter, and his assistant entered the courtroom to a rumble of unified disdain from the balcony. Here was the personification of their enmity, a portly man in a thrifty gray suit who looked over his crescent spectacles with narrow, pale eyes. His physique labeled him as anything but a fighter, but in his face John perceived the spirit of war. In that brief moment when Coulter peered over his shoulder at the balcony, in that second when his eyes swept across those seated on the first floor, John saw the ridge of his lips hint slightly upward. He was confident, perhaps even smug, and as he walked forward, John wondered if in his balled left fist he did not carry a rock with which to smite his enemies.

After all parties had arrived, and the charges were again read, a foreboding silence enveloped the courtroom. The only motion whatsoever came from Darcy, who squirmed in his new suit of clothes, scratching a little, like a snake eager to dispatch his old skin. The judge swung his gavel twice, and Darcy stilled.

"Mr. Coulter, you may proceed with your opening argument."

Coulter kept his head down, slowly sifting through a few sheets of paper on his desk, appearing more like an unmotivated accountant than a breakwater for the condemned. He sat still just long enough for the balcony to begin to rumble and the prosecutor and judge to hunch forward, then rose slowly, flipping his glasses toward the desk, pacing toward Judge Castille with long steps. His eyes were wide, his lips flat, and his bearing calm.

"It has come to my attention that many people here in Charleston, South Carolina, take umbrage with my presence at this trial. That, in fact, I am not wanted here." The few groans of agreement from the balcony caused him to smile. "Then it might surprise you to know that I, too, do not wish to be here. No, I find this trip an obligation, not an opportunity." His voice dropped in pitch. "A sad call to duty."

He turned away from the judge, toward the assembly. "You see, no lawyer in Charleston was angered, outraged, or embarrassed enough by these egregious charges to step forward and confront the foolhardy men who would disgrace the courts by bringing them. So," he continued, his voice almost conversational, "I am here.

"Almost a hundred years ago, before this great country won her freedom, a heinous murder took place in Boston at the hands of the British troops, an act so cold and unconscionable that we came to call it the Massacre. And yet even then, in an era of outrage and oppression, it was a Bostonian who took on the challenge of defending some of the soldiers already convicted by public opinion. He recognized that only in defending every man equally did we express to the world our fairness and our freedom. The lawyer was John Adams. And the soldiers he represented, not guilty. I challenge any man in this courtroom to debate Adams's patriotism or dedication to this country." He paused. "Yet, where are the Adams's of Charleston?" He looked about the courtroom. "Where are they today, when the reputation of their city hangs in the balance with this trial?" He walked back toward his desk and stared at his own empty chair. "Absent, it seems. So sickened by a system as to force their truancy. So, I am here.

"Many of you most likely think that I have come to your city on behalf of the abolitionists, to attack and condemn slavery from within its fortress." His eyes walked among the benches. "There you are incorrect. While my personal views may run counter to yours, they have no place in this courtroom, no bearing on this trial.

"No, what brings me here should be of as great a concern to you as it is to me, and by God, above all to Mr. Calhoun." He paused. "I have come here to tell you of traitors in your midst."

He raised his hand high over his head, his fist balled up except for the thumb. "Bounty hunters," he exclaimed loudly, then released his index finger. "And crooked slave masters." He held his arm straight for a few seconds. "These are the perpetrators of your most dire problems." He looked softly toward the defense desk. "Darcy is merely their victim. And who knows, any of you may be next.

"These groups of men live by no code of honor, and in doing so transcribe their sins unto you—guilt by association. And what is their sin? What is their transgression?" His face grew rigid and cold. "They accomplish their objectives by *any possible means*." He turned back to the judge. "For the unscrupulous slave master the statement applies to their will for increased wealth. Since, of course, it is well known that their wealth is directly proportional to the number of slaves they own, these men see no boundaries in their acquisition of laborers. They will lie to get them, and they will most certainly steal." He paused. "They will get their man, by any possible means.

"And the bounty hunters, men whose job it is to catch fugitive slaves, they also appropriate those words. They make money only through capture, and then by returning the captured man for a fee. But there is no system in place to ensure their maintenance of legality. No one to make sure the men or women abducted are who they say them to be. But what is their concern? With the complicity of a planter who himself is getting a slave for a bargain, why should the bounty hunter worry about the Negro's true status?" He paused. "They will get their fee, by *any possible means*.

"So how does Darcy Calhoun fit in? Very sadly, but very simply. He is *their* victim. This kindhearted farmer chose only to help a man in need. A wounded, beaten man who just so happened to be black. But Darcy was kind to the wrong Negro. He should have been more measured, more calculating in dispensing his generosity. Why? Because a group of bounty hunters and a slave master were chasing a supposed runaway. And by God they would catch him, or at least his replacement, *by any possible means*."

Coulter took a deep breath. "So there is your crime, or rather should I say, bad luck. Helping the wrong man. And as contemptible as is the system that would charge a man with such a ludicrous crime, more contemptible—in fact, criminal—is the fact that no one within that system would willfully and competently choose to defend him." He threw up his arms haphazardly. "So, I am here. Your decision, not mine." His voice became fire. "And, by God, *I* will defend him *by any and all possible means.*"

The judge paused a moment before looking to the district attorney. "You may proceed, Mr. Alford."

Alford affected nonchalance as he stood behind his desk, the same manner John had witnessed when questioning him in Breckenridge's study. His cheeks were flushed, a result of alcohol and not heat, he guessed. Alford gently tapped his finger on his desk, and his smile grew.

"Your Honor, this is truly an open-and-shut case. Now, whatever argument Mr. Coulter might choose to use to defend his client is really of no consequence. The evidence is simple. Darcy Nance Calhoun came across a runaway slave. Fact." He slapped his hand hard down upon his desk. "That runaway slave was not off on some daytime stroll, but rather running, his clothes in tatters, his body bloody from the chase." His hand swung down again. "Fact. Then, though he had never seen him before, the defendant invited this unknown, fleeing man inside his home for protection, even while men's yells and the baying of dogs played in the background. Fact." He shook his head and leveled his tone, emoting a false shock at the claim's audacity. "And after all of that, once confronted by the search party and specifically asked if he had seen a runaway Negro, he denied it. He said he knew nothing of it. Only when the search party recognized a trail of blood leading into Mr. Calhoun's cabin and decided to investigate did they find the runaway standing right there in his living room—the same fugitive slave reported missing not two weeks before from Mr. Bodean's custody!" His hand, this time, merely patted the table. "Fact."

Alford walked back to his chair and turned to address the judge. "Your Honor, Darcy Calhoun has broken one of our most basic laws of property—a crime that endangers our social order. Punish him to the utmost for what he has done. Your Honor, the state asks that you impose a sentence of death in this case."

The scattered applause was quashed by a gavel strike and the judge's dark stare of warning. As it quieted, he continued. "Very well, then. Mr. Alford, call your first witness."

"The State of South Carolina calls Mr. Thomas Bodean to the stand."

The man was led in from outside the courtroom by a bailiff. Bodean was a healthy older man, dressed impeccably. He walked forward and stood in the witness box, where he was sworn in.

Alford sauntered forward with a smile. "Mr. Bodean, thank you for being here today. Will you please tell the court your occupation?"

Bodean's drawl was thick syrup. "I am a planter. I live and work in Union County, Georgia."

"And how are you involved in this case?"

"The fugitive is my property. He escaped from my land in the second week of May."

"What efforts did you make to capture him?"

"After our local search did not turn him up, I placed advertisements in all the papers within a couple hundred miles. I also sent out word and a description to bounty hunters in the area to be on the lookout."

Alford walked back and picked up a paper from his desk. He read from it. "Runaway from Bodean Plantation in Union County in May last. A Negro man named Tiller; had on when he escaped a Negro homespun shirt and breeches. Took with him his blanket. Tiller is a short Negro with large scars on his back and shoulders. Whoever delivers the said Negro shall receive twenty-five dollars currency reward." He walked forward and handed the paper to Bodean. "Is this the wanted ad you had printed?"

"It is."

"Well, then, Mr. Bodean, you must have been quite pleased when you found out this slave, Tiller, was captured. Tell us, how did you get word of it?"

"I only learned of it the day he was returned to my plantation. He was brought by Mr. Flannety, who requested the bounty for the capture. After I saw the slave for myself, I was happy to hand it over."

"So there is no question that the slave returned to your plantation was, in fact, the one who ran away? This Tiller?"

"No question whatsoever."

"And the man who returned him to you, Mr. Flannety, did he tell you where he was captured?"

Bodean glared toward Darcy. His voice offered contempt. "He said he was captured in the Carolina lowlands. Being hidden in a white man's cabin."

"Thank you, Mr. Bodean, that is all I have."

As Alford took his seat, the judge leaned forward. "Mr. Coulter, you may proceed."

Coulter walked very slowly toward the witness box. Bodean waited with a frozen expression, like a man sitting for a photograph, unsure of when the shutter would click. Coulter did not speak. Rather, he just cast his eyes back and forth between the witness and the floor. Bodean looked ready to burst.

"Tell us, Mr. Bodean, how are the living conditions on your plantation? How are the slaves treated?"

Bodean's tone revealed a low burn. "My slaves live well. They are treated fairly and decently."

A counterfeit smile lifted Coulter's face. "Are they? Excellent. But explain to me then, how is it that the only specific identifying characteristics you chose to list in your want ad for this slave, Tiller, were the large scars across his back and shoulders? Were those merely an accident, or an example of your fair and decent treatment?"

Bodean leaned forward. "Tiller has always been a troublemaker. Sometimes with troublemakers we have no choice but to beat some sense into 'em."

"Ah," he breathed, mimicking an outburst of understanding. "A lashing is educational, then. Very well, what did the man Tiller do to deserve his lashings? And remember your oath, sir."

"Once it was for stealing food. Another time he tried to escape."

Coulter nodded and half turned toward the courtroom. "Hunger and freedom. And what a grievous pair of sins those are. One might say they are at the core of man's needs." He paused. "Unless, of course, the man is black." He turned completely back to the witness. "And what punishment did Tiller receive for his most recent attempt at freedom?"

"He was lashed," Bodean spat.

"As he was last time after he tried to escape."

"Yes."

"Well, Mr. Bodean, logic then would tell us that lashing does not seem to impart enlightenment. It is not much of a deterrent. I mean, you lashed him last time, and yet he still tried another escape."

"I told ya, he's a troublemaker."

"Right, right. So, if this troublemaker tries yet another escape and you capture him again, is there to be another lashing?"

"There won't be no other attempts. Tiller has been warned of the consequences."

"Ah, something more ingenious than a lashing, perhaps. Tell us, sir, what are those consequences?"

There was venom in Bodean's words. "If he is caught again, he will lose his right ear."

"How civilized," Coulter replied, allowing time for the thought to settle on the crowd. "And the time after that?"

"His left ear," Bodean snapped even louder.

"Yes, I'm sure we all have heard of these increasing reprisals of mutilation. First the lashing, then disfigurement, and if all else fails, castration. But I must say, Mr. Bodean, these seem drastic measures to me. After all, how difficult should it be to keep people at a place where they are treated so decently and fairly as your plantation? I would not have thought it necessary." Coulter took a deep breath and a step back. "How many slaves do you have on your plantation, sir?"

Bodean's cheeks were now red. "Almost fifty."

"Yes. And of those fifty, how many were born into your custody?"

"Seventeen," he answered immediately.

"And Tiller, was he one of those?"

"No. I bought him here in Charleston ten years ago, when he was fifteen."

"From whom did you buy him?"

"A trader named Murdock."

"A slave trader?"

"Yes," he growled.

"And where did this slave trader say Tiller came from?"

"From a plantation in North Carolina."

"What proof did he give?"

"Proof?"

"Yes, proof. How did you know he, in fact, *did* come from a planta-tion in North Carolina? It is interesting that this slave went on the market just as he reached the age of productivity. How did you know that he was not illegally abducted, like so many others? Stolen from their homes, their families, their free lives? Believe me, sir, acts such as these arc well documented. So I ask again, how did you know *for certain* where he came from?"

Bodean's tone was harsh. "The trader gave me his word."

Coulter nodded. "The word of a slave trader. Pardon me if I don't accept that as gold." He began to walk back to his desk as if he were finished. He stopped abruptly, and turned to Bodean with a harsh glare. "Oh, just one other question, sir. How many of your other slaves have you been forced to lash for running away?"

Bodean forced an angry smile. "None."

"You mean no other slaves have tried to escape?"

"That's right. None."

Coulter nodded slowly, then looked up to the judge. "Your Honor, if we are to treat Mr. Bodean's testimony as truthful, if we *are* to accept that he treats his slaves decently and fairly, then a problem does arise. The man Tiller, whose acquisition is questionable at best, seems dis-satisfied—for the lack of a better word—with his bondage on that plantation. And, unlike the other slaves, he has made a continuing effort to escape to freedom. Now what reason could there be for this? If I asked Mr. Bodean, he would only answer by telling me that the man is a troublemaker. But I believe there is more to it than that." He raised his voice. "Is it not possible that Tiller was once free, illegally abducted and then forced into slavery at the hands of a scurrilous slave trader and Mr. Bodean himself? And, as we all know, if a man was once free, then he cannot become a slave. Therefore, Darcy Calhoun may have done nothing illegal in helping this man. Nothing illegal whatsoever." He shot a glance of contempt back at Bodean. "I have no more use for this witness."

Judge Castille took a moment, then looked back to Alford. "Redirect, sir?"

Alford stood up with an incredulous smile. "Mr. Bodean, did you or did you not purchase the slave, Tiller, legally?"

"Of course I did."

"And you have the papers to prove it?"

"I do."

"Very well. That is all I have for this witness."

Bodean, wearing a mask of fury, was dismissed from the courtroom. The next witness called by Alford was Mr. Luke Flannety, a rough-looking man of about thirty who had chosen not to shave for these proceedings. Once he was sworn in, Alford approached.

"Mr. Flannety, you were the bounty hunter who captured the slave on Mr. Calhoun's property. Is that right?"

"That's right," he slurred. "Me and my men."

"How exactly did your search lead you there?"

"We's got word that there was a runaway 'bout three miles north of Bixby. Heard it was the man gone missing from the Bodean land. So we's set out to capture him. We caught a brief sight of him just after we crossed the Anderson stead, but he managed ta slip away into the forest. That's when we got the dogs. They trailed him up near the Calhoun property. At first, my man Hooks was the one who done asked Darcy Calhoun had he seen him. Darcy told him, no. But when I arrived I saw the tracks on the porch. They was bare tracks, Negro tracks, you could tell. So I called over my men, and we tied up Darcy Calhoun. Then we went inside and found the man we was looking for. He was just standing there, not doing nothing. Fit the description, though. So we tied him up, too." Flannety shrugged. "That was 'bout it. Afta that, I just took the slave back to the Bodean property and got our reward money."

"On the trip back to the Bodean property, did the slave ever mention his name?"

"Yes, sir. We asked him, and he said it was Tiller."

Alford nodded. "And that man, the man whose cabin that Tiller was found inside, is he here in the courtroom today?"

"Yes, sir." He pointed a crooked finger at Darcy. "That's him right over there."

"I have nothing further."

Coulter rose slowly and ambled toward the prosecutor's desk. He picked up the paper that Alford had read to the previous witness. "Tiller is a short Negro with large scars on his back and shoulders." He looked up at Flannety. "That's quite a general description. Tell me, when you first caught sight of this man, Tiller, was he wearing a shirt?"

"Yes, sir. Sure was."

"So, since you couldn't see his back and shoulders, you had no way of knowing if he had any scars."

"No, sir."

"Then the description you were working off was that you were after a short Negro." He threw his arms up in the air. "That probably reduces the number of potential candidates in the nearby counties to about a hundred thousand, wouldn't you say?"

"I wouldn't rightly know," Flannety answered slowly, confused.

Coulter exhaled a breath of frustration. "All right, then, tell me this. What alerted you to this man in particular three miles north of Bixby? It certainly wasn't because he was a short Negro."

"No, sir. A man from those parts got word to us that there was a suspicious acting nigga. He said that when he called out for him ta stop, that the nigga walked away twice as fast."

"And that is what alerted you? That a Negro man walked away quickly from someone."

"Yup. The Negro should know to stop when a white man tells him to." His look for understanding in Coulter found no reflection. "But later, when we caught wind of him near the Anderson stead, he actually started ta running. That's when we knew we had our guy for sure."

"Because he ran. Because he ran from five armed men on horseback and a pack of angry dogs. Mr. Flannety, if you put one hundred men in that situation, ninety-nine would run." He took two angry steps toward the witness. "What is it that you do, sir?"

"That I do?"

"Yes. Your job, sir. Your trade, your occupation. What is it?"

"Well, I'm a bounty hunter."

"Full-time? You mean there is no work that you do outside of chasing down Negroes?"

"I do odd jobs now and again. But that's 'bout it. I don't really need ta do nothing else."

"So it would be fair to say that hunting fugitives is your primary source of income? It's how you make your money."

"Yes, sir. Mostly."

"And would it also be fair to say that you don't get paid unless you catch your man?"

"Not a dime."

"I wonder then, how many runaways in all have you captured?"

Flannety squinted and looked up at the ceiling for retrieval. "Not exactly sure. Probably ten or twelve."

"And of all of those men you've captured, how many didn't turn out to be who you were after?"

"None. They was *all* who I was after." He looked up and smiled. "I's real good at what I do."

Coulter paused for just a moment. "Or very bad." He looked back to the judge. "Your Honor, this man's very occupation is an indictment of the system of slavery. It is because of men like him that the Negroes are *forced* to run. For what is the other option? Mr. Flannety just said he has never not captured someone who he was after. But with descriptions so broad as to send him looking for a short Negro, it is no wonder. How could he *not* catch such a man? As you well know, Negroes captured as fugitive slaves are not allowed to speak on their own behalf. So, any white man with a set of manacles and a rifle can earn himself a quick twenty-five dollars by finding himself a Negro who fits a general description. And the complicity of the slave owners only invites this unscrupulous behavior. For twenty-five dollars, they can acquire a slave worth hundreds." He pointed toward Flannety. "Until men like this are held responsible for their actions, until Negroes are allowed to speak on their own behalf, your society will be plagued by this incredible immorality. And you shall reap what you sow." He wiped the running sweat off his forehead with the back of his hand. "I am through with this witness."

The judge, exhibiting no emotion, looked to the district attorney. "Redirect, sir?"

"Not for this witness, Your Honor. I would like to point out, however, that the prosecution has subpoenaed the four other men present at Mr. Calhoun's cabin when the runaway was found. In order to move this trial along quickly, I am willing to excuse them from testifying so long as the defense concedes the fundamental point expressed by Mr. Flannety. That they found Mr. Bodean's property inside Darcy Calhoun's cabin, and that Mr. Calhoun attempted to conceal that fact."

Judge Castille looked to Coulter. "Well, sir, is there agreement?"

"No, Your Honor."

And so it went. John Sharp watched as the four others were called to testify, none so smart or well spoken as Mr. Flannety. They all offered the same description of events, though one man, a short, pale fellow named Atticus Jones, was continually admonished for speaking of the defendant as a nigger lover. From Coulter they all received condemnation, sometimes in curt sentences, sometimes dressed in erudite prose that left only open jaws and frustrated squints from the witnesses. John found the defense to be quite bold and intriguing. He had expected a more universal condemnation of slavery as a whole, an attack on the entire system. What he got instead was a concentrated barrage leveled at one singular aspect. The idea was well crafted and prepared. As John knew, it didn't take a flood to break a dam; one loose brick at the core would do it. He wondered where Darcy Calhoun fit in.

After the last of the bounty hunters had finished testifying, Mr. Alford again rose. "Your Honor, the prosecution rests."

"Very well, Mr. Alford. Mr. Coulter, you may call your first witness."

"The defense plans to call only one witness, Your Honor. We call Darcy Calhoun."

A light mumble from the balcony followed Darcy to the witness box, where he was sworn in. He looked uneasy standing there, his hands gripped tightly on both wooden rails and his eyes unsure of a target. He bit his lip and furrowed his brow as Coulter approached.

Coulter's voice was calm, but strong. "Mr. Calhoun, would you please tell us where you are from and what it is that you do?"

Darcy swallowed, and his fingers tightened around the wood railing. "I has me a bit of land just south and east of Cowford." His voice wavered from nervousness. "I grow a plot of cotton there in the season, and work me a garden near year-round."

"Do you live with family?"

"No, sir. All my local kin done passed, my momma most recent. I live there by myself."

"All by yourself? That seems an awful lot of work."

"I manage," he answered, his words somewhat stuttered. "I's healthy."

"And tell me, are you a religious man, Mr. Calhoun?"

"Oh, yessir. I ain't missed church on Sunday in almost three full years. I's always the first one to arrive, sometimes 'fore the reverend even. 'Tis what I look forward to most."

"And Darcy, have you ever been arrested before?"

Darcy shook his head quickly. "No, sir. Neva."

Coulter took a step away from the witness box. "A hardworking, God-fearing man who has never had any trouble with the law." He fired his next volley at the prosecutor. "I see South Carolina has dedicated itself to rooting out the truly sinister elements among her society."

The judge glowered at Coulter. "Mr. Coulter, confine yourself to questioning the witness."

The lawyer turned back to Darcy. "If you would, Mr. Calhoun, please tell us how the incident with the man, Tiller, came to pass."

Darcy took a deep breath and stood straighter. "Well, it was late in the afternoon, and I went to the porch to fetch me some water. That's when I starts ta hear it—a ruckus sort of, coming from the trees to the south. Soon after I heard it, I started ta see the branches shake. Then, but a second later, is when the Negro man broke into the clearing."

Coulter cut in. "And when you first saw him, surely you saw the placard around his neck, the sign on him that said he was a slave."

Darcy's brow tightened. "No, sir. It ain't work like that. Slaves, they walk around just the same as other black folk. They ain't got no signs or nothing."

"They don't? Then how are you supposed to be able to tell them apart? The free from the slaves?"

Darcy's mouth hung open for a moment, his eyes squinting. "Well, ya can't, I guess."

"I see." He paused. "So this black man came into the clearing. What happened then?"

"Nothing for a minute. We just sort of stared at one another, kind of in shock I guess. It's then that I saw how tore up he was. His clothes was all ripped and he was bleeding pretty good on account of all his cuts. He didn't have no shoes on, neither. He was in a miserable state."

"And you had no idea who this man was?"

"No, sir."

"No idea whether he was a free man or a slave?"

"No, sir, I ain't neva saw him before in my whole life."

Coulter nodded. "So what did you do?"

"Well, afta a moment, I sort of waved my arm at him, so he'd know it'd be all right for him ta come to the cabin. That's when he starts ta walking toward me. He was limping sump'n awful, and bleeding heavy from the gash on his foot."

"Did you know that he was being chased?"

Darcy nodded slowly. "Had me a pretty good idea. Ya see, I could hear the hounds barking a ways off, and I kind of felt the rumble of horses."

"Yet you invited him inside anyway. Why?"

" 'Cause he was hurt." Darcy grew quieter. "Thought maybe I could help him."

"And did you stop at all to think of the repercussions? What might result from your actions?"

"No, sir. Wasn't thinking 'bout much at all. Not more than dressing the long cut he had running the length of his foot."

"So he came inside your cabin. Is that when he told you he was a runaway slave?"

"No. He ain't neva said nothing like that. In fact, he ain't neva said nothing at all. The two of us nary spoke a word."

"What did you do, then? Simply stare at one another?"

"No, sir. I fetched him a cloth so that he might clean up his wounds. It wasn't but a moment after that that the man on horseback starts ta yelling outside."

"Oh yes, the bounty hunters. What did you do when you heard that man yelling?"

"Well, I went out onto my porch. That's when the man asks me if I'd seen a Negro run through those parts."

"And what did you tell him?"

Darcy bowed his head just slightly, his words trailing off. "I told him I ain't."

"Why, Darcy? Why wouldn't you just tell him that the Negro was inside?"

"I don't know, fo' sure. The man, the Negro, ya see he was beat up sump'n awful. And the guy chasing him on horseback, he looked pretty mean. I wasn't sure what he was gonna do if he got his hands on the Negro. Whether he was gonna kill him right there, even." Darcy took a long breath, his eyes hollow, his chin tucked to his chest. "I just couldn't bring myself ta give him over. Not in the shape he was in."

The courtroom was still for a moment, as those in the balcony momentarily forgot to wave their fans. One could almost hear Darcy's heavy breaths coincide with the heaving of his chest.

"And the rest," Coulter continued, "is it how the bounty hunters testified?"

Darcy nodded slowly. "Yessir. They tied me up once they caught sight of the footprints, all bloody as they was. Then they went in and dragged out the Negro. That was the end of it."

"The end of it," Coulter repeated sullenly. "Only were that so." He walked back slowly toward his desk. "I only have one more question, Mr. Calhoun. I wonder, are you sorry for what you have done?"

Darcy looked back up—out past the lawyer's tables and over those congregated on the first floor and balcony—locking on the large glass windows elevated at the rear of the hall. He seemed much more sure of himself than he had when John had asked the same question. He almost appeared relaxed. "Sorry?" he whispered. "Every man has him an awful lot to be sorry for in not always keeping the Commandments. But, by trying ta live piously and going ta church, we try ta make amends for what we's done wrong in the eyes of God." Darcy stalled, standing motionless, his eyes still staring out the large windows at the back of the courtroom.

"Darcy?" Coulter prompted.

His gaze fell back, level. "I think a man just knows when what he's done wasn't right. God plants that seed of guilt right there in his chest so that there ain't no way of not knowing. But no matter what people keep saying ta me—telling me how sorry I should be—I still ain't felt that feeling." He locked eyes with Coulter. "No, sir, I ain't sorry. I figure God'll let me know when I should be."

Coulter smiled. "Thank you, Darcy. The prosecutor may proceed, Your Honor."

"Or perhaps you are wrong, Mr. Calhoun," Alford said as he stood, wearing a wry smile. "Perhaps God abandoned you when you abandoned Him." He approached the witness box. "There remain a few parts of your story that aren't too clear to me. You see, you act as if this search party that came across your land was nothing out of the ordinary. That this type of thing happens frequently. Is that the case?"

"No, sir. I ain't neva seen nothing like it before."

"Oh. So the whites who live in your area are not known to just mount up and chase down packs of free Negroes?"

Darcy's brow furrowed. "I ain't neva heard of it."

"Why, then, do you suppose that they were chasing this Negro? I mean, surely it must have occurred to you that he was some sort of fugitive."

"Like I said, I didn't stop ta think about it. Not for a moment."

"How convenient for you." Alford paused. "The other issue that confounds me is the fact that you say you and the slave never exchanged words."

"That's right, sir. We ain't talked."

"And that doesn't strike you as strange, Mr. Calhoun? One would think that when encountering a man involved in something so . . . odd as this, that one could barely keep their mouth closed from all the questions. 'Who are you? Why are you running? Who are the people chasing after you?' You never thought to ask him any of these things?"

"No, sir. It all happened so quick that I just came up tongue-tied. Him too, I guess."

Alford threw his hands up in the air. "That is absolutely preposterous. It forces us, then, to make one of two conclusions. Either you are flat-out lying—concocting a story that conceals your complicity—or you lack any measure of common sense. That you are, in a word, stupid." Darcy slumped at the last. "So which is it, Mr. Calhoun?"

"Objection, Your Honor," Coulter barked. "If we are to reduce ourselves to name-calling, then I assure you, I can come up with an adjective or two more cutting than stupid to describe the prosecution."

"Very well, Mr. Coulter. Mr. Alford, refrain yourself from anything that might be construed as insulting."

"Of course, Your Honor." He looked back at Darcy. "So are you, in fact, telling the truth?"

"I done swore on the Good Book."

"Tell me, yes or no, are you lying?"

"No, sir. I would neva . . ."

"No." Alford cut him off. "Only while assisting a fugitive." He took a step back and stuck his thumbs in his jacket. "But let us assume for a moment that your story is true, that you *are* so far out of step with the rest of society." He turned and faced the assembly. "What are we to do? Does that mean we are to free him and wait for the next time when he is not smart enough to recognize his circumstances?" He looked back at Darcy. "Let me put it to you this way, Mr. Calhoun. If one man kills another with his bare hands, with a punch, let us say, is it reasonable for him to say he is not at fault because he didn't know his own strength?"

Darcy squinted. "I ain't sure I know any man who ain't aware of they's own strength."

"And I am not aware of any who unknowingly assists fugitive

slaves." He leaned over Darcy. "So I ask you directly, if a man commits an outrageous crime, whether he is aware of it or not, isn't he still guilty?"

Darcy's mouth was partially open, his face entirely confused. "I . . . I don't know, sir."

"Of course you don't. You don't seem to know much of anything. You don't know if a black man running through your woods chased by a pack of hounds is a fugitive. You don't know not to lie about him being in your cabin. You don't know guilty from innocent. You don't know right from wrong. Heck, I can't tell if you even know enough to come in out of the rain! Your ignorance seems awfully convenient." He turned to walk toward his desk. "But for the rest of us, his ignorance is a danger. And ignorance of the law is no excuse. No further questions of this witless . . . I mean witness, Your Honor."

"Redirect, Mr. Coulter?"

Coulter bounded up quickly, nearly knocking his glasses from his nose. There was a blotch of red on each cheek, and his lips were compressed into a white line as he walked forward. He appeared to be making an effort to control his voice.

"I find it very odd that the prosecutor chooses to associate cruelty with intelligence and compassion with stupidity. Mr. Alford seems so sure of his infallibility, as if Moses came down from Mount Sinai with South Carolina's fugitive slave laws on the stone tablets. Mr. Alford is so convinced *he* knows right from wrong." Coulter shook his head. "By God, compared to that I find it refreshing to hear a man admit to uncertainty."

He walked toward Darcy. "*I don't know*," he quoted, then paused. "The statement seems innocuous enough—no sign of abject stupidity. But what a reaction it draws. I wonder if because in a system of tyranny there can be no room for skepticism or doubt. You have to buy the whole package. The walls might start to crumble if the citizens don't march along in lockstep. The danger comes if someone steps out of line and says, '*I don't know about this.*'"

John felt a prod to his arm. Owen's face was a question mark. John turned a palm upward and shook his head.

"Mr. Alford describes Darcy's actions as dangerous. He contends that this society is somehow endangered by his ignorance. Maybe this institution is endangered by just the opposite. If the people of South Carolina would start to think a little, they could allow doubt to creep into their thoughts about the morals of the system and the dastardly acts of its henchmen. Mr. Alford might dismiss it as stupidity, but when you start to realize something is wrong, first you shake your head and say, 'I don't know.' That's when you start to think. Then you take a good hard look at it."

He stopped just before the witness box. "Darcy, Mr. Alford, and indeed many others, would like us to believe that you are just plain stupid. I wonder if you would help me prove them wrong."

John Sharp, from his seat ten rows behind the lawyer's desk, was now rigid with tension. He could feel Owen's concerned glances fall on him every few seconds, but could not take his eyes off Darcy Calhoun. It was all unraveling.

"So tell me, Darcy, do you often study the Scriptures?"

"Yessir. As often as I can. My reverend, Reverend Rose, he goes over 'em with me every Sunday afta church. He helps me learn 'em, on account of the fact that I can't read."

"So you have memorized some passages?"

"Yessir. A few."

Coulter nodded. "Would you recite a Psalm for the court to prove this?"

Darcy paused, his forehead crinkled. "Well, which one is it that ya wanna hear?"

"How many do you know?"

"Around thirty or so."

"Is that right?" Coulter announced enthusiastically. "Thirty. I wonder how many men in this courtroom could say the same." He turned to the prosecutor. "I wonder if Mr. Alford could recite a third that many?" He turned back to Darcy. "Very well, Mr. Calhoun, do you know Psalm 13?"

He nodded with a manner of pride. "Yessir."

"Might we hear it then?"

Darcy closed his eyes, his lips almost smiling, and he began to speak.

> *How long wilt thou forget me, O Lord? for ever? how long*
> *wilt thou hide thy face from me?*
> *How long shall I take counsel in my soul, having sorrow in*
> *my heart daily? how long shall my enemy be exalted*
> *over me?*
> *Consider and hear me, O Lord my God: lighten mine eyes*
> *lest I sleep the sleep of death;*
> *Lest mine enemy say, I have prevailed against him; and*
> *those that trouble me rejoice when I am moved.*
> *But I have trust in thy mercy; my heart shall rejoice in thy*
> *salvation.*
> *I will sing unto the Lord, because he hath dealt bountifully*
> *with me.*

Darcy's eyes opened as he finished, and his smile faded slowly.

"Thank you, Darcy," Coulter responded, just above a whisper, still loud enough to reach the top of the balcony. "Now, if it please the Court, I can ask Mr. Calhoun to recite all other twenty-nine Psalms he has memorized to prove the fact that he is far from stupid."

The judge leaned over his raised desk. "That won't be necessary. I'm sure that the prosecution is willing to concede to Mr. Calhoun's vast knowledge of the Psalms. Mr. Alford?"

"Yes, Your Honor," he half sighed. "We so concede."

"Very well, then," Coulter continued, "then allow me to reiterate a few final points. Darcy, when you came across this Negro, did you know if he was free or slave?"

"No, sir. I didn't know one way or the other."

"And when confronted by the search party, why did you not just hand him over?"

"I was worried as to what they might do to him."

Coulter took a step back and lifted his voice to a crescendo. "Open-mindedness and compassion." He looked about him, locking eyes with a few random faces in the assembly. "Open-mindedness and compassion. Those are the words that most accurately describe Darcy Calhoun's actions. Stupidity is not. Perhaps he was just open-minded enough that in the moment of indecision, with an injured, terrified man standing outside his cabin, Darcy's mind made the leap from 'I don't know' to 'I don't know about this.' "

He turned slowly, taking in all of the assembly. "Look into your hearts. Look at the circumstances of the trial. Can you say, 'I don't know about this?' If you can, you are at least as smart as Darcy Calhoun." He tugged at his jacket and straightened his tie. Then he walked back toward his desk. "The defense rests, Your Honor."

Judge Castille pushed back a stack of papers and leaned forward. "I will give you both a moment to prepare your closing arguments." He looked to the witness box, to Darcy. "Mr. Calhoun, you may return to your seat."

Owen Conway turned to John as a buzz of quiet conversation filled the courtroom. "What in the hell was that?"

"I don't know."

"Why would he do that?" There was anger in his muffled tone. "He showed how a simple man could be confused. His best chance was to play that up. Why would he go and imply that Darcy was as smart as everyone else?"

"I know," John answered, his eyes on Darcy, his voice soft. "I fear the defense just proved that his motives exceed the mere outcome of this trial. The man couldn't have a mental deficient as a champion of the abolitionist cause. It wouldn't play well in Philadelphia."

Owen placed balled fists on his lap and looked maliciously toward the back of Coulter's head. "The bastard."

Neither John nor Owen spoke again over the next few minutes. Occasional whispered barbs of insult were released from the balcony and rained down upon both defendant and defender. Whether or not they heard them, neither man flinched.

"All right," Judge Castille then announced, settling the courtroom. "You may proceed, Mr. Coulter."

Coulter stood up and walked to a spot five feet from the judge's tall desk. "Your Honor." Coulter paused until the judge looked up and met his gaze. "Darcy Calhoun is a good man. If not for the blinders strapped on by this system, every man in the courtroom would see that. He *is* a good man, a man with few aspirations beyond God and the bit of land he tills. A man who loves deeply the animals in his care. No, he was not blessed with a glib tongue or a scientific mind, but that does not diminish the fact that he is a man of principle." Coulter took a step back and peered up at the judge's bench. "It is a difficult task, Your Honor, to erase the values instilled in us as children. The value of right and wrong. The value of assisting those in need. The bedrock of our morality may be buffeted by the passage of unjust laws; it may be weathered by public pressure and castigation, but it can still dwell deep within us at the core of our being."

He pointed a finger at Darcy and raised his voice with an almost pleading quality. "It still dwells in Darcy Calhoun. Darcy retained the values of his childhood. He assisted a wounded man in need. He did not know of that man's past or circumstances. All he knew was that he needed help. In rendering that help, Darcy harmed no one.

"Here in South Carolina some of you would say that Darcy Calhoun has a malady. You see, Darcy is color-blind. The man in need, the man Darcy helped, happened to be a black man. Darcy didn't see the color, he only saw the man. But perhaps Darcy is not the one with the malady. Perhaps it is you."

He stood still for a time, his eyes locked on Judge Castille, refusing to blink. "Today, we find out if the sickness can be cured. If the South can begin to heal itself." Coulter walked back to his desk and sat down.

Castille quickly turned to Mr. Alford, as if to dispatch a bad aftertaste. "If you will, sir."

Alford arose with the same humorless smile he had worn so often that it now seemed part of his character. He looked at Coulter. "He harmed no one." He let that sentence hang in the air.

Alford's eyes swept the courtroom. "No, this is not a case of murder. Nor is it a rape. Indeed, the crime itself seems to be reasonably free of victim. After all, Mr. Bodean's slave was returned to him. Mr. Flannety received his reward. And no one was physically harmed during any of it." He paused. "But, despite all that, I believe that this is a crime of *the* most heinous variety. A crime that attacks our society at its core, that tugs at the roots of our way of life. On occasion of murder, as dastardly an act as it is, there is but a solitary victim. Such is the same with a rape or a robbery. But here, here in this instance, we are all the victims. For, were there to be no penalty for the actions willingly undertaken by the defendant, chaos would ensue. Imagine a countryside full of fleeing Negroes, you, yourselves, helpless to do anything to stop their exodus. Imagine the collapse of the plantation system under such conditions—where runaways are rewarded with kindness and shelter each step along their journey to the North. Our economy would crumble. And we would be targets of vicious attacks of retribution by the rampant blacks. The horrors of the Habersham County uprising would play out in every county and hamlet south of the Mason-Dixon." He looked back at Coulter and scoffed. "He harmed no one, indeed.

"Mr. Coulter offered you a long theoretical speech, but let us now speak of fact." Alford turned to the judge and raised his voice just slightly. "Darcy Nance Calhoun violated the Fugitive Slave Act. Of that there is no question, no ambiguity. The facts have been laid before you, Your Honor. There is but one possible verdict—guilty as charged." He walked toward his desk, gifting a smile to Coulter along the way.

Judge Castille took a moment arranging some papers before him, then addressed the court. "I shall take a moment to review the charges and decide my verdict. Until then, the court is in recess." He banged his gavel, then exited through the door behind him.

With the authority now gone, segments of the balcony reverted to the behavior common among unwatched children. They whoomped and laughed; a few began tossing peanut shells toward the defense table. Darcy turned just once, long enough for John to see the years of endurance and the fresh pain behind the eyes.

"Let's get out of here," Owen suggested in disgust. "We can wait downstairs in the lobby until the verdict comes back."

"Very well," John answered, staring at Darcy in case he again looked back. He was glad he did not.

The two reporters separated in the lobby. Owen spotted a reporter from Washington whom he hadn't seen since the trial's hiatus, and John went after Woodridge.

The Bostonian's face seemed free of the concern he had shown during their last meeting. John kept his voice low.

"All's well, I hope."

"As well as can be expected under the circumstances," Woodridge responded.

"What have you thought of the proceedings?"

Woodridge smiled. "I thought the defense did extremely well." He seemed to react to John's raised eyebrow. "He certainly wasn't given much to work with, after all."

John hoped he meant the circumstances, not the man, and nodded halfheartedly. He avoided eye contact by glancing at his watch as he asked his next question. "Any news around town?"

"Little beyond the trial. I'm sure you were aware of the fires the other day. One really ravaged those warehouses. And then there have been rumors, pretty far-fetched, about a guarded shipment down at the wharf." He must have seen a flicker of change in John's expression. "Have you heard of it?"

"Yes." John felt his mouth go dry. He paused to clear his throat. "I went down there to check it out. I heard talk that it was some planter's art collection getting ready to be shipped north." He shook his head dismissively.

Woodridge smiled. "Well, I managed to get a good pretrial interview with the defense team. Coulter gave me some good statements that he couldn't exactly use in the courtroom."

John tried to look appropriately impressed.

"By the way, I heard you were a guest at Willowby," Woodridge commented, matching John's expression. "Has the enchantment worn off yet?"

"I would say that events here certainly put it in perspective."

"I'll bet." Woodridge checked his watch. "I'd best be getting back to the courtroom. I can't imagine the ruling will take much longer. Good to see you, Mr. Sharp."

Now standing alone, John began to look about the crowded lobby. His gaze bounced from cluster to cluster, briefly taking note of the men he recognized. Then his eyes stopped dead. A chill swept through him, and he clenched his jaw. There, standing alone thirty feet away, was Tyler Breckenridge. He had his predatory look again. His gaze was directed solely at John.

Breckenridge began to walk toward him, his expression now congenial.

"Good day, John," he said somberly, extending his hand.

John shook his hand, attempting to force words past his constricted throat. "Hello, Tyler."

"I did not notice you until just a moment ago. I hope you are doing well."

"Fine, thank you."

"I'm terribly sorry I missed you yesterday. I sent a man to find you—to your boardinghouse—but he informed me that you were out."

John clenched his fist at his side. "Yes, I'm afraid I was quite busy."

"Indeed," Breckenridge answered quizzically. "I was not aware anything important transpired last night."

John stared deeply into the planter's eyes, holding them for an uncomfortable moment. "You should know as well as any man that at times like these, important moments are all around us." As he finished, he forced a tepid smile.

Breckenridge did not smile back. Instead, he took a half step forward. "Yes, John, pivotal moments do abound. However, it is important that those are not confused with more ordinary happenings." There was no inflection in his statement whatsoever. "One must keep a wary eye and cautious judgment."

"Yes, one must. My experience in Charleston has most certainly taught me that."

John no longer noticed the sounds around him. As he and Breckenridge stared at one another, he was aware only of the pounding of his heart and his slow, heavy breaths.

"Well, then . . . ," John began.

Breckenridge exhaled. "John, join me for supper tonight. I feel as if there are a few things we should discuss."

"Unfortunately I am extremely busy. What with the trial and all."

John's posture stiffened as Breckenridge put his hand on his shoulder.

The planter's tone was grave. "John, I would be indebted to you if you would join me for dinner." He passed a soft smile. "After all, you do have to eat. I can send my man for—"

"Really," John said firmly, "I cannot."

Breckenridge lifted his hand from John's shoulder and took a step back. "Very well. Clio will be disappointed."

"Send her my best."

Breckenridge nodded. "Good day then, John."

"Good day, Tyler."

The planter turned and ascended the stairs toward the courtroom.

Most of the audience had returned to the courtroom. Owen Conway was among the last of the stragglers as he slid into his seat beside John.

"I ran into old Mabry in the lobby. His paper called him back to D.C. when the trial was postponed. I wanted to pick his brain on what's been happening in the capital this last week."

"Any new scandals?" John asked, distracted.

"No." Owen waited for John to look at him. "I wanted to know what's been happening politically." Owen leaned closer and lowered his voice to a whisper. "Some members of Congress and some folks at his paper are up in arms over rumors they've heard about a meeting in Tennessee. Only representatives of southern states were invited. His editor thinks it's all about secession." Owen paused for effect and raised his eyebrows.

"I heard a rumor about the meeting at the party," John acknowledged. "It doesn't exactly make me feel any better right now."

Owen nodded in agreement. "I saw you talking to Woodridge and some rich guy out there."

"The rich guy was Breckenridge."

Owen's eyes widened. "Do you think he suspects that you know something?"

"From the way he acted, I would say yes."

"Jesus, John, be careful." Owen glanced around briefly to be sure no one was watching them. "What about Woodridge?" Owen continued. "Does he know anything? Did you fill him in on what we learned?"

"No. I'm not sure I trust him."

"Why? He's on our side."

"Maybe not." He looked at Owen. "Do you remember who he said he worked for?"

Owen took a moment. "He said he was a freelancer, did he not?"

John nodded in agreement. "From Boston, as a matter of fact. Do you know what the word 'freelancer' translates to south of Mason-Dixon?" He paused. "Abolitionist."

Owen replied. "So what, you don't like abolitionists?"

"Not particularly. I don't like any man who sees the world in absolutes—where every issue is black and white. It turns reason into zealotry." John hesitated a moment as a man filed past him in the row ahead. "Don't get me wrong, these men down here are no damn different, no better. They have their own moral absolutes. That's why they don't compromise. That's why there's about to be a war."

The court reporter reentered the courtroom, as did several bailiffs. The anticipation of climax quieted the rambunctiousness from the balcony. Upstairs there was a sea of murmurs, no word so loud as to be decipherable. Downstairs, where John and Owen sat, there were no words at all. It was nerves, he knew. Nerves that dispatched the genteel small talk these men claimed maintainable even under a barrage of cannon. Nerves that carried doubt; a doubt heretofore hidden behind an arrogant nonchalance. John found the hypocrisy contemptible.

The reason for the worry was almost humorous. Were it not for his connection with the man himself, John would have reveled in the fact that a kind and simple backwoods farmer could humble the Carolina elite. But he did know him. And he cursed himself for caring.

Silence followed the judge as he climbed the steps to his desk. He sat still for only a moment, casting his eyes across the court before him, stopping eventually on Darcy Calhoun.

"Will the defendant please rise."

Stolen whispers hid beneath the creek of sliding chairs as Darcy and Coulter stood. Darcy fidgeted with his hands behind his back in the endless seconds that followed.

"Mr. Calhoun, you have been charged with breaking the fugitive slave laws of this state and nation. On that charge, this court finds you guilty."

Applause broke out in the balcony. Many of the planters and businessmen stood, shaking hands with those around them. A score of hands reached to slap the back of the prosecutor, while a sprinkling of feet—eager reporters, most likely—rushed toward the exit. John craned to get a better look at Darcy. He was still; his lawyer leaned in beside him, whispering something behind his ear. His hands no longer fidgeted, but rather, hung still at his sides. It was only when the gavel struck that he moved at all.

"Order!" Judge Castille yelled. "Order in the court!" He waited for the moment of jubilation to subside. "Now, on the matter of expediency, the court orders the sentencing hearing to take place tomorrow, Saturday, at two o'clock in the afternoon. Until then, this court is adjourned." The gavel fell a final time.

As all stood, and the gaiety began to play again, John watched the bailiff walk toward Darcy, carrying a set of manacles. As they were locked on, Darcy stood in profile. His lips moved quickly, his head responding to certain words with a light forward twitch. Owen, watching the same scene as John, need not ask this time. Darcy Calhoun was praying.

"Well, it wasn't like it was a surprise, you know," Owen said, chasing the words with a hefty sip of ale.

They sat at a table in the back corner of Hawk's Pub, just down the street from McClellan's. It was as dimly lit now as it had been in full night. The hour was seven, and they had been there, in the same spot, since the end of the trial.

"I mean, there was no real chance they were going to find him not guilty," Owen continued. "The real issue is the sentencing. That's where his chance is."

John took a sip from his glass and spoke through the hoarse tone that follows whiskey. "That Coulter is a real bastard. He took any chance Darcy may have had and tossed it out the window in favor of his precious ideology."

Owen waited a moment, then spoke calmly. "There never was a chance, John. Not really. Darcy lost that case the day they found the Negro in his cabin. John Quincy Adams himself couldn't have gotten him off."

John slapped his glass heavily against the table. "It *still* burns me. To try out some philosophical defense on a man unconcerned with philosophy . . ." He returned to his bourbon. "Play God with someone else. You should know. You met him. Darcy was too simple to grasp what was really going on." He took a long, deep breath.

"I know," Owen answered. He waited a minute, allowing the anger to dissolve from his friend's face. "Will you go see him?"

"Tonight? How could I?" He again tapped the glass. "What would I tell him? That everything will work out?" He took another sip. "Or that if he is killed, I shall be sure to make it so there is due outrage in the North? What a comfort that would seem." John stared down at the table, growing calm after a moment. "I wouldn't know what to say to him, Owen. I just wouldn't know."

"Yeah," Owen said, finishing his ale. "Neither would I."

John took another long drink of whiskey. He rocked the glass back and forth in his hand. "I tell you this, part of me hopes that ship *does* launch tonight. Part of me hopes they do go ahead and attack Moultrie. Then we can get this whole damn thing over with." The number of drinks consumed increased John's sense of fatalism. "The sooner it starts, the sooner it finishes. The southerners will be out of it as soon as they've used up their munitions. It's gonna happen anyway, you know. The way these people talk makes it inevitable." His voice grew hushed. "Plus, if they do it now, maybe they'll forget about Darcy."

Owen stared at John and waited until his eyes rose to meet him. "If it comes, it comes. But don't wish for it. Else you're as foolhardy as these damn crackers." Owen pulled out his pocket watch and checked the time. "It's starting to get late. Late enough that I should catch some sleep if I'm going to spell you later at the wharves." Owen stood up. "You're staying and watching till when?"

"Three. That's when I'll come and wake you so you can take over."

"Remember, though, come and get me the minute you see anything. No matter what time it is." Owen patted John on the shoulder as he headed for the door.

John nodded but sat still, staring into the dregs of the whiskey glass as he swirled it around and around on the uneven wood table. He was thinking of Clio.

Clio Breckenridge, sister to Tyler, daughter of Charleston—how did she fit into this strange world of vengeful ideology and seditious conspiracy? She was incapable of duplicity, he was certain. Her genuine warmth and humor and her lack of artifice were the qualities that had drawn him to her from the beginning.

She abhorred talk of war. He had seen her gentle nature in her care for the elderly at Willowby and in her concern for her neighbors. The conspirators may have met in her home, but she would know nothing of the planned attack.

John pictured her as she had looked on their picnic at Fox Hall, with peach flowers on her bonnet and a flush in her cheeks from the wine. She had spoken ruefully of the loss of civic improvements and the arts as men grew preoccupied with war. If his suspicion of this conspiracy proved true, if the attack was carried out, marching ranks and caissons would trample her parks, and cannon bursts would replace her fireworks. Clio's graceful world would never be the same.

For a while, John entertained the notion of trying to get her out of Charleston. New York was out of the question, but perhaps she would relocate farther north. Virginia, maybe.

The problem was that she probably would not leave her brother. John and Clio had known each other but a few days, and he felt there was a growing attachment between them. But John knew that her bond with her brother was older and stronger.

He was not sure if she would believe him if he told her of Tyler's involvement in the plot. And after the attack, what would she choose to believe then? He replayed their conversations in his mind. One thought stopped him cold. They had been behind the screen at the party talking about secrets—the use she and Tyler made of them, and the fact that all of the neighbors knew each other's. ". . . all but Tyler's and mine," she had said. Could she be a party to her brother's manipulations?

John suppressed a shiver in the shadow of doubt.

The city was almost silent now. Beneath the lap of the waves and the mournful tone of the harbor buoys, John could hear the comings and goings of the denizens of the darkness—the soft squeaks of the wharf rats and the scuttling of the giant cockroaches called palmetto bugs by the gentile of Charleston.

John checked his pocket watch. It was a quarter to three. It did not appear that the *Port Royal* would sail tonight. The last of the crates had been loaded an hour earlier, after which the stevedores departed and the militia guards went belowdecks. A solitary sentry remained on watch. The man had not moved for a while; John thought he might be asleep.

John hypothesized that the lack of activity would move back the timetable for the attack. More troops would doubtless come on board before the ship sailed, and the munitions would have to be offloaded at the other end, Fort Sumter. It was probably a good time to pass the watch to Owen.

John arose stiffly from his perch on a crate in an alley that had provided a sheltered view of the wharf. His legs had grown restless over the last hour, and now when he tried to walk they were stiff and unsteady. The effect of the bourbon had worn off several hours ago, and his mouth was as dry as cotton. He felt like hell, and in another hour the glow would begin in the east, announcing a new day in Charleston, South Carolina.

John's footsteps echoed through the empty streets. At least, he thought it was an echo at first. He slowly realized that the report was off—just a little. Was someone following him? He changed the cadence of his steps. There could have been a missed beat or two before he resumed an even pace. He halted and looked behind him. The footfall ceased, and he saw no one.

John had been followed before as he chased down stories in New York City. In the Five Points, where the usual motive was robbery, an athletic walk, an air of confidence, and a coat that just might conceal a weapon had always been enough to divert a predator to another target.

John had no such advantage here. He was the only target available on an otherwise deserted street, and John had a pretty good idea that robbery was not the motive of whoever was skulking behind him in the dark. But the flutter in his stomach soon gave way to anger. He would not simply walk along and play the role of the victim.

As he passed a corner storefront, he turned the corner abruptly and quickly removed his shoes. Then he doubled back, ducking into the alley that ran behind the businesses. He looked for a hiding place with a view and found one when he spotted a packing crate that offered a step up to the roof. He lay flat and waited.

The man who entered the alley was not tall or well built, but the pistol in his belt gave him the confidence of a giant. He walked about casually, peering into corners, peeking behind the packing crate; he could have been looking for his cat. The light fell on his face; he was a nondescript little man, totally unknown to John.

The man exhaled loudly in frustration, then chose a vantage point between buildings that offered a view of the alley and the street. He waited a good five minutes before a second set of footsteps approached.

"Did you let him see you?" The voice seemed vaguely familiar.

"No. I always kept a good block behind him. And one street ova. Must have him a girlfriend around here somewhere."

"Not likely. He probably heard you. I told you you need a new pair of boots."

"Maybe. But what now?"

The second man sighed. "Well, I don't see much point in waiting around here. He ain't going anywhere anytime soon. We'll find him tomorrow."

The second man scanned the alley. He looked up at the roofline, and John was amazed that he hadn't been spotted, because he could see the man's face very clearly. It was Breckenridge's man Rogers.

TWENTY

⟳

John Sharp walked downstairs to the front room of the McClellan boardinghouse just after eight in the morning. His joints ached, his stomach was queasy, and his head felt funny—as if the skin on his scalp was too tight. The night he had experienced, followed by only about two hours of sleep, could produce that effect. Compared with the turmoil in John's mind, and the twisted sheets of his unmade bed, McClellan's parlor offered an ordered tranquillity. A breeze ruffled the curtains of an open window, circulating the light aroma of ham that lingered from the night before. He walked past the window, stopping for a moment to feel the soft wind against his face, then slowly moved to one of the chairs tucked beneath the bare dinner table.

John set his elbows on the table and laid his head upon his open hand. Owen had been awake when he returned last night. The Irishman had been sleepless as well, and was more than willing to take up the post at the docks. He ignored John's cautionary warning. "It's you they've been following, not me," he said with a wink. "If I had been tailed, I'd have known it in an instant."

A friendly face peeked out from the kitchen door. "I knew I heard someone walking about," McClellan said with a wide grin. "You sure are up awful early, Mr. Sharp."

John forced a smile. "I am sorry if I bothered you. I've had a hard time sleeping."

"Nah, ain't no bother. Everything's all right, I hope."

"Oh, yes," he answered without conviction. "All is fine."

McClellan looked back at the kitchen for a moment, then again to John. "You know, all of breakfast won't be ready for least another hour and a half. But what say you I fry you up some bacon and a couple of eggs? That ought ta keep your belly from growling."

"I don't wish to put you to any trouble, Mr. McClellan."

"Ain't no trouble at all. I'd be glad to do it. You just wait here. I'll brew ya up some coffee, too. Won't be but a minute."

While McClellan prepared his breakfast, John rifled through a three-day-old copy of the *Charleston Gazette*. He settled on the wanted advertisements for fugitive slaves. Eight were listed. By description, all were virtually indistinguishable from the others, all except one man missing three fingers on each hand. Enough to keep men like Flannety busy, he thought. And enough ambiguity to ensure his success.

McClellan delivered a plate of scrambled eggs, crisp bacon, and several generous slices of cornbread. John was halfway into the meal, thinking that McClellan handled impromptu breakfast pretty well, when the bells began to ring.

It began with one, far away but insistent. Then the steeple bells joined in, uniting in a cry of alarm. The sound reverberated in John's chest, leaving him speechless. McClellan rushed back into the dining room cradling the coffeepot.

"Oh, heavens," the innkeeper whispered. "Not another fire."

The bells, in some tone or manner, imparted an urgency that transcended the fire alarms. John leaped up, nearly overturning his chair, apologized to McClellan, and rushed out the door, forgetting his hat and coat.

He stood in the middle of the street, scanning the horizon in all directions. He saw no column of smoke anywhere.

"My God," he breathed. "They've gone and done it. In the full light of day, they've gone and done it."

The few people on the streets rushed in all directions. John knew precisely where to go. He ran down State Street, cut over on Queen, then sprinted down the East Bay, passing each wharf in a blur.

He listened for distant cannon fire and the sound of artillery, but the pealing of the bells drowned out all other sounds but his own panting breath and the pounding of his shoes on pavement.

John felt the rush again—the thrill of the chase when pursuing a story. Back in New York, at the hint of a breaking story, the footrace was on from the halls of Printers Row. The magnitude of the event did not really matter. With a fast-breaking story, it was simply paramount that you get there, that you see it for yourself, get the scoop, and lock whimsical thoughts like context back in the room with your pen and paper. That's why John Sharp ran hard along the East Bay, consumed by nothing but the threat of lost time.

The warehouses at the end of each dock blocked view of all but the masts of the nearby vessels. As his sprint continued, it was Fort Sumter that came into view first. John slowed to a fast walk to prevent the buffeting that accompanies a run from distorting his perception. But Sumter seemed peaceful. There was no smoke, no flash of fire from her guns. John looked quickly toward the necks of Sullivans and Morris Islands. There was no activity there either. The bells stopped ringing. There was no sound of gunfire, no sound at all.

"What in the hell?"

He started to run again, down the remainder of the East Bay. He passed the final warehouse that blocked view of the *Port Royal*, then stopped dead in his tracks. The ship had not moved.

John heard the slap of footfall behind him and turned quickly. It was Owen, who had the look of a man who had been running in circles. He hunched forward with his hands on his knees to catch his breath while looking in disbelief at the ship and John in turn.

"I don't get it," John said, shaking his head.

"Perhaps it *was* only a fire," Owen gasped.

John turned around and again scanned the horizon over the entire peninsula. "There's no sign of smoke. And the bells. You heard them. They were different from the usual fire alarms."

Owen nodded, still panting. "So what then?"

Looking back down the East Bay, John noticed the pedestrians all moving quickly toward the west, with virtually no exception. John pointed to the street as a whole. "We follow them."

They ran again, following the path of dozens toward the center of Charleston. They saw an older man, walking slower than the rest, and stopped briefly beside him.

"Excuse me, sir. Could you tell us what's going on?"

"Some sort of news," he replied. "Important news, or else the bells wouldn't have rung like that. Everyone's going to the wire office to find out what."

"Thank you," John said, and the men continued on.

Owen managed to stammer a few words between breaths. "You don't suppose . . ."

"Secession?" John continued. "Perhaps the men meeting in Nashville have made their decision."

"Shoot!" Owen exclaimed, both worried and excited. "Then let's hurry up and get there."

A throng of hundreds were gathered around the wire office as John and Owen approached. Many looked like they had been shaken out of bed. Soon more arrived at their backs, pushing them further into the mass. The anxiety, the whispers, the looks of confusion, all told John this type of announcement was far from common. He looked at his watch. It was 8:57. He guessed the word would be announced on the hour.

Owen leaned in beside his ear. "John, you know I'm not one to needlessly worry. But I'm not stupid either."

"What do you mean?"

"Well, if this is what we think it is, and they're about to say what we think they are, don't you think we're in a bit of a precarious position? I mean, with us being northern reporters."

John scanned the faces around them. They had definitely been noticed, and the looks weren't friendly. The accusatory stares and vengeful glances implied suspicion of Yankee malfeasance in the announcement to come. John nodded immediately at Owen's suggestion.

"Yes, perhaps we *should* listen from a bit of a distance."

They threaded their way out of the crowd, settling fifty feet from the rear of the commotion.

Owen looked to John with a huge smile. "Think you can still run?"

"Fast enough, if circumstances demand it."

Owen smiled. "We'll see."

At nine o'clock, after the bells of Charleston had tolled the hour, a hush fell over the crowd. A breeze stirred, and a whispered phrase swept through the assembly like a rustling of dry leaves.

"It's the president."

Three men came out of the telegraph office. One elbowed his way through the crowd toward the courthouse. Another headed in the opposite direction.

"It's the president."

The remaining man dragged a box out onto the sidewalk, creating a makeshift rostrum. He withdrew a scrap of pink paper from one coat pocket and a brass bell from the other. He muttered to those around him to move back, to give him some air.

"It's the president."

"Hear ye! Hear ye!" The uniformed telegrapher rang the bell. He swung it in a grand manner, bending his arm ninety degrees at the elbow. The action was an anachronism, harkening back to the days when news had traveled on horseback rather than the wire. The telegrapher cleared his throat. "This wire was received from Washington, D.C., at 8:35 a.m. today."

The crowd fell utterly silent.

"President Zachary Taylor is dead of complications from a stomach illness. Vice President Millard Fillmore will be sworn in as the thirteenth president of the United States. No further information is available at this time."

There was only silence.

But the president had *only had food poisoning*. Something about bad fruit or bad milk. John glanced about him, mute and confused like the others in the crowd. The president was dead.

John's mind scrambled to place the event in context. Taylor was not the first to die in office. No, William Henry Harrison had caught a cold on his inauguration and had died about a month later. John remembered it; he had been about twelve at the time. That situation had felt different, however, for there had not been time for Harrison to assume the identity of the president in the mind of the public. Taylor, on the other hand, had been a powerful presence, and his death would create a vacuum. What was going to happen? John felt numb. The president was dead.

As the shock began to dissipate, murmurs of excitement ran through the crowd. The atmosphere around the wire office took on a strange dynamic, neither celebratory nor mournful. This was news of great importance—news to be shared, news to be spread. Bricklayers, bankers, and haberdashers now took off at a trot, eager to be the first to impart the news to their own circle. "The president is dead."

John and Owen wandered through the streets of Charleston. The clutches of townsfolk discussing the event did not seem to mind their intrusion. Many seemed eager to be interviewed. John's question was always the same: "How did you hear the news?"

"Those bells woke me out of a sound sleep. I had just enough time to throw on pants and a shirt and make it down to the wire office. You could of knocked me ova with a feather when I heard. Stomach illness? Hell, do ya think someone could've poisoned him?"

"I was busy fixing breakfast with Hetty. My young 'uns, Billy Bob and Georgie, come running into the kitchen all out of breath with the words tumbling ova each other trying to get it out. Georgie said the president was dead. Billy Bob said he'd been swearing at the vice president. 'Course he got that wrong. Then Hetty took the skillet of bacon off the stove, folded her hands, and started saying a prayer for the president's soul. It made me think about when George Senior died. She had been frying the bacon then, too."

"I was out in the stable with our groom when the bells started tolling. He thought my sorrel mare might've stepped on a nail. We didn't get to the wire office in time ta hear the announcement, but I ran into Bob Crawford on his way back. The whole thing sure makes me nervous. There are power grabs, you know, in other countries when the leader dies. Down in Mexico. Over in Europe. I learned about it through some readings. Beheadings and the like. 'Course, I figure we're too civilized for that here. I just hope things go smoothly. That they get Fillmore sworn in right quick."

John looked at his watch and turned to Owen. "It is about two hours until we are due in court. Do you think they'll postpone the sentencing?"

"You would think so, but we'd better be there anyway." Owen checked his notebook. "I think I'll use the time for a few more interviews. Thought I'd check out the taverns."

John nodded. "The taverns should be busy. Southerners use any occasion for a drink—celebrations or mournings."

"Which one is this?"

"Damned if I know."

"Are you coming along?"

"No. I don't want to walk into the courtroom with an afternoon high." John paused for a moment. "I think, perhaps, that there is a man who might give me some answers about all of this. About what we can expect."

"You're not talking about Breckenridge again?"

"Of course not. I meant Mannion, the editor of the *Charleston Gazette*. I want to get his take on this."

Owen nodded. "So how about meeting back at the boardinghouse at one?"

John nodded, and they went their separate ways.

John nearly collided with Joshua Mannion at the front door of the *Charleston Gazette*. Mannion invited John inside, then led him to a vacant office.

"Mr. Sharp, I only have a minute."

"That is all I need."

He gestured to a chair for John. "How may I help you?"

John sat. "Mr. Mannion, since hearing the news of the president's death, I have been attempting to understand the local reaction. The signals I am receiving are mixed, to say the least. Prior to today's news, I would have said that President Taylor was truly hated down here. Yet today, I am hearing a great deal of shock and some apparent sorrow at the man's death."

"Mr. Sharp, there was certainly no love lost between the average Charlestonian and President Taylor. Many believed his recent hard-line antislavery actions to be nothing short of traitorous—since, as it was, he was a child of the South. I have no doubt that all here wished him out of office. Just not in *this* manner. In general, I would say that our citizens feel a genuine regret that the man has died, but they also feel relief."

"But what relief? The new president, Fillmore, is a Yankee. A New Yorker, for heaven's sake. How much better is that?"

Mannion smiled. "While it is true that geography is a great divider, agreeable politics see no borders. Millard Fillmore, while a Yankee, has long been seen as more pliable than his predecessor—more apt to negotiate on pressing matters. Already, since the announcement, I have heard many disparate voices willing to take the time to fairly evaluate his policies. With Zachary Taylor, that possibility was long dead. There is potential for new life here, Mr. Sharp." He paused, taking another sip. "Though I have always been an optimist."

There was a knock on the door, and a man with an ink-stained apron poked his head in. "Sir, we need you."

"Very well. Mr. Sharp, I am sorry—"

"Just one more question please, Mr. Mannion. Before, at the party, the warning you gave to me about an event . . . Is it still imminent?"

He paused for a moment, as if studying the question acutely. He looked back up, sliding his glasses up the bridge of his nose. "No, Mr. Sharp. I no longer believe that it is."

At a quarter to one, fifteen minutes before their planned meeting time, John stood on the front porch of his boardinghouse, awaiting Owen's arrival. His smile must have been visible from a block away.

"So what?!" Owen shouted from across the street. "Have you already lined up a personal interview with President Fillmore?"

"Hardly," he answered, walking quickly to meet him. "It's something else."

"What?" John watched Owen fidget like a hyperactive child. "What?" he repeated more insistently.

John placed a hand on Owen's shoulder and spoke softly but with suppressed excitement. "I have just come back from the wharves. They are unloading the *Port Royal.*"

Owen looked at him speechless.

"They are loading the cargo back into wagons, and they're carting it away."

Owen grabbed John's shoulders and shook him. "I don't believe it! It's not gonna happen!"

John was caught off guard by his own laugh. "No," he stammered, attempting to collect himself. "It seems we may have dodged disaster."

Owen threw himself down onto McClellan's front stoop. He stretched his legs out straight before him and extended his arms to the side, shoulder high. He took a huge breath and exhaled loudly. "I feel like someone just moved a millstone off my chest. I haven't been able to take a deep breath for days." He reached for a cigarette. "Who would have thought that a chance event could have such an impact?"

John shook his head. "I wonder how often that is the case. Food poisoning!" He shook his head again. He found himself grinning at the irony. He was only a little ashamed.

"Do you see how this changes everything?" Owen straightened up. "This could bode well for Darcy at the sentencing. These southerners have their blood. The president they all despised is dead. Perhaps now is a time for reconciliation."

"Perhaps," John agreed. "A lax sentence could serve as an olive branch to the new administration."

Owen followed a whoop with a cackle. "It's all working out for old Owen, just like it always does." He stood up and patted John on the chest. "Hey, I'm suddenly starving. Let's hurry and get some food so we can make it to the courthouse in time."

John agreed, and they walked back toward downtown Charleston, both suddenly free of the fatigue, and with the first hint of optimism they had felt for days.

The powers that be *did* deem it fit to go forward with the sentencing, even on such an occasion as this. The courtroom itself was far from crowded—open gaps in the balcony and the benches below spoke to the suddenly diminished role that Darcy Calhoun now assumed. Coulter and his assistant conferred quietly at the defense table, apparently oblivious to all others. They looked as if they could have been discussing their train schedule. John sat beside Owen, yards away from the nearest spectator. He could not help but make a hasty scan of the downstairs for Tyler Breckenridge. He would like to have seen the look on his face. To his regret, Breckenridge was absent.

"You know," Owen started, "they lowered the flag outside the courthouse to half-mast. I'm actually surprised they did it, what with their passionate hatred of the man himself."

"Etiquette," John replied. "Have you noticed the black armbands, too?" He nodded at their prevalence in the lower section of the courtroom. "Southerners do not err in matters of etiquette."

A minute later, Darcy was led into the courtroom from a side door. The suit was gone. He again wore a farmer's standard work outfit—high britches braced by suspenders and a loose, collarless cotton shirt.

"That's a relief," Owen whispered. "Yesterday he just looked silly."

As Darcy walked to join his counsel, he seemed surprised by the sparseness of the crowd. He looked repeatedly back to the first-floor benches, his eyes squinting, his mouth slightly ajar. As he saw John, his expression changed. His eyes rounded and his cheeks trembled lightly. It was a question, John knew, and his only answer was a half smile and a nod of reassurance. It was not lost on John that Darcy's gaze had sought him rather than Coulter.

As the judge entered, everyone rose. Judge Castille, normally a man given to an expression of stoicism, looked tired and agitated. He banged the gavel harder than usual.

"We are here for the sentencing of Mr. Darcy Calhoun." He turned to the defendant. "Mr. Calhoun, you have been found guilty of violating the Fugitive Slave Act. Today, this court shall decide your punishment." He looked to the prosecutor, the red-cheeked Mr. Alford. "Sir, does the state still ask for the penalty of death in this matter?"

"We do, Your Honor."

"Very well. Before I make my ruling, Mr. Calhoun will have the opportunity to speak on his own behalf. Now keep in mind, Mr. Calhoun, the question of your guilt has already been decided, so please confine your statements only to the issue of sentencing. Do you understand that, sir?"

"Yes. Yes, Your Honor."

The judge looked at Coulter. "You have explained this to your client?"

"We have, Your Honor."

"Then, Mr. Calhoun, please approach the witness box so you may be sworn in."

Once Darcy removed his hand from the Bible, Judge Castille looked down toward him. "You may proceed with your statement, sir."

Darcy clutched his hands on the rail of the witness box as his words began to stammer. "Umm, well, ya see, I . . . I ain't a man given well ta speaking in front of others. Especially . . ." He stopped and swallowed. "Especially so many as this." He paused for as many as ten seconds, his eyes darting to countless inanimate objects. Then he looked back at the judge. "Sir, Your Honor, would it be all right if I told a story? I mean . . . I mean, I think it might help to explain things. And, well, I speak better when I's telling a story."

"Yes, Mr. Calhoun. You may."

"Thank ya, sir. The story . . . The story is from when I was a boy and still living in North Carolina. I ain't real good at judging my age at times, never has been, but I's guessing . . . Well, I's guessing I was about nine or ten at that time." Darcy eyes were on the floor as he spoke. " 'Twas during a real terrible drought. A drought near twice as bad as the one we's had here more recent. That drought, back then, had lasted almost two years. Well, two summers at the least.

"My family . . . My father and mother and me, we was never rich. Never close to it. But those summers was the worst off we ever was. By the second, we'd done killed off all our livestock on account of food, not that we'd had many animals to begin with. Our garden had done dried up, too, and many a time my momma was fixing suppa from nothing more than a couple spoonfuls of flour, a bit a lard, and some water." A humorless smile passed over his face. "It's funny, when you's hungry, no matter what else is going on, there ain't nothing you can do to stop your mind from thinking on food. Even now, so many years passed as they have, the thing I remember most from then was just how hungry I always was."

He took a deep breath. "Since I wasn't getting enough to eat at home, I began ta . . . Well, I starts to scavenge 'round the woods and places for extra food. I first began to chew on pig wort." He held up his hands, making a circle with his thumb and index finger. "Ya know, those plants 'bout the size of a dollar that grow close to the ground. Found that I could chew on dozens of 'em, but it still did little to fill my belly." He cast his eyes to the ceiling for just a second. "Afta that, I started to put my mind t'ward finding cattails. You know, the bushy tops of the reeds that grow in the lowlands along the rivers. I found that you could slit thems open and then eat out the insides of 'em." His hands mimicked the action. "They tasted like . . . Well, they ain't tasted good, but they did heaps more in filling me than did the pig wort.

"Problem was, a couple of other kids from school seen me munching 'em. And, well, I gots to be made fun of. Quite frequent, as a matter of fact. Kids start ta calling me half raccoon. Half coon 'cause they said I eat like the animals do, even though I ain't never seen no 'coon nowhere near a cat's tail."

Darcy looked over his shoulder, back at the judge. "I tell you all of this to try to explain why I did what I did."

As Darcy lay a considerable pause, the judge looked at him inquisitively. "In this case?"

"Oh, no, sir. No, Your Honor. Why I did what I did back then. You see, our teacher, she kept her a basket of apples up at the front of the classroom that she gave out to the students from time to time, on account of good work. Well, one day, I was made to stay after the other kids 'cause I hadn't yet finished my studies. My teacher, she left the classroom for a while, tending to some other business I gather, and I was awful hungry. You see, ever since the kids start to call me half raccoon I had stopped my eating of the cat's tails. So I was hungrier then than ever. Well, I walked me up to the front of the room and I took me three of those apples, all which I stuffed in my trousers. I remember 'twas three, 'cause I was gonna take one home for my momma and my papa, and then one for me.

"Those apples—they was the yellow ones, ya know, all big and juicy—well, they was 'bout the best tasting fruit we's ever had. My mom and pop never did ask where I got 'em. Guess they figured not ta question such a blessing." Darcy rubbed his hand across his forehead to wipe away the sweat. "The next day at school, the teacher was awful mad. She asked me had I stolen some apples. I told her that I had taken three, but it was just on account of how hungry I was, not out of no meanness or spite. Well, despite what I said, she was fuming mad. She done made me stand up in front of the class and admit to what I had done. Then she says, 'Not only does he eat like a 'coon, but he steals like one too.'" Darcy's expression stayed stolid, but John could hear a slight crack in his voice. "Steals just like a 'coon."

Darcy stared down at his hands, watching a finger slide across the wood railing. Then he turned back to the judge. "Now, Your Honor, you may be wondering how I think my story runs into my present state. But, ya see, I think they is both similar. I was always a religious boy, was since I can remember, and the way I looked at taking them apples, well, it wasn't as bad as stealing. I thought me . . . Well, I thought the Bible taught us that those with plenty shall help out those with little. And ya see, in my present case, I just figured that the Bible told us ta help other people when they's in need of it. To always offer a helping hand to those in need." He turned back forward. "But I guess I just ain't smart enough to understand that there's more to it than just that. Wasn't smart enough back then, and I's not smart enough now." He paused. "I was punished for taking them apples, in a way I could never forget. But I bet the teacher forgot 'bout them apples in a day or two." Darcy paused and furrowed his brow. "I know I's to be punished here today, too. I guess all I'm saying is that I ain't actually sure as to why. That's all. I just ain't sure as ta why."

The court was as quiet as a church. After Darcy had not spoken for a while, the judge leaned forward. "Mr. Calhoun, is there anything else you would like to say?"

Darcy raised his head. "No, sir. I guess not."

"Very well," Judge Castille said softly, politely. "You may return to your bench, Mr. Calhoun, but remain standing."

As Darcy returned to the defense table, his two lawyers stood to join him. Their expressions showed a professional gravity. The court's attention was riveted on Judge Castille.

He sighed audibly as he began. "When sentencing, a judge must weigh the nature of the crime against the nature of the man. Darcy Calhoun, for all intents and purposes, is not a bad man. While his somewhat secluded lifestyle has perhaps shielded him, and negatively so, from society's standards, he is none the less a decent individual. And I have no doubt that the action prompting this trial was an aberrant one." Judge Castille looked sternly toward the man sitting in the front bench to his left. It was the mayor of Charleston. "Were Darcy Calhoun to be released, I have no doubt that we in the legal system would never hear from him again."

The anger apparent on Castille's face intensified as he continued to stare at the mayor. It was then that John knew.

"No," he whispered in a breath.

Castille now looked back to the center of the courtroom; the creases around his mouth seemed deeper. "But the nature of this crime is not the same as most. As the prosecutor suggested, it does not victimize only one or two, but our society as a whole. And while Darcy Calhoun might never again commit the same act, a show of leniency would only encourage others to behave in a similar and reckless manner, destabilizing our order. That we cannot afford. Therefore, weighing both the evidence and the statement made here today, this court has no choice but to sentence Mr. Darcy Calhoun to the maximum penalty allowed by law." His voice was softer. "Death by hanging. The sentence is to be carried out with due speed, Monday, the eleventh of July, at ten in the morning. This court is hereby adjourned."

The light patter of applause in the balcony stopped almost immediately when no others joined in. There was just a soft murmur of conversation downstairs, as men began to arise quietly, a few at a time, and shuffle toward the door.

Owen sat silently. He leaned forward until his elbows rested on his knees, then he rocked back and forth, just a little, his attention focused on the floor.

For his part, John Sharp sat perfectly still. He felt the color rise in his face. He felt the mist in his eyes. He did not know whether to blink or not, on the chance that Darcy would look back at him. Darcy turned just once on his way out of the courtroom. It was a solitary glance aimed only at one man. As John locked eyes and leaned forward, Darcy cocked a slight smile. "It's all right," he mouthed through trembling lips, then turned away and exited through the side door.

Owen and John did not speak as they walked hastily down Broad Street. They stopped only when they were called upon, a few hundred yard's distance from the courthouse.

"Mr. Conway, Mr. Sharp, a moment please." Prescott Woodridge walked quickly toward them. His disposition seemed far too agreeable. "Well, this ought to provoke a fury in the North, wouldn't you say?"

John saw a tightening of Owen's jaw. "No concern for the man, eh, only the cause?" He said it almost mildly.

Woodridge was taken aback. "I am not *happy* with the ruling, Mr. Conway. I only mean that—"

"That his death can be made into a positive," Owen responded.

"Well . . . Yes. And what is so wrong with that? It is far better than a meaningless death."

Owen smiled, but it came across more like a frown. "Meaningful death. Meaningless death. Is it all about prizes, all about moral victories?" he asked softly. "Who has the most feathers in their cap in the end? Do you think that if there were a hundred Darcy Calhouns, you would actually win?"

"If they were all so brave, then perhaps."

"Bravery? He did not ask to be part of your cause. He did not ask for the situation laid upon him. He was a pawn for the abolitionists, and you know it." Owen turned to John and sighed. "Come on, let's go to the tavern."

They put their backs to Woodridge and began to walk away. "Mr. Sharp, please," he called out.

John stopped. "Owen, I'll meet you there."

Owen grunted, then walked off.

Woodridge walked up beside him. "I do understand Mr. Conway's frustration. I mean, it has been a hell of a day for all of us, starting with the death of the president. I sure didn't see that coming. But the trial—well, I thought the outcome was a foregone conclusion. I thought you and Mr. Conway knew that too."

John's eyes, seemingly unfocused since the trial's conclusion, now locked on Woodridge. "I have met Darcy Calhoun. I have talked with him personally. I know him. His life is no less precious than yours or mine."

"Forgive me if I seemed callous. I was not aware of the extent of your contact with the defendant. But you must agree, the sickness of a system that would allow a man like Darcy to be accused, let alone convicted, is the real evil here. Their barbaric laws and courts are the ones to blame, not the abolitionists."

"Perhaps they would not be so barbaric were they not provoked. You know that men with your politics purposefully incite the South at times. You invite responses such as this."

Woodridge softly grasped his arm. "Mr. Sharp, I know from the few times I have met you that you are a decent and honorable man. It is your anger that speaks now, not your reason. The South strikes at the North like a fighter in a dark room. They are desperate and afraid." He dropped his hand. "Think about it, John. The only time a thought or idea is truly feared is when it is realizable. And that realization comes closer every day, with every action like the one just made in the courtroom."

"So you *are* happy that Darcy is to be executed."

Woodridge sighed. "Again, you look past the main issue. When we achieve our goal at the end of the road, there will be no more travesties like the one that befell Mr. Calhoun today."

"No. But until you get there, the road will be paved with them." John felt his anger taking control; he briskly tipped his hat. "Good day, sir."

John was about thirty feet away when Woodridge called out to him. "I know all about you, Mr. Sharp." John stood with his back to him as Woodridge approached. "I know where you've been and what you've seen. I can only imagine how hard it must have been to fight off the seduction of the luxury that a plantation estate and the mansions of the East Bay can offer."

John turned around swiftly, his face frozen with rage. "I was not seduced."

Woodridge lifted his lips into a coy smile. "Prove it."

"How?"

"Meet me here tomorrow, promptly at ten in the morning. Bring three dollars with you, and I assure you, if you were ever at all enamored with these people, I shall change that forever."

John stood still, confused.

Woodridge began to backpedal. "Ten o'clock. You won't regret it. Oh, and try to look like a southerner." In an instant, he was gone.

The atmosphere at the tavern was lively. There were rousing songs, clinking glasses, and a smattering of laughter. Seated in the shadows of a back corner, neither John nor Owen were in the mood.

John was drawing rings with his finger in the spilled salt on the table. "A thought has been bothering me." He looked up at Owen. "You know how we had talked earlier about the possibility of the South sending a message by acquitting Darcy? That it might offer an olive branch to the new president?"

Owen shook his head. "Damned if I can figure out what kind of message they're trying to send."

"Maybe they are drawing the line over this fugitive slave issue— particularly after the killings in Georgia, where the ringleader got away. Maybe that is what this trial has been about all along—to send the strongest statement possible to the powers in Washington, *whomever they may be,* that the South will not continue to tolerate northern sanctuary for escaped slaves."

Owen shrugged. "Right now my head hurts. I'm not up to second-guessing them."

The men lapsed into silence. Both were preoccupied with deaths, recent and impending. It was almost unbearable to overhear the toasts and the congratulatory remarks over Darcy's sentence. Yet both of them knew that the announcement of another man's death had narrowly averted a disaster. The source of his contradictory emotions were not lost on John as he stared down at his bourbon.

"You know," John mused, "before I came down here, I rarely drank. Only at parties or special occasions, really. But from the moment I set foot in Mahan's office he had a bourbon in my hands. It's been mostly the same, ever since. While I was out at Willowby, they continuously plied me with alcohol. Drink after drink. Right now I don't know if it's making me feel better or worse." His thoughts faded into another sip.

John's eyes were drawn to an incongruity near the doorway. A man was standing on his toes, scanning the room, but his presence was so out of context that it took John a minute to recognize him. It was Michael Allen, the mayor's assistant. John sat watching him until the eyes found his. Then Allen motioned to him silently, inviting him outside.

John excused himself from Owen and made his way to the door. As he squinted at Michael Allen in the sunlight, he felt a little ashamed of himself. His eyes were drawn to details he normally overlooked when talking with an intelligent man on a matter of importance. He saw scuffed shoes, a rumpled shirt collar, a hat in need of brushing. It was the disparity that made him notice, of course, for Allen had been fastidiously groomed on their previous meetings. John had perceived him to be a public servant on the rise.

Allen spoke in an earnest whisper, with a furrowed brow and eyes that looked very tired. "I think it would help Darcy if you came to see him. Tomorrow, I mean."

"I don't know how I could help him," John stammered nervously. "I mean, I know I should go, but I have no idea what to say."

"The words aren't important."

John sighed. "I'll come. I'm just afraid that uncomfortable silence and hollow reassurances will not do the man a lot of good." He knew he was hedging. "You will have a good minister, right? A man of strong faith like Darcy?"

"We'll have a minister. But I think you are the one who could help him the most." He paused. "He talks about you, you know."

John looked up.

"He repeats to me the things you have told him. Stories. Words of encouragement. He quotes you—the words are obviously not his." Allen looked hard at John. "It would make a difference."

John nodded. "I will come tomorrow night. You can tell him that."

Allen exhaled. "Thank you."

John watched the mayor's assistant walk away. The tired gait, the droop of the shoulders, belonged to an older man.

TWENTY-ONE

⌒

John met Woodridge and another man at the intersection of Broad and Meeting, promptly at ten.

"I'm glad you decided to come," Woodridge said with a smile.

"Yes. Now if you could tell me why I . . ."

"Ya got my money?" the nameless man interrupted. He was tall, with pronounced buckteeth that made his upper lip and mustache perfectly convex.

"This is Mr. Brandi," Woodridge said. "He will be your guide this morning."

"To where?"

Woodridge's face became serious. "To the workhouse."

"The workhouse? I did not think such a place was open to the public."

"It ain't," Brandi said. "That's where I come in. That is, if you's got my three dollars."

John reached for his wallet and handed over the money.

Brandi smiled, peeling back his upper lip like a wet tarp. "Now listen. This is how it works, and if ya don't like it, then you's can find another guide." Brandi stared John over, focusing on the outfit. "Your clothes should do fine. Ya look pretty dandy, almost southern. So, we's going to the workhouse 'cause you is a planter looking for a missing slave. Get it? They's sorta know me there, so there shouldn't be no questions. But if there is, you let me answer 'em. Don't talk at all. If ya do, they'll know you's up to no good." He laughed. "And you ain't wanting that ta happen. When you's ready to leave, you just whisper to me, and I'll tell 'em your runaway ain't there. But remember, no talking. Ya got it?"

John looked to Woodridge, his brow furrowed in doubt.

"He is honest," Woodridge insisted. "And he knows what he's talking about."

"Very well, then. Let us waste no more time."

They walked a distance across town to a rather isolated area. Brandi pointed ahead to a wooden building—somewhat of a warehouse, it appeared—then looked to John. "That's it. That's the workhouse. You ready?"

John turned to Woodridge. "Are you coming also?"

"No. I have already seen it, and once was more than enough for my eyes. Perhaps one too many times for my memory as well. I shall wait for you here."

John turned back to his guide. "Very well, Mr. Brandi. Then let us proceed."

He walked into a haze—not smoke or vapor, but a dense chalky cloud that smarted his eyes and stung his throat. He blinked to let his eyes adjust to the interior of the barnlike room. The only light came from long window slits high up near the ceiling. It fell in narrow shafts, like spotlights on a stage, illuminating a few feet, creating shadows in sharp contrast. Human forms moved back and forth through the light, their backs bent under the heavy weight of sacks.

A huge millstone dominated one side of the room. It was driven not by water or by oxen, but by men. The men worked in silence, walking in continuous circles, in and out through the light and shadow.

On the other side of the room was a large treadmill. Men and women were chained in place, climbing endless steps to nowhere. The repetitive nature of the millwheel and treadmill was a concept straight out of hell, for no action was ever completed. Minutes stretched to hours with the eternal turning of the wheels.

John walked forward, ostensibly searching for his lost slave. He heard the grunts of effort, the grinding of the wheels, and the sweeping sound as the women brushed the crushed rock into sacks. There was no human speech except for an unintelligible singsong soliloquy, fading in and out. It seemed to echo from various corners of the building.

The appearance of the human forms was most bizarre; they looked like the negative images of a daguerreotype—white where black should be. John thought they looked painted at first. Then he realized that the chalk was caked to the sweat on their faces and bodies, with their black eye sockets making a sharp contrast—like skeletons in a medieval painting of the *danse macabre*.

John could see a man being beaten, his hands tied to a beam in the center of the room. He walked closer and stood just feet from the victim, facing the black overseer with the whip. Spatters of blood fell on Tyler's fine cream suit.

"Better move away from there," the taskmaster called.

John moved even closer. The man with the whip could now see the flecks of blood on John's face and clothing. He stopped, with his limp arm now hanging at his side. His eyes were afraid.

John walked about the room, looking at the faces. He felt that he owed them that; a look in the eye, some recognition of their suffering. But no one looked back. Their eyes were too far gone.

The smell of the place evoked a memory of the time that John had set foot in a knacker's yard, where used-up animals were sent to die after a lifetime of labor. It was necessary to use them completely, long after the spark of life was gone—tan the hides, render the fat, grind the bones to glue. Any man or woman who left this place would be as spiritless as those animals, serving their masters on and on when their lives were over.

The odd singsong was closer now—like one person carrying on two sides of a conversation. It came from a wraithlike woman, who twirled in the drunken circles of some strange dance.

"The baby done drowned. Went home ta Jesus! . . . The fat was a-burning in the old frying pan."

"She is mad," the taskmaster said. "There is nothing to be done with her."

John stared silently for a few more moments. "I've seen enough," he then whispered under his breath. He turned on his heel sharply and strode for the door, leaving a trail of bootprints among the barefoot impressions on the floor.

"The baby done drowned . . ."

The door slammed shut behind them.

John walked out with a resolution of stone. Indeed, Brandi had a difficult time keeping up with him as they strode back toward Woodridge.

"Horrible, is it not?" the abolitionist asked gravely.

"Horror doesn't even come close."

"I dare say that I could endure only seconds more than you, Mr. Sharp. It is not a place of subtlety."

Brandi, clearly not up for an ideological discussion, interrupted. "If that's all you'll be needing me for, then I'll be on my way. Ya let me know if ya need me again, Mr. Woodridge. Same special rate as always." Out came another bucktoothed smile. "Three dollars." He turned and walked away.

Woodridge put his arm on John's shoulder. "There," he said, pointing back to the workhouse. "In there is the true face of slavery. It is not the image of happy children singing or cultured servants. That is the anomaly—found on one of those few scattered show plantations. Slavery is . . . Well, as you said, beyond horror. A bloody affront to the decency of civilized man."

John had heard barely a word. He did not have to. He had drawn his own conclusions, conclusions that settled harshly in his stomach. The workhouse was a catalyst for reawakening the anger he had fought to settle overnight. Now all of it, the trial, the deaths, the dishonesty, came back in a surge—a surge of hate focused on only one man.

John looked at Woodridge. "Thank you for showing me this, but I must go immediately."

Woodridge seemed taken aback. "Where?"

"To see someone."

"John, unwise choices are often made in the heat of anger. Should you not wait?"

John began to walk off. "I know what I'm doing."

"Be careful then!" Woodridge shouted, apparently quite aware of John's destination. The next words were only a whisper. "For God's sake, be careful."

John pounded on the door of the Breckenridge mansion. A liveried slave answered after a moment.

"Is Mr. Breckenridge home?" John asked curtly.

"Yessir," the man answered, then noticed the blood. "Are . . . are you all right, sir?"

"Tell Mr. Breckenridge that John Sharp asks for an audience with him immediately."

"Yessir. Won't you come in and wait?"

John nodded and walked inside. He waited in the parlor for only a few seconds. The same slave then returned. "Mr. Breckenridge will see you now in his study."

As John pushed back the study door, Breckenridge stood. The beginning of a smile dissolved. "Good Lord, John, are you all right? You are covered in blood."

John walked forward. "I am well aware of that. It is part of the reason I am here."

Tyler quickly sensed John's mood. His voice became quiet, almost somber. "Won't you sit? Can I fix you a drink?"

"No. And I prefer to stand."

Tyler walked past John and softly closed the study door. "Then what can I do for you, John?"

"You can tell me why you invited me to stay at Willowby. You can tell me what it was that you were trying to keep me from finding out."

Breckenridge's reaction showed no sign of shock or discomfort. "John, I'm not exactly sure I understand what you're talking about. I invited you to stay at Willowby so that you might see more, not less. I thought that, as a reporter, you were entitled to both sides of the story. I was not keeping you from anything."

John smiled a nasty smile. "You are a liar, sir."

Breckenridge remained calm, taking a seat behind his desk. "I am sorry that you feel that way, John, but you are entirely incorrect."

John was a bit deflated by the staid reaction. He wanted a fight. "Is that so? Then you southerners have a polluted sense of honesty, Mr. Breckenridge."

"I fear that you have me somewhat at a disadvantage. For if you do not expound upon these allegations, then how am I to respond?"

"The ship and its cargo," John exclaimed. "That is the reason you detained me out in the country. So that I would not become aware of it."

"What ship?"

John grew more annoyed. "The *Port Royal*, of course, moving back and forth to Fort Sumter. Docked at the only wharf in Charleston that has been under day and night guard by professional militia."

"Why would the *Port Royal* concern me? Or you, for that matter?"

"You know damn well why. You knew of its intended purpose. I saw men of power and influence sneaking out the back gate of your house the night before the trial, the night the *Port Royal* docked for its final load. You were part of the conspiracy."

Tyler nodded very slowly in confirmation of a thought of his own, rather than acknowledgment of John's accusation. "So our trust turned to suspicion so quickly that you felt the need to watch me surreptitiously. What a shame."

John stared at him coldly. "Let us not forget who started watching whom first. Were it not for *your* initiative, you and I would be but strangers."

Tyler looked at him with sharp, powerful eyes. "Yes. And without my continued watching, they might be fishing your body out of the Cooper River."

A chill ran through John. The statement clenched his throat for a moment. "Besides," he said, attempting to disguise a swallow, "I was only waiting that night to see you after your guests left. I had just put the pieces together about what was going on, and I wanted to talk to you about it. Those present at the meeting left little doubt of your involvement."

"And were you a witness to the meeting itself?" Tyler studied John's face. "No, of course not. For if you were, we would not be having this discussion." He took a sip from the glass before him. "I believe that you are a good reporter, John, but you are young. You must not make assumptions about events that you yourself did not witness. It mars your professionalism."

"I saw the cargo. I saw the ship," he spat back. "*It* was no figment of my imagination."

"Yes, you saw a ship with a guarded cargo. But what happened with it?" He paused. "What really happened here, John? You are so busy speculating that you've lost track of the facts. Facts—they are the key to every story."

"How's this for a fact. There was a second fire the night your warehouse burned. A smaller fire over on Elliot Street that started after yours. When you saw it, you were angry and you sent your man for the fire engine. *To Elliot Street*. Not to the firehouse on King Street. You had previous knowledge of that fire. You knew where the engine would be."

Breckenridge looked quietly at John for a moment. "That is quite an intuitive leap." He paused. "What you fail to consider, however, is my knowledge of this city. The firehouse faces north, toward Elliot Street. When the alarm was raised, that would be the first plume of smoke they would see."

John realized that Breckenridge was not about to honestly discuss the meeting or the fires. He walked over and sat in the chair across from the desk. He had a new tactic. "You want to discuss facts? Fine. How about the fact that the last appointment of Horace Simpson's life was with you?" Breckenridge did not react. John continued. "The meeting was set for an isolated spot, with a view of the dock where munitions were being loaded on the *Port Royal*. Simpson ran from the scene and died. Witnesses place you at the scene of his death. What were you doing with Simpson?"

Breckenridge leaned back in his chair. "I will not dispute your facts in this matter, John. But I will take issue with your assumptions.

"I was set to meet with your colleague. I was to determine his suitability for an exclusive interview with Darcy. You may recall that Darcy's holding cell is on a jetty just a few blocks beyond the site of the accident. When Mr. Simpson didn't show, I went looking for him." Breckenridge turned one hand palm up. "You know the rest."

John grimaced. "You seem to have all the answers." He leaned forward. "You mentioned Darcy. I assume you know that his execution is set for Monday. That is tomorrow."

Tyler took a breath and spoke slowly. "I know. It is something that brings me considerable grief."

"Grief? The man lived but two miles from your property for the last ten years. He made . . . he made the pig your mother gave him into a domesticated pet. The man was practically your ward, the way you looked after him. And all you can come up with is grief?"

Tyler looked down at his glass. "What else do you expect me to say?"

"I expect you to say that you did nothing to help him. I expect you to say that you chose politics over a man's life. That's what I expect."

Breckenridge, just for an instant, looked vulnerable. "But that is not the case."

"Isn't it? Do you know that some of the first names I learned upon arrival here were the ABC's of Charleston? In case you don't know, the B is for Breckenridge. Yet you, namesake of one of the most powerful families in all of Carolina, could not help a simple, kind man avoid the undue punishment he received. What good is the power, Mr. Breckenridge?"

"That," he said, looking back up at John, his will again buttressed, "*is* a good question." He took a long, heavy drink of his brandy. "Power, like everything else, is finite. No man, no matter how powerful, can control all that he wants to. It is true, John, that my family position offers me influence—a considerable amount at times. But there is a limit. Unfortunately, saving Darcy stretched beyond it."

John's voice was combative. "He was just a simple farmer."

"No, he was not. He became a symbol, John. You know that as well as I. The speeches you heard on the street, the near riot after his hearing, the way his name was uttered with pure malice, these were not responses to a farmer. Dozens of men of my stature could not have quelled the call for his blood."

John's expression was pained. "Then why did you let me believe there was hope?"

"Because there always was."

"Then why weren't you in the courtroom to hear the verdict?"

"Because," he said frankly, "I do not handle disappointment well."

John shook his head in disgust. "How noble that your wish to avoid disappointment precluded Darcy Calhoun from finding a friendly face in that courtroom full of jackals. How noble that it was left to me, a New Yorker who had met the man but twice, to provide support and glances of encouragement. How lonely must he have felt in that ultimate moment of fear and abandonment." John calmed and settled back into his chair. "But at least you did not suffer the horror of public disappointment."

Tyler sat still, his hands interlocked. "You are right, John. I should have been there." The next words hinted of frustration. "I am capable of bad choices."

Countless insults coursed through John's mind, but he swallowed them all. None, he thought, would make Breckenridge any more contrite, if, in fact, he was at all.

Seconds into their silence came a knock on the study door. A slave stuck his head in. "Mr. Breckenridge, sir, yo' meeting."

"Cancel it," Tyler answered with a hint of temper.

"Very well, sir," the slave responded, closing the door again.

"Now I have a question for you," Breckenridge said, leaning just a bit forward. "Why are you covered in blood?"

John took a sadistic joy in his answer. "The workhouse." He watched as Breckenridge's eyes tightened. "I was there today. Yes, Mr. Breckenridge, I have now seen the true nature of slavery—the treadmill, the millstone, the whippings . . . the torture. Willowby is but an illusion, whether you choose to believe it or not."

Tyler was silent for a moment. "I now understand your anger. After what you have seen, it is entirely justified." He took a measured sip of brandy. "The workhouse is a degradation to us all. I abhor it, as do many others. Indeed, there is a group of us committed to having it demolished."

John muttered a half laugh. "Your hands are already too dirty to be washed clean. You are a *slave master*, and the workhouse is the end result of slavery. You are no different from the planters who *do* send slaves there. All that you have, from the day your great-grandfather started that plantation, has been acquired through the victimization of others. Your wealth, your enlightened lifestyle, are based upon your complicity and perpetuation of that horrific system. You are as guilty as they are. The workhouse is as much your family's sin as any others."

Tyler sighed. "And I would have thought *you* would know better than to assign guilt by association."

"What does that mean?"

"Perhaps you forget, John, that I lived in New York for a short period of time. When I met you, your name rang a bell. While I know that the last name Sharp is not at all uncommon, your obvious intelligence and formal manners still managed to pique my interest." John's eyes fell to the floor as he continued. "It was your uncle, was it not? Your uncle who sank both the family fortune and your father's reputation in a case of fraud. Your uncle went to prison, your father's bank went under, and you . . . You were forced to drop out of Yale and then became a reporter." His tone became soft, sympathetic. "Please understand that I don't bring this up to embarrass you. In fact, you should feel no embarrassment whatsoever. After all, you did nothing wrong. But, I must imagine there were some—probably many—who began to treat you differently because of your familial association. That wasn't right. And neither are your accusations of me."

John looked up, his voice trembling with a thousand shades of anger. "How long have you held on to *that* in the hope of using it? Was that the trump card you always carried, ready to play when my opinions ran counter to yours? Every further second I spend with you erodes my remaining respect."

"John, I am sorry, I only—"

"And you are wrong! There is a great difference between knowing a scoundrel and inviting him over to dinner. Yes, there was scandal in my family's past, but I have worked hard to distance myself from it. You . . . you invite its company. How many men who came to your party . . . how many of your friends are the same ones who beat and torture indiscriminately? Self-absorbed men who posture and play their power games while sucking the life out of others."

"It is true," Tyler replied calmly. "Some who have entered my home may be unscrupulous. You see, John, I entertain people I wish to influence. But you are wrong to think them my friends." He paused while he caught John's eye. "I choose my friends carefully."

"And those you entertain, friend or not, how do you reconcile their ongoing barbarity with their oh so genteel civility?

"I got a glimpse today of slavery's hideousness—men worked like oxen and beaten without remorse—and I wonder how long it shall haunt me. Men like you see it daily, choosing to bookend those images with lavish parties and garden strolls. How, in the name of heaven, is that possible?"

Tyler looked directly into John's eyes for seconds. He did not blink. "My only moments of peace come when I don't think about it. Sometimes I just don't think."

"And the mistreated slaves, the ones who have no choice *but* to think about it, what is their recourse?"

Tyler sat statue still. For once he made no effort to respond, and the silence dragged on.

"There is no answer, Mr. Breckenridge. You and your fellow southerners have become the jailers of the world's largest prison."

"It is interesting that, as a reporter, you are filled entirely with accusations and barren of answers. Perhaps it harkens back to your days with the penny press, when such behavior was standard." Tyler smiled as he refilled his brandy. "So what exactly is it that I should do, Mr. Sharp. It seems you have no dearth of opinions." As John did not answer, he continued. "Shall I free every one of my slaves?" he asked. "Surely that would raise my esteem in both your eyes and the abolitionists. But," he continued, holding the word up like a kite, "that is an impossibility. Not only is it illegal, but also, the minute that word spread, I would be besieged by every relative I have, all insisting that I be committed to some manner of mental institution." He took a hefty drink and hummed. "Even George Washington, a man known to morally waver on the issue despite his status as a planter, waited until his death to free his slaves. The father of our country, a man of unquestioned virtue and valor, chose not to wage that battle in life. So perhaps *now* you get a clearer picture of the intricacies and obstacles." He stared at John like an astute teacher. "Would it not be better to work to repair the faults, then, instead of condemning universally?"

"It is too late for that. The faults are too great, and the system unfixable."

Tyler shook his head, his tone lightly roiled. "I must say, John, you are quite wrapped up in your cloak of moral certitude."

"Perhaps my morals have survived because they were not awash in this corruption."

"No," Tyler answered, his voice utterly serious. "Yours is a different brand of corruption altogether."

"What are you talking about?"

"Industrialization. Capitalism. The life's blood of the northern economy. It differs from slavery only in name."

John's tone was dismissive. "That is preposterous."

"Is it? Or is it so dangerously similar that outright repudiation is your only shield?"

"Your comparison is ludicrous. The two systems are night and day."

"In theory, yes, of course, but what about in practice? The anger you presently feel is blocking your objectivity."

"Men in the North are paid laborers, *not* slaves."

"Are they not? Many work sixteen-hour shifts, laboring in dank, unhealthy conditions unsuitable for animals. Some children begin work as young as the age of five or six, some of them physically strapped to machines that only their tiny fingers can operate. And what is their reward? The exhausted men and women, the overworked children, what do they get? So meager a wage that they barely subsist. In many ways they are *worse off* than slaves."

"It is not all as bad as you now claim."

"Really? Or do *you* choose not to think about it because of the despair that such thoughts might bring?" He leaned back in his chair.

"Just as you explored this city, I also explored New York. I, too, journeyed to the darker side. I wanted to see where my cotton went. I found exhausted workers laboring beside dangerous machinery, filth and fumes filling every breath. It took me months to get over the sound of the coughing . . . it bothers me still." He chased the sentiment with more brandy. "The workers get torn up by those machines all the time; they lose hands, arms, sometimes their lives. Do you know what compensation their families get?" His voice faded to a whisper. "Seven dollars and fifty cents. The equivalent of three month's pay. The industrialists' price for a human life. Quite cheap, don't you think?"

John took a moment. "Not all places are so brutal. What you describe is an anomaly."

Tyler locked eyes. "Much as the workhouse, wouldn't you say?"

John was muted by the response. He got up, walked over to the bar in the corner, and poured himself a bourbon, nearly overfilling the glass. "Very well, then," he said, walking back to his seat. "But in New York, when I walk down the street I can look up at a tree without the fear of seeing a hanged Negro. And I have never seen a man attacked who was not allowed to raise his arms in self-defense, unlike Charleston."

"Do not speak to me of violence, John. There are ten times as many murders as we have lynchings here. Gangs rule the neighborhoods with the point of a knife. Explain to me what good it does for a man to raise his arms in self-defense, when he is attacked by twenty others?" He tapped his finger on the desk. "Yes, John, there your argument is hollow. Charles Dickens himself described the Five Points as the worst slum he had ever come across, and New York has countless others that mirror it. But what? Is that too just another anomaly outshone by the glories of the industrial boom?"

The patronization burned John's chest. "You are missing something here. Shiploads of immigrants, many escaping famine, come to northern cities because there is a possibility of a better future. There is hope." He took a hefty pull of bourbon. "Down here, hope is locked away by the heartless who occupy the mansions along the East Bay."

"Heartless? When my slaves are hungry, they are supplied with food. They do not lack for clothing and shelter. When one comes up ill or lame, he is well taken care of, ofttimes by the finest doctors available. And when they are too old or infirm to work, they are not forgotten. They are well cared for until the last of their days. Heartless," he scoffed. "Tell me the names of your industrialists who do the same. Until you can, you speak the word *heartless* only with hypocrisy."

"And the hope . . . the dreams? How do you supply them with those?"

"Mr. Sharp, do you know how many blacks live in Charleston?"

"Nearly fifteen thousand, I believe."

Tyler nodded. "And did you know that nearly two in ten of them are free?" He waited for acknowledgment. "Many of them were once slaves. If not them, then their fathers or their grandfathers. And, as slaves, they were not required to work so many hours as the laborers in the North. They were allowed free time, and some used it productively; they grew gardens, raised their own livestock, or learned a trade. All of these things they were, and still are, allowed to do on their own behalf, for their own gain. My man Johnson, the metal worker, he is but months away from purchasing his freedom. And he will gain it with a skill that will transfer to considerable monetary success in a city like Charleston. Countless others have trod and will tread the same path."

John sat still for a moment, still angry, nursing his bourbon. The next thought came quick, almost as an eruption. "If all are so happy, then what of the uprisings? And if the treatment is so good, then explain to me how a whisper of unrest in the black community translates to harsh oppression by the whites?"

Tyler seemed prepared for the question. "I said before that our world was not perfect. And yes, while such incidents shake the general public, they remain quite rare and rather small in scale. I do not know what happened to initiate the disaster in Habersham County, nor do I care to speculate. But it is amazing to me how easily outsiders describe any actions of violence in the South as cataclysmic, while dismissing similar situations in their own backyard as merely incidents of an unfortunate nature. Is violence not the same everywhere?"

"Not when it is the oppressed who revolt against their oppressors. *That* is news."

Tyler laughed. "And the actions at Astor Place, where the mob of the disenfranchised lay siege to a group of the wealthy, that wasn't the same? Or now will you tell me that it really *was* just an actor's dispute—a war of words that got out of hand?" John had no response. "Dozens more died on that occasion than did in Habersham County, and in fact, there it was the poor who did the dying. I find it odd, John, that in New York you all seem to favor protecting the rich, while in the South you are suddenly concerned with the welfare of—how did you put it? The oppressed. Funny, in New York they are just called ruffians."

John's anger was now frustration. "I fear that this is an argument that I cannot win. You have had years to rationalize a defense of your system, and I must admit, you do it extremely well. My only weapon is morality, and it seems you are even capable of twisting that." John set his empty glass on Tyler's desk and stood.

Tyler stood as well. "But don't you see, it is not an argument that I am after. It is only a discussion. How else can we change things? How else can we stop this short of conflict?"

John relaxed as he stood, absorbed by a sudden feeling of peace. "We can't. I must say, I didn't feel that way before arriving in Charleston, but now it is clear. The polarization is too complete, the bond already severed." John walked over to the door and opened it. "You must realize that too. For as well as you judge human nature, I fear you are merely fooling yourself."

"I cannot stop trying. There is still a chance that men like us *can* make a difference."

John looked at Tyler Breckenridge. He saw in his eyes what he had seen that night at Willowby after the party. He almost pitied him. "You could not even save a simple farmer. How are you to stop a war?"

Tyler's eyes dropped as John closed the study door.

Clio Breckenridge stood very still, facing him in the hallway. She wore one of the little straw sunbonnets with flowers that John had seen her wear in the garden, as well as a pinafore with embroidered daisies over a plain yellow dress. She looked at him with her lips slightly parted, her face pale, her eyes very wide. She looked like a child.

John hesitated a moment, then started toward the door.

"Wait!" she called.

She reached up and put a finger on his chin, turning his head. She spoke very softly. "Are you hurt? Have you been in a fight?"

John took a step back. "No." He had to clear his throat. "I just got too close to . . . a situation. I had better be going."

"No. Let me take care of this." She took a handkerchief from her pocket and moistened it with water from the pitcher on the hall table. She dabbed his face gently, as if the blood were his own. "Now give me your coat." She began to help him remove it, and he did not resist. She removed her pinafore and placed it on a chair with his coat. "Walk with me?"

He nodded and offered her his arm. They left the house silently.

They walked down King Street, east toward the Battery. Neither of them spoke for a while.

"I need to ask you something," John finally said. He turned to look at her. "Did Tyler ever tell you about my background? About my family?"

Her brow furrowed a little, but she met his eyes directly. "Yes. Tyler told me that first night before dinner that your family had experienced some difficulty over a bank they owned. He said that it had nothing to do with you."

"Why do you think he told you?"

Clio tilted her head a little, as if the answer was obvious. "He wanted to spare you any questions that might make you uncomfortable."

John nodded, but offered no other response to Clio's questioning look. They walked in silence for another block.

They heard a sharp bark. A young black Labrador retriever squeezed under the gate of a neighboring house. It obviously knew Clio, because it bounded up playfully, vigorously wagging its entire hindquarters.

"This is Tillie," Clio said, performing the introduction. "No gate can hold her, but she is perfectly harmless." Clio bent to stroke her head. "Oh, dear! What do you have?"

The dog deposited a white glove at her feet.

"Thank goodness, it is only a glove." She looked at John with a flush of color. "Last time she brought me a 'garment' off the clothesline, it was of a personal nature. Imagine how I felt returning it to the doorman." She gave an impish laugh and John was forced to smile. He patted Tillie's head.

A young black woman came quickly through the gate and grabbed Tillie by the collar. "I'm sorry, Miss Clio."

"Just a glove this time," Clio quipped.

The woman flashed a smile as she departed with the glove and dog.

Clio smiled up at John and placed her hand upon his arm. "I was observing the Summer Triangle again last night," she began in a serious tone. "I am contemplating pursuing a course in celestial navigation . . . For when I go to sea."

She then began to list anticipated ports of call—Far Tortugas, Barbados, Port Royale. John stiffened at the last destination, but soon realized that she was only listing notorious pirate lairs.

They were at the Battery now, and numerous small sailboats were visible out in the bay.

"Have you ever sailed?" John asked.

"Yes, often," Clio responded, obviously pleased that John had initiated conversation. "But not so much recently. How about you?"

"I sailed a skiff as a child."

"Tyler and I used ta sail a great deal when we were children. In the beginning, Tyler was a terrible sailor. Daddy wouldn't let us go out unless we had Bramley, Tyler's man, with us. Tyler would always forget and turn the rudder the wrong way, and Bramley and I would get hit with the boom. For years, whenever Tyler had bad news for me, he would preface it with, 'Prepare to come about.' He hasn't said it for a long time. When there came to be too much bad news, we didn't joke about things like that anymore."

Her tone was light, but the last remark caused the tension to rise again in John. He was quiet as they watched the boats sailing toward Fort Sumter and Sullivans Island.

"You know," Clio remarked as they resumed walking, "you had quite an impact on Mary Ellen and her friends. I had to confiscate a positively lurid novel about New York that was circulating among them."

John smiled and shook his head.

Clio continued. "They now all want to be 'special correspondent' to the *Charleston Gazette.* I think they envision a series of travel articles from exotic cities. Mary Ellen had planned to ask you for pointers on traveling incognito that night you had come to dinner—the night of the warehouse fire."

"Did you ever learn anything about that?"

"Our warehouse foreman and his assistant were called away ta help with a carriage accident a few minutes before it started, so we don't know for sure what happened. Some people say it was set deliberately, like other fires around town. Tyler says we can't be sure. It may have started in the Wilkens warehouse next door."

They were walking along the Battery now, bordering White Point Gardens. Across the park, John could see the mansion where he had observed the party his first night in Charleston. It was unquestionably a beautiful home, but today, in daylight, the magic was gone. So much had happened since that night; it seemed like another lifetime.

Clio continued to converse with him, like a sickroom visitor speaking with an invalid. It made John remember the first time he had seen her—when she had helped the old black woman from her cabin to rest under the trees at Willowby.

When they approached the Breckenridge home, their steps slowed, and both seemed to be searching for something to say. Clio stopped, and John could feel the pressure of her hand on his arm. Her face was earnest.

"John, I do not know what happened between you and Tyler, but please know this. Tyler is a good man. He tries very hard to do the right thing."

John answered slowly. "I know that you are a loving sister. I know that you believe that is true."

She looked at him wordlessly for a moment. Then she gave a sad little smile. "Spoken like a man who chooses his words carefully." She paused for a long moment, staring off into the distance, then back to John. "You know, one of the things I liked about you from the beginning was your sense of humor. You were so funny." She stifled a laugh in recollection. "You reminded me of the way Tyler used to be . . . But then Daddy died, and Tyler changed. Now you have gone and changed, too."

Hours later, Michael Allen walked John somberly through the first of the two locked doors. Before he opened the second, John whispered to him. "How has he been?"

Allen turned and stared at John for a moment, expressionless. Then he returned to the task of unlocking the second door.

"Darcy, you got a visitor," he said with spirit as he moved to open the cell.

Darcy Calhoun sat on his cot, his knees pulled up against his chest. He was staring up at the small barred window at the back of the cell. It was not until John walked inside that Darcy seemed to notice him.

"Oh, hello, Mr. Sharp. How—"

"Please just call me John, Darcy."

"All right, John," he said distantly, again staring up at the window. His words picked up as if he were already in a conversation. "Ya know, I used to oft wonder about family. My own, I mean. I used to think on it a lot 'round when I was twenty or so—having a wife and children. Sorta stopped afta Momma died." He laughed. "Heck, I think she might have been the reason I was thinking on it at all." His laugh waned quickly. "I's kind of glad now that I don't have one, though. It'd be awful painful on dem. Heck," he said, his voice falling to a whisper. "It'll be hard enough on my dogs." He stared out the window a second longer, then looked at John. "What 'bout you, Mr. Sharp? Oh, excuse me. What 'bout you, John? You thinking you's ever going to have a family?"

"I don't know. Someday, I hope."

"Yeah, I guess that's the sort of answer I'd have gave two months ago. All of this starts ta make your thinking weird. You ask strange things and the like."

"I understand," John said with a small smile. "So have you had any other visitors?"

Darcy nodded. "My reverend, Reverend Rose, he done come out

here yesterday, afta the sentencing and all. We's talked for a long time, mostly 'bout God and heaven and the glory of the afterlife. Then he read me some Scriptures, and then we's said some together. It was awful nice of him to come. He had to leave, though, on account of getting back for all his services. I understood."

"What about today? Have you seen a minister today?"

"Uh-huh. A nice man, Reverend Trch. When he come in, he sorta tried to make a joke. He says his last name ain't got no vowels in it, and then he starts to chuckle. You know, since I can't spell, I don't know me too much 'bout vowels or nothing. But I started to laugh anyways. I didn't want him feeling silly." Darcy smiled and John too. "Also today, earlier this morn—real early actually, just afta the sun come up—Mr. Allen and Mr. Pickering, the other man who guards me, they took me on a walk along the river." Darcy stared at John and half chuckled. "I wasn't suppose ta tell no one that, but I think you is trustworthy."

"I won't tell a soul," John said. "So how was the walk?"

"Oh, it was real nice. Real nice and pleasant. Ya see, I ain't never seen that much water, John. I know it sounds strange, how close to it I's lived all my life, but I never before had seen the ocean. I liked it." His face carried a quizzical expression. "Mr. Allen and Mr. Pickering sorta acted funny, though. They kept getting awful nervous when I got close to the rail—nervous like I was gonna jump in or I had bad balance. I don't know what had 'em so worried. I told 'em both I couldn't swim."

John smiled as his insides ripped, Darcy's simplicity so innocent, so endearing. He quickly reached into his pocket. "I almost forgot. I brought you some licorice." He handed over the crumpled brown bag. "I didn't know if you even liked licorice. I hope—"

"I do, John," he said simply, stuffing his nose inside the top of the bag and taking a huge whiff. "I'm much obliged." He set the bag next to him. "But if ya don't mind, I think I'll save 'em for later. Always did enjoy sump'n sweet right 'fore bed."

"Of course, Darcy. Enjoy it at your leisure."

Darcy turned quiet, once again staring out at the orange-red sunset through his window.

"There is something else, also." John reached his hand into his pocket. "You see, my grandmother was Catholic. And when I was a boy, it seems all I could do was talk about traveling. All the places I wanted to see and visit. Well, one day she set me on her lap and she handed me this." John pulled a gold chain out of his pocket with a gold medallion on the end.

Darcy looked enamored. "It's beautiful."

"It's a Saint Christopher medallion. It's to protect you . . ." John took a moment to reinforce his voice. "It's to protect travelers on their journeys."

Darcy's eyes flashed up at John, then back down at the medallion.

"It was very dear to her. And now, I very much want for you to have it."

Darcy reached his hand forward, then jerked it back. "Oh, I just couldn't. Not sump'n so precious as that. Your grandmother wanted that for you. It's just too much."

John spoke with gravity. "I want *you* to have it, Darcy. It would mean a lot to me if you accepted it." He paused. "Please."

Darcy smiled wide and reached forward slowly. His laugh was childlike as he took it in his hands. "Can't remember a time when I received a gift such as this. Neva one so beautiful." He began to rub his fingers over the engraving on the medal, adding a bit of spit to increase the shine. As he stared at it for a while, his eyes began to water. He looked up to John a moment later with small droplets stuck precariously to his sparse lashes. "Thank ya, John. Can't tell you how much this means." Darcy raked a hand across his face and wiped his nose on his sleeve.

"Of course, Darcy. Of course."

Darcy took a moment to compose himself. He took a deep breath, stealing occasional glimpses of the medallion before casting his eyes elsewhere. "So tell me, John," he said, clearing his throat. "How long have you been a reporter?"

"A little over three years."

Darcy smiled. "Do you have any more stories, then? I mean, ones that ain't too serious?"

"Yes. A number, as a matter of fact."

"Would ya tell me a couple? I just love hearing them kinds of stories."

"Of course, Darcy."

Darcy curled in his knees and stared out the window as John began to speak. He told Darcy about P. T. Barnum and the building of the American Museum. He told the story of the Tom Thumb, the first successful American steam locomotive, and its breathtaking race across New York State.

"Imagine ladies in the open cars traveling at the blinding speed of eleven miles per hour!"

But Darcy did not react to the telling of the stories. Indeed it seemed as if he was not listening at all. Only when the speaking stopped—during a dramatic pause or between tales—did Darcy turn sadly toward him. It was his calm voice, not the stories, that Darcy wanted to hear.

In the middle of John's account of a newspaper prank gone awry, Darcy looked at him seriously and interrupted.

"John, is we friends?"

"Yes," he answered immediately. "Of course we are friends."

Darcy's eyes went down, then back up. "Are we, or is you just saying that 'cause of the . . . 'Cause of the circumstances?"

John pulled his chair closer to the cot and put his hand on Darcy's forearm. "I am proud to call you my friend, Darcy. Damn proud."

Darcy nodded, but did not look at him. "I can't say I's had many friends during my time. I mean, I's friendly with people and all, but not too many friends."

John squeezed tightly around his forearm, unsure what else to say.

"I heard a man once say, he says a man's life can be judged by the number of friends he done made during his days." He looked at John. "Ya think that's true? Ya think that's how a man is to be judged?"

"No Darcy. I believe it is the value of friendships, not the number. The number is meaningless."

"Yeah," he responded, a smile lighting his face. "I think yo' right. Tell me more of your stories now. I like hearing 'em."

John talked for the next half hour. John drew from Americana;

tales about Johnny Appleseed and Rip Van Winkle. Then he told about Kit Carson's travels through the Wild West. Reality or fiction, to Darcy it was all the same.

"What will ya write about me?" Darcy asked during one of the pauses. "I mean, what sorta things will ya say?"

John was unprepared and sat silent for a moment. Then he smiled, speaking slowly. "I will write about a good man, a farmer, who lived in the Carolina lowlands. I will write of the obstacles he faced in his life: the deprivation, the taunts, the loss of a childhood friend. I will tell of his piety, and how that translated into a love of all creatures. How he took a pig in a time of hunger and turned it into a beloved pet. How he jumped into a swollen creek to save a drowning mule, nearly killing himself in the process. How much he loved his dogs. I will tell of a man who took preserves to the people of Cowford in a time of giving, and a man who was always the first to church and the last to leave. A man who could not read, but who learned the Scriptures by heart." John swallowed heavily. "But most important, I will write of a man who was faced with such a moral decision that it would have brought nearly anyone to his knees. But not this man. This man did not abandon his beliefs, not for an instant. I will write of a man who chose the ultimate sacrifice over any sort of compromise." John looked at Darcy and smiled. "That is what I will write about Darcy Calhoun."

"I like that," he whispered. "I think my momma would be proud to hear such words. Thank you, John."

As John inhaled, his breath hitched. "No need to thank me, Darcy. I only write the truth."

A moment later, Darcy reached under his pillow and pulled out his Bible. He handed it to John. "Would you mind reading me a little?"

"Of course not. What would you like to hear?"

Darcy smiled. "I was always fond of the Psalms."

John began to read from the first chapter. Darcy closed his eyes as he listened and recited along with those he knew. Just after John finished Psalm 23, Darcy opened his eyes, a smile on his face.

"That's a good place to stop," he said. "That one was always my favorite."

John handed him back his Bible and watched as Darcy again tucked it away. "Are you scared?" he asked softly.

"Scared," he repeated, tucking his knees back against his chest. "Well, John, I ain't worried 'bout where I's ending up, but I'm a bit frightened of the journey." His eyes drifted to the ceiling and a small smile brushed his face. "Back when I was a little boy, maybe five or so, our family set to move from one end of North Carolina to the otha. Now this was back in the time when boys all tried to scare one another with all sorts of stories. Stories of highwaymen and bandits and all the mischief they done caused. Well, once it come time for us to up'n leave, I was crying and shaking like I neva done before. My daddy told me I was being silly, and that I should get such silly thoughts out of my head. But that didn't help. So my momma come over, and she's a bit more understanding. She tells me there ain't no such thing as high-waymen and the like in that part of the country. But I still didn't believe her." He chuckled. "Ya know, it's funny, at that age we think what other kids is saying is pure truth and that our parents is just all wrong. But anyways, afta that didn't work, my momma starts ta talk about the place we's heading. She starts telling me 'bout the hills and mountains, 'bout the streams and lakes all full a fish, all 'bout how beautiful and exciting the place we was moving to would be. I starts to listen, then, 'cause what she's saying sounded so good. Then she tells me that if along the way I ever get worried or nervous, that all I need to do is think 'bout where it is that we's heading—how beautiful and exciting all of it will be." Darcy paused, looking back to John. "It was good advice, you know. I think it still is."

"Yes, Darcy. I think that is wonderful advice."

Darcy nodded, then began to fidget with his hands. "But there's sump'n I wanna tell ya, John." He paused and went quiet.

"Yes, Darcy, anything."

"Well, I'd sorta like it if you wasn't there tomorrow morning when it happens. I know you's a reporter and all, and you's supposed to do stuff like that, but I'm asking you not to. I think it might make me feel worse, not betta, for you to have to watch."

"All right, Darcy. I won't be there."

"Thank you," he exhaled in a relieved breath. Then he smiled. "I's thinking that it's about time that you set on yo' way. I've already done chewed up most of yo' evening—"

"No, Darcy. I wanted to be here. And I'd be happy to stay if—"

"No, no. I think I'd like to be alone now. Got some more thinking I's gotta do."

"I understand," John said, standing up.

Darcy stood as well. "There's just one last thing. There's sump'n I want you to have." He twisted his lip. "Do you think you can get out to my old cabin one last time?"

"Yes, of course."

"Well, there's sump'n there I want ya to have."

"Darcy, I am flattered by the thought. But wouldn't you rather have it go to your kin? I'd be happy to go get it and then—"

"No, John, this is for you. There's only one thing 'bout it that you have to agree to. You can't give it away to no one, never. I's only wanting you ta have it."

"Yes, Darcy. I wouldn't consider it anyway."

"All right, then. Once you get inside my cabin, you're gonna have to push the kitchen table outta the way. Underneath, there's a long piece of floorboard with a big brown knot on it. Don't worry, it's the only knot 'round there. Underneath that, that's where I keep my valuables."

"How will I know what to take?"

"Oh," he smiled, "there's only one valuable thing in there. You'll know what to take."

He nodded slowly. "Very well, Darcy. And thank you."

"No, John. Thank you. You's the only person through all this who kept treating me like I was a man. I ain't neva gonna forget it."

John's throat clenched. "I will not forget you either, Darcy."

Darcy walked forward and wrapped his strong arms around John, squeezing him tightly. John's grip was comparatively weak.

"Good-bye, Darcy," he said in a raised pitch.

"Good-bye, my friend. And God bless you."

John left the cell. He did not turn around.

· · ·

Once outside the jail, John turned and stared toward the placid water of the Ashley River. The slight chime of the harbor buoy was the only sound above his labored breathing.

"You all finished in there?" a voice asked from behind him.

Surprised, John turned and saw a man atop a wagon. The light was dim, but he could still make out the reddish hair and pockmarked skin. "Yes. Why do you ask?"

The man hopped down from the wagon and walked around back toward the bed. A yelping sound came from a large crate at the rear. "Mr. Breckenridge done sent me." He fiddled with the latch of the crate, then, a second later, two dogs jumped down from the wagon. "He sent me to bring Mr. Calhoun his dogs fo' the night."

The two animals bounded playfully, obviously delighted to be out of the crate. Breckenridge's man had a difficult time controlling them, for the leashes were an obvious novelty to which they were unaccustomed.

"I'm sure Darcy will be thrilled," John said, torn between joy and pain.

The man made for the door. Just as he got there, he looked back, his right arm jerking from the animals' tugs. "You need a ride anywhere? I won't be inside but for a minute."

"No, thank you. I could use the walk." John stopped. "But one last thing, Mr. Rogers."

"Yes, sir."

"I will be leaving Charleston soon. I just wanted to thank you—for saving my life."

Rogers looked a bit taken aback. "That wasn't me. That was Mr. Breckenridge."

"I realize that he told you to follow me, but I wanted to thank you for your part in it."

Rogers paused as if considering. "Think nothing of it, sir," he finally responded. "Good night." He turned and bent to untangle the leashes. Then he coaxed the dogs inside the building.

John walked to an isolated spot a hundred yards away where a line of trees ran beside a low wall. Hidden by the shadows he dropped to one knee. There, the tears and the prayers came pouring out.

• • •

John met Owen Conway at a prearranged spot—the tavern with the "wrong door" where they had met John's first night in town.

Owen looked at John's face as he sat down. "I'm so sorry, John."

John looked up and shook his head. "No, don't be. I'm glad I saw him." He laughed just a bit. "At times, I think he felt the need to raise my spirits."

Owen poured from a half bottle of bourbon on the table, a generous splash into each glass. "Think he is gonna be all right?"

"I think he is at peace." John took a pull of bourbon and cleared his throat.

Owen raised his glass slightly and looked to John. "To Darcy Calhoun, then. For all his shortcomings, still the tallest man in Charleston."

"In all South Carolina," John added before clinking glasses and completing the toast. "Tell me, Owen, do you leave tomorrow?"

"Yeah. On the noon train. I could afford to stay longer, but I just don't want to. I've had enough of this town."

"As have I. But before you leave, I must ask you for a favor. You are going to the hanging, are you not?"

"Begrudgingly," he answered bitterly, taking another drink.

"Darcy asked me not to go. I was hoping that you might be so kind as to leave me a note of the formal details. The time and other such essentials."

"Sure, John. Of course. So you won't even be in town?"

"No. Darcy also asked that I travel to his cabin to retrieve an item. Of course, I agreed. But I shall not be back before you leave."

Owen refilled his glass. "Consider it done, my friend. And you, when will you be leaving?"

"The day after. Tuesday at noon. I will not stay a minute longer than necessity dictates. New York has never sounded more appealing."

"So this is it, huh, sport," Owen said quietly. He raised his glass one last time. "To New York." His inflection was odd as he spoke the name of his hometown, as if it had changed in his absence and he wouldn't recognize it anymore.

"Tell you what," Owen said after draining his glass. "You know the Old Mill Tavern, the one on Boundary just north of Houston?"

"Yeah. It's got a pretty seedy reputation."

Owen smiled. "Yeah. What say we meet there a week from Wednesday at nine o'clock."

"I'll be there." John extended his hand. "To better days."

Owen nodded. "As elusive as they may be."

A mahogany closed carriage pulled by a fine chestnut team stood just up the block from the McClellan boardinghouse. As John approached the sidewalk, a uniformed servant stepped from the shadows beside the porch. He bowed slightly and nodded toward the carriage.

"The lady wishes ta speak with you, sir."

John recognized the blue livery of the Breckenridge household. "Certainly."

John climbed inside the carriage.

"Thank you for agreeing to see me, Mr. Sharp," Clio said when she was sure John was comfortably situated. "I won't keep you long, but we might be cooler and a bit less conspicuous if we take a turn around the block."

"That will be fine, Miss Breckenridge."

She waited until the carriage began to roll. "I will be leaving Charleston tonight for Willowby. I have no desire to be here tomorrow."

John nodded. "I understand."

John looked at her, and his lips curved into the trace of a smile. She wore a dress with a jacket in a muted shade of blue-gray and a small matching hat with a feather. Her hair was pulled tightly back with no loose wisps of curl, in a manner some might consider severe. If anything, it made her look younger, more fragile.

Her face and tone were serious when she spoke. "I want you to know that I asked Tyler what happened between you." She looked down at her gloves. "He had difficulty speaking of it, and he did not tell me the whole story."

She looked back at John. "But he did tell me he thought that you felt betrayed by what has happened here and by the people you have met." She looked John in the eye. "This is true?"

John's throat felt tight. He could only nod.

Her tone became lighter, and she forced a little smile. "Tell me about some of the people you have met here. Some that you liked."

"I have met many people here that I have liked."

She smiled again. "Name a few."

"Why, you and Mary Ellen, of course."

She made a little circular motion with her glove.

"And an old woman named Buella, Cletis McClellan, Maude and Harry Regan—"

"You're going to have to help me out here," Clio interjected. "I won't know who they are if you only give me a name."

"Sorry," John continued. "Cletis McClellan is my innkeeper, and the Regans own a bakery. They were kind to me after I was hit in the head with the brick. You want me to go on? All right, a black boy named Samuel who taught me to keep cool by putting cabbage leaves in my hat. A newspaper editor named Mannion. Some tough-looking militia named Buster, Wiggins, and Hoot, who bought me a drink even though I was a Yankee. A man named Beauregard Throckmorton, who invited me to a backwoods party on a Sunday night. Then there are Darcy's jailers, who show kindness in spite of the job they must do . . . And Darcy, of course."

"Of course. I asked you this because we are all so different, John. We are individuals, just like the people you know back home. The events that just happened here do not define us. If, God forbid, there is a war, if your president sends his cannon south, our men who march to meet them won't be faceless men to you. They will be individuals like those you have met—wearing cabbage leaves in their hats."

The carriage rolled to a stop. John was quiet for a moment. "I understand what you have told me, Clio." He paused again. "You were the right person to remind me, because I don't think there is another individual like you in all the world."

When he disembarked from the carriage, Clio extended a gloved hand through the window. As John took her hand, she remarked, "I just want you to know, Mr. Sharp, that you do fall short of the gentlemen here in one important area."

"And what is that, Miss Breckenridge?"

"They are all very keen on writing poetry. You have never produced a sample of your poetry—or any writing, for that matter."

"When I return home, I shall remedy that, Miss Breckenridge. You may rely on it."

TWENTY-TWO

⌒

It was a windy morning, a little cooler than normal. The sun was shining, but low clouds tinged with purple blew across the sky, casting moving shadows over the crowd like enormous birds of prey. About four hundred had gathered—businessmen, workingmen, militia, and a sprinkling of blacks. Few women were present, certainly no ladies.

Owen Conway had witnessed public hangings before. He had arrived prepared for a circus atmosphere of spectators jostling for position, choruses of noisy catcalls, and vendors hawking wares. The Charleston crowd seemed subdued, to Owen's thinking. Many wore black armbands for the death of a president they did not like. It appeared that in the sentencing for this crime Charleston had made its statement; the actual penalty seemed almost an anticlimax.

There were a few rowdy types present, several groups of youth a few years shy of twenty who looked like they had not been to bed after a night of heavy drinking. They issued a few slurred demands to "Hurry up and hang 'im," then shouted general comments on the parentage and personal habits of abolitionists. Several better-dressed bystanders told them to mind their manners. "Shh! Folks are singing hymns here!"

They were. There was a group of about thirty of them, wearing robes and standing to one side of the gallows. There were men and women, some white, some black. Somebody said that they were from St. Michael's. The hymns had a strange folksy quality alien to Owen's Catholic ear. He wasn't sure if they made him feel better or worse.

At ten o'clock, the bells from the eight steeples of Charleston began to ring. As they finished tolling, Darcy Calhoun emerged from a door of the building. A constable stood at one arm, a minister at the other. Darcy carried a Bible.

He wasn't wearing a suit today or his old clothes. Someone had apparently bought him a new shirt and pants, nothing fancy, but respectable. He glanced briefly at the crowd, which was buzzing now, and looked up at the gallows. He wrinkled his forehead like he was thinking really hard. Then he tucked his chin and walked forward, slowly, deliberately, his eyes focused on the middle distance as if on something only he could see. If he heard the crowd at all, he did not let on.

He wavered a little on the steps, and the minister took his arm. The minister was reciting the Twenty-third Psalm. They climbed to the top of the scaffold where the hangman was waiting. The crowd was very quiet. The constable read the sentence. When he asked Darcy if he had anything to say, Darcy licked his lips and said, "No, sir."

The breeze picked up a little, and with it came drops of rain; not a downpour, but a gentle sprinkling in full sunshine. Darcy looked up, surprised. His expression changed. He was a farmer again at that moment, grateful for raindrops in the midst of a drought. He looked toward the choir and smiled a little. They were singing, "Shall We Gather at the River." He looked out at the crowd standing in the rain and smiled at them too. Maybe he saw the black armbands of mourning—maybe he thought they were for him. He turned and said something to the minister beside him, who started as if surprised.

The hangman placed the hood over Darcy's head, and Owen turned to look away—as if it wasn't Darcy anymore. Owen took slow, painful breaths as the rain fell on his face and the minister read a prayer. Then there was a sharp crack as the floor dropped away, and the choir ceased its hymn in mid-line. Then, only silence, but for the creaking hinges of the trapdoor.

Owen encountered the minister as they walked away from the square.

"What did he say to you . . . there at the end?" Owen asked him.

The minister seemed preoccupied. It took him a minute to answer. "He quoted to me word-for-word the line of a prayer I had read him in his cell. 'God's mercy, like the gentle rain, falls from heaven . . .' "

John Sharp had left Charleston just after eight in the morning. He rode the rented horse hard, traveling south. A light, chalky cloud followed him like a ghost through the soft hills and small towns of the Carolina lowlands. The pounding of hooves and rhythmic breathing of man and horse were not enough to deaden the volume of his thoughts. They were dark thoughts, bitter as bile, of violence and retribution, in words too coarse to be spoken.

As the hour of ten approached, John pushed the mount harder, then harder still. He sensed the time and did not check his watch. He sensed it from the rising sun and the spell of nausea that only worsened with each passing mile. Only later did John realize the folly of relying on his senses rather than his timepiece. For, instead of knowing the exact moment and facing it just once, he imagined Darcy climbing the steep, narrow steps over and over.

John slowed as he neared the town of Cowford, just after eleven; it was the horse's will, not his own. He vaguely remembered the path to Darcy's cabin, guiding the beast through the heavily wooded terrain toward the stream that drew a path to his destination. They merely walked the last half mile. With proximity came apprehension. He was no longer in a hurry.

When he came upon the cabin, he dismounted, secured his horse, and began a slow walk up the slight incline toward Darcy's porch. He stopped on the steps, staring down at the caked imprints of bare feet that now seemed fossilized. No rain had blown in to wash them away. He leaned over and softly ran his finger over one of the impressions.

"Good that they should still be here," he whispered.

He chose not to go inside. Not yet. He took a wide swing around the side of the cabin, walking toward the long rows of cotton plants. Today there was no worker, no slave sent from Willowby to maintain the fields until Darcy returned. But with the help of the sky, the cotton would grow. And in the profit conscious world of the planters, the cotton crop would be brought in.

Darcy's garden was a different story. What had matured had been picked, but in the absence of rain, the hand-watering had obviously stopped a few days back. The peas, the pumpkins, and the squash vines withered; and the little caterpillars ate the green bean plants.

John walked back to the front of the cabin and climbed up onto the porch. The washboard atop the water barrel had been knocked aside. The water's rust-colored surface was now tickled with the ripples of countless developing insects. He saw other marks of neglect, unnoticed on his previous visit. Several shingles had come loose from the roof, the front window was cracked, and one of the porch boards sagged. The cabin had a lonesome feel, an abandonment that seemed longer than Darcy's two months away.

He walked inside slowly, cautiously, as if expecting some manner of surprise. There was none. The main room looked just as he had left it, a bit dustier perhaps, but still Spartan and straight. He looked at the table in the room and peeked briefly beneath it. Not yet, he thought. Not just yet. Careful to avoid the dried mud prints scattered across the floor, he walked down the short hallway to Darcy's bedroom. It was dark—darker than he remembered. But the shaft of light from the open door illuminated the cross on the far wall. It glinted gold in the half-light. John smiled. That was why Darcy chose to hang it there, off center. He chided himself for not realizing it on his first visit.

With a deep breath he stared at the room one last time, then closed the door slowly, allowing the cross to fade to darkness. The door clicked shut.

He walked back to the main room and set about his task. He dragged the large round table six or seven feet toward the window. Looking back at the circle of undusted floor, the knot Darcy described was clearly visible. He approached it, dropped to his knees, and probed the knot on the eight-inch-wide floorboard with his finger. As he lifted, the two boards beside came up with it. The space below was pitch-black and smelled of earth. He removed the floorboards and laid them to the side. Then he lay on his stomach, stretching his arm into the dark hole. He felt nothing, not even a floor below it. He reached in all directions but still found nothing. Perhaps whatever Darcy had left was already gone.

John stood up and walked over to the windowsill, where an oil lantern sat beside a box of matches.

"Please light," he said as he fumbled with the lantern and a lit match.

It did, but there wasn't much left of the wick, so the illumination produced was little brighter than a candle. He returned to the hole, again dropped to his chest, and slowly lowered the lantern into the small, dark cavern. Except it wasn't so small. The space below was nearly as large as the cabin itself. There was a black dirt floor almost four feet below, and a box that had been placed near the hole to serve as a step. The circle of light was limited, but John could just make out some shapes on the near wall.

John stood up again, this time to take off his jacket. Then he descended gingerly into the darkness. When he reached the dirt, his head and shoulders were still above the floor level of the room. Lowering the lantern with care, he slowly submerged into Darcy's hidden storeroom.

The shapes on the near wall turned out to be burlap sacks. Two were filled with corn, and a third was half full of pecans. Next to the sacks was a box containing jars of preserves.

"All right, so I'm in the vegetable cellar," John said aloud.

He looked around. In the distance, he could see a mound and a box on a far wall. He started to make his way toward them, hunched, nearly squatting. He held the lantern in one hand and braced himself on the dirt with the other. About halfway there, he nearly banged his head on a lantern that hung from a central beam. He fumbled in his pocket for the matches and tipped over onto one knee. This lamp worked a bit better than the other. A light glow now bathed the entire storeroom.

His clumsy traverse of the crawlspace seemed hardly worth the effort when the mound proved to be nothing but a pile of old clothes, mostly homespun, which smelled of mildew. The box contained more old clothes, though these appeared cleaner and in better shape. Inexplicably, John began to rifle through them. What he found surprised him. They were not all men's clothes, not even all adult. Near the top he found a pink shawl, a worn work shirt with contrasting patches, a pair of child's trousers, and a red bandanna. Darcy's mother must have been one of those people who never threw anything away.

At this point, his back and leg muscles were protesting, and sweat tickled his neck and forehead. He had managed to snag a few cobwebs in his hair. His frustration was palpable.

"What in the hell are you trying to give me, Darcy? Some old clothes? Food?"

Oh, heavens, he hoped it wasn't the preserves. John glanced back in that direction and wiped the sweat off his face with his hand. He spit out the dirt that fell to his lips.

John gave up on his suit pants and knelt down on the dirt floor. Darcy had said there was only one thing of value down here, and John would know what it was. It was obvious that it was gone.

He looked carefully around him and noticed only one unexplored feature in a corner of the storeroom. He had overlooked it in favor of the box with the clothes. He crawled over to it now and discerned it to be a blanket spread out over something. He felt the hair on his neck stand up.

His hand began to shake as he reached forward to pull back the blanket. Beneath it was a pallet with a straw-stuffed pillow at the head.

"My God!"

His glance swept the room quickly now. The food, the clothes, the lantern, the bed. He had goose bumps. He could barely make out something on the wall over the pillow. He brought up the lantern for a better look. Etched into the wall were notches—all different, some deep, some long. He began to count them. He stopped at twenty.

"Darcy Calhoun, you son of a gun. Your valuables were people."
John turned around and sat Indian-style with the lantern between his legs. He began to laugh.

He sat there for several minutes, rocking a little, marveling in the work of a man who had convinced the world that he was only a farmer. Then he began to crawl back out, past the beam to blow out the lantern, past the pile of discarded slave clothes, past the food stacked in the corner. As he began to stand into the opening, he found one final surprise. Hanging from a nail, just to the side of the trapdoor, were strands of crafted string. He picked them up—there were about ten—and set them on the wood floor of the cabin. They were Darcy's maps. And they were all exactly the same.

"They never were for you, you crafty bastard. They were for them. A map to their next stop."

John picked them up again and returned them to the nail below. One, he took and put in his pocket.

"I hope you don't mind, Darcy," he said. "But I would like to keep just this."

John jumped out of the hole and slid over to pick up the wood panel he had earlier removed. He gently set it atop the hole, running his hand over the top to make sure it was again smooth. Then, as he turned, a sight captured his eyes and twisted his gut. Five feet away, just on the outskirts of where the table had earlier stood, was the last set of muddy tracks left by the slave.

"You were so close," he whispered. "Five more minutes, and . . ."

The thought forced a heavy swallow. All of this, all that had transpired, could have been different with just a little more time. He slammed his closed fist onto the floor, again and again, until finally the pain eased the tightness in his chest.

John sat on Darcy's front step for about an hour, fingering the knots on the string and dealing with all he had just learned. He felt somewhat peaceful now, more peaceful than when he had arrived, and he enjoyed listening to the splashes from the nearby creek and the litany of birdsong coming from the trees.

John found himself thinking of the men and women who had come here and found refuge in Darcy's cellar. They had exchanged their slave clothes for Darcy's collection of hand-me-downs and left with a sack of cracked corn, pecans, or jerky to follow a string map to a new life. What became of them? What became of men like Jebediah Jones? The friends and family they left behind would count them lucky if they never heard of them again. Living or dead? They would never know.

His horse whinnied and stirred nervously at its tether. John felt it a second later, the heavy beat of hooves quickly approaching. He did not react, except to stuff the string back in his pocket.

The sound of the gallop stopped, and John saw nothing, not for at least a minute. Then from the direction of the fields a familiar black horse appeared, and atop it, Tyler Breckenridge. He walked the animal to within a hundred feet of the cabin, dismounted, then made a slow walk toward John. His manner was again smooth and flawless, his expression unreadable and yet relaxed—it was as if the meeting between them yesterday had not taken place.

John looked at him as he approached. He did not stand. "Did they . . . ?"

"Yes," Tyler answered simply. "The sentence was carried out."

John looked down at his hands and nodded. He did not speak for a number of seconds. "Tell me, who is in charge of his burial?"

Tyler was now about ten feet away. "I asked that I be allowed to tend to it."

"And where . . ."

"In my family plot. On the grounds of Willowby. That way he will be well looked after."

John nodded again, this time looking down. "Are there any trees there?" He stammered a bit. "Darcy told me once, offhandedly, that he would like to be buried beneath a tree."

"Yes." Tyler smiled. "There are quite a number."

"Good. He would like that."

The next moments passed in silence. Tyler Breckenridge stood as if he were posing for a portrait—one leg slightly bent, the other straight, his eyes cast off in the distance. John realized that despite everything, the man still mesmerized him.

John stood, dusting his hands against his pants. "I best be going. I need to get back to Charleston."

Tyler nodded and waited until John had taken a step toward his horse. "So you know," he said matter-of-factly.

John turned abruptly and looked hard at the planter. "Know what?" he asked defensively.

Breckenridge laughed lightly. He touched his finger to his cheek. "The dirt. It gives it away, John."

John smeared his hand across his face, only worsening the smudge. "I don't know what you are talking about."

Tyler retrieved something from the inside pocket of his jacket and dangled it before him between thumb and forefinger. It was a string with knobs and extensions—one of Darcy's maps.

"I'm sorry I had to have Jenkins appropriate this from the pocket of your suit. With my luck you would have followed the damned thing."

Tyler lifted his eyes and nodded, ambling a step or two closer to the cabin as John stood in silence. "It has been going on for a number of years now. Six years, if I am not mistaken. It probably started after Darcy's mother passed." He looked back at John. "I had wondered if Darcy would tell you. I had a feeling he might."

"But how—" His words froze there.

Breckenridge clasped his hands at his back. "How did I know? One of my workers told me of it. He had witnessed some strange comings and goings. It did not take much investigation to figure out what was going on."

John sat still, gawking slack-jawed toward the forest of trees. He sat back down on the steps.

"There was more, of course," Tyler continued. "Darcy made a big show of always being hungry." He chuckled. "In addition to his garden, he bought a considerable quantity of nonperishable food. There was no way he could have eaten that much."

"You make it seem so simple," John interjected, just above a whisper. "But Darcy sure wasn't stupid. He managed to fool everyone else."

Tyler shook his head. "He was no actor, John. And though he wasn't stupid, he was not particularly smart either." He looked down for a moment, then back up at John. "Darcy was just smart enough to make use of the fact that people grossly underestimated him."

It was hard to keep his head from spinning. "Then this . . . is this why you did not help him? Is this why you allowed Darcy to die?"

Tyler flinched a little. Most would not have noticed it, but by this time, John had some practice reading Breckenridge's expressions. He said nothing. Instead, he walked over and sat down on Darcy's steps a few feet from the reporter. Then he turned and looked at John, waiting for him to meet his eyes.

"What I told you before in my study was true. I did everything within my power to save Darcy." He looked off. "It all began to go wrong when Smith, his first lawyer, handed him over to an abolitionist. Then, when Coulter concluded his defense by having Darcy recite Psalms to prove his mental competence—that's when I lost my battle. I had called in favors from every powerful man in the county. But I came up short. I couldn't garner enough support to make the difference."

John's mind raced backward, and he felt his stomach clench. His question was just above a whisper. "Did I do anything? Did my presence here or in town influence what happened?"

Tyler sensed something in John's question. He hunched forward a little, mimicking John's posture, his elbows on his knees. He met John's eyes and held the look. "No." His voice was kind.

John realized at that point that he could make a choice—to believe all of it, or nothing.

"Perhaps I should qualify that," Tyler continued. "You gave support and comfort to someone who needed it . . ." His mouth twitched a little, and his tone became lighter. "And wearing that impossibly black wool suit of yours, you managed to pull a half-gone militia private out of a mob that would have been more than willing to make you its target."

A half-realized thought suddenly became clear. "And then *you* pulled *me* out."

"Yes."

"Why?"

"I don't know." Tyler said with a half laugh. "I didn't think about it, I just did it."

John nodded slowly. As he stared at Breckenridge, he looked at him as he had never done before. It was a strange insight, yet there were still so many contradictions. He gestured toward the cabin. "I still do not understand why. Why you allowed this to go on beneath your nose? You are a planter. A slave owner."

"I warned you before not to draw guilt from association."

John looked back at the footprints on the porch, his brow furrowed as he tried to make sense of it all. Tyler watched him, then spoke quietly.

"I'll tell you how I acquired my firsthand knowledge of what was going on with Darcy. I was eighteen and had been out drinking with my friends." There was a rueful pause, whether from longing or embarrassment, John could not tell. "I was coming back late along the lane between Darcy's cabin and the path to North Creek on Willowby. I was riding too fast and was too young to know better, when my horse lost its footing. We both went down hard, and I managed to hit my head on something. When I came to, I was in a shallow ditch, my horse was gone, and my head felt as if it was in pieces." He smiled at John. "You know the feeling.

"So, as I was lying there, incapacitated by the oddest of circumstances, I saw a black man walking across the path. There was a full moon, so I could see him quite well. He was young and his clothes were too big for him—rolled up at the sleeves and pant legs. I knew he wasn't one of ours.

"I wasn't thinking very clearly, but I knew that I needed help, for my knee was dislocated and I was a good three miles from the nearest cabin. I called out for him to stop, and he did. The man looked terrified, twice more than me, I'm sure. He probably thought at first that I was a ghost, rising up out of the field like that and white as a sheet.

"I asked him where he was from and where he was going. He said his name was Marcus and that he was a free man. He said he had to get to a job in Charleston. Then I told him who I was and said that if he would help me get back to Willowby, I would see that he got a ride to Charleston.

"I knew from his response that he was lying, because I read his fear—much greater for the discovery of a planter's son than an apparition. But instead of running off, he helped me. By the time he got me up and had my arm draped over his shoulder, I could tell that he was hurt as well." Tyler paused and looked off at the trees. "I was taller than him, and his shirt was loose at the neck. I could see welts down his back as wide as my thumb."

As he continued, Tyler looked ill at ease. "You don't get to be eighteen and not know that slaves get beatings like that every day. I had seen it happen. Our former overseer . . ." He broke off. "Well, at that point, I had just had enough.

"When we got to within earshot of the cabins, I told him that he could go if he didn't want to wait for the ride. He looked me in the eye for a long time. Doubt, fear, hope—they were all manifested in his expression. Then he asked me if we were far from where the North Road cut across the East Road to Charleston. I told him, and he took a little string with knots out of his pocket." Tyler smiled and ran the strands of Darcy's map through his fingers. "Then we both thanked each other, and I wished him Godspeed."

Tyler took a deep breath. "You asked me a question in the study that, at the time, I did not answer. You asked me of the mistreated, and their possible recourse." He fanned a hand toward the cabin. "I couldn't tell you then, but this was my answer. For Darcy, at least, the course of action was simple and clear. I protected him when I could."

John sat completely still, the shock still fresh. Then he started to shake his head.

"Do you still mistrust me, John? If so, stop to consider this. I have just put my reputation in your hands." He smiled, as if it were somewhat unimaginable. "I have confessed everything, and at what gain to me? You are free, of course, to return to New York and write of the complicit southern planter. The man who did nothing to stop escaping slaves. My neighbors might not think too much of it, but your abolitionists might send me down a medal."

"But your actions . . . Are you not one?"

"No. I am not an abolitionist. They are too reckless, too impatient. Men who demand immediate change usually have nothing to lose, and no responsibility for making things work afterward." He voice dropped. "Slavery has existed here for a long time. Our economy is built on it. The South must now change over time, John, just as the North did. To emancipate the slaves suddenly would mean economic death to all of us. That is the reason so many here lash out at such calls with threats of their own. They fear what would happen were things to change too quickly. We need time, John. More time."

"That is what I fear we are running out of." John paused. "That ship, the *Port Royal*, I am convinced that she would have made action to precipitate war were it not for the death of the president."

Tyler smiled. "Hypotheticals," he mused. "Millard Fillmore is now the president, and I believe that bodes well for us all. I believe that he can hold us together."

"Tyler, there is something I must know. Simpson's death—"

"It was an accident. He ran out in front of a fire wagon."

"And your appointment? What was that about?"

"The explanation I gave you before was a reasonable one." Tyler paused. "But as an alternative—perhaps it could have involved a leak." He paused again. "As in a dam. A breach is about to occur, which will release a torrent. The devastation will be incredible. So what does one man do?

"Perhaps he arranges for a man with a good eye to take a look. He might raise an alarm so that men will come to reinforce the dam. Then, later, when the flood has subsided, men can work to heal the breach so that the collapse never occurs."

"Then why wasn't I . . . alerted?"

"It was too late. At that time, an alarm could have made the situation worse."

"Tyler, how long until another Zachary Taylor comes along? How long until a hard-willed, uncompromising man again comes to power? What then?"

"Good heavens, John," Tyler said with a smile. "You have become so terribly dire. You nearly sound a southerner."

"It will happen, Tyler. At some point."

Tyler blinked slowly. When he spoke, his voice was almost a whisper. "We are a nation of civilized men. At least, for the most part. I do not believe that civilized man's natural proclivity is for war. Diplomacy has to be the key. That is why I pray that men like you and I will be given enough time to make a difference."

Tyler was silent for a moment; he looked around, taking in the trees, the stream, the cotton field. His voice was normal when he turned back to John. "So, will you write of this?" He gestured toward Darcy's cabin.

"I could not if I wanted to. I swore it to Darcy."

Tyler only nodded.

After a moment, John made a motion toward his horse. "I really must be getting back to Charleston."

"Help me with something first." Tyler walked to his horse and retrieved several items bundled behind his saddle. As he walked back, John could make out what they were. They were torches.

"What are you going to do?"

"End this," he responded. "So that Darcy's secret dies here. You understand the necessity of it." He sparked a match and lit the pitch at the end of one torch, then touched it to the other, igniting it as well.

John took the torch from Tyler's hand. He watched the planter hold it to the dry wood under a corner of the porch. It caught quickly. Then Tyler walked to another corner of the house and lit it as well. John followed Tyler's actions, and when he walked up the front steps and pushed the door open, John threw his torch inside. Then Tyler set fire to the roof.

The men walked back to their horses. John stood with his back to the cabin; he could no longer bear to look at it. But Tyler stood before him, facing the flames. He did not look away.

"I have to believe that Darcy felt some victory in the struggle itself, if not the outcome," he said.

The man who rarely showed emotion now stood watching the fire with a look of profound sadness. John could see the yellow of the flames reflected in Tyler's eyes as he watched Darcy Calhoun's cabin burn.

After a little while, the men mounted their horses, walked them in a wide circle around the fire, then rode off across the cotton field to the south. The wind must have been at their backs, for the smoke stung John's eyes for a very long time.

TWENTY-THREE

ᕦ

John Sharp settled his account at the McClellan boardinghouse and prepared to leave for the train. As he opened the front door—his suitcase in one hand, a half-crumpled letter in the other—he was met on the stoop by a familiar face.

"Samuel, what are you doing here?"

"Well, hello there, Mr. Sharp. I hope ya don't mind, but I took the liberty ta ask Mr. McClellan which day it was that you was leaving. And, since I figured you'd be catching the noon train, well, I's decided ta come by." He paused, then blurted abruptly, "To carry yo' bag, of course. You don't have ta pay me or nothing. You's already given me more than enough."

John set down his suitcase and smiled. "Thank you, Samuel. I would greatly appreciate it."

Perhaps forgetting the weight of the suitcase, Samuel hefted it with a pained expression. But, once righted, he moved efficiently toward the street.

"Meant ta tell ya, sir, that you coming here has left me with nothing but good fortune. You see, not only did I's get ta do some reporting for ya, but also, Mr. McClellan, he seen me coming by a lot looking for ya, and he tells me that he could use an errand boy from time ta time. Says I impressed him with how conscientious I was." The boy smiled wide. "Didn't know what the word meant at the time, but I went and asked folks. Turns out ta be a good thing."

"Indeed it is. The word fits you well. And I'm glad you got more work. I'm sure it will turn out to be Mr. McClellan's blessing."

Samuel switched arms with the bag. "So, will ya be coming back ta Charleston soon?"

"No. I don't think it likely."

Samuel nodded, continuing to struggle with the bag over the next few blocks. He later looked up at John with a quizzical expression, perplexed by the change in the man who had been so talkative when they met.

The boy broke the silence. "How'd them cabbage leaves work out fo' ya? You ever have another use for 'em?"

"They were wonderful, Samuel. They cooled me considerably." He looked up briefly at the overcast sky. "But it's strange. After a few days I became adjusted to the heat. I did not need them anymore."

Samuel began to laugh. "That makes sense. Wasn't gonna tell you or nothing, but the time you was so struggling with the weather, that was nothing. I'd have bet you was the only man in Charleston wearing cabbage leaves on them days. Most wait till it's much hotter."

John looked down at the boy and smiled. "Is that so?"

"Yessir," he answered, continuing to laugh.

They spoke little for the remainder of the short trip to the railway station. As they approached it, Samuel pointed out a bench. "You might like ta sit there to wait, Mr. Sharp. It gets awful hot inside that little building, and the train ain't set to leave fo' another hour."

"That sounds fine, Samuel."

The boy set down the suitcase and curled his fatigued arm three or four times. "Would you like me ta wait with ya, sir? I'd be more than happy."

"No, Samuel, you run along." He dipped his hand in his pocket and pulled out two quarters. He shoved them into the boy's hand.

Samuel's eyes flashed wide. "Oh, no, sir. That's too much."

John silenced him with a wave of the hand. "Samuel, your services have been a bargain. You were truly indispensable." As the boy's brow crinkled, John smiled. "It's another good word. It means I couldn't have gotten along without you."

"Thank ya, sir."

John stuck out his hand. "It was nice meeting you, Samuel."

They shook hands. "And you too, Mr. Sharp. And I's wanting to tell ya, the next time you does make it down here, even if it is a long time, you look me up, sir. Samuel Grass. I won't be no suitcase porter by then. I'll be a big man. And I'll treat you to the finest home-cooked meal your eyes have eva come across."

"It's a deal, Samuel," he answered with a smile. "I look forward to it."

Samuel bounded away, obviously giddy with his newly acquired wealth. Suddenly he stopped. He turned and ran back to John, his breaths panting as he spoke. "I almost forgot. Meant to tell ya, Mr. Sharp, that things is changing here. There ain't no more curfew on black folks, and all manner of folks is starting ta act like they was. You know, friendly on the street and all. Everything's going back ta normal." John did not react. "Well, I just thought you'd like to know."

"Yes, Samuel," he said distantly. "Thank you."

As Samuel walked off again, John looked down at the half-crumpled envelope in his right hand. He had already read it, but now opened it and read it again. It was Owen's account of Darcy's death. Owen's crass bravado was obviously just a mask for a lyrical soul. His story was sensitive and revealing. There had obviously been a great deal more to both men than met the eye.

The stationmaster interrupted John's thoughts. "Excuse me, sir. I need ya to sign these papers." He gestured behind him as two men wheeled out a dolly bearing Simpson's wooden casket. "They'll load it in the baggage department. You just keep the receipt with ya for the other end."

John folded the receipt and placed it in his coat pocket. His eyes were again drawn to the nearby church spire—the first one he had seen in Charleston. The steeple bell began to toll eleven o'clock.

He waited with Simpson by the tracks for the train to come.

EPILOGUE

In the first weeks after taking office, President Millard Filmore dispatched troops to two locations, the Texas–New Mexico border and, because of worrisome rumors, the federal forts off Charleston, South Carolina. He also authorized General Winfield Scott to develop a contingency plan in the event of secession and uprising in South Carolina.

In September, the Congress passed a collection of separate bills that came to be known as the Compromise of 1850. They provided for the following: California was admitted as a free state; New Mexico and Utah were organized into territories with future status as free or slave states to be determined by popular vote of the residents; the U.S. government settled boundary claims with Texas, while assuming its $10 million preannexation debt; and the slave trade was prohibited in the District of Columbia. Finally, Congress strongly reinforced the fugitive slave laws in the 1850 Fugitive Slave Act.

The president declared the compromise a "final settlement" on all disputes. The first four laws were concessions to northern interests, but the last provided a virtual carte blanche to slave owners and bounty hunters pursuing fugitive slaves. Ulysses S. Grant later said that nothing so galvanized northern opinion against the South as the imposition of these draconian laws.

In the next years, public opinion in South Carolina moved back toward moderation, and Unionist sentiment briefly gained strength.

Abraham Lincoln won the 1860 presidential election with 40 percent of the popular vote. He did not receive one electoral college vote from any of the slave states. By the time of his inauguration in March 1861, the newly formed Confederate States of America had elected its own president, Jefferson Davis.

On April 12, 1861, Confederate batteries fired upon Fort Sumter. Deaths in the ensuing Civil War would exceed 600,000.

How *Fire Bell in the Night* Got Published

Gather.com is the social networking site where adults connect around shared interests ranging from travel to cooking and politics to parenting. On Gather.com, you'll find an engaged community of book lovers and writers who read and publish some of the highest-quality user-generated content online. Special groups offer author advice, book reviews, insiders' publishing information, and a virtual writing workshop, all for free.

Leveraging the strength of its members, Gather.com launched the groundbreaking First Chapters Writing Competition in January 2007. The prize: a first-time fiction author would receive a publishing contract with the Touchstone imprint of Simon & Schuster. Over 2,600 Gather.com members submitted manuscripts to be evaluated and voted on by their peers, who narrowed the entries to five finalists. The quality of the submissions was so high that Simon & Schuster published two novels, one of which you're reading today. Join the online discussion about *Fire Bell in the Night* at http://firebell.gather.com. You can find the other winning novel, *The Way Life Should Be* by Terry Shaw, wherever books are sold.

If you want to influence the next books that get published, visit http://firstchapters.gather.com. Upcoming First Chapters competitions will focus on the romance and mystery genres, launching fall 2007. Join the conversation around the latest novels and cast your vote for the next bestseller at www.gather.com.

Congratulations to Geoffrey S. Edwards
from the following Gather.com members:

Ty T.

Stephen Prosapio

Nana to Seven cutie pies

Beth H.

Trudy P.

Julie G.

Lori F.

Pat S.

Andy Z.

Arlene H.

Ken W.

Pat S.

Ian Bradley

Geeta M.

Sheila D.

James R.

Ann B.

Judi F.

K. B.

Samantha B.

Susan J.

Kathryn Esplin-Oleski

Moira K.

Jessie Voigts

Sonia M.

Christine Zibas

George Corneliussen

Eric D. Goodman

G. Photog.

C. A.

Michael DeFilippo

Latasha W.

Kerry Dexter

Noble Collins

Amy B.

Brian F.

L.A.R.

Anthony Samuel P.

Marge H.

Patti C.

Kathryn S.

Yolanda H.

Cara V.

Cindy the Anti-Trite

Susan Marie

Jage P.

Shirley Cheng

Judi J.

Kate K.

Mae W.

Diane B.

Karen R.

Isabella H.

Mary S.

Rae A.

Jasmin J.

Jennifer B.

Ms. Meacham: Money Maven

Beverly Meyers

Catherine B.

Lisa B.

Lisa M.

J. K. Sather

Val Fox, VP of marketing at
Gather.com

Edward Nudelman

Catherine M.

Cee D.

Dave S.

Roy W.

Rand P.

Barbara S.

Deb D.

Jen A.

Venessa G.

Gail S.

Clellie T.

Sandra D.

Cathie A.

Andy Anderson

A. C.

Andrew Madrid

Jak J.

Alyson W